DIANNE OREN

How to Date a Mermaid

A sweet contemporary romantic comedy

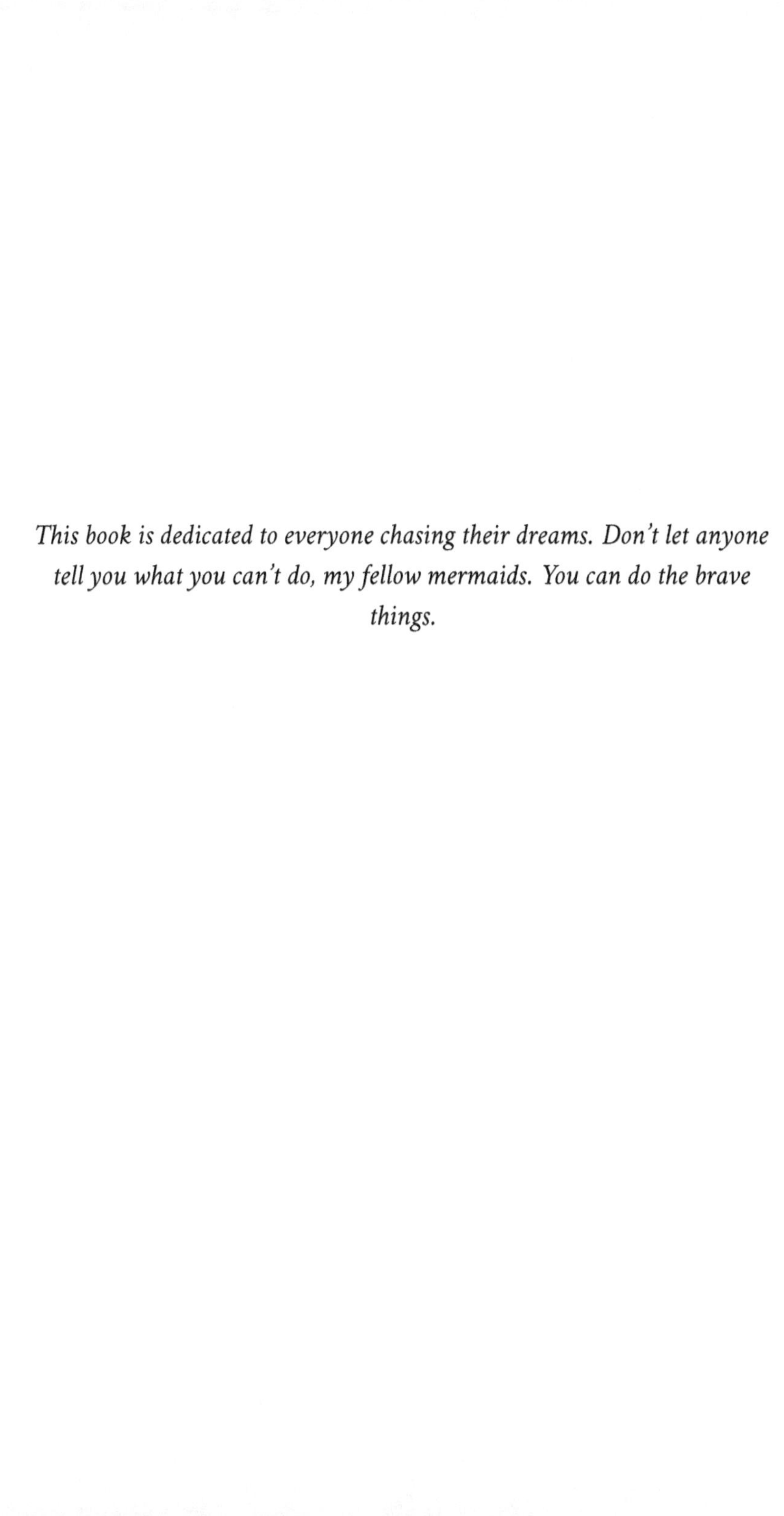

This book is dedicated to everyone chasing their dreams. Don't let anyone tell you what you can't do, my fellow mermaids. You can do the brave things.

Content Warnings

This is a sweet romantic comedy, so you're getting a feel-good story with no sex, swearing or spice and a guaranteed happy ending.

Because I want all my readers to feel safe, the following topics are discussed in this book:

Loss of parents (past), growing up poor, being a child in foster care, creepy dude finding excuses to touch female colleagues, workplace bullying.

Contents

Chapter 1	1
Chapter 2	15
Chapter 3	35
Chapter 4	46
Chapter 5	58
Chapter 6	69
Chapter 7	84
Chapter 8	95
Chapter 9	115
Chapter 10	131
Chapter 11	147
Chapter 12	161
Chapter 13	180
Chapter 14	200
Chapter 15	214
Chapter 16	226
Chapter 17	241
Chapter 18	259
Chapter 19	274
Chapter 20	288
Chapter 21	307
Chapter 22	323
Chapter 23	337
Chapter 24	355

Ashley's next... 368
Chapter 1: Fake It Till You Make It 369
Acknowledgments 383
Special Dedication 385
About the Author 386
Also by Dianne Oren 387

Chapter 1

Marina

"I blame you for this," I moan, flopping my mermaid tail in Ashley's direction.

She gives me the side-eye from the driver's seat.

"Not my fault if you drew the short straw this morning, my friend," she shoots back with a grin. "Someone has to be the mermaid. We can't all be the sailors."

The top of her convertible is down on this gorgeous California day. It would be perfect if we were on the beach or in the park. Anywhere else except stuck in a huge traffic jam in the middle of the Golden Gate Bridge with a mermaid tail trapping my legs together in a purple, glittering vice grip. I wiggle in frustration.

"My legs are sweating," I complain. "And I've lost count of how many truck drivers have taken my picture. Why aren't we moving? We've been stuck in this same spot for an hour."

"Thirty minutes tops," our friend Scarlet deadpans from the back seat. Ever the realist.

Seated next to Scarlet in the back seat, our positivity princess Merry tugs at the collar of her sailor suit.

"I'm with Marina. I wish we'd changed before we left. I could be getting some sun. Look on the bright side, girl. At least you're getting a tan in the mermaid costume."

I tilt my head back at her. "Redheads don't tan," I remind her matter-of-factly, randomly twisting a fiery strand of my long hair around a finger. "And I'm the most ridiculous-looking one in the bunch today, so please don't envy me."

Scarlet rolls her eyes at all of us. "The bride's creepy uncle was looking at you like you were a snack," she offers up with a grumble. "It was either get out of there quick or fight him off. He wasn't worth screwing up my manicure."

"Fair point," I concede. "But I am miserable in this thing and I want out."

The car horns quiet, but from our vantage point, we can't see why. The mile-long bridge has an arch to it, and we're on the north side. The deck slopes up and blocks our view of whatever the problem is. Not to mention the huge monstrosity of a very fancy bus that's stopped a few cars in front of us, making our view even worse.

Ashley turns pale and we all turn our heads to see what she's looking at. The police are moving up the bridge, looking like they're delivering some very bad news.

"This can't be good," Scarlet grumbles, her perfect blond bob moving with precision as she shakes her head.

"You never know," Merry chimes in. "Could be good news."

Ash gives her a look, which is only going to encourage Merry. I try to fight the smile creeping up on my face. If I smile now, it'll only ensure Merry goes from zero to sixty on the road to Extra Town. Secretly, it's one of the things I love most about her. She sees the good in every situation.

Several people step out of their cars, stretching their legs and muttering in frustration.

Ashley pulls her long blonde waves up off her neck. "Nope. Definitely not good."

"I beg to differ. Here comes my next ex-boyfriend," Merry says under her breath, pointing a finger in one particular officer's direction. "Hello, Officer Honey Buns…"

I laugh softly and crane my neck to see him. Yep. Exactly her type: blond hair, tan complexion, muscles for days…and the way he fills out that uniform. Wow. He doesn't smile as he approaches, his eyes hidden behind aviator sunglasses. It's completely disappointing, because now I can't tell if he's noticed the predatory glint in Merry's eye.

"Ladies," he greets us as he approaches, eyeing Merry as she brushes her shoulder-length chestnut brown hair away from her face. "As you've likely guessed, there's a pretty bad accident on the south end of the bridge. The tow trucks have just arrived, but we estimate it'll be another thirty minutes before it's cleared."

Ashley grabs her sailor hat off the dash and beats the steering wheel with it while Officer Honey Buns gives her the side-eye. Scarlet whistles sharply, trying to rein her in. Ash shoves the car door open and gets out. The officer looks back at the rest of us.

"We'd like you to stay in your vehicle, but if you do get out to stretch your legs, please don't leave this immediate area. We'll come back through to give you an update again soon."

I do a double take as Merry literally bats her eyelashes at him like Miss Piggy. I stifle a laugh. His eyes dart around to each of us.

"What's with the costumes?" he grumbles.

Merry's the next one out of the car, shoving her door closed with a hip and leaning against it with a coy smile aimed at the officer.

"We were singing at an engagement party."

Officer Honey Buns raises his eyebrows at her.

"We have all kinds of different performances we do," Scarlet offers as she props her feet up on the backseat. "Sometimes we're princesses, sometimes we're show girls…"

He keeps looking between the sailors and me in my mermaid tail. "And…this time?"

Merry points to me. "Marina drew the short straw, so she had to be the mermaid today," she begins. "We all hate the thing…but it looks great, so we take turns wearing it. Mermaids…or sirens…could lure sailors with the sound of their beautiful voices."

Officer Yummy smirks. "That sounds a little creepy for an engagement party."

My eyes flick over to Merry, who is starting to look a little unnerved that he isn't surrendering to the siren song her ovaries are obviously singing.

I smile up at him from my perch on the front passenger seat. "The bride and groom met on a cruise," I explain. "Specifically, in the karaoke bar where they ended up singing sea shanties together. So, the bride hired us to perform a few at the party."

"Yeah," Ashley chimes in. "Until her creepy uncle got handsy, and we had to make a run for it."

"Not *run*, exactly," Merry offers after Officer Honey Bun's chiseled jaw twitches. "He just wouldn't stop bothering her. He was practically drooling, and then he started to touch. So we grabbed our stuff and bolted to the car instead of changing first."

He nods. "Well, don't go luring any sailors while you're on the bridge, okay ladies? Stay close to your vehicle, and we'll try to get this wrapped up as soon as possible."

He moves on, Merry watching his departure with wicked amusement.

"Officer Honey Buns could've been my next bad decision," she says with a low sigh.

"Could've been?" I ask.

She shrugs. "Too grumpy. He's more honey badger than honey buns."

Scarlet giggles in the back seat, and I turn my attention to Ashley as I wiggle around, trying to get comfortable.

"Ash, can you *please* put the top up so I can get out of this tail? This thing is driving me nuts."

"Uh…" she starts, looking pensive. "Pretty sure it's broken."

All heads whip to face Ashley.

"What? But you put it down this morning," I say, desperation in my voice.

"Yeah, but it got stuck when it was almost all the way down, so I just sort of shoved it the rest of the way and sat on the lid to keep it inside." She sighed, biting her lower lip. "I'll take it to the dealer tomorrow."

"Daddy's gonna be mad, Ash," Merry purred, finally breaking her gaze away from Officer Honey Badger's departure.

Ashley's family is wealthy beyond anything the rest of us experienced growing up. Especially me. Although she grew up privileged, she isn't the spoiled little rich girl people expect her to be. Sure, she still lets her dad give her expensive gifts sometimes, and she can be so incredibly dramatic about the littlest things, but she's a fierce friend and one of the kindest people I've ever met. Rather than accept a guaranteed position at her father's finance company, she went out and earned her teaching degree. Now she teaches third grade and shares an apartment with me in a not-so-great neighborhood in the city.

Scarlet climbs out of the back seat and stretches. Great. Everyone else can get up and move around, but I'm stuck here in these fishy flippers. My legs are starting to sweat.

"This is beyond boring," Scarlet groans.

"It's great people watching, though," Ashley grins, nodding at an elderly woman shuffling around in unicorn pajama pants, lime green Crocs, and a t-shirt that says, 'If fat adds more flavor then I'm delicious'.

We all glance over and laugh.

"I hope I'm that bold when I'm her age." Scarlet laughs. "She's awesome."

I smile and leave the girls to shuffle around the car in their sailor suits. I've spent my entire adult life *not* being bold. I excel at flying under the radar and avoiding attention. Well, most of the time. I do realize that my current mermaid situation makes that nearly impossible, but we all really need the money we get from these lucrative little side gigs.

More and more people get out of their cars as we wait for the wreck to be cleared. Merry's doing lunges in front of the car. Ash and Scarlet move next to my door, wondering aloud at what kind of person drives a giant bus like the one blocking our view.

"Probably a Kardashian," Scarlet mutters. Ash and I giggle.

"C'mon," Ash objects. "They're all about first class. They wouldn't be caught dead on a bus."

I raise my eyebrows and nod at it. "It's a pretty first class bus."

It's a monster. Something an NFL team might take from the airport for an away game. Shiny black exterior with silver accents and trim. There's no lettering on the sides or back like it would have if it was owned by a charter company, which tells me it must be privately owned. A few of the windows are open on the side, but the screens are the type you can't see through. The whole thing screams luxury.

"Maybe it's Dolly Parton!" Ash cries with a huge smile.

I giggle again. "Wouldn't she have her face on the bus? I mean…it's Dolly."

"Pfft," Scarlet sputters. "And have crazed fans chasing you down when you're just trying to go to the store?"

"Yeah," Merry chimes in from her spot in front of the car. "Because she'd take a whole bus to go to the store."

I wiggle again in my seat and close my eyes. Gratitude. Gratitude. Grati-freaking-tude.

Merry starts tapping a single rhythm with her knuckle on the car hood, swaying back and forth to the beat. We all look over curiously. Merry is our instigator. Whenever we're up to something, she's usually the one who starts it. Scarlet almost immediately squeals and runs over to join her. Now there are two sailors knocking on the hood while Ash and I exchange bewildered looks.

"C'mon, ladies," Merry growls in a comically low voice, wiggling her eyebrows at us both.

Ashley shakes her head. "You've spent too long in the sun, Merry… what are you doing?"

Scarlet starts humming a tune, and a light bulb goes on for me and Ash. They're thumping out the beat to 'The Wellerman', one of the sea shanties we sang at the party.

"We're bored," Scarlet cries. "Let's have some fun!"

Ashley looks at me with raised eyebrows. "Yeah?"

"No way!" I cry out. "You guys, no! I am not singing 'The Wellerman' in the middle of a bridge in a mermaid costume. You're insane."

Ash runs over to join them and now there are three. Three possibly soon-to-be ex-friends, all swaying back and forth and knocking out the rhythm of 'The Wellerman' on the hood of Ashley's car, looking at me with pleading eyes.

"No!" I whisper-shout with wide eyes that are doing absolutely nothing to make them stop.

Ash thrusts out her bottom lip, which looks ridiculous at any time, but especially with her in a sailor suit. Scarlet giggles, and Merry decides to double down. Welcome to Extra Town.

"You know we're just gonna get louder until you do the thing," she says with an evil chuckle. "So c'mon, girl…do the thing!"

People around us have begun to notice the three sailors knocking on the car hood, rocking back and forth to the beat. Curious glances are aimed our way. I cross my arms over my chest and shake my head.

"People are watching!" I argue, knowing how ridiculous I sound. I'm running out of reasons to say no, and they know I can't resist their ridiculous antics. They know me too well. I make a mental note to make new friends. Boring ones who never sing in the middle of bridges.

Ash rolls her eyes. "People watch us all the time when we perform and you don't care then," she argues back. "And you guys call *me* dramatic?"

A woman and her little girl step closer to see what the fuss is about. Merry, knowing my weakness for all tiny humans, lifts her chin in their direction and mouths 'For the kids' at me. Right in my Achilles heel. I'll remember that. The little girl watches me with curious eyes, and I cave like a house of cards on a windy day.

I heave a sigh of resignation and fling open the car door, prompting all three sailors to squeal and cheer. I pull myself to a standing position and shut the door, my heart skipping a beat when the little girl's mouth falls open. She takes in the beautiful, sparkly mermaid tail, and the sweetest smile spreads across her face. Her mother grins at me in delight, and I can't help but smile back. I wave at the little girl, and I'm rewarded with a shy wave in return.

With as much dignity as I can muster, I start wiggle-walking until I'm next to the hood of the car. I jump up and land my left hip on the hood, and Scarlet reaches out and offers a hand to pull me fully onto it. I give the little girl another smile and bend my knees, tucking my feet underneath my right hip. The tail splays out behind me, glittering in the sun. People start moving closer, eager to see what we're doing.

I give my friends a quick scathing look, and Scarlet sticks out her tongue. I break into a laugh, and they all nod at me. Ready when I am. So much for not calling attention to myself, right? Here we go. I snap myself into performance mode, looking at the people around us as if I'm telling them the most amazing story…and I begin to sing.

"There once was a ship that put to sea," I begin, paying special attention to the little girl who is now dragging her mother as close to us as she can get. "The name of the ship was the Billy O' Tea. The winds blew up, her bow dipped down, oh blow my Billy boys, blow…"

"HUH!" Merry, Scarlet, and Ash grunt simultaneously as they launch into a dance and join me in the chorus.

"Soon may the Wellerman come to bring us sugar and tea and rum," we sing together. The harmony we manage when we sing this song always gets my heart beating fast. As much as I don't like attention, I have to admit that singing in front of an audience is exhilarating.

More and more people draw near now, but we're used to an audience. We've performed this countless times. Merry turns to the crowd and claps the rhythm over her head with her hands, motioning for them to join her. They do, of course, because we're all trapped on this bridge together, and everyone is more than happy for a distraction. Heads begin to pop out of the windows of the giant bus ahead of us. I don't recognize any of them, but they're far enough away to make it a challenge. I turn my focus back to the crowd.

Gesturing dramatically with my hands, eyes wide, I begin singing the second verse. I sing about the huge whale coming close to the Wellerman, feeding off the energy of my friends as the crowd increases in size.

As we launch into another chorus, the girls begin dancing all the way around the car, making their "HUH!" grunts in time with the song. I look down at my new little friend, whose precious ear-to-ear smile is more than enough to keep me going.

I sing the next verse, telling the story of the whale hitting the

Wellerman with its tale and the crew harpooning the whale in return. I lean forward a little, at times addressing my words only to the little girl, such delight shining from her sweet face.

The girls make another lap around the car, dancing and grunting, and I can't help but break into a laugh. I don't know if it's the spontaneity of the performance or the fact that we're in the middle of one of the most famous bridges in the world, but we've all amped up our performances to a Broadway-level experience. The crowd pushes in just as there's a bit of a commotion at the back. I'm unable to see what might be happening. I just hope it's not Officer Honey Badger and his friends coming to arrest us for being a public nuisance. That'd be my luck the one time I actually do something spontaneous.

I continue with the next verse. The crowd parts at the back, as if making a path for the whale I'm singing about. I sing about the battle between ship and whale that took forty days.

Do I hear...singing?

Trying not to break the rhythm of the song, I watch the crowd continue to part for someone I still can't see as I finish the verse and let the girls do another lap around the car during the chorus. Instead of joining in this time, I put my hand up to shade my eyes as I strain to see what's happening at the back of the crowd. Whatever it is, the audience begins cheering and screaming, smiling and shaking their heads as if they can't believe what they're seeing. Cell phones turn in that direction to record whatever's happening.

I exchange looks with the girls, who've also noticed the commotion, but they motion for me to keep going. I definitely hear singing. It's a man's voice. Gravelly and rich. And he's quite good, actually. We're used to dealing with drunk party-goers creating distractions, so I keep smiling and begin the final verse about the mighty whale and valiant crew still fighting out at sea just as the crowd parts in front of me.

A lone figure steps into the clearing in front of the car where the girls are dancing, and my stomach drops like I'm on a rollercoaster. My heart beats wildly and I stop mid-verse, eyes wide in shock as I look into the smiling face of Zach Adams, one of the biggest indie rock stars of our time, and lead singer of The Royal Rebels. From the collar-length rich, dark brown hair, perfectly trimmed stubble and sexy dark eyes to the fitted black t-shirt and jeans, he looks exactly like he does in every news article and magazine cover I've ever seen of him. There's a power and grace about him that I didn't expect, especially for a man so big. He's at least six feet tall and incredibly fit. Muscles are everywhere, and they're gorgeous. My throat goes a little dry. His eyes are fixed on me as he sings and walks through the crowd. I find myself wanting to slide right off this hood just to be closer to him. The pull is magnetic.

I look up into a sea of cell phones as people everywhere begin recording what unfolds. Suddenly, everything feels like it's in slow motion as he draws closer to me. He leans in slightly and lowers his voice.

"C'mon, Siren," he growls with a grin that sends little shivers across my skin. "We have to finish strong."

He jumps up on the car hood and sits with me just as Officer Honey Badger and several other policemen appear on the edge of the crowd. I feel Zach's warm, strong fingers close around my hand, and I turn to look up at him. His dark brown eyes meet mine, and he smiles again, nodding with encouragement. He dips his forehead until it's nearly touching mine.

"Ready?" he rasps with another squeeze of his hand.

I feel a strange calm that I can't explain. I look down at the girls, who are all grinning from ear to ear in as much disbelief as I am, and I nod.

"Let's finish strong." I laugh softly, smiling at Zach as we face the crowd together.

We finish singing the last verse together, and I find myself projecting my voice stronger and louder than ever before to match his. Our voices blend perfectly, and the adrenaline of performing with such a perfect partner hits me full force. It's one of the most thrilling sensations I've ever experienced. Like our energies are not only feeding off each other, but giving the other's voice more power.

Together, we finish the final chorus with the girls. They don't circle the car this time. They stay in front of it while we all sing together. Merry motions for the crowd to join in, and many of them do, and the crowd erupts in applause and cheers.

We all burst into laughter at the end, the girls rushing toward us and high-fiving us. Merry gives me a side glance and mouths "O-EM-GEE" at me, and I laugh again, shaking my head in denial. Did this just happen?

Zach turns to me as the crowd starts calling for an encore. His eyes are like magnets for mine, pulling me in. He looks down briefly, realizing he's still gripping my hand. He lets go, and I resist the urge to grab his hand again, loving the contact.

"That was incredible!" he says above the noise of the crowd. "Brilliant!"

His gravelly voice and British accent are going to be the last thing I hear before I faint on this hood. This is all too much for me, but I feel myself smiling back at him as if in a dream.

"Likewise," I say breathlessly, unable to pull my gaze from his.

"Uh, guys?" Scarlet shouts above the noise. I look up and see Officer Honey Badger and the others moving through the crowd authoritatively, gesturing for people to get back to their cars.

The people closest to us begin to push forward, still cheering. Scarlet, Merry, and Ash take bows and instinctively back away from them, making their way to the car and jumping over the doors to get in.

"Oh," Zach mutters, realizing at the same time as me that we're about to get mobbed by dozens of adoring fans. He grabs my hand again, standing up and looking down at me. "Let's get you in the car, Siren."

I look up at him with pleading eyes. "My legs are pinned together by this tail. A little help?"

He nods and takes my other hand, pulling gently and hauling me to a standing position on the hood of the car. I wobble a little, and he lets go of my hands to grab my waist and steady me. My hands drift up to his broad shoulders on their own.

I look over to find Officer Honey Badger fighting through the crowd toward us as the remaining crowd still chants, "encore, encore, encore."

Uh oh. Honey Badger is mad. I glance toward the little girl in time to see her mother haul her up on a hip, both of them waving goodbye as they return to their car. I wave back just as a dozen fans reach us. The car lurches suddenly, and I wobble again. Zach's arms tighten around me as I look up at him with a worried expression.

"Sir, please return to your vehicle immediately," one of the officers calls to us.

Zach looks down and nods. "Of course, officer," he says, turning back to me.

He carefully removes his arms and makes sure I'm steady, then he jumps off the hood and offers me a hand. I look down at him, trying to figure out how to best maneuver my way off the hood. I glance behind me to see if I can just sit on the edge of the windshield and drop down into the passenger seat. Nope. No way.

More officers appear, successfully turning most of the crowd back toward their vehicles. I look down at Zach just as the car is jostled again, and I'm knocked off balance. A scream escapes my lips as I go flying off the hood and land squarely in the arms of the world's biggest rock star.

Chapter 2

Zach spins around quickly with me in his arms, taking one step toward the passenger door, when more fans swarm in and block his path. Police officers are making their way to us, but we're getting pushed farther away from the car. I wrap my arms around Zach's shoulders. Dear God, he smells like a day at the beach. Salt and sea and…is that sandalwood? It's intoxicating. I look behind him as he backs away from the car. We're getting closer to Officer Honey Badger but farther away from my friends.

"Please, everyone," he shouts with a practiced grin on his face. "Let me get the mermaid back in her car."

No one listens. More people shove their way between us and the car. He keeps backing away.

"Please let us through!" Zach yells a little more forcefully.

Cell phones are out and recording. People are shouting out song requests in some sort of mass someone-famous-is-here hysteria. None of them seem to care that the police are closing in. We're a good two-and-a-half car lengths from Ash and the girls now. At least they're safely inside the car, even if they are yelling at the crowd and gesturing wildly like sailors on leave who can't get in a bar. Scarlet whips out her cell phone.

"Mr. Adams," Officer Honey Badger says from right behind us.

Zach turns to face him.

"If you could just get back on the bus and out of sight, we'll get the rest of the crowd under control."

A stricken look comes over his face as if he's blaming himself for the chaos.

Well, actually…

Zach nods. "Of course, Officer," he says, turning away and taking off in long strides toward the bus.

Wait, *what?*

"Hey!" I cry out, pointing toward the car. "I need to go that way!"

He looks down at me, a soft smile on his full lips. My pulse rate is all over the place.

"I know, love," he says huskily. "But right now, we need to get out of sight before we start a riot…so I'm going to have to ask you to trust me."

The last thing I see before Zach steps up into the bus, carrying me like I'm no burden at all, is Ash and Merry watching with their mouths wide open and Scarlet recording the entire thing.

The bus driver gives me a wink as Zach whisks me inside the bus. He takes a few steps inside and gently lowers me to my feet. My right hand has a mind of its own, and I lightly skim my palm across his muscled shoulders. I don't know how it happened. Truly. A slow grin spreads across his handsome face as if he knows exactly what I just did. My cheeks warm, and I let him go.

Zack steps over to the nearest window to look outside and see whether the police have gotten everyone back in their cars. For the first time, I notice his three bandmates sitting on plush chairs in the living area of the bus. They're all watching me with lazy grins on their faces.

I put my hands on my hips. "What?"

They keep smiling. The one closest to me thrusts his chin at Zach.

"Catch yourself a mermaid, Zach?"

I roll my eyes at him, and then my eyes meet Zach's as he turns around. He stops dead in his tracks, his expression softening. As if in slow motion, the corner of his full mouth tilts up in half a smile. He gestures behind him at the window.

"They're still trying to calm things down," he explains.

I can see police officers still moving around outside the window. People are making their way to their cars finally. Good.

Zach takes a step towards me, placing a broad hand on his chest. "I'm Zach," he says softly, extending a hand. His expression is warm. Expectant.

"I know who you are," I answer, placing my hand in his with a laugh. His long, strong fingers wrap around my hand, and it nearly disappears. There's a crackle of energy between us. Warmth creeps up my cheeks.

Zach shakes my hand slowly, his warm brown eyes locking with mine. For a moment, everything seems to still...like we're the only two people here. His grip on my hand is calm. Reassuring. Natural. I cock my head to the side, wondering if he feels the same, and he suddenly lets go.

"I'm Marina," I offer coolly.

"These are my bandmates. Rick, Jimmy, and Sam...this is Marina."

My eyes meet his again at the sound of my name on his lips, spoken almost reverently. I quickly look away. What is this feeling between us? Does he feel it too? With as much dignity as I can muster, I wiggle walk until I'm close enough to shake each of their hands.

I can't believe it. The Royal Rebels in the flesh. These guys have been on the covers of magazines. Featured on countless documentaries and gossip shows. They seem completely normal. Not an entitled celebrity vibe among any of them.

"I can't believe I'm standing in The Royal Rebels' tour bus," I say quietly, stifling an awkward laugh. What are the odds?

"Can I get you some water?" Zach offers. "Or something else? Pop? Juice? Tea?"

He seems almost nervous. I smile and shake my head.

"No, but thank you. I really just need to get back to my friends."

Zach nods in understanding and glances back out the window.

"Oh!" he mutters softly, then takes a step to move around me as if he needs to speak to the driver.

Suddenly, the bus lurches forward a few feet, and I'm knocked off balance again. Zach reaches out and wraps his arms around me just in time to save me from falling. I grip his muscled shoulders, willing myself to keep my hands still this time. He whirls around gracefully and deposits me in a plush chair, then gives my hands a reassuring squeeze.

"Let me just see what's happening," he purrs, turning and walking towards the front of the bus. I turn to find his three bandmates watching me with interest.

"My friends and I entertain at parties on weekends sometimes," I explain, gesturing at the mermaid tail. They continue to stare in silence. "For extra money."

I laugh softly, realizing how ridiculous I sound to these guys. None of them has to work a second job just to make ends meet. And here I am, trying to act like a normal person having a regular conversation when my legs are trapped in mermaid hell. Nothing to see here. Just your average girl having a chat with a rock god and his band.

"Seems like a pretty cool gig to me," Rick replies with a grin.

One half of the Rebels' hit songwriting team, Rick looks like some kind of Viking god turned rock star. He's just as tall and muscley as Zach, but with blond hair and crystal blue eyes. He's incredibly handsome, and yet I don't feel the same pull towards him that I do towards Zach. Of course, this means exactly nothing because I do not date. I don't need any more drama in my life.

"I love that you were singing The Wellerman," Sam says. He looks like a younger version of Kevin Costner. "And dressed like a mermaid...with sailors? I get it. What a great idea."

I grin ear to ear. "Word of mouth has started getting out now that we've done a few, and we're getting more jobs," I offer. "This costume makes normal movement impossible, so we're always arguing about who has to wear it. I lost today."

"Not from where I'm standing," Zach's gravelly voice sounds from behind me as he comes back into view.

Little chills run down the back of my neck. I'll bet this guy could talk about indigestion and it would still sound sexy with that British accent. Which means I have to get away from him. As quickly as possible.

I stand up, my mind already working on how I'm going to get off this bus without him carrying me. He gives me a smile that makes me feel like a teenager at a boy band concert and hands me my cell phone. I look up at him, raising my eyebrows in question.

"One of your friends sent a police officer over with it just as traffic started moving," Zach explains, pointing to it. "It's been vibrating like crazy."

I break my gaze from his, open my lock screen, and see a handful of unread text messages. I tap on the first one, and the bus lurches forward again, sending me careening straight into Zach's chest. Out of the corner of my eye, I see Jimmy catch my cell phone before it hits the floor. My cheek hits a wall of solid muscle, and I start sliding, my face skidding down his shirt as I struggle to grab hold of him and pull myself up. With a deft move I can't even fathom, he twists around, puts one arm behind my knees and the other at the small of my back, and lifts me up again.

Rick laughs. "Whatever you're getting paid for wearing that thing, you need a raise."

Zach swings me around and sets me down in the chair again, then takes the seat next to me. All eyes are on me, I realize. I turn to Zach.

"How am I getting back to my friends?" I ask as Jimmy hands my phone back to me. "I assume there's a plan?"

The bus is moving steadily now. My cell phone vibrates a few more times.

Zach nods, looking to his bandmates and then back at me.

"I think the most logical thing to do is for your friends to follow us to the stadium," he begins. "We're in town for two big performances and some personal appearances over the next few weeks. They're letting us keep the bus there. There's a tunnel at the stadium we can pull into so the helicopters can't see us."

My eyebrows shoot straight up to my hairline. "What?"

Jimmy laughs and points a finger up toward the sky. "You can't hear them?"

I listen for a moment. Sure enough, it sounds like hornets outside. My eyes dart back and forth between Zach and his friends.

"Why are there helicopters?" I ask breathlessly, a sense of impending dread crawling up from my gut to my throat. This is not good. I do not have a good feeling about this.

"There was one above the bridge, probably reporting on the accident," Zach explains. "But then it moved to us when it saw the crowd swarming. Suddenly, there were…a few more. I have a feeling we'll be tonight's top story on the news."

I throw my face into my hands. *No, no, no, no.* I shake my head, feeling tears well up behind my eyelids.

"It'll blow over in a few days," Rick offers in a consoling voice. "We're used to it."

I raise my head finally, looking at Rick with wide eyes.

"Well, I'm not," I counter, shaking my head and looking at all of them. "This can't happen. My job…my *real* job…this *can't* happen…"

My heartbeat leaps at the mere thought of being caught up in some kind of viral video. The firm frowns on any kind of notoriety. I will absolutely be fired.

Zach looks at me with understanding and lifts a hand as if he's going to touch me, then decides against it. He levels his gaze at me. His eyes are so dark I can barely see his pupils. They're beautiful in a way that makes me just want to stare into them all day and forget about everything else.

"Marina," he says, almost a whisper. "Let's think about this for a minute. What's real here? What's the truth?"

The spiral my mind is caught in stops completely. I blink at him for a moment.

"What?" I ask, my voice trembling.

His throat bobs. "In this moment. Right now," he says in a soothing voice. "What's the truth? What do we actually know?"

I blink again, not sure how to respond. He flexes his hand, gives me a pensive look, and places his fingers on my hand.

"Have you lost your job yet?" he asks coolly.

I shake my head. "No."

He nods slowly, never taking his eyes from mine.

"Right," he says simply. "We haven't even seen the media coverage. We don't know if they got a good shot of your face."

"There were cell phones everywhere," I shake my head, my voice still shaky.

He shakes his head gently, his warm brown eyes burning into mine. "What are the facts, love?"

Something in the emotion behind his eyes reaches into my chest and wraps around my heart, calming me. I take a deep breath and he nods.

"We don't know enough yet," I say quietly.

He gives me a small grin and releases my hand, sitting back in his chair.

Jimmy leans over and catches my eye. "It's gonna be okay, Marina. We deal with this all the time."

I look at him skeptically, shifting in my seat. Looking out the window, I can see that we're still on the bridge and not moving very fast at all. Zach slips his gaze to the window and seems to read my mind again.

"Don't take this the wrong way, Marina," he starts with a wicked grin, "but if I were wearing that thing, I'd be dying to get out of it. I don't have anything that would fit you, but I do have a pair of joggers and a t-shirt you can borrow if you'd like."

I raise my brows. "Joggers?"

Sam chuckles. "Sweats, man! When are you going to talk like an American?"

Rick and Jimmy laugh. Zach rolls his eyes and looks at me for my answer.

"They're in my closet just back there."

I look behind him, down a long hall that leads to the back of the bus. He nods and stands.

"Yes, we sleep on the bus a lot when we're touring the U.S.," he offers. "So there's a bedroom with a door at the back where you can change in private."

I look between the four of them. "A bedroom? Just one?"

Jimmy laughs. "The Duke gets the bedroom. We've got bunks."

The sudden realization hits me that he's not *just* a rock star. What have I done? I really hope I'm not going to end up dealing with the aftermath of a viral video of the two of us. I've seen enough of him on the news to know that his parents are also a duke and duchess in the United Kingdom. He's basically royalty. This is surreal. And it's a news story in two countries. No, thank you.

I stand up and nod. "Sweatpants sound amazing. Yes, please."

Zach gestures to the hall. "After you, Siren."

Once I get a real look at how far the back of the bus is, I heave a big sigh and shake my head. "Actually, that looks really far."

Zach looks confused for a moment, and I kick my foot, making the large mermaid tail flop against the floor. A big, floppy fish anchor holding me down.

"Maybe I should just grin and bear it," I say, looking at the chair in resignation.

Zach reaches for me hesitantly. "May I offer assistance?"

"Doesn't anything faze you? You seem completely unbothered that a mermaid on your tour bus needs to borrow your…joggers? Is that what you call them?"

The guys snicker.

Zach watches me carefully, his warm eyes creasing just slightly as he smiles.

"I *am* unbothered."

I nod my permission, snaking an arm around his neck and telling myself it's completely out of convenience and nothing else that I'm allowing this…let's face it…drop dead gorgeous man to hold me in his arms again. He picks me up immediately, stalking down the hall as the guys all yell, "See you soon, Marina!"

I laugh out loud, trying not to take a huge whiff of that sea salt, sage and sandalwood scent that's so intoxicating. I fail. Miserably. We pass two open bays with bunks on either side. There's also a small kitchen area. He comes to a stop at the end of the hall and lowers me gently. I pull my arms away from him, feeling a blush crawl up my cheeks.

"Thank you," I mutter, suddenly feeling a little self-conscious.

Zach nods and reaches over to open the door. "Let me get you those *sweatpants*," he says with a grin. He even makes sweatpants sound sexy with that flawless British accent.

The door opens to reveal a surprisingly spacious bedroom. Muted tones of gray and cream decorate the space, and natural wood cabinets flank the king-sized bed. It's neat and clean, not at all what I expected from a rock star's bedroom.

Zach steps in, walks over to the cabinet on the far side of the bed and opens it. Several drawers line the inside. He flips through two before he finds the sweatpants and a t-shirt, snatching them up with satisfaction and pacing back over to me. He hands them to me with a smile.

"You fold your sweatpants," I murmur with a smile, taking them from him. His fingers brush mine and my gaze flicks up to find him watching me.

He nods. "So?"

I hold his gaze and my smile. "That doesn't seem very rock star of you."

He raises his eyebrows. "Do you know many rock stars?"

I tilt my head as if I'm counting through my list of many friends, then shake my head. "You're the first one."

"Well, then we're even," he murmurs. "You're my first mermaid."

I laugh softly, and he grins like a Cheshire cat, then steps out of the room. He gestures at the bedroom.

"All yours, Marina," he says softly.

I nod and take two wiggle-walk steps into the bedroom when I feel his touch on my arm. I turn to face him with my hand on the door.

"Unbothered," he purrs. "But completely bewitched."

He turns and walks down the hall, his gait overflowing with confidence. He shakes his head to himself and mutters, "Siren," as I close the door with a soft laugh. I lean on the back of the door for a moment, trying to let my brain catch up with the events of today.

I'm alone in a rock star's bedroom. On a bus. On the Golden Gate Bridge. This day just gets weirder and weirder.

I reach back and unzip the mermaid tail, then quickly shimmy my way out of it.

Aaah!

"Yes!" I whisper as I toss it onto the bed.

I gently pop the sparkly purple flats off my feet and pace the room, digging my toes into the thick, luxurious carpet and letting my legs enjoy their freedom. My phone vibrates again, and I unlock my screen to look at my text messages. They're all from Merry.

Merry: Officer Honey Badger to the rescue! We got him to run your cell to the bus.

Merry: Text me when you get a minute...we want to make sure you're okay, girl.

Merry: Honey Badger came back with a message from the bus driver to follow along. You can get off the bus at the stadium.

Merry: He is so pretty, but a total honey badger. Mean. Sassy. Will probably fight me. Bummer.

Merry: Okay, are you so enraptured with the rock star that you can't text back?

Merry: Let us know you're okay because we are DYING FOR DEETS!!!

Merry: If you don't answer me in the next 5 minutes, you're wearing the mermaid for the rest of our gigs all year!

I laugh and hammer out a quick text.

Me: I'm fine. Sorry to worry you guys. This bus is amazing! I'm changing into a pair of sweats so I can walk like a normal person. And NO...I will not be wearing this death trap all year. LOL. See you soon!

I tap out of my texts and toss the phone onto the bed next to the mermaid tail.

There's a plush chair in the corner, and I step over to it. A stack of books sits atop a small table, and I can't help but snoop. British naval history mostly. Famous shipwrecks. No wonder our sea shanties lured him out of the bus. There's a picture of Zach and his parents in a silver frame. They're all dressed up, looking very…royal. They're standing on a finely manicured lawn, and I can just make out some kind of palace or palatial estate in the background.

I shake my head. I wonder what the Duke and Duchess of Wherever would think of me, growing up in the foster care system without a penny to my name. Aging out of it because I was a wild teenager nobody wanted. Not to mention…my brother. I force down the lump that forms in my throat every time he pops into my head.

Not now, Marina. Not now.

I steal one more glance at the picture before grabbing the sweatpants and my phone from the bed. Zach grew up in a world of tea parties and polo ponies. We couldn't be more different. He couldn't be more out of my league. A good thing, actually, since I swore off dating two years ago and I've kept to my word. Not that someone like Zach would ever be interested in some nobody dressed as a mermaid.

I inwardly chastise myself. I'm *not* a nobody. I'm a loyal friend. A dedicated employee. A good person. At least I am now. I'm secure enough to see that I'm not the same caliber as the celebrities and supermodels throwing themselves at someone like Zach. And that's okay. None of that appeals to me. I don't like drama. I don't like messes. I had enough of all of that as a kid.

I slip my legs into Zach's sweats, and I'm instantly swimming in them. They're soft, though, and I can move freely. And they smell like him. My mind immediately wants to wander off into Zach-land, wanting to know more about him. Wanting to spend more time in his presence. I know what it's like to be held in his arms…sort of.

But what would it really be like to be wrapped in those arms and kissed by those lips? There's something that's equally exciting and calming about him, and I have to admit feeling attracted to him. Very attracted.

No, Marina.

I roll the waistband of the pants a few times so they stay up and I can see my feet, then slip the t-shirt over my head. Now the scent of him hits me full force, and I feel the rest of my resolve crumble into dust. Just for a moment, I think as I bunch the fabric up in my hands and press it to my nose. I close my eyes and inhale deeply. He smells like beach sunsets by the fire. Salty, woodsy, fresh and clean. I could smell this scent forever.

I hear laughter coming from the living area, and I let go of the shirt, smoothing it down with my hands. Time to go. I slip my feet back into my flats and neatly roll up the mermaid tail, grab my phone, and square my shoulders. Time to make small talk until I can meet up with the girls and say goodbye to Zach and his friends for good. I wonder if they'd let us take a selfie with them for posterity's sake.

I open the bedroom door and walk down the hall to the living area, being extra careful with my steps. The bus is traveling at normal speed now, and I can see we're off the bridge. I take a seat in the chair next to Zach. Everyone smiles at me, and Jimmy points at my legs.

"That must feel better, yeah?" he asks with a grin.

I nod. "It's a pretty costume, but a horrible experience."

Zach looks at me with what seems to be regret, pulling all my attention his way.

"I think I owe you an apology," he says.

I blink back my surprise. "Why?"

His eyes scan my face, as if trying to discern something. "Your reaction to the helicopters," he explains. "I should have thought about what I was doing. About the attention I would bring just stepping out of the bus. I just heard your voice, and I had to see where it was coming from. *Who* it was coming from."

His passion for life amazes me. It also reminds me that we're from two different spheres. He lives for himself. He's wealthy, famous, and doesn't have to deal with dictator bosses or worrying about making rent. My early life taught me all the ways I did not want to live. Poor. No autonomy. No control. Now that I have a precious little bit of what I've fought for since my eighteenth birthday, the idea of doing anything to compromise it sends me into a panic. So I make every effort not to stand out. He lives in the spotlight. For me, this could be catastrophic. For him, it was just a duet on a bridge with a woman he'll never see again. That's all. A lump forms in my throat. Truthfully, I wish I had the luxury of being a little more like him.

"It's fine," I say in the voice I use to appease people a million times a day at work. "I work for a very conservative company, that's all. They would…well, there could be serious repercussions for me if things got out of hand."

All eyes are on me again, and I can feel half a dozen questions hanging in the air. No one is brave enough to ask them. I'm about to start up some small talk about the bus when Sam claps his hands and rubs them together like he's concocted an evil plan. While not as strikingly handsome as Zach and Rick, Sam is a regular guy with a bit of a Dad bod…but there's an energy about him that makes you want to smile.

"Right," he says with a grin. "Then I think we're duty-bound to give you some tips and tricks on how to evade the paparazzi, Marina."

I grin at him. "Yeah?"

Rick nods in agreement. "We snuck a peek at the news while you were changing," he reveals. "It doesn't look too bad right now. Most of the footage is of Zach because he's Zach."

I look around at all of them, hopeful that it's just as they say. I just can't afford any negative attention, and my boss is a demon in four-inch heels. I nod as if the act of doing it will ward off any bad mojo from today.

"Anyone who knows you personally may spot you in some of the footage we saw," Zach says calmly, looking like he wants to reach for my hand again. "But the *media* doesn't know who you are. They would still have to search for you and find you in order to cause any real problems."

My eyes widen again as I think about every terrible scenario, including the real fear of losing my job. That's exactly what would happen if I broke the cardinal rule of *bringing unwelcome attention to the firm.*

Zach's warm, strong fingers close over my hand again.

"We're going to show you how to make sure that doesn't happen," he says gently as I look into his eyes. I feel like a ball of tight energy is spinning around in my gut every time our eyes meet. "And we have a few tricks up our sleeves as well."

I take a big, shaky breath. "I'm listening."

"The press," Sam begins with a grin. "At least the kind that follow us around, aren't too bright sometimes. They see what they want to see."

Zach nods. "So we help them come to the right conclusion."

I frown at Zach. "I'm not following…"

"We hide in plain sight," Jimmy offers.

"For example," Zach says quietly. "As much as I absolutely hate the idea, you might want to keep your hair up on your head for a few weeks."

I raise my eyebrows. "Putting my hair up is going to solve this?"

Jimmy laughs. "*Cover* it up, Marina. They'll be looking for a redhead with long hair."

I grin slowly. "Okay, I can do that."

Zach shakes his head, and I turn back to him.

"And you hate this idea?" I ask with a frown.

Zach's eyes drift over my long red hair, and an expression I can't quite identify falls across his face. He shakes his head again.

"It's a crime to hide anything about you, Marina," he rasps. Not smiling. Not joking. "Especially that beautiful hair."

I feel the air in the room change. It's charged as if there are little invisible sparks flitting back and forth between the two of us. It pulls at me, and I resist it. I clear my throat.

"Okay, what else?" I say lightly, looking at Jimmy pointedly.

"Do you drive or take public transportation?" he asks.

"This is San Francisco," I say with a laugh. "Do you have any idea how expensive it is to own a car here? Parking fees everywhere, let alone the price of gas."

He nods. "All right then," he begins, looking thoughtful for a moment. "Don't go down to the bus stop until the last possible moment. Maybe change hats on the bus and put on a scarf so you look a little different when you get off than when you got on."

I laugh out loud. "Wow," I say with a shake of my head. "This is starting to feel like I'm running from the CIA."

They all chuckle. Zach leans forward.

"You'll only have to do it for a few weeks," he says gently. "By then, the press will have lost interest, and they'll be on to the next big thing."

I'm about to ask another question when the driver yells back to us. "We're here!"

I smile excitedly, dipping my head to look out the window, relief flooding through me. I'm rewarded with a view of the stadium looming ahead. The bus slows to a stop, and I hear the driver exchanging words with someone. He thanks them and we're moving again. The light dims everywhere as the bus enters a huge tunnel under the stadium. We slow to a crawl, then make a long turn, and the bus finally stops.

I stand, wanting to run for the door. I need to get away from Zach and his…everything. This has been a weirdly fun experience, but Zach unsettles me in a way I can't comprehend, and that's something I absolutely cannot allow. Before I take a step toward the door, I offer Zach and his friends a polite smile.

"It's been amazing to meet all of you," I say with genuine sincerity, then turn to Zach. "Have fun at your concert this week."

Zach blinks. "The benefit concert? That's not for a couple weeks. But we managed to book a handful of other appearances in the area as well, so we'll have plenty to do."

"Well," I say softly, taking a step away. "Thank you for coming to my rescue."

Zach looks at me like a poker player contemplating his next move, then extends his hand palm up. I lightly place my fingers in his hand, and he pulls my hand to his mouth, planting a light kiss on the back of my hand. My pulse reacts like a jackhammer as his soft lips touch my skin.

"It was an honor, my lady," he says with a twinkle in his eye, that British accent wrapping itself around my heart again and squeezing.

My fight-or-flight response is fully triggered by the full-fledged sex appeal emanating from this man. I laugh softly and pull my hand away, regarding them all one last time.

"Well," I say as I turn toward the door. "Goodbye. Enjoy your time here."

I turn and head toward the door, focusing on putting one foot in front of the other.

"I'll walk with you," Zach says quickly, closing the distance between us.

As I take the few steps that lead off the bus, I feel the heat of his body behind me like a shadow I can't shake. I hit the ground in the tunnel just as Ashley pulls the car up behind the bus. I make a bee line for the car, but I stop when I hear multiple footsteps behind me. I turn around to see Rick, Jimmy, and Sam are following as well. Great.

The girls trot over to Zach, and high fives are exchanged all around, and again when they meet Jimmy, Rick, and Sam. Merry and Scarlet decide to monopolize Zach for a few moments, so Ash and I decide to chat with the guys. I study Rick for a few seconds. He's looking at Ashley like he just saw an angel, and I have to fight back a grin. How sweet is that?

"I have a few more tips for you if you'd like," Sam says to me. He rubs his hand through his scraggly light brown hair. "When you're on the bus, let's say you've changed your hat and put on a different jacket. Walk a little differently when you get off the bus. If there's a back entrance to any building, use it. Make it as hard to find you as possible."

I nod solemnly. This feels like so much. All of this just because I was spontaneous one time. This is exactly why I always make a plan and stick with it. See what happens when I don't stick with said plan? Now I have to worry about my viper of a boss finding out, so I'm thinking about disguises and walking with a limp when I get off the bus.

Any unplanned attention aimed at the firm is unwelcome, Marina, I can hear her hissing.

"Hey," Ashley says quietly. "You okay?"

I nod automatically, fixing another placid smile on my face. "Fine. Just anxious to get home. Zach and the band have so much to do…we don't need to be in their way."

Jimmy laughs. "Are you kidding? Have you seen the way he looks at you?"

I blink up at him in surprise.

Rick shakes his head, pats Jimmy loudly on the back, and shoves him away. "Don't listen to him, Marina. He's just weird."

Zach, Merry, and Scarlet come over to join us. Scarlet's smiling so big I think she might explode.

"We're going to the benefit concert!" she squeals. "Zach's gonna give us VIP tickets."

He laughs softly, turning to me. "The benefit concert and the big Rebels concert the week after, if you'd like. Tickets will be waiting for you at the Will Call gate. How many should I leave?"

I look at him in confusion. "Four, I suppose?"

He nods. "Of course, but would any boyfriends want to come? Certainly some of you ladies are spoken for."

Ashley throws up a hand. "Oh, I'd love a ticket for my fiancé!"

Zach nods, then looks at Scarlet with a curious expression. She shakes her head. Merry waves him off. Then he turns to me.

"And what about you, Marina?" he purrs with an infuriatingly charming gleam in his eye. He knows exactly how obvious he's being. "Boyfriend?"

My green eyes meet his beautiful, I-see-you-Marina brown eyes. It should be illegal to be as handsome as he is. I can't afford to flirt with this man. It doesn't matter if those eyes pull at me with the power of a thousand magnets. Zach is a storm waiting to toss me around at sea, and I can't let that happen. Ever.

"I don't have time for men," I say, a touch of coldness in my voice.

I watch his expression change from one of surprise to understanding, just like every other guy who gets ideas about me. Good. I'm good at keeping strict boundaries, and I mentally pat myself on the back as I add another brick in the wall between me and Zach.

Ashley looks a little surprised at my tone. She smiles at Zach.

"Marina is studying to be a lawyer," she explains.

I give her a look that tells her to stop giving details as I nudge her towards the car.

Jimmy walks over to Zach. "I just took a peek. No helicopters outside."

"Great!" I cry, turning back toward the car with Ashley. "Let's get out of here before they come back."

I prod Ash, trying to get her to hurry it up. She whirls around to face me.

"What is up with you?" she whispers. "You're being really weird."

I open her car door for her and nudge her towards the seat.

"No, I'm not," I insist. I totally *am*, but whatever.

I look up to find that Merry has hung back and is talking to Zach again. Whatever they're talking about, he's listening with way too much interest. I hit Ash's horn and Merry looks up with a frown.

"Let's go!" I yell a little too quickly, then run around to the passenger side and get in.

Scarlet climbs in the back seat and looks me up and down. "What are you wearing, dude?"

"Zach loaned me some clothes so I could move normally," I explain. "I'll figure out a way to get them back to him."

Merry finally comes back to the car, and we're ready to go. I wave at Zach.

"Thank you again!" I call over the windshield.

He waves at me, a sly smile splayed across his face. The guys wave as well, and Jimmy yells, "See you at the concert!"

Ha. Not for a million dollars. The girls can go if they'd like, but I'm not getting within one hundred yards of Zach Adams, his muscley shoulders, or his beachy campfire vibes again. No good can come from this. I throw one last wave in the air, and as Ashley steers the car out of the tunnel and toward the stadium exit, I feel confident that my little Zach encounter is over and done with for good.

Chapter 3

Zach

I wave, watching Marina walk to her friend's car like I'm one of the four horsemen of the apocalypse and she needs to get as far away from me as possible. She's absolutely swimming in my clothes, which, combined with her bedazzled shoes, looks absolutely ridiculous. Yet she walks to the car with the confidence of a model wearing haute couture. I'm grinning so hard my face literally hurts. Who is this woman, and why do I suddenly need to know everything about her? She leans into the convertible and taps the horn, impatiently signaling her friends with the most adorable frown. I'm in big, big trouble. Huge.

"Hey, smitten kitten," Jimmy chuckles, his expression smug.

I think about denying it, but there's no point. Even if it wasn't written all over my face, Jimmy knows me too well. I smile at him and nod, smacking my hand over my heart for emphasis.

"I think I'm in trouble, mate," I confess, watching the car disappear down the tunnel.

He bobs his chin at me with a knowing look. "You coming up with a plan?"

"Absolutely," I say without hesitation.

He laughs out loud, then slaps me on the back and moves over to a small group of stadium crew that have gathered, yelling back, "Better be a good one!"

Rick and Sam join him. I wave to the group and turn back toward the bus. I need a minute. I need time to figure out a way through this. I step inside the bus, a plan already forming in my head. Thankfully, I'm not starting from scratch. While Marina was occupied with the guys, I took the opportunity to go talk to her friend Merry. Once I introduced myself, I tried my usual tactics to get information and failed miserably. Marina's inner circle is strong. After watching me make some of my best detective moves, she calmly looked down her nose at me and proclaimed that she knew exactly what I was trying to do.

I was then put through a vetting session where she threw rapid-fire questions at me to see whether I measured up. I'm not sure which answer did it, but I eventually passed her test.

At that point, Merry noticed Marina looking our way, so she turned to me and said, "I like you, Zach, but she'd kill me if I told you anything. But I also love that you give so much back to the communities you play in, and you seem like a good guy. That deserves something. So if you happen to show up at the Golden Gate Park branch of the San Francisco Public Library on Tuesday at 5:30 pm for song night in the children's wing…you better not tell her where you heard about it."

With that, she bounded off toward her friends without another look at me, a mischievous smile on her face. Marina is beautiful, talented, *and* she sings to children? I am in such big trouble.

I reflect back to that first moment on the bridge, when the last bit of the crowd parted, and I saw her sitting on the hood of that car. The costume was a surprise, yes, but it was her voice that lured me out of the bus. And when I *saw* her, when I saw the pure joy on her face as she sang to the crowd…I was a thousand percent hooked. Reel me in, I'm done. I didn't care about the crowd, the traffic, or anything else. I just wanted to bask for a minute in that green-eyed sunshine and never think about another thing again.

A knock on the door pulls me from my thoughts.

"Zach!" Rick calls through the door. "You okay with a quick meeting with some stadium guy at five? I don't know what he wants, but he's wearing a suit."

I laugh. Rick doesn't pay attention to titles or status, which is just one of the things I love about my friend. I stand and stretch, calling back, "That's perfect."

Work. Good. I'm grateful for the chance of any distraction. When it comes to music, I fly by the seat of my pants. My creativity has its own mind. All I have to do is let it go, and it does its own thing. But in all other areas of my life, I'm a planner. I think, I plan, I execute. Right now, I'm fuzzy on the whole thing…so a creative distraction is welcome. Then, I'll get back to planning.

I just need to be sure about the plan. I need to work out every detail because something tells me I only have one shot to catch this mermaid.

***

Marina

"No means no," I tell Ashley for the umpteenth time as I pour coffee into my drink tumbler on this gloomy Monday morning.

She scowls at me. I pull three packets of sweetener from the box, shut the drawer with my hip, open them, pour their contents into the tumbler, and then toss the empty packets in the trash. I reach into the fridge for the creamer, and she's still scowling at me.

"I don't have time for complications," I say emphatically.

I finish mixing my coffee, add ice, throw the plastic straw in, and screw the top on.

"He's not a complication," Ashley argues, her crystal blue eyes looking right through all my excuses. "He's a man. A *gorgeous*, famous, rich man who couldn't take his eyes off of you!"

I tilt my head to the side and squint at her. "The very definition of 'complication'. No, thank you."

I grab an elastic band from my purse and twist my hair up into a knot on top of my head, then take a sip of my coffee. *Mmmm.* Perfection. See? Coffee never lets you down. Men, not so much.

I shrug into the coat I left hanging on a nearby bar stool and pop a baseball cap on that says "Alcatraz Swim Club". It's a snug fit, thanks to the bun, but it works. I sling on my laptop bag, grab my purse and coffee, and offer Ashley a smile on my way to the door.

"You guys should go to both concerts if you want," I say with a sigh. "You'll have an amazing time. I want you to go. But I am not getting anywhere near Zach Adams again. Final answer."

With a firm nod, I step out of the apartment and leave Ashley with a bewildered look on her face. My heart sinks a little as I descend the stairs to the lobby of our apartment building, partially because a big part of me already wants to be around Zach more. He's handsome and charming, and he was very kind on the bus. In a way, it's reassuring that there's a little struggle going on in my heart between shutting him out and letting him in. The girls like to give me a hard time for the fierce boundaries I keep up when it comes to men. I struggled so much as a teenager, often making things worse for myself because I overreacted and lashed out at everything. I'm no longer in the business of causing myself drama, and inviting the attention of one of the biggest rock stars in the world would definitely bring drama. I wish the girls understood just a little of that, but all I've heard since we left the stadium yesterday is how Zach couldn't stop staring at me and how amazing it would be if we started dating.

Dating?

The idea is ridiculous on multiple levels. First, rock stars don't date penniless executive assistants. I've seen the kind of women usually on Zach's arm. He's always in the media. Second, my friends (whom I love dearly) are all being over dramatic. Yes, there were a few times I think I saw Zach looking at me with a glint of attraction in those gorgeous brown eyes. No, nothing is going to come from it. For two reasons: because I'm sure he looks at a lot of women like that and because I have no time in my life for anything that threatens my normal.

Remembering what Zach and the guys told me about making myself scarce in the eyes of any media snoops, I wait in the lobby of my building and watch out the glass door until I see my bus coming up the street. Just as it pulls up to the curb, I step outside and right onto the bus. I tap the payment pad with my card and take a seat on the aisle, turning away from the window.

The bus pulls onto the street as I reflect on my second near-panic attack while watching the news last night with Ashley after we dropped Merry and Scarlet off. Just as I feared, our impromptu concert was all over the news. Ashley barely kept me calm by pointing out that most of the content was focused on Zach because he's such a celebrity. But there was one gossip show that made a point to ask who the mermaid was. They zoomed in on my face, which was terrifying to see on the five o'clock news. Ashley, working hard to talk me off the proverbial ledge, pointed out that my hair was elaborately curled and pinned up with jeweled combs and that I was "in full glam" having come from a performance. I don't look like that every day. Maybe it would be enough.

In all likelihood, they'll be so focused on Zach that they won't give me another thought—but I'm determined to take all the precautions

I can to ensure I'm never found. I pull the baseball cap off my head and reach into my work bag, pulling out a beige cloche hat I found at a secondhand store when I went for a walk after my near meltdown yesterday. I slip the ball cap into the bag and put the cloche on, then shrug out of my reversible trench coat to flip the navy side to the beige and slip it on again. Boom. Better than the CIA.

Nearly a half hour later, the bus pulls to a stop at Trans United Tower. Home of several huge corporations, it's a massive building that lends a signature element to the San Francisco skyline. The top five floors are all for the highly conservative law firm of Taft & Kennedy, where I work as the executive assistant and designated whipping post for the infamous Alexis Taft. Yes, *that* Taft. The one whose name is on the door.

Alexis, or Ms. Taft as we peons are required to call her, is a five-foot three-inch tornado in Louboutins. She never has a hair out of place and is always clad in designer suits. Ms. Taft only accepts perfection. She's the youngest partner at the firm, the only child of the great Leopold Taft, our founder and former mayor of San Francisco, and she holds my entire future in her hands. She likes to dangle it in front of me like a child playing with a new kitten.

I step off the bus and head straight to the ladies restroom in the lobby, removing the cloche and putting it in my work bag. I take my hair down completely, run a brush through it a few times, then set to work winding it up in the tight chignon that is the standard hairstyle of all women at the firm. I give it a quick spritz with some setting spray I keep in my bag and eye my reflection in the mirror. There. Not a hair out of place.

On any normal day, I opt for very little makeup. A little mascara and a little lipstick. I let the spray of freckles show across my nose and cheeks, a by-product of my natural red hair. I'll never have flawless skin, and I'm okay with that. I grab my bags and head for the door.

Covered in gray marble, the huge lobby is overwhelming. And I do mean covered. The floors are dark gray marble. The security and reception desks are a lighter gray marble. The walls...gray marble. Chrome trim and fixtures provide some contrast, as do the lush cream rugs and cream leather couches in the waiting area. A few fake spiky-looking plants in giant gray pots fill the corners of the lobby. It's cold and a little ominous, but it's all by design.

It actually helps me get into work mode. As soon as I step inside these doors, I'm all business. I make an effort not to forge friendships at work. I'm polite. Respectful. Hard-working. Dependable. That's all they need to know about me. This firm pays their executive assistants a significantly higher wage than other firms, and I'm barely making it as it is in a city that's notoriously expensive to live in. I need every penny I can get, especially since Ashley's boyfriend Greg recently became her fiancé. As happy as I am for her, I'll be without a roommate within a year, and I can't afford to stay in my apartment unless I get a promotion or a pay raise. A new roommate is not something I'm prepared to think about. It's hard enough for me to let people in, and the idea of letting someone move in with me that I only know through a few interviews...well, no thanks.

The firm, rhythmic click of my heels on the marble floors echoes in the vast space as I make my way to the bank of elevators. The security guard nods at me in greeting, and I give him half a smile before I disappear into an elevator and push the button for the 48th floor.

Within minutes, I'm at my desk. Ms. Taft is already in her office, of course. When I first got this job, I wondered if she had a button under her desk she pushed so a bed appeared, allowing her to just sleep here. Once she trusted me enough to run personal errands for her, which is both a blessing and a curse, I was given access to her twelve-million-dollar apartment in Nob Hill. You know, so I can stop by Hermes and pick up her $30,000 special edition Birkin bag and drop it off with her dry cleaning.

"Don't even sit," she calls from her office in a tone I've learned to dread.

I mentally run through a list of possible crimes and come up empty. Unless, of course, she happened to see the news. She doesn't care about the entertainment world, though. Even I would be surprised if she looked up at the TV because of a story about a rock star and a mermaid. It can't be that.

Can it?

Right. I grab my notebook and a pen and rush to her office.

She's frowning slightly at her laptop when I walk in, gesturing at one of the plush chairs in front of her desk with a perfectly manicured finger. I sit, trying to ignore the morning news playing on the large flat screen mounted on the wall. The two anchors are discussing a police chase that happened late last night.

Ms. Taft looks up, her gaze raking over me from head to toe. I can feel her going through the checklist she gave me on my first day at work: hair, face, suit, shoes. I try not to feel self-conscious. I know how to "groom myself for success", as she calls it. All perfect.

"The Montclair Group is looking for new representation," she says with a predatory gleam in her eyes. "Taft & Kennedy *will* get that contract."

She says it without a hint of doubt in her voice. It's a done deal to her. The most successful marketing and media firm in the city will be our newest client. I nod silently.

"Ethan Montclair and I went to school together," she elaborates, smoothing a perfect finger over one of her perfect eyebrows. "In fact, our parents were hoping something might happen between the two of us but…well, we were both very focused on other things."

I nod again, reserved and obedient, waiting for my orders.

"I've reached out," she says matter-of-factly. "He's a bit busy this week, meeting with other prospective firms, I'm sure. We're meeting for drinks next week—and he's promised to come here to hear our formal proposal on the 28th."

She pauses for dramatic effect, studying the diamond watch on her wrist. I mentally do the math. Whatever she's planning, we have about three weeks to get everything in place.

"We *will* be ready," she declares with a lift of her chin. "I'll need you to ensure everything is perfect here. I'll have everyone else working full time on the proposal. We'll cater breakfast in the executive conference room, but I think we'll go out for lunch after the proposal to celebrate closing the deal."

I nod firmly. "Absolutely, Ms. Taft," I say eagerly. "I'll take care of everything."

She holds my gaze with a slight glare, and I will myself to maintain eye contact. When she's satisfied that she's terrified me into submission, she nods. As she turns back to her desk, she glances up at the television.

"Wow," she says, grabbing the remote for the television and hitting pause.

My heart pounds in my ears as I turn in slow motion to find a frozen image of Zach and me on the bridge. It's blurry, but my red hair is there. Most of the picture shows Zach, but there's a slightly obscured view of the side of my face.

Ms. Taft points at me with the remote. "You have a twin out there," she says with a scoff.

I shake my head, looking at the image as if it's completely ridiculous.

"She's wearing way too much makeup," Ms. Taft deduces, "and her hair is just ridiculous. But she looks a lot like you."

I'm a riot of emotions on the inside, but I somehow manage to keep my face calm and reserved. Bored, even. I take a good look at the image on the television and roll my eyes.

"I don't have any family," I say with a shrug. "No sisters or anything."

Ms. Taft considers for a moment, pursing her lips in thought. She flicks the television off and drops the remote on her desk. I breathe a very quiet, very slow sigh of relief.

"I don't understand this hysteria over some rock singer creating a stupid scene on the bridge," she grumbles. "Who cares?"

I smile and shrug, praying it's enough of a response to make her drop the subject. She raises her chin at the doorway and excuses me. I stand immediately and hurry to the door.

"Marina," she calls sternly.

I turn to face her.

"I will not accept anything less than perfection," she warns ominously. "We must do everything to impress Ethan and his colleagues. If anything goes wrong with this meeting, I will hold you responsible."

I swallow deeply, my throat bobbing.

"But," she continues. "With great success comes great rewards. Do your part well, help us get this contract, and I will make sure you're rewarded well."

I straighten my spine with determination and square my shoulders. "I won't let you down, Ms. Taft," I declare, stepping out of her office and closing the door behind me.

Fear of discovery aside, it's all I can do not to skip back to my desk. My heart is beating so hard I can almost hear it. She bought the notion that the news footage wasn't me, so I'm relieved beyond words. But this meeting…this is a huge opportunity. Not only because her favorite way to reward people is to throw money at them, but because it might open the door for me to ask for help with law school. A letter of recommendation from Taft & Kennedy would carry a lot of weight with all the law schools I'm interested in.

I sit at my desk and open a drawer, pulling out my favorite notepad and pen. If there's one thing I do well, it's rolling out the red carpet when they need me to. It's time to do a little research on our guest—because I'm determined to make this meeting the high point of Ethan Montclair's time here. He'll be begging to give us the contract by the time I'm done.

Chapter 4

Marina

I clutch my work bag on the bus ride home as if it contains the CIA answer files on every mystery in the world. My regular work day is normally crammed full of things to handle for Ms. Taft, but I managed to do some internet research on Ethan Montclair between projects. I printed everything out, stuffed it in my bag, and plan to spend the evening reading. But first…home, comfy clothes, and whatever food I can scrounge up.

Just before my stop, I change my hat, take my coat off, and drape it over my arm. I step off the bus and dart into my building, bounding up the stairs to my apartment with renewed energy. With any luck, Ashley is already home from work, and I can bounce ideas off her.

As soon as I'm inside the apartment, the heavenly smell of Ash's lasagna hits me full force. I grin from ear to ear, take my hat off, toss my bags in the entry, and practically run to the kitchen, throwing my arms around her. She laughs and shoves me away.

"I love it when you make lasagna!" I cry, grabbing a glass and filling it with water. I pull a bar stool up to the small kitchen counter and plop myself down.

Ashley throws a few frozen breadsticks on a cookie sheet and puts it in the oven with the lasagna that smells ready to come out. Yum. She eyes me curiously.

"What's up with you?" she asks coolly. "You seem…happier than usual."

I squirm with excitement. "I am! Good things are on the horizon, Ash. If I make one little meeting a success at work."

I fill her in on the details of the contract with Montclair and Ms. Taft's offer to make sure I'm rewarded if I pull it off. Ashley rolls her eyes at the mention of my boss, who she completely hates.

"Ms. Taft," she scoffs as she pulls two plates out of the cabinet. "That woman is evil. And her offer is too vague, Marina. She'll make sure you're rewarded? With what?"

I think for a moment. Ashley doesn't wait for an answer.

"A thousand-dollar bonus?" she muses. "A new car? Jelly of the month club? It could mean anything."

"Oh!" I exclaim as I remember my near heart attack today. "She saw the news footage this morning, and I nearly died. Luckily, she's too self-absorbed to even imagine that her quiet, meek assistant could be dressed up like a mermaid and singing with a rock star in the middle of a traffic jam."

Ashley giggles.

"She paused the video to show it to me," I say excitedly. "I thought I was caught for sure. But she just wanted to show me that I have a twin out there somewhere."

"She doesn't think any of her people have a life," Ashley muses. "You should have asked her for details on what rewarding you means…it gives her too much freedom to back out."

"No one asks questions when it comes to Ms. Taft," I explain. "But I've seen how she rewards people, Ash. Huge bonuses. Promotions.

All I want is a letter of reference for a good law school. Well, and I wouldn't turn down a bonus."

Ashley leans her hip on the counter and folds her arms across her chest.

"You don't have to worry so much, you know," she tells me, a look of genuine concern on her face. "We haven't even set a date for the wedding yet. Greg is too busy. It's going to be awhile before you need to think about a new roommate or another apartment."

I smile at Ash, cupping my chin in my hand and leaning my elbow on the counter. I look around at our apartment and smile. It's insanely expensive to live in this city, so it's small and in a questionable neighborhood at best, but it's ours. I could live farther away, outside the city, but then I'd need a car and all the expenses that carries. Being roommates with Ash has been the perfect solution for me, and, to be honest, I don't know what I'm going to do once she moves on with her life.

"I'm not worried," I say in the standard, airy voice I use when I'm worried and don't want people to know. "I'll be fine."

She nods with an expression that shows me she knows I'm full of it. "Yes, you will be…because I'm not going to let you down."

I make a face. "You're not letting me down by living your life, Ash," I say softly. "If Greg is the one for you, then I'm happy for you. You belong with each other. You shouldn't need to worry about me."

"But I do. You've worked so hard to gain your independence, and I know you worry about backsliding. I just feel like you're always waiting for the other shoe to drop. For the next bad thing to happen… and I want you to know that I will never let anything bad happen to you, Marina. You're my best friend."

Without a word, I get up from my perch, walk into the kitchen, and throw my arms around Ashley again. She squeezes me back hard in one of those really great, super strong friend hugs. Suddenly, I'm on the verge of tears and desperately need to change the subject. I let go quickly.

"Can we eat that before it burns?" I say with a laugh, grabbing the plates and setting them on the counter.

"Oh geez!" Ashley gasps, grabbing the oven mitts and rescuing the breadsticks first. She pulls the lasagna out next, then gets silverware from the drawer and puts them out for us. "C'mon, tell me about your big plans to win the contract while we let that cool a few minutes."

***

Twenty-four hours later, I've done more research on Montclair and his inner circle, and the media still hasn't let the mermaid story die out—although right now, the theory is that Zach hired me as part of a publicity stunt. The attention is still mostly on him, which is both a blessing and a curse. I don't know how many videos I watched of him on my phone last night while drifting off to sleep, but it was enough to make me dream about him.

I'm full of inspiration as I step outside the apartment and pop open an umbrella. The library is ten blocks north and since it's raining just hard enough to need an umbrella, I'm not in danger of being identified by anyone. It's chilly out, even with the jeans and cozy gray sweater I changed into when I got home, and I pull my jacket tighter while I walk. I'm grateful for the chance to just be silent for a while. The sounds of the city are my only companion. The pitter-patter of rain. A car honking in the distance. The musical ding of a cable car somewhere nearby. The sound of my boots on the sidewalk. I let it wash over me like a kind of music, lulling me into a sense of calm so I can think. My mind begins ruminating over my duet with Zach on the bridge, his invitation to the benefit concert this Sunday, and my reluctance to go.

Ashley knows me better than anyone. In fact, she's the first close friend I've ever had. We found each other in college, both of us instantly feeling like we'd known each other forever. There's something about Ashley that I know I can trust, even in my first year of college when I had just aged out of the foster care system. Before Ash, I tried to minimize my interactions with everyone in my life. Having long been labeled a problem kid, I spent most of those years living in a group home for troubled teens. New kids came and went like there was a revolving door on the place. Some kids were lucky and were adopted by families, but most of us were stuck there until our 18th birthday.

While many of the girls in the group home I lived in went right back to the families they'd been taken away from as children, my situation was different. My only family was my brother, and I believed he was far better off without me. So I reached for the only lifeline I had: a college education, thanks to grants and assistance available only to newly minted adults who aged out of foster care. Soon after, I met Ashley one night in a coffee house on campus when she spilled her drink on her laptop, and I jumped in with a trusty pack of tissues.

She knows my whole story. She knows how I struggled after my mom was killed in a car accident. She knows about my brother and the absolute shame I feel over the whole situation. When she realized I didn't have a family, she welcomed me into hers—which consisted of her and her father, her mother having died from cancer years before.

The following year, Scarlet and her mother landed in our lives. Merry came soon after, along with her entire crazy family. Now I have this sort of patchwork family, all of whom love me and want me to succeed—and I know Ashley means it when she says she's not going to let anything bad happen to me. Any one of my found family would take me in, but after growing up a burden…first to my overworked, underpaid mother, then to six different foster families, and finally to a state-funded home…I am prouder than the average person to be standing on my own two feet. I'm going to do everything in my power to be ready to handle Ashley moving out, which is why it's so important that we get the Montclair contract.

I spot a familiar polka-dot raincoat ahead of me and realize I'm already at the library. Little Miss Amanda, a precocious five-year-old, is holding her foster mother's hand as they walk up the sidewalk together. I smile as I walk up the steps to the library, having been so lost in my thoughts I don't even remember the journey here.

***

Zach

I step inside the library doors, and the smell of books hits me instantly, bringing a quick smile to my face. I love libraries. As a kid, the one in our family home was my favorite place to spend time. Of course, when you're a child and you're growing up on your family's ancestral estate…no other kids for miles but a pesky younger brother…where else would you go? Pirates, cowboys, kings and queens, musicians, and sailing ships were all waiting for me in the family library.

I walk into the main room of the library and take a moment to absorb my surroundings. Large oak tables are neatly lined up along either side of me, with brass lamps providing close-up lighting on each one. A large circular reception desk is in the center, and library employees are moving about, loading books on carts, or helping people find materials. The second floor looks down on the first, and antique wood railings border the opening that looks down to the reception area on the first floor. The distant thump and slide of books being pulled out and re-shelved, it's impossible to tell which, echoes gently all around me.

"Can I help you find something, sir?" a library employee says from just behind me.

I turn to find a woman with honey-blond wavy hair, bright blue eyes, and a kind smile waiting for my answer. I smile back.

"I'm here for song night," I answer quietly, half expecting her to eye me with suspicion because I don't have a child with me. Instead, she nods with a warm expression.

"I was just about to head down there myself," she says. "You can walk with me."

I step back and motion for her to lead the way, and soon she's leading me down one of the many corridors on the east side of the main room.

"I'm Danielle. Is this your first time here?" she asks as we walk.

I don't miss it when her eyes dart around us. Yep, she's wondering why a grown man with no child is interested in song night, and I instantly like her. I decide to put her at ease.

"I'm a…friend of Marina's," I say pensively.

Her kind eyes light up instantly. "Oh, how wonderful!" she exclaims softly. "She'll be happy to see you."

We reach a foyer just outside what is definitely the children's wing. Crepe paper flowers and brightly colored butterflies are stuck to a three-dimensional tree coming up out of the center of the floor. She leads me to one side of it, gesturing to a brunette clerk behind a small desk.

"Cherie will check your cell phone for you," Danielle says matter-of-factly.

Cherie waves a small ticket at me as if I'm supposed to know what to do. I look at Danielle in confusion.

"Check my cell phone for what?" I ask with a confused grin.

She guides me closer to the desk.

"We don't allow cell phones in the children's area," she explains. "Some of the children who come to song night are in the foster care system. No cell phones, no photography."

"No exceptions," Cherie offers from behind the desk with a bright smile, holding her hand out. "I'll keep it safe until you're ready to go."

Without another word, I pull my mobile from my jeans pocket, silence it, and place it in Cherie's hand. She gives me half of the ticket she was waving and now it all makes sense. She sticks the other half of the ticket on my phone and puts it in a drawer.

I feel an arm loop around mine and I look down to see Danielle grinning up at me. "Shall we go see Marina, *Mr. Adams?*"

My expression gives me away before I can say anything, and she places a reassuring hand on my arm.

"Don't worry," she whispers. "I won't give you away. Although you're so famous, that may not make a difference."

I let her lead me into one of the rooms that spokes off the foyer. My eyes immediately find Marina, who is sitting on a small stool and talking to two little girls who've brought her a book to look at. Her hair is loose, falling in flattering waves that frame her beautiful face. Her green eyes light up as she listens to the girls tell her a story, and suddenly, my heart rate is all over the place. I feel a gentle pinch on my hand, and I look down at Danielle.

"Marina is special," she says in a serious tone, her eyes full of concern as they study me.

I nod. "I couldn't agree more."

She gives me a warning look. "Just making sure we understand each other," she says, walking away to greet some of the other adults milling about the room.

Thankfully, Marina is so engrossed with the children she doesn't notice me. I find a spot in the corner and lean against the end of a bookcase, unable to keep my eyes off her as more children file into the room, followed by their parents.

"Marina!" a little boy yells at the top of his lungs as he runs at her from the entry door. A young woman trails behind, shushing the boy to no avail. She grabs the back of the boy's shirt to stop him from plowing right into Marina.

Marina smiles sweetly at the boy, patting the stool next to hers. He sits obediently, and the young woman steps away and slumps against a table in the back of the room.

"Brandon, I'm so glad you're here," Marina tells the boy, who is fully enraptured. Can't say I blame him. "Can you sit right here and help everyone remember that there's no shouting in the library?"

He gives her a knowing look. Nothing gets by this kid. He says something to her, but I can't quite hear it. She puts an arm around him and gives him a gentle squeeze. He looks up at her, and I suppress a laugh. I know that look.

Don't steal my girl, kid.

I watch her engage with the children over the next several minutes, feeling my heart slip farther and farther away from me with every eyebrow raise…every soft laugh…every toss of her hair. She is a natural with these kids, and it's obvious how much they love her. She is absolutely enchanting and I am in way over my head.

"All right, everyone, it's almost time!" Danielle calls out as she comes to the front of the room. "Please take your seats and put on your listening ears so Miss Marina can sing for us."

The kids rush to the center of the room in an adorable mob of ponytails, ball caps, and scuffed sneakers. They eagerly line up in neat rows, then sit down. All except Brandon, who's still trying to steal my girl. I need to keep an eye on this kid.

As if reading my thoughts, Marina whispers something to Brandon and he looks disappointed for a moment, then sits on the floor right in front of her. As he stands up, his gaze falls on me and I can tell he recognizes me. His eyes light up in a way I know all too well. I'm only saved because Marina taps him on the shoulder and reminds him to sit down. She looks out at the sea of children in front of her.

"Hi everyone!" she greets in a melodious voice.

"Hi, Miss Marina!" the children answer together.

"I think tonight we'll start with one we can all sing together," she says. "Are you ready to sing with me?"

She's rewarded with a chorus of yeses, squeals, and cheers. She laughs softly.

She begins singing "The Itsy Bitsy Spider" and the children immediately join in. Again, I'm lured in by her honey-smooth voice. It's clear and pure, with a quality that instantly calms me. I can't help the huge smile that comes as she uses her delicate hands to mimic the spider crawling up the water spout and the rain that washes him back down. The children do as she does, their voices strong and sure, their smiles wide as they end the song together and burst into applause.

"Very good!" she praises them, laughing genuinely and giving high fives to the kids in the front row. Brandon makes sure he gets his in there, then whirls around to see if I'm still here. When Marina begins speaking, he turns back around to give her his full attention.

"Wasn't there a song someone wanted last time that we didn't have time for?" she asks, scanning the children's faces. Several little hands shoot up straight in the air.

"Katie?" Marina calls, pointing at a little girl with long blond braids.

"Kensly wanted that Cinderella song!" she says with a near-toothless grin.

Several kids around her nod their heads in eager agreement. The girl looks down at a slightly younger girl next to her, also with blond braids, and smiles. Big sister looking out for little sister, no doubt. Something squeezes at my heart a little.

"All right," Marina says softly. "Before I sing it, what did we learn from Cinderella?"

Every hand shoots back up in the air. Marina begins calling on a few of the kids to share their answers.

"Be kind to everyone," a little girl answers.

"Gus is fat!" a boy yells, then laughs.

Brandon raises his hand and Marina calls on him. "If magic was real, I'd wish you were my fairy godmother," he says with a shy grin.

I can tell by Marina's expression her heart melted a little over that one. I silently contemplate tying this kid's shoelaces together in retaliation.

When Marina begins to sing "A Dream Is A Wish Your Heart Makes", everyone goes still. Even the kids, so wiggly and full of energy, are fully mesmerized by Marina's soft, lilting version of the classic song. As she sings, she looks around the room, making eye contact with the kids as if the lyrics are meant only for them. Each child smiles when she gets to them, and whatever is squeezing my heart grips a little tighter. I rest my head against the bookcase I'm leaning on, a wide smile on my face as I listen to her beautiful voice.

As she gets to the final verse, her eyes drift up to mine suddenly. To her credit, she doesn't miss a beat of the song, but her spine straightens, and her shoulders push back. Those bright green eyes burn into mine, and she has that look again. Like she's on high alert and ready to run. I feel my smile fade a little, and I tilt my head at her, shaking my head just a little to let her know I'm not planning any grandiose bridge karaoke tonight. She seems to get my message and relaxes a little.

The children and their parents burst into applause when she finishes the song, then turns to the audience and bows her head slightly. Brandon looks back at me again, then smiles and gives me a little wave. I wave back quickly and motion for him to turn around and pay attention to Marina. He does, thankfully.

I spend the next forty minutes watching Marina completely enthrall the room full of kids and their parents. Or guardians, I realize, since Danielle shared that some of these kids are in foster care. Between songs, Marina asks them about their favorite books or what they like to do after school, and then she manages to sing a song that has something to do with that. Occasionally, her eyes meet mine. Like when she led the children in singing "If You're Happy and You Know It" and she raised her eyebrows at me to make sure I was clapping along. I absolutely did.

Marina tells the kids there's only time for one more song, and there's a collective chorus of groans. All the adults laugh, some getting coats and jackets ready. I look at my watch. I can't believe it's nearly been an hour. Marina is in her element, laughing and chatting with the kids. I can feel myself slipping more and more under her spell. She laughs softly at something one of the children says, and I feel myself grin in response. I can't take my eyes off Marina, and that's exactly why I don't see Brandon stand up and point right at me.

"Can Mr. Zach sing the last song with you?" he asks loudly, a huge smile on his face.

Chapter 5

Zach

As if in slow motion, all eyes turn to me. My mouth drops open. Brandon just stands there with a pleading grin on his face, having no idea what he's done. Marina's eyes are as big as saucers, and I feel an immediate need to fix this. I just don't know how. I look around at the parents, some of whom are obviously excited at my presence. I say a silent prayer of thanks that they don't allow mobile phones in here, or I'd be the cause of Marina's worst nightmare right now.

"I came to hear Marina sing," I hedge, shaking my head. "She doesn't need my help."

Brandon groans, then folds his little hands together and shakes them at me. "Pleeeeeeez?" he whines. "My dad and me listened to all your songs all the time."

Something in his tone has me looking over at Marina, who nods at me with a soft smile and gestures for me to come to the front of the room. Suddenly all the air leaves my lungs, but I somehow manage to propel my body forward and awkwardly fold my 6' 2" frame to claim the tiny stool next to her.

Brandon throws his arms around me in a bear hug. For a little guy, he's incredibly strong. I put my hand on his back and give him a few pats. Danielle appears out of nowhere and expertly moves Brandon to my side, whispering something to him about giving side hugs to strangers and then fading into the background again. I give his shoulders a little squeeze, and he gives me a huge smile. Then, he runs over and settles back down on the carpet. I look over at Marina, and I see tears welling up as she watches him. She turns away and smiles at the kids.

"Well, I guess we should ask Mr. Zach what children's songs he knows," she says with a gleam in her eye, turning back toward me.

All at once, kids begin yelling out song titles.

"The Wheels on the Bus!"

"Frozen!"

"Are you a Swiftie?"

"Let's Shake!"

She looks at me, and I grin helplessly, shaking my head. "I don't know any of those." I look down at Brandon and add, "Sorry."

Brandon gives me a very star struck thumbs up.

Marina appears thoughtful for a moment, then leans closer. She smells like coconut and sunshine, and I have to fight the urge to bury my face in her hair and inhale. Somehow, I think that might be a tad over the line.

"What about 'You Are My Sunshine'?" she whispers over to me.

I clap my hands together excitedly. "I know that one!"

Marina and the kids all laugh, and I smile back at them with a thumbs up. Brandon jumps up and gives me a high-five. Danielle reappears, thrusting an acoustic guitar at me with a wink. Where is she coming from? Is there a magical little Danielle door that she pops out of, instantly holding whatever it is that's needed? Where did the guitar come from?

"Mr. Elliott had to miss song night tonight," she explains. "He usually accompanies Marina. Would you like to use this?"

The children break into applause, so I pull the guitar onto my lap and look to Marina for guidance. Her calm green-eyed gaze meets mine, and my pulse is pounding. I sing in packed stadiums without giving it a second thought, but this? This is something else entirely. A room full of children and the most beautiful woman I've ever seen…that's pressure on very unfamiliar ground.

"Ready when you are," she says with a shy smile, my heart doing that familiar squeezy thing again.

I nod, and begin strumming out the opening of the song. Marina begins with the opening verse and I join her, our voices intertwining perfectly. We sing together as if we've done it for years, smiling at each other and at the kids as we harmonize our way through the familiar song. Several of the kids sway to the music, sweet smiles on their faces. The room bursts into applause when we finish.

Marina and I take a bow for the kids as Danielle reappears.

"Thank you all for coming to song night," she says with her arms wide open. "Make sure you have all your things as you exit, kids. We'll see you next month!"

Brandon runs over to me again. "Are you coming to sing next time too, Mr. Zach?"

The same young woman steps up to Brandon with his jacket, smiling shyly at Marina and me.

"C'mon, buddy," she says quietly. "It's time to go home. You can have a story before bed."

Brandon stomps his little foot. "I want to stay and talk to Miss Marina and Mr. Zach!"

Marina leans forward, and Brandon looks at her with a wobbly lower lip.

"Brandon," she says gently, keeping a soft expression on her beautiful face. "You know the rules, my friend. But I'll tell you what: if I hear from Aunt Grace that you did all your homework and made good choices, I'll let you pick the very first song next time."

His face lights up. "Really?"

Marina laughs softly and nods. "Really. Do we have a deal?"

Brandon looks at me. "Will Mr. Zach be back next time?"

All eyes turn to me, except Marina's. She doesn't even look at me as she shakes her head and says, "Mr. Zach is a very busy man. He's just visiting our city right now."

I immediately want to jump in and deny it. I want to say I'll be back. I'll sing for the kids. I'll do anything if it means I can sing with Marina again, to spend a little more time in her presence. Truth is, she's right. I *am* just visiting. I have no reason to believe she'd even want me to extend my visit, let alone stay here indefinitely. And why am I even thinking about this right now? I have a band. I live in hotels and on my tour bus most of the time. What's going on with me? Still, I find myself leaning forward and putting my hand out for Brandon. He puts his tiny hand in mine, and I shake it gently.

"It's been lovely meeting you, Brandon," I say with a wide smile. "I don't know how long I'll be here, but if I am still in town for the next song night, I would love to come back and sing for you. If it's okay with Miss Marina."

Marina looks at me as if I just told her she has to live the rest of her life in that mermaid tail I rescued her from. Hmm. When she realizes she has an audience, she puts a smile back on her face and nods at Brandon.

"Of course," she says. "Now go with Aunt Grace, and I'll see you next time, okay?"

Brandon nods and obediently slips his arms into his jacket. He takes his aunt's hand and waves goodbye to us, then walks towards the door.

The room bustles with activity as tiny hands wave goodbye to Marina, and parents swoop in with coats and jackets. Several of them tell their tiny charges to say thank you. A few of the parents steal a glance at me, giving me big smiles and nods of approval. I thank them, but maintain my focus on the action of the kids in the room, an old trick that sends a subtle message that this is not the time or place for autographs. Sometimes it works, sometimes it doesn't—but tonight it does, and that's all I care about. After several minutes, Danielle has ushered the last of them into the foyer and Marina and I are alone.

She's silent at first, chewing on her lip and obviously trying to figure out how I found her. Just as I'm about to confess, she turns to me.

"Merry," she says with a shake of her head. "That's what you were talking about in the tunnel, isn't it?"

I hold my hands up in surrender. "To be fair, she spent most of the time interrogating me about my intentions."

She squints at me. "Intentions?"

I lean a little closer, incapable of resisting the pull of her beautiful eyes. "Towards you."

She scoffs, but I don't miss that her gaze drops to my mouth for a split second. "What intentions would you possibly have towards me?"

I tilt my head with a smirk and open my mouth to reply, but she holds a hand up.

"Don't answer that," she mutters.

Danielle comes back in, handing me my mobile with a pensive smile.

"I hate to tell you," she begins quietly, "but a few of the parents are hovering outside the children's wing, probably waiting to see if they can get pictures or autographs."

Marina's shoulders sag, and I suddenly feel guilty about coming. I look around us.

"Is there a back way out of here?" I ask, then turn to Marina. "No one has any pictures of us here. There's no story for the media if there aren't pictures."

I turn to Danielle with a hopeful expression. She grins.

"I can let you out the historian's office. It has a door that exits directly to the alley out back," she says, patting Marina on the shoulder.

Marina's gaze darts up to Danielle. "I guess I'll just stay at the library for a while until the parents realize he's gone and there's nothing to see."

Danielle looks at her with surprise etched on her face. I shake my head.

"I have a car service," I explain. "I can drop you at home."

She barely looks at me. "No, thank you. I'll be fine."

"Are you mad at me?" I ask boldly, leaning forward to meet her eyes.

When she looks up at me, I can see the shield she's built around herself as clearly as if it was a real, tangible thing. I stiffen.

"No," she says simply. "But the less we're seen together, the better. I do not want the media to find me."

I nod slowly. "I understand," I say softly. "But I can get you home without attracting media attention, I promise."

She shakes her head. "I don't live far. I walked here, and I don't mind walking back."

Danielle gasps. "Marina, it's pouring outside now. No one wants to walk in that."

I give a grateful wink to Danielle and turn to Marina. "Please? I'm a Brit. I have to be chivalrous. It's in my DNA."

She doesn't want me to see the corner of her mouth tip up in a half smile, but I do. I feel like I won the lottery. She looks up at Danielle in a silent plea for help, but Danielle is firmly on Team Zach. She nods as if to say, "go with the handsome man who's clearly obsessed with you." At last, Marina turns back to me.

"Fine," she mutters. "But please stop showing up wherever I am."

I narrow my eyes at her and smirk. "I've only done it once."

She raises her eyebrows. "What about the bridge?"

"That was *your* fault," I tease, standing and stretching after sitting too long on the tiny stool. I wink at Danielle, and she suppresses a smile.

Marina stands as well. "*My* fault? How do you make that out?"

I raise my eyebrows and place my hand on my heart as if I'm testifying as the defendant at a murder trial.

"There I was," I begin with a touch of drama, "relaxing on my quiet little tour bus, when I was ensnared by a siren and her captivating song."

I'm rewarded when she rolls her eyes and laughs. "*Little* tour bus… ha!"

I laugh, pulling up my phone and starting a text message to the driver I hired for my time in the city. He answers back immediately.

"He'll be here in five minutes," I say with a grin, turning to Danielle. "Would you mind telling the driver where to bring the car?"

Danielle nods and I dial the driver, handing the phone to her as she motions for us to follow. Marina grabs her jacket and a handbag so large she can crawl inside of it. I gesture for her to go first and I follow. Danielle speaks in hushed tones to my driver, then hands my phone back to me. We're guided down two more hallways and into another foyer. This one opens to three offices. Danielle pulls a set of keys from her pocket and opens one of the doors, motioning for us to come through. We follow her up to a large, ornate wooden door, and she unlocks it. I step forward.

"May I?" I ask, and Danielle steps back with a little blush on her cheeks. I fight back a smile. I don't know what it is about American women and British accents, but I'll take it. Especially if Marina likes it too.

I open the door just enough to peek out. The alley behind the library is deserted and dark, rain pouring down in a deluge. There's no overhead shelter, so it's no wonder there's no one back here. I close the door and find Marina watching me expectantly.

"All clear," I say in an even tone.

She nods and drops her bag for a moment, getting ready to put her jacket on. Without a word, I step forward and gently take it from her. Her eyes shoot up to mine in surprise as I hold it open for her. I smile down at her, wondering what kind of men she's been around that would make her surprised to be with a gentleman. Not that she's *with* me. In fact, she always seems to be running from me. She slips into her jacket and I force my fingers to let go instead of doing what I really want to do and grip the jacket so I can pull her straight into my arms.

"Thank you," she murmurs, stepping back quickly and wrapping her arms around herself.

My phone beeps, and I check my messages.

"He's here," I say softly.

Marina grabs her bag, and I quickly take Danielle's hand, shaking it. "It was a pleasure to meet you, Danielle," I say with a smile. "I do hope we meet again someday."

She blushes again and laughs. "All right, you," she says, giving me a good-natured shove. "Remember what I told you."

I nod with a twinkle in my eye. "How could I not?"

I turn to Marina. "Ready?"

A quick nod is her only reply. I open the door and look outside once more. The car is there, and not a soul in sight. Excellent. I swing open the door and step outside, opening the back passenger door for Marina. She dashes out quickly, covering her face from the rain, and gets in the car. I slip in behind her, shut the door, and we're safely away from any prying eyes.

"Thanks for the lift, Dave," I say to the driver, an affable chap I've rather come to like. He nods at me in the rear-view mirror, waiting for instructions.

I turn to Marina and she's pretending to be fascinated by something outside the window, in the dark alley, where there's absolutely nothing to see. Her arms are folded across her chest and she's doing her best to give off every "stay away from me" vibe she can conjure.

"Marina?" I say softly, and she reluctantly turns to face me. "Where are we taking you?"

She stares at me for a long moment. "I'm having second thoughts," she says firmly. "If I give you my address, you'll be able to show up any time."

I consider my reply long before I open my mouth.

"I'm sorry if I alarmed or upset you by just showing up tonight," I say gently.

She watches me silently.

"I wasn't even sure I was going to approach you after you sang," I explain hesitantly. "I just couldn't resist seeing you again. One more time."

I can see she believes me by the change in her eyes. She relaxes a little, and the corner of her mouth tilts up just slightly.

"And then Brandon called you out," she says with a low laugh.

I chuckle.

"He really did, didn't he?" I grin, remembering the simultaneous feeling of surprise and horror when he pointed that chubby little finger at me.

She's quiet again, looking like she wants to say something a few times, but fighting it. She looks at the driver and then back at me.

"Dave," I say softly, not taking my eyes off Marina. "Can we have a minute?"

"Of course, Mr. Adams," Dave replies, and the privacy screen goes up.

Finally, those green eyes focus solely on me.

"Why?" she asks simply. "Why can you not resist seeing me? Nothing can ever come from this."

I tilt my head at her, genuinely surprised. "How can you know that?"

She bursts out laughing and shakes her head at me. I decide to try a different approach. I turn my body so I'm facing her.

"Marina," I almost whisper. "The first time I met you, you were singing your heart out in the middle of a traffic jam on the Golden Gate Bridge dressed as a mermaid. If that wasn't enough to get my attention, you have the voice of an angel."

She scoffs, but doesn't say anything else.

"I know my life must seem bizarre to you," I say hesitantly. "I know our lives are very different. I'm not asking you to change yours...or do anything, really, other than give me a tiny bit of your time."

"For?" she asks, eyebrows raised.

"Coffee?" I answer with a smile. "A drink? Dinner, if it's not too much to ask?"

She watches me wordlessly, and there's something in the way she's guarding herself that makes me wonder what her story is. Does she always expect the worst from people? Is it just men? I'm feeling incredibly protective all of a sudden.

"Where could we possibly go and not be spotted by someone? You're too famous," she argues.

Challenge accepted.

"It's your city," I counter. "Perhaps you know of a place where we can sit, chat, and not be bothered?"

The moment she has an idea, I see it play out on her face.

"You've thought of something," I say with a grin.

She hesitates, as if trying to calculate whether I'm worth the risk she's taking. She pulls out her mobile phone and types out a message, then looks over at me.

"Maybe," she says coyly. "I'll give you an hour. If she's there."

I raise my eyebrows. "She?"

Marina opens her mouth to reply when her phone chirps. She looks down at the screen, and I can't tell if she's disappointed or relieved by the message she sees. She nods at me.

"Okay, I know a place where we can go," she says almost grimly.

I knock on the partition. Dave lowers it.

"Dave, the lady has an address for you," I say, gesturing at Marina.

Marina gives the address, and Dave punches it into the dash computer, which shows an estimated travel time of twelve minutes. We fasten our seat belts, and my brain goes into overload because I have about eleven minutes to figure out how I'm going to get Marina to lower her defenses enough to want to see me again.

Chapter 6

Marina

The car is too quiet as the driver pulls out of the alley behind the library and onto the busy San Francisco streets. I should think of something to say, but I have no idea what I'm doing. I shouldn't even be in this car. With him. I should be walking home so I can study the materials I printed on Ethan Montclair over a plate of leftover lasagna.

Still, an hour won't hurt—and I really, *really* want to know what's up with this guy. Something inside me won't let go of it, which is funny really…because I can't let go of *his* reasons for not wanting to let me go. It's almost like we're obsessed with each other. We can't figure one another out.

"Brandon mentioned he *used* to listen to my music with his dad," Zach says softly, a quizzical look on his face. His deep brown eyes are both soulful and unnerving.

I nod. "His father was killed in a car wreck six months ago," I reply quietly. "He never knew his mother. Aunt Grace is the only family he has."

Zach nods in understanding, empathy etched onto his face.

"She looks so young," he says quietly.

"She's 23," I answer. "My age. With a five-year-old and a job that doesn't pay near enough to support them both. Truthfully, she's struggling."

He seems to get lost in thought for a moment, rubbing his palms across the tops of his jean-clad thighs. The muscles in his biceps and forearms flex and bunch as he moves, the tight sleeves of the long-sleeved t-shirt he's wearing doing nothing to disguise it. I wish I didn't notice.

"Danielle mentioned some of the children tonight are in foster care," he says softly.

I nod.

"The library has a few programs that offer free or low-cost activities for them," I explain. "I volunteer to manage this one."

Zach's eyes go wide, and I beam a little proud smile.

"This is *your* program? You created it?"

I nod again. "Foster kids have a special place in my heart," I say, not offering any further explanation.

He's thoughtful for a moment. "I can see that."

The car gets quiet again.

"And you?" he asks. "Have you been able to stay clear of scrutiny at work? No one has discovered you're the mermaid in the viral news story?"

I shake my head. "Not yet," I hedge. "But my boss paused the news footage of us this morning to show me I have a twin out there."

He blinks back his surprise. "He didn't put it together?"

"*She* lives in her own world, really. A singing mermaid is not something she'd spend time thinking about, and, given my office persona, I think it's too far of a reach for her to make."

He tilts his head. "Your office persona?"

I shrug. "This job is a step on a ladder for me," I explain. "I have my foot in the door of San Francisco's most prestigious law firm. If I play my cards right, I can get a recommendation to the law school of my choice and possibly a better job within the firm. My office persona is who they want me to be, not who I really am."

His eyebrows knit together. "How?"

I shrug again. "I shop at thrift stores near high-end neighborhoods so I can afford the designer suits and shoes that get their respect. My hair is always in the same style, efficient and professional. I wear very little makeup, have no friendships with people at the office, and do whatever they want me to do when they want me to do it. I'm the assistant they turn to for everything now because they know I'm all about the firm and I'll get the job done. It's exactly what I want them to think."

"No friendships at the office?" he says incredulously. "So what do you do on a Monday morning when someone says they had a great weekend and they obviously want to talk about it."

I laugh softly. "I usually give them a polite smile and say something like 'how wonderful to hear' as I walk out of the break room and back to my desk."

He laughs out loud.

I smile proudly. "When you're always in motion, you're harder to pin down."

His face lights up like I've just given up a secret, and I find myself wondering why. I wait for him to say more, but he just nods.

"And what if someone asks you how your weekend was?" he asks, looking like he already knows my answer. It's unnerving.

"I just say it was great, or I cleaned my apartment or…something generic," I reply. "They don't really care, they're just being polite."

The car slows to a stop, and I look out the window. Nonno's Italian Bistro looms outside, its festive Italian decor lighting up the street.

"Can you pull around to the rear entrance, please?" I ask the driver, not missing Zach's quizzical glance.

The driver pulls into the small parking lot and turns around the back of the building, stopping close to the back door. An awning covers a large part of the back entrance, shielding it from the rain. He gets out of the car before I have a chance to open my door, then trots around to my side and opens the door with a smile.

"Ma'am," he says with a quick nod.

Wow.

"Thank you," I answer, stepping out of the car just as Merry comes out of the back door of the restaurant.

Zach slides out of the car and stops short when he sees her.

"Oh!" he says with a grin. "Hello again!"

Merry waves, holding the door open for us. The smell of freshly baked breadsticks and delicious sauces hits me full force. I smile but manage to give Merry a mock glare as I step inside.

"I'll speak with you later, Merry," I tell her in what I think is an ominous tone, but she smiles at me like she's not worried in the least.

Merry walks us through the kitchen. As soon as her grandpa sees me, I smile. He throws his arms in the air and cuts a path through all the kitchen workers, wrapping me in a zesty, pasta sauce-smelling hug. I hug him back. Nonno DeLuca is one of my favorite humans on the planet.

"My little beauty, Marina!" he yells over the kitchen clamor in his lovely Italian accent. "It's about time you come to see Nonno!"

He notices Zach trailing behind us and releases me, then steps between us. Zach looks at me nervously as Nonno squints at him.

"Who is this?" Nonno asks, pointing a stubby finger at Zach.

"That's Marina's friend Zach, Nonno," Merry interjects. "They just came for a quiet dinner, that's all!"

"No fuss," I object quickly, but it's already too late.

Nonno whirls around, his face exploding with joy as he puts his meaty hands on either side of my face and squeezes.

"Marina, bella!" he cries out, gently shaking my head as he squeezes my cheeks together. "You *finally* have a date!"

Zach bursts out laughing, and I try to glare at him, but I'm sure it makes me look even more ridiculous. I grab Nonno's hands and pull them away from my face with a kind smile.

"No, not a date," I interject helplessly, but he's already reaching for Zach's hand to shake it.

Zach introduces himself, and Nonno wraps him in a bear hug when the handshake is over. How do I make this stop? How?

"Nonno!" Merry yells, laughing. "Let him go!"

Does he listen? No. Nonno never does. He grabs my hand and Zach's and brings them together like we're three-year-olds on a playground being told to make friends. Zach's warm fingers instantly wrap around my hand, and my traitorous fingers respond in kind.

Despite my level of embarrassment being at DEFCON-1 right now, feeling Zach's hand wrapped around mine makes me want to giggle like a teenager on her first date. My heart is pounding like crazy. I hate how good this feels. How natural. It's safer if I don't like it. Zero attraction would make this whole evening more manageable, but he's like a magnet. A big sexy Marina magnet, dragging me towards him no matter how much I try to run.

"You two!" Nonno croons. "You will have the best date! Nonno make it perfect. Merry, get a table."

Merry hugs her Nonno and herds him back into the kitchen. "Nonno, go and cook! I've got this."

Nonno keeps yelling from the kitchen. "Marina, eat some breadsticks! You too skinny!"

I feel an overwhelming urge to bury my face in my hands, but one of my hands is still linked with Zach's. He smiles down at me and steps closer.

"For what it's worth," he purrs, lowering his mouth close to my ear. "I think you're perfect."

I feel a traitorous blush creeping up my cheeks, and I look away just as Merry motions for us to follow. I start to pull my hand away, but Zach keeps a hold of it with a gentle squeeze as we follow Merry. We're escorted into the restaurant, which is bustling with customers, but we're on the other side of a screen made of ficus trees. No one can see us. We're escorted to the family's booth, which is behind a partition so Merry's family members who work at the restaurant can take breaks and not be seen by customers. Usually, the table is covered in papers and clutter from one or more members of her family, but tonight, it's pristinely clean. The green upholstered booth seat curves around a semi-circle table. A small vase of fresh flowers, just like those that adorn the customer tables, is in the center, and there are place settings for two. My heartstrings tug a little at all the trouble Merry went through to make space for us.

"Your table for the night," she says lightly, grabbing a menu from a holder nearby and handing it to Zach. "Marina knows the menu well, so this is for you. I'll be back in a bit."

"Thank you," Zach calls after her, then turns to his menu. "What are you hungry for?"

"Normally lasagna, but Ashley made some yesterday, and I'll be eating leftovers for days."

He grins. "You ladies are big Italian food fans?"

I nod firmly. "Pasta is the solution to all of life's problems, and I'll die on this hill."

He throws his head back and laughs, and I don't miss the jittery feeling that springs into my chest at the deep, throaty sound of it. However much I might not want to admit it, Zach has an energy about him that makes me feel good just being near him. I can see why he's beloved by so many all over the world. He just puts everything out there for all to see. I haven't been that way in a very long time.

"How about something to share? What's good here?"

I raise my eyebrows and scoff. "Everything," I say. "But you seem like a spaghetti and meatballs kind of guy."

He tilts his head at me. "Oh, I have to hear the explanation for this. Why do I seem like a spaghetti and meatballs guy?"

Now it's my turn to grin like a Cheshire cat. "You know, messy and all over the place."

His grin is wide as he chuckles. "Ouch!"

Merry reappears, raising an eyebrow at me as if she caught me flirting. I'm *not* flirting. I narrow my gaze at her as a reminder that we're going to talk later about her inviting Zach to the library. She still doesn't look sorry.

"Lasagna?" she asks, pointing at me.

I shake my head. "Ash made some yesterday."

"I think we'll share the spaghetti and meatballs," Zach interjects, a secret smile directed at me.

My toes curl in response.

"I'll put that order right in," Merry drawls, wiggling her eyebrows at me as she exits.

As Merry leaves, I turn my attention back to Zach…whose gaze has called those butterflies back again. I flatten my palms against the coolness of the table.

"I promised you an hour," I say coolly. "What would you like to talk about?"

He shrugs. "Everything."

I laugh softly. "Can you narrow it down a little?"

He studies me for a moment as if he's trying to figure out how far he can go. What questions are okay, and what questions are too much. Like he knows me already.

"How long have you been singing?" he asks quietly.

I shrug. "As long as I can remember."

He smiles again, and I feel like it's just for me. Anyone else might see it and think it's just a smile, but for me? That smile is reaching across the table and whispering in my ear...*I completely get you.*

My whole life, I've felt like I had to explain myself—and yet even when I intentionally give him the briefest answer possible, he hears the whole message. I've been singing my whole life, and I don't remember a time when it didn't feel completely natural to sing. The look on his face tells me it was the same for him.

"And you never wanted to sing professionally?" he asks me with a tone of disbelief.

"Once upon a time, maybe," I say with a shake of my head. "But life changes things. Besides, I can't *really* sing. I'm just okay."

Zach's eyes grow wide. "What? Tell me you don't believe that."

I nod. "That's how it is," I explain. "One of the high schools I went to was in a very affluent neighborhood. I was in the school chorus while I was there. All the girls who were really serious had voice coaches their parents paid a fortune for. A few of them actually had agents. They were really serious. I just wanted to sing."

He tilts his head. "If you have natural talent, you don't need a voice coach, Marina."

I shrug, hoping he changes the subject. I don't like talking about the past. *My* past.

"What did your parents say?" he asks softly.

I flinch, immediately hoping he didn't notice. He waits for me to answer, his face giving me no indication he saw my reaction. But I can't answer. In fact, to my horror, my throat begins to tighten, and I don't think I could speak even if I wanted to. I look down at my hands, willing my eyes not to fill up. I shake my head wordlessly, hoping he moves on.

"Nonno, please!" Merry yells back at the kitchen, stomping our way with a basket of breadsticks.

She puts the basket on the table, sees my expression, and raises her eyebrows at me in silent question. I give her a slight nod.

I'm okay.

I was actually starting to relax and wasn't expecting the question. That was all.

"He's been fussing at me back there to bring you breadsticks since you sat down," she says, shaking her head. "I'm trying to figure out a cookie recipe I'm playing with, and he's freaking out because you're going to die from starvation."

We both laugh, and I'm grateful for the distraction. I take a deep breath and then another. Merry jabs a finger at the basket, and I take a breadstick and pass the rest to Zach.

"Your food should be out shortly," she says with a grin. "Please don't hate me."

With that, she runs back to the kitchen and I wonder what surprises are in store now.

"Oh...wow..." Zach mumbles around a mouthful of breadstick.

His eyes are closed, and he's obviously having a moment. I understand completely. There's nothing like Nonno's breadsticks or anything else he makes for that matter.

"Okay," Zach says with a nod, wiping his mouth with his napkin. "No more burning ambition to sing? You'd make a lot more money with that voice on stage than in any courtroom."

I frown at him. "I don't want to be a lawyer for the money."

His eyes light up at my reply. "No? You work at a fancy law firm. And you're desperate to ensure our little duet isn't discovered by them, so I thought—"

"You're way off base," I reply, more than a little disappointed in him for thinking I'm motivated by money and equally so in myself for caring about what he thinks of me. "I need this job for all kinds of reasons. First, because Ashley's engaged. They haven't set a date yet, but that's coming. I can't afford to live by myself right now. Scarlet and Merry don't need roommates, and there's no one else I trust. I need to be ready to find an apartment I can afford when the time comes. That means I need a promotion and a raise."

He's completely still, his attention fully focused on me, so I continue.

"Second," I say, holding up two fingers like I'm ticking items off a list. "If I'm going to make a difference as a lawyer, I need to get into the best law school I can. I had good grades, but a letter of recommendation from the most respected law firm in San Francisco carries a lot of weight. If I impress my boss, I can get those things, but she doesn't like drama. The firm doesn't like anything remotely scandalous or frivolous or…viral. If they put it together that I'm the mermaid, I can forget about a raise, a promotion, or a referral for law school. And I could lose my job. It all goes down the drain."

He's grinning at me ear to ear, but not in jest. If I didn't know better, I'd say it was pride shining in his eyes. But that can't be right. He doesn't know me. I'm nothing to him. Maybe it's the breadsticks. I'm going with that. It's a Nonno breadstick high.

"You are going to be an amazing lawyer, my lady," he croons in that ridiculously sexy British accent.

"Why do you say that?" I ask a bit breathlessly.

Although I hate the effect he has on me, I also really want to know what he thinks.

He leans back and admires me for a moment. I'm not sure if it's the light in those warm brown eyes or the smile on his handsome face, but he makes me feel valued. Seen. I've never felt that way around a man before. It's both thrilling and unnerving.

"You have such passion for the things you care about, Marina," he says almost reverently. "You lit up just now, fighting to make your point. To make your voice heard."

I can't help the small smile I feel turning at the corners of my mouth. "I lit up?"

His eyes rove over my face. "Like a bonfire on the beach, Siren."

I laugh at the sound of his nickname for me and shake my head.

"I'm no siren," I say pointedly.

He leans forward, bracing his forearms on the table. The muscles in his arms flex as he folds his hands in front of him, and I have to fight not to watch them.

"I completely disagree, counselor," he teases, eyes full of mischief. "I was an innocent man, relaxing in my own space, when your voice lured me outside. I followed it, unable to resist, until I found you. And now? I'm trapped. And I don't think I'll ever be the same again."

The sight of Merry coming out of the kitchen with a giant platter is enough to stop me from replying. Not that I could say much if I wanted to after that speech. As much as I'd love for even part of that to be true, I know it isn't. I've never provoked that kind of reaction in any man. I feel my instincts for self-preservation kicking in. I start talking myself off the ledge. He's flirting. It doesn't mean anything. He does this with a lot of women.

"Here we are," Merry sings as she sets a family-sized platter of spaghetti and meatballs between us. The meatballs are arranged in a heart shape.

She catches the incredulous look on my face, grins, and turns around immediately.

"Don't be mad at me," she calls. "Nonno's orders!"

Zach and I look at each other and laugh out loud. He crooks a finger at me.

"You're going to have to come closer," he says, gesturing at the massive plate. "Nonno has seen 'Lady and the Tramp' one too many times."

I pick up my fork and scoot a little closer. This booth is massive. It's not unusual to find at least five of Merry's family members in it on any given day, but with Zach here it feels small and I don't want to get too close. In *any* way. Because, for the first time in a long time, I know I'm in some danger here. Zach isn't someone who is easily put off by my usual tricks. Add to that his obvious good looks, his considerable charm, and the whole British thing…well, I'd be an idiot if I didn't admit it would be very easy for me to catch feelings for him.

Wordlessly, I twirl up a fork full of spaghetti, stab a meatball, and shovel the whole thing in my mouth. Zach's eyes go wide in delight and I have to fight to keep from laughing. Good. Let him see my not-so-ladylike way of eating spaghetti. If he's turned off, then I get what I want. Otherwise, I'll have to keep building walls. Either way, I win.

"I don't think I've ever had a dinner date with a woman who actually ate much of anything," he says as he loads up his own fork. "That was refreshing."

I point my fork at him. "This is not a date."

He nods while he finishes chewing. "I am out to dinner with a beautiful woman, whom I didn't think I'd ever get to see again, and I'm having a lovely time. There's great food, stellar company, and I feel happier than I've felt in a very long time. This is a date."

I shake my head and repeat, "It's not a date."

I load another fork full of spaghetti and take a bite. Nonno's spaghetti is my favorite thing to eat on this Earth.

Merry comes over with a bottle of wine and two glasses. She wordlessly fills them, winks at me, and retreats back to the kitchen. She waves when Zach thanks her.

"This is the best spaghetti I've ever had," Zach grumbles over his plate.

I nod. "There's none better. Nonno is a magician with food."

He watches me for a moment, then digs back in for another bite. "Call it what you want, Marina," he says with a devilish grin. "I can't stop you. But this is a date to me."

I raise my chin. "Fine. You enjoy your date with a mermaid who doesn't exist, and I'll just stay over here having a chat and a few bites of spaghetti with this guy I just met."

As soon as the words are out of my mouth, I cringe—because Zach's eyes light up in amusement. Challenge obviously accepted. Did I mean to issue a challenge? No. Am I going to back down? Also no.

"All right, let's chat," he says with an intimidating grin. "Can I tell you all about my date?"

I roll my eyes at him.

"I have to tell someone," he continues. "She is so beautiful. And she's smart. She's studying to be a lawyer, and she's going to be a brilliant one. And her voice? She could fill concert halls with that voice, but she has no such designs. She sings to children…which I adore. There's literally nothing I don't like about this woman."

I scoff. "Yet."

He tilts his head at me curiously but says nothing. Loading up another fork full is safer than talking right now, so that's what I do—and for a few moments, we just eat in relative silence.

I see Nonno poke his head out of the kitchen to watch us for a few minutes. Merry eventually scolds him back into the kitchen, and I bite back a laugh. I never had a relationship with either of my grandfathers because I never met them, so when I met Nonno and he instantly made room for me in his heart I was powerless. The man is a giant ball of love.

I watch Zach from behind my lowered lashes. I find him… confusing. And charming. Fun. Mildly irritating. And, let's face it, so gorgeous. And he smells amazing. This feels ridiculous. And wreckless. Having dinner with this man is the last thing I should be doing right now, and yet here I am. I can't seem to resist the pull of him, like the tide every night under the moon.

"May I make a suggestion for our second not-date?" he asks softly.

I roll my eyes again. "Zach."

He laughs softly. "You're going to love this idea."

I raise my eyebrows. "Doubtful, because I'm not going."

"Don't you even want to hear what we're doing before you say no?" he croons. "You might really want to do it."

I raise my chin in defiance. "No, I won't."

Undeterred, he takes a sip of his wine, nods his approval, and squares his shoulders.

"I want to take you out to a recording studio," he says bluntly, a grin slowly spreading across his face. "Just the two of us. To sing and have a great time without being stuck in the middle of a bridge. Where no one else will see us."

Okay, I kind of want to do that. A lot. Back when I was a teenager, my favorite daydream was being discovered while working as a backup singer for Justin Bieber and then recording albums and touring the world with him. As it turns out, life threw me a million curve balls when I was thirteen, and the whole thing with the Bieb didn't work out, but I have to admit it would be really fun to see inside a real recording studio. And sing with Zach again.

"How would that work?" I ask, hating myself for the elated look on his face.

He knows he's got me.

"There's a studio in the city I've used before," he explains. "I'll rent it out for the entire day, so it's empty for hours before we even get there. I know the owner. He's a good chap. There's zero risk of media leaks with him. It'll just be the two of us, so we can stay as long or as little as you want. I'll send a car to pick you up."

I take a sip of my wine, going over the risks in my mind. There doesn't seem to be much risk if we're not out in public together—especially if I'm getting picked up at work in a car with darkened windows and meeting him there. I chew on my lip, feeling my resolve weaken. Finally, I look up to find him watching me with a hopeful expression.

"No one can ever know," I say lowly, a slow smile spreading on my face. "Promise?"

He grins again, prompting a little dropping sensation in my stomach, and I say a silent prayer that I'm not making a huge mistake.

Chapter 7

Zach

The sun streaming in through the bedroom window of my hotel suite has me grabbing a pillow and shoving it onto my face. I don't mind late nights, but my brain just would not shut down after my non-date with Marina last night. Her beautiful face, fixed in that adorably stern expression when she was scolding me for calling our impromptu dinner a date pops into my head, and a wide grin spreads on my face. That spontaneous duet on the bridge was a gateway drug. Spending time with her yesterday only made me want even more. I even had a dream about her last night. We were on the bridge again, but this time, she didn't try to run away from me at every turn.

I groan, roll out of bed, pad across the plush hotel carpet to the window, and throw back the curtains. The city of San Francisco is laid before me, bathed in sunshine as people rush around the streets and go about the day's business. I glance at the clock. It's 10:30, so Marina is already at work. I wonder if she's having a good day. From our limited conversation about her work environment, I gather it's quite a challenge but one she's willing to endure. Last night, after

I got her to agree to a second non-date at the recording studio, she alluded to the fact that she's part of a big project that could mean a pay rise or promotion if she does well. I know she'll be focused on all of that this morning. In fact, she mentioned she wouldn't even take a lunch break today. That bothers me, but it also gives me a great idea.

I grab my mobile off the nightstand and open a new text message. Marina and I exchanged numbers last night. Since we stopped at Nonno's restaurant, she wouldn't let me take her home. She insisted with fierce independence that she would be fine, so I insisted she text me when she got home so I'd know she was safe. Merry happened to be there and chose to back Team Zach in the mobile number debate, so I won. Thankfully. And Marina did, indeed, text me when she arrived home and was safe.

I think for a moment, and then begin typing.

Zach: Good morning, beautiful. Hope you're having a great day at work. How's the project going?

I wait a moment. Then another. Just as I'm about to give up on receiving an immediate reply, I see three little dots wiggling and smile.

Marina is typing...

Marina: Good morning. I'm still only in the research phase, really.

Zach: Still no time for lunch today?

Marina: Right. I need to read up on this prospective client, and I won't have time after work. The girls are coming over tonight.

Zach: Lovely! You ladies seem more like sisters than friends. It's nice to see.

Marina: They are the best. What are you doing with your day today?

I smile. She's curious, and maybe…just maybe…starting to look at me as more than the rock star personality the media shows to the world. Whatever the case, the fact that she is not sending me curt, one-word replies is a good sign, and I'll take it.

Zach: Me and the boys have an appearance at City By the Bay Records. We're signing autographs until our fingers bleed.

Marina: I love that store. There's an independent coffee house next door called Cuppa Love. I recommend everything on the menu.

I laugh out loud. As much as she tries to rein in her personality around anyone who isn't in her inner circle, Marina has a passion for life that's music to my soul.

Zach: Maybe you could narrow it down for me. What's your favorite thing there?

Marina: The Fog Lifter. Their signature grind blended with cinnamon and sweet cream.

Zach: Thanks for the recommendation, Siren.

Our chat goes quiet, so I step over to the closet and grab my clothes for the day. Thankfully, the appearance in at the record shop calls for our usual attire: anything we want. I grab a pair of jeans and a henley from our first concert tour and turn on the shower. While it's warming up, I do a quick search for Nonno's and make an absolutely necessary call before I get ready to start my day.

***

Marina

Ethan Montclair is one smarmy dude. Ms. Taft is off-site today (which is code for the very expensive, non-inclusive spa she loves), so I'm reviewing all my research at my desk. Between the parade of women, the broken marriages, and the shady business deals he's been involved with, I feel like taking a shower with a bottle of bleach and a wire brush. I sit back in my chair for a moment, pinching the bridge of my nose and willing myself not to get the headache I feel creeping across my skull.

I take a deep breath and stretch, looking up just in time to see Merry walking towards me with a takeout bag from Nonno's.

What?

She smiles as she trots over to my desk, stealing a glance at Ms. Taft's office door.

"Where's the Evil Queen?" she whispers.

"Not here today," I say, my stomach growling loudly when the scent of Nonno's spaghetti hits my nostrils. I gesture at the bag. "You didn't have to do this, but I am totally glad you did. I'm starving!"

She stifles a giggle and shakes her head. "I didn't do it."

I nod as I open the bag and pull out an envelope of breadsticks. "Nonno, then," I say. "Please give him a huge hug for me."

She shakes her head again. "Nope. Not him."

My eyes meet Merry's just as the realization hits me. I point a breadstick at Merry.

"No!" I gasp, wide-eyed. "Are you freaking kidding me?"

She squeals and sits in the guest chair next to my desk. "He called this morning before we opened. Nonno answered the phone before I could get to it, so be warned."

"What?" I ask quickly. "Why?"

She grins and wiggles her eyebrows. "Nonno yelled 'He's a keeper!' and sang all through kitchen prep this morning."

We both burst out laughing. Sweet Nonno. He's probably already planning my wedding. Merry reaches into the bag and puts a foil container of spaghetti on my desk, along with utensils and napkins, then reaches back into the bag for another container. She winks at me and stands up.

"You want me to put the canoli in the fridge?" she asks, her whole face lit up.

My mouth drops open, and I gasp, my eyes darting from the container to Merry and back again.

"He got me *canoli?*" I whisper reverently.

Merry nods. "He basically asked what your favorite things are and then ordered it all."

I take a bite of my breadstick, speechless and completely unable to control the smile spreading across my face. In my whole life, I've never had a man fuss over me like this. It's kind of…nice.

Merry grabs a breadstick from the bag and takes a bite. I scoot the container of spaghetti between us.

"I can share!" I say quickly, taking the lid off. "Have lunch with me?"

She shakes her head.

"No need," she coos. "I have to get back, but he offered me whatever I wanted on the menu. I told him I get to eat for free, so he left me a $100 tip for delivering it."

I feel like my eyes are about to pop straight out of my head. I lower the breadstick in slow motion. Merry pats me on the shoulder.

"You've got a keeper!" she teases.

I try to hold in my laughter and end up snorting, causing us both to laugh out loud. I stifle my laughter quickly and wave my hand.

"No laughing!" I whisper.

Merry rolls her eyes. "These people have no souls. I'll be right back."

I watch her disappear into the executive break room with the canoli. Merry's been here a few times, usually to drop off dinner for me when I was working late at night for Ms. Taft. She knows her way around the office.

I sit back in my chair and take another bite of my breadstick. The heavenly scent of the spaghetti wafts in my direction, and my stomach grumbles again. This is definitely better than the stale energy bar that's been sitting in my desk drawer for months. Merry comes back and gives me a quick hug.

"I have to run," she says. "Be sure to text your boyfriend to say thank you."

I laugh again but remember to keep it down. "Very funny!"

She blows me a kiss and makes her way to the elevator as I finish my breadstick. I take the lid off the spaghetti, unwrap my utensils, then grab my phone and snap a quick picture of it. I text the picture to Zach.

Marina: The height of British chivalry. Thank you so much.

I glance at my watch. It's nearly one o'clock. He's probably at his appearance, surrounded by fans, but he'll get it eventually. As I'm setting my phone down on my desk, it vibrates in my hand.

Zach: I couldn't stand the idea of you working all day without a meal, Siren.

Who is this guy? I shake my head and sigh.

Marina: I think I can survive missing a lunch or two. :-) But this is really very sweet and I'm very grateful. How's your autograph session going?

Zach: I broke away for a few minutes to text you back. Imagine what they would do if they knew I was standing here texting the infamous mermaid. :-)

Marina: Tease me all you want. I know my secret is safe with you.

Zach: For a chivalrous Brit, that means a great deal, my lady.

***

"He wants to *what?*" Scarlet squeals, plopping onto the couch and grabbing her margarita off the coffee table.

Merry grins from her spot on the floor. "They're disgustingly cute together," she says with a shake of her head. "You should have heard him when he called Nonno's this morning to order her lunch. He's got the love bug."

"Guys!" I call from my perch on the couch. "Focus. This emergency conclave is for you to talk some sense into me, not encourage me to be reckless."

Ashley shakes her head and hands me a fresh margarita. "We *are* trying to talk sense into you," she insists, plopping into the middle spot on the couch beside me. "We're trying to give you all the *please date the handsome, rich rock star who can't stop staring at you* vibes."

"He's also a duke," Scarlet mutters with a grin.

"He's not a duke," I say flatly, giving her the side-eye. "His father is a duke."

All three of my friends look at me as if I have a horn growing out of my forehead.

Ashley nudges me with her foot, an incredulous look on her face. "He looks at you as if you're the only woman on this planet. And he's gorgeous. Tell me you're not the tiniest bit curious about where this could go."

Okay, I'll be lying if I say I haven't thought about it. But it's an impossible situation. He doesn't even live in San Francisco. How would that work? Nothing can come from this but heartbreak. *My* heartbreak, to be exact. And I've had enough heartbreak for a whole lifetime. Loving something and having it torn away from me is the worst feeling in the world. I'm not signing up for that.

"This is so romantic," Ashley says with a grin. "He wants to take you to a recording studio? You sang together the first time you met, and then again when he surprised you at the library. He can't get enough of your voice. You really *are* a siren!"

"And he's *nice*, Marina," Merry pushes, taking a sip of her drink. "Despite his celebrity status, he has a reputation for being a genuinely kind human being. And that's not the $100 tip talking. There are stories all over social media of him helping disadvantaged people. He refuses to comment on it or use it for publicity. The stories get out from the people he helps, not from his publicist."

I don't watch much television. I certainly don't watch any entertainment gossip shows, but Merry does, and I know she knows what she's talking about. And she's a huge fan of The Royal Rebels.

"I love that he sent you food today," Scarlet croons. "It's so sweet."

All three of my friends eye me expectantly, and I feel it to my core. They would never steer me in harm's way, and they're very much aware of my sometimes irrational need to control things.

"I just don't see what can come from this," I say with a flutter to my voice. "If we do hit it off, what happens then? We're from two completely different universes."

Ashley meets my gaze, and I know what she's thinking before she even opens her mouth. And she's right. She gives me a look to encourage me to keep talking.

"And…I'm afraid…of maybe catching some feelings," I say quietly, looking down at my hands and shaking my head.

"I get that," Scarlet says. "But this isn't some guy hitting on you in a bar. As much as I love it when you send those guys scurrying away with their tails between their legs, I don't think Zach is the type to scurry away. He's different. How do you really feel about it?"

The answer springs up immediately, even if I don't want to admit it. I take a deep breath.

"I like him. A lot."

Within seconds, Ash scoots over on the couch and wraps her arms around me. She doesn't say anything, she just hugs me. Next is Scarlet, who gets up and runs around to squeeze me from behind the couch. Merry puts her drink down and scoots across the floor until she can wrap her arms around my legs.

I start to giggle. "You guys are ridiculous," I say with a sigh and a huge smile.

"We're proud of you," Merry declares, her breath tickling my knee cap. "You said a brave thing."

One by one, they let go and smile at me.

"You said a brave thing," Ashley agrees. "And so now you can *do* a brave thing. Right?"

I look at her, and a pensive smile begins to form on my face. "Go out with the rich, handsome rock star?"

Merry squeals. "Yes!"

Ash and Scarlet nod their agreement.

I'm torn between cursing the absolute nuclear-strength butterflies I get any time I think of Zach and just letting them fly. Truth is, I'm intrigued by him. I want to know more about him, and not the stuff I can learn by searching the internet. I want his stories. I want his time. And I definitely want to sing with him again. Don't get me wrong, I love singing with the girls, but there was something about that moment on the bridge when our voices came together so effortlessly. Even at the library, with a song as simple as "You Are My Sunshine", we sounded beautiful together. I loved every minute of it.

Okay, so maybe I've been building boundaries for so long I've forgotten how to open the door once in a while to let someone in. One thing's for sure: just thinking about opening up to someone new is petrifying. Which is exactly why I know I need to push myself just a little bit. The truth is I've survived a lot more than the average twenty-three-year-old, so I can survive a date with Zach Adams.

Can't I?

I guess I'll find out tomorrow after work.

***

For anyone else, a day at one of the most luxurious spas in the city would put a smile on their face. Not Ms. Taft. She rolled into the office this morning, looking like someone took her Birkin bag and threw it into the bay. She barked orders at all of us all morning, went for a long lunch, and she stomped back into her office an hour ago. She's been in there ever since. I have strict instructions not to allow any visitors.

I have my favorite notebook out, and I'm writing a chronological to-do list for the big meeting when two paralegals come out of the executive kitchen and chat over their freshly refilled coffee mugs.

"It's probably not even someone local," Janie whispers. "Maybe she was driving into the city for some kind of publicity thing or modeling gig and ended up being in the right place at the right time."

"Whoever she is, it's such a fun story," her friend Allison answers. "Zach Adams is so gorgeous. And he just walked away with her in his arms like that kind of thing happens every day."

Both women laugh. I focus on my computer and keep a neutral expression on my face. Everyone knows I don't participate in office gossip, but I don't want to invite them to include me by making eye contact and seeming interested. But I *am* interested. More than I should be.

"I hope it wasn't a publicity stunt," Janie continues. "I'm such a romantic."

"Me too, girl." Allison giggles as they wander back to their desks. "Something like that just randomly happening? It feels like it was meant to be."

"Yes!" Janie squeals. "I wish we knew who she was. I'd love to see an interview with her."

"With *both* of them…"

They're a safe enough distance away for me to let out a quiet laugh. Imagine what they would think if they knew the all-business, never-chatty executive assistant to Ms. Taft was the mermaid at the heart of the viral video everyone is talking about. This is the third conversation about it I've overheard today. It feels like the story is gaining momentum, not calming down.

My head is screaming at me to text Zach and cancel our date. People are still too interested in the story. It's a risk I shouldn't be taking, especially in the middle of the Montclair deal. Ms. Taft is depending on me. If I pull this off, I can take a huge step towards law school. I shouldn't even have to think about it.

My gut, though, disagrees. And my heart. They've teamed up and have decided that my head doesn't need to be involved in making decisions about Zach. I can't explain it except to think this has never happened to me. I have no idea what I'm doing, which is unlike me. And there's a very real part of me who doesn't care, which is *very* unlike me. The only thing I can say is that any time I'm around Zach, I feel a pull. He calls me Siren, claiming that my voice lured him out of the bus that day—but he's like a rip tide, pulling me farther and farther out. All I know is that, right now, my curiosity has more power than my instincts for self-preservation. I only hope this doesn't end with me being pulled so far away from shore that I can never get back.

Chapter 8

Marina

Instead of stepping out onto the city streets to catch a bus at the end of my day, I take the elevator to the parking garage under the building. There is a designated waiting area for ride share and car service vehicles, so I head that way and find two cars idling. I recognize the SUV that rescued Zach and me from the library, but I double-check the license plate number against the one Zach texted me about an hour ago. As if on cue, Dave steps out of the vehicle and opens the rear passenger door for me.

"Good evening, Dave," I say with a smile, throwing my bag in and sliding into the seat.

"Miss MacArthur," he says with a quick nod.

Dave pulls the SUV out of the parking garage and into traffic as I relax against the plush leather seat and watch the city roll by. I have to admit, it's really nice having someone pick me up at work instead of riding the bus home. I could get used to this. I don't have to worry about changing hats or turning my coat inside out. I look forward to the day I don't have to think about that kind of thing anymore, which

95

is hopefully very soon.

My phone vibrates in my hand and I look down to see a text message from Ashley.

Ashley: Hey, have fun tonight! Remember…you don't have to marry him. No one's trying to rock your boat. Just have fun!

I smile and shove my phone in my bag. Several minutes later, we pull to a stop on California Street. An awning over the door says "Golden Gate Studio". My pulse picks up at the thought of getting to see inside a real recording studio. Dave gets out and opens the door on the sidewalk side of the car for me. I slide my way out just as the door to the studio opens, and Zach appears.

"Thank you, Dave," I say softly as I close the distance between Zach and me.

Zach just stands there, looking a bit confused. Like he's never seen me before. I step closer.

"Is something wrong?" I ask quietly.

"I almost didn't recognize you," he says, stepping back to take in my entire appearance.

Only then do I realize that my appearance is, indeed, quite different from what he's used to. My hair is still pulled back in a tight chignon, and I'm wearing a designer red suit and four-inch high heels. Zach is used to casual Marina…or mermaid Marina. Not the buttoned-up, stern version of me that works at Taft & Kennedy.

"Have I shocked you?" I ask with a laugh, stepping inside as he holds the door open for me.

Zach steps in behind me, and I look around the small lounge area. It's comfortable and welcoming but otherwise nondescript. There's a single hallway that leads back to what I assume is the recording studio.

"Is this your office persona?" Zach asks with a soft smile.

I nod, smoothing a hand down my straight red skirt. "All the women are expected to wear suits and heels. We all put our hair up in a chignon. I don't even think about it anymore. It's like wearing a uniform, I suppose."

He offers me a lazy smile. "I don't think I'd fit in at your office."

I take advantage of the opportunity to look him over, from his slightly tussled collar-length dark brown hair to the perfect scruff that's grown along that gorgeous jawline, down to the vintage long-sleeved t-shirt, well-worn jeans, and boots. I shake my head and grin.

"Not one bit."

We laugh together, and he gives my hair another peculiar look.

"Here," I say quickly, reaching up and pulling my long hair out of its confines. "I didn't bring anything to change into, but maybe this will make me look like less of an angry corporate clone."

I shake my hair out and comb my fingers through it.

"Better?" I ask, not really needing an answer.

He stands there, staring at me for a few moments as if hypnotized.

"Much better, Siren," he says as he heads down the hall and motions for me to follow. "Let's give you a proper tour."

I smile softly at the sound of my nickname and follow him. There are a few doors leading off of the hallway, but they're closed, and I can't see more. At the end of the hall, there's another small lounge area. The walls are covered in framed record albums signed by various musicians and singers. I take a moment to look them over. Frank Sinatra. Johnny Cash. Ed Sheeran. There are artists from every decade here. I feel Zach watching me, and I glance over to see him regarding me curiously.

"Did you ever imagine singing in a recording studio when you were little?" he asks, leaning against the door jamb.

I smile again, turning back to the wall of record albums as I study them.

"I used to get in trouble for daydreaming in school when I was very young," I say as my eyes pass over records by the Bee Gees, Eric Clapton, and Taylor Swift. "It was always some version of me becoming a famous singer and making millions of dollars so I could help my family."

"Oh?" he says from the doorway.

I nod, slowly moving along the wall. My eyes reverently pass over each artist's name.

"We'd buy our own house," I continue. "We'd never have to live in a run-down apartment again or deal with crazy neighbors. Mom wouldn't have to work at a cruddy diner and be on her feet all day. My brother would be able to play baseball. We'd go to a safe school. Kid's stuff."

Zach is quiet, which prompts me to turn around. He just stands there, watching me thoughtfully.

"Sounds like a nice dream," he says softly. "Are you still close to your family?"

My heartbeat increases when I realize I walked right into a conversation about my past. My family. That I no longer have. Our eyes meet and I get stuck on the words that want to come out of my mouth. I open my mouth to say something, then close it again.

"You don't like to talk about your family…" he guesses.

I consider for a moment, then ask, "Do you like to talk about yours?"

He shrugs. "I don't mind. My origins aren't exactly a secret."

I nod with a smile. "Yes, you're a royal."

He lets out a hearty laugh, and its sound reaches into my ribcage and pulls at my heart. I try to school my features into a neutral expression, but I feel slightly panicked at how quickly this man is breaking through my defenses.

"Technically, yes," he answers, prompting me to raise my eyebrows at him.

"Zach, we're all set!" a voice yells from behind the closest door to us.

With that, Zach steps over and opens the door. He motions for me to enter first, and I walk into a rather spacious recording studio. We enter into the area where the producers and technicians work the equipment, giving the music whatever kind of feel they're going for. Dials and buttons and switches stretch across a huge instrument panel. Just above it is a glass window overlooking the actual recording studio where the artists sing or play instruments. A tall man with rich bronze skin and no hair extends a hand to me with a huge smile.

"Hello, Marina," he says warmly. "I'm Bo. Welcome to my studio."

I shake his hand. "Thank you so much, Bo. This is amazing. I've never seen a real recording studio."

"Well, in that case, let me give you the deluxe tour!" he says, motioning for me to step closer to the instrument panel.

For the next several minutes, Bo takes me through an overwhelming orientation of every switch on the panel. I'm fascinated and definitely way, way out of my comfort zone—but it's fun, and for a moment, I wonder if some door inside the deepest part of my defenses didn't swing wide open the moment I decided to sing in the middle of that traffic jam. I'd normally be home with my nose in a book.

What have I started?

Movement out of the corner of my eye gets my attention and I notice that Zach has moved into the actual recording studio and is playing Fur Elise on the keyboard. Bo sighs beside me, then winks.

"He's showing off for you," he says with a grin. "Don't tell him I said that."

I laugh and roll my eyes, making sure to thank Bo as I step into the recording side of the room. Zach is still playing around with the classic Beethoven piece as I approach.

"I'll bet you've never played that at one of your concerts," I tease.

He laughs and stops playing.

"You would be correct," he admits. "But I did play it in concert at school. Mum was very proud."

I smile and nod, taking in my surroundings. The walls are covered with sound-proofing materials. There's a drum set toward the back of the room with a microphone suspended from the ceiling, and there's another microphone on a stand at the center of the room. Various musical instruments are set up all around the outside of the room, ready to play.

Zach gets up from the stool he's sitting on and comes over to me, gesturing at the mic.

"Shall we have some fun?" he says with an infectious grin, making me laugh.

I nod. "Yes, let's."

Zach looks through the window at Bo and gives him a thumbs up. Bo grins and hits a switch, leaning over to a small mic.

"You want this recorded, bud?" Bo asks over the intercom system.

Zach looks at me with questioning eyes. I smile.

"Do I?" I ask with a laugh.

He shrugs. "You're the boss."

It doesn't take me long to think about it. When will I ever have the chance to be in a recording studio again? A memento of this experience would be nice to have.

I nod excitedly, glancing at Zach and Bo. Bo laughs and gives me a wave.

"I got you, girl!" he says with a sweet grin, making me laugh. I watch as he flips a few switches and then flashes us a thumbs up. "Zach, you can use the remote right there on the piano to hit the record on/off switch."

Zach looks over and grabs a small remote, waving at Bo as he walks out of the control room, and the door closes behind him.

"Normally, he'd stay in the control room, but we're on a non-date, and I asked for privacy. He's going to hang out in his office unless we need him."

I give Zach an eye roll, and he reaches out, wrapping a warm hand around my elbow as he gently guides me to stand in front of the mic. He adjusts the height of the mic stand, his eyes meeting mine. He's close enough that I can smell that intoxicating sea and salt mixture again, and I have to fight the urge to lean closer. He pauses for a moment, not moving away from me. We're close enough that I could take a half step and be in his arms if it weren't for the mic stand between us. I hate how thrilling it is to be this close to him.

"What shall we sing?" he asks quietly, his eyes looking down into mine.

My eyes land on his lips, and I can't look away. Handsome isn't the best word to describe him. Maybe ruggedly beautiful is a better term. And now my mind has gone blank. I can't think of a single song written by any artist on the face of the planet. Ever. Zach grins and backs away, taking a seat at the keyboard again.

"Who are your favorite artists?" he starts. "Or what's your favorite kind of music?"

I shake my head and laugh. "All of it."

He appears thoughtful for a moment, then his fingers begin to move on the keyboard. I recognize the melody, but I can't place it. I'm about to give up when he gets to the chorus, and I squeal in excitement. It's "Just Give Me A Reason" by Pink. I start singing the chorus, and Zach joins in.

Just like before, our voices blend perfectly. I'm sure it's the professional recording studio we're in because we sound absolutely amazing together. My heart leaps as we hit every high note together and harmonize beautifully. By the time we get to the bridge, I burst out in joyous laughter. Zach stops singing and shakes his head at me.

"What's this?" he asks, settling his hands on his thighs.

I can't stop smiling. "This is…I don't even know. That was amazing."

He sits at the keyboard, watching me carefully. "We sound good together, don't we?"

I nod. "It's incredible," I reply, feeling breathless. "I mean…I have so much fun singing with the girls when we do our little side gigs, but this is something entirely different."

I can tell by his expression that he feels the same. He laughs under his breath, and I watch him curiously.

"It's refreshing to see this kind of reaction from someone who's not a professional singer," he explains. "It can be so fun to find that person who matches you perfectly. I'm glad you see it too."

"I'm sorry I got a little overwhelmed by it all," I say with a pensive smile. "I didn't mean to ruin it."

His expression grows serious. "You've ruined nothing. I don't believe it's possible that you could ever ruin anything, Siren."

I let out a sarcastic chuff. "You'd be surprised."

He raises his eyebrows in question, but I don't offer an explanation. He glances away for a moment, then claps his hands together.

"Right. Shall we test ourselves? How about another genre? Country? Rap? Opera?" he grins wildly at the last one.

I laugh. "Opera, ha! As if. Country? Can the Duke of Rock sing country?"

He rolls his eyes and immediately begins playing "Wagon Wheel" by Darius Rucker. His voice is rich and warm and I close my eyes, as if it'll help me hear the music better. I get lost in the sound of his voice. It's so soothing and beautiful. Suddenly, the music stops, and I open my eyes to find him grinning at me.

"Free concert's over, time to work," he chides. "Who's your favorite country artist?"

I don't even have to think about it. "Kenny Chesney all day long."

He takes a moment to think. "How about 'You And Tequila'?"

I jump up and down. "Yes!"

He grabs a guitar from a nearby stand and begins strumming out the intro to the song. I turn so I can look at him while we sing. He plays beautifully, looking up at me as he begins singing the Kenny Chesney part of the song. A slow smile spreads on my lips as I listen.

I join him at the chorus, and that now familiar thrill wraps around me as our voices come together. I can't keep the smile off my face as we sing. His smile is softer, his eyes darker. Keeping his gaze locked with mine, he stands and slowly walks over to stand on the other side of the mic. I feel it when the energy changes in the room. The air between us crackles with sparks that seem to tease along the surface of my skin. Through it all, we just keep singing along to the easy rhythm of the song, our gazes never breaking away from each other.

It feels like our voices are living, tangible things, flowing into the air and then twining around each other in a kind of dance. It isn't lost on me that the lyrics speak of two people trapped in a dangerous dance of their own, unable to get enough of each other. His eyes drift down to my mouth and I nearly forget the lyrics. I feel that familiar tug from the logical part of me, telling me to back away from him and make an excuse to leave early, but my gut instincts keep me rooted where I stand. Somewhere in my heart, I know Zach is different. And so I ignore my head and keep singing, content to give myself this evening with Zach without putting the weight of all my fears on it. For once, I just let it be what it is.

Zach strums out the final strains of the song and I don't even try to stop the smile that spreads across my face as I close my eyes and we sing the last notes together. I open them again to find him staring down at me, his jaw slack and his eyes full of so much emotion that I look away. I clear my throat and step back a bit.

"That was a good one," I say confidently, smiling up at him as he studies my face with those bottomless brown eyes. He nods. The air feels tight between us.

"Should I even bother trying to find something that's a challenge for you?" I tease, trying to break his laser focus on me. "You're very versatile."

A slow grin spreads on his face. "I don't know much opera."

I give him a satisfied nod. "Well, it's good to know you're not perfect."

He laughs softly, setting the guitar aside a moment, then turning back to me with renewed interest.

"What did you mean when you said I'd be surprised about your ability to ruin something?" he asks softly, his expression sincere.

Whether the intimacy of singing together has worn down my defenses or something else, I feel myself wanting to share at least part of my story. In the short time Zach and I have spent around each other, he's shown me that he's a caring person. His intentions are honorable. Somewhere in my gut, I feel it.

"I was quite a handful when I was a teenager," I begin, my voice small as I talk about a time I'd much rather forget. "My mom died when I was thirteen. We never knew our dad. We didn't have any other family, so my little brother and I went into foster care. Because of my behavior, I went through several foster families before social services gave up and put me in a group home for troubled teens."

Zach's expression is all compassion as his eyes scan over my face. I wait for him to ask me for details. I wait for him to start digging, ready to shut him down. He doesn't. He gives me the space to share what I want to share.

"I'm so sorry you lost your mum," he says in a near whisper. He reaches out cautiously, taking my hand. "That must have been hard, especially at such an age."

Zach's fingers are warm and reassuring as they squeeze my hand gently. His thumb rubs lazy circles across the back of it, quelling the nervous rhythm of my heart. I nod, unsure of what to say. I'm not a person who opens up easily, but it's as easy with Zach as it was with Ash, Merry, and Scarlet. Certain people just feel safe.

"And your brother?" he asks softly.

I shake my head, words definitely failing me. Tears spring to my eyes, but I refuse to let them fall. His throat bobs, and he wraps those big, warm hands around my biceps and gives me a gentle squeeze.

"I have a brother," he says gently. "Harry. Not the prince."

I blink up at him to find a mischievous grin on his face. I offer a half-hearted smile in return.

"Is he as tenacious as you?" I ask with a slight breathlessness to my tone. His hands are just slightly kneading my shoulders in a gesture that's as comforting as it is hypnotic.

"He is," Zach says with a grin. "You sort of have to be when you're born into the aristocracy. Otherwise you end up just bending to their ridiculous rules and have no life of your own."

I take a moment to study his face. The handsome features, the eyes that pull me in every time he looks at me, the lips that make me wonder too many things I shouldn't wonder about. I'm equal parts thrilled at the idea of being kissed by that mouth as I am afraid of it ever happening. Suddenly, I realize I'm staring and flick my gaze back up to his eyes.

"What are we singing next?" I ask.

For a moment, Zach looks thoughtful, like he's trying to find a way to keep the topic on our families. He gives my arms a final squeeze and releases me, reaching back for the guitar again.

"I defer to the lady," he says, putting extra emphasis on his British accent.

I laugh and shake my head. "I chose the last one. It's your turn."

Zach lets out a full, throaty laugh, and I'm captivated.

"Who was your biggest crush when you were a teen?" he asks.

I cringe.

"I don't want to say," I admit with a little laugh. It only encourages him.

"Siren…" he teases, picking a few notes on the guitar. "Out with it."

I close my eyes and mutter, "Justin Bieber."

I'm rewarded for my bravery with another hearty laugh, the sound of which shimmies into my bones and makes my toes curl. I beam up at him.

"What d'ya got?" I ask with a laugh.

Without hesitating, Zach gives me a wink and begins expertly strumming out, "Baby". Just like that, I squeal like a twelve-year-old and jump up and down, earning another laugh from Zach.

I jump behind the mic and begin singing the song, giving Zach a look when he doesn't join in. He smiles and shakes his head.

"Don't know the lyrics, love. This one's all you."

I nod and throw myself into the song. There's just something about this one that lightens my spirit and makes my heart happy. I dance behind the mic as I sing, gesturing at Zach like he's the first love who broke my heart. He grins at me as he strums out the song, and seems to be having a good time just watching me being silly. As soon as he finishes playing the end of the song, he swings the guitar to the side and applauds.

"Bravo!" he yells, whistling and clapping like he's at a real concert.

I dip into a low curtsy, which is a real challenge in these heels, but I reign supreme. Zach and I both laugh. I feel like a weight has been lifted off my shoulders, and I realize it's been a while since I allowed myself to just let go and have fun. Have I become so fiercely focused on my goals that I've forgotten how to loosen up and just have a good time? It sure seems like it. Maybe there is something to say for just going with the moment and doing what you feel. I've lost that part of myself.

"That was so fun," I say through my smile. "Thanks for not laughing at how monumentally uncool that was."

Zach shakes his head. "Nothing uncool about doing something you love, Siren. I love how much that made you light up."

"Like a bonfire on a beach?"

He grins at my use of his phrasing, and I wonder if he knows that's what he smells like. Fresh sea air, salty and smoky. Suddenly, I want him closer. Am I going to do anything about it? No. Am I going to stop thinking about it? Not likely. He puts the guitar down again and sits on the stool, and for a moment, we're just quiet and enjoying each other's company. It's time enough for me to realize how much I really like him. The urge to share more about myself comes back.

"I don't know where my brother is," I say suddenly.

Zach's eyes meet mine. There's no judgment in his eyes. Just interest and compassion.

"The first foster home I was in," I continue, wringing my hands, "was hard for us both at first. The Lewises."

I lower my gaze to the floor as I say their name. I haven't really thought about them in a long time.

"Were they mean to you?" Zach asks quietly.

I shake my head.

"They were decent people." I sigh. "Max...my brother...he and I were scared. I was thirteen, he was nine, and our mom was the only family we'd ever known. All of a sudden our entire world shifted, and we were living with two strangers who wanted to be our mom and dad. I was angry. I wanted my mother back."

Zach stands and steps over to me, taking both my hands in his. "Of course you did."

I shake my head again. "They did everything they could to help us get settled, but it was all such a shock. With our mom, we didn't have much. She was all we had, and she had to work so hard to support the three of us. That meant it was up to me to look after Max."

I close my eyes when I mention his name, anticipating the feelings of guilt that I know are coming. What kind of a sister does what I did? I feel a squeeze on my hands and look up at Zach, watching me with such empathy in his eyes.

"We did everything together," I continue. "Homework after school, and then I made dinner. Mom usually came home for dinner, and then we'd watch TV for a while before bed. Max always wanted me to sing him to sleep."

Zach nods, smiling softly. "Who wouldn't?"

I give him a half smile. "We went from living in a one-bedroom apartment with mom to living with two people who weren't our parents. Mr. Lewis was a surgeon, so they lived in a really nice neighborhood. I remember the first time Mrs. Lewis took us grocery shopping. She was very kind. We went up and down every aisle and she told us to show her all the things we liked or wanted to try. We walked down the baby aisle, and the baby formula wasn't all locked up in a cage. That's when it really hit me."

"How different your lives were?"

I nod. "It just made me so mad. I kept staring at that baby formula and thinking that I'd rather be back in that terrible neighborhood with the locked-up baby formula if it meant having my mom back. Suddenly, I had two new parents, and Mrs. Lewis didn't work, so she had time to help Max with his homework. *She* made dinner. She insisted I should have time for my friends, but I didn't have any friends."

"You didn't have time to just be a kid before," Zach offers with another gentle squeeze. "It makes sense that you felt a little lost."

I nod again. "Well, once we got settled, Max wasn't so lost. Our dad left when Max was born, so he never had a dad and I barely remembered him. Mr. Lewis and Max formed a bond pretty quick, which was tough for me to watch, but I was happy for him. I wasn't angry at him. I was just angry at the world. And I started acting out."

Zach nods.

"I started getting in trouble a lot. And one night, I overheard the Lewises talking about me. I had officially become too much to deal with, but they didn't want to say anything because Social Services' first goal is always to keep the kids together. If I got removed from their home, they would take Max away too—and they loved Max. I thought about how hurt Max would be if we were taken away from the Lewises, especially after losing our mom, and I knew I couldn't risk that."

"Of course not."

"So I ran away," I say with a tone much lighter than the topic at hand.

Zach frowns. "Were you caught?"

I nod. "Several times, but my teenage mind was made up. I decided that Max was better off without me. I didn't want him to lose the family that loved him, so I never told anyone what I heard that night. I told our caseworker I didn't want to be with my brother, and I hated the Lewises, which wasn't true, but I knew it would work. She put me with another family. I ran away again, and a few more times until they put me in a group home and threw away the key."

Zach's hands drift up my arms and stop at my shoulders. His thumbs make lazy circles as he watches me pensively.

"The Lewises adopted Max," I say softly, smiling as much as I can. "They wanted me to write to Max so we could at least keep in touch, and I did that for a little while. Eventually, my anger and guilt got the best of me, and I stopped writing. When I finally snapped out of it, they'd moved away."

Zach's eyes dart around my face as I look up at him. I shrug and shake my head.

"So that is why it's hard for me to talk about my brother," I say with a heavy sigh.

Without another word, Zach pulls me in and wraps his arms around me. It doesn't even occur to me to resist. I wrap my arms around his waist and settle my head against his chest like it's the most natural, normal thing in the world. Oh, this feels too good. That lovely sea salt and sandalwood smell envelops me, and I inhale it like a healing balm.

"I'm so sorry, Marina," Zach says gently, holding me tightly in the best hug I've had in a very long time.

I could stay here forever. Literally. Just stay wrapped in his arms and never have to deal with the rest of life again. No more horrible bosses. No more worrying about the next bad thing to happen. Just this. Sure, eating might be a problem and I'd need bathroom breaks, but otherwise. Just this.

"Thank you for sharing that with me," Zach murmurs against my hair.

I nod, not trusting myself enough to say more, and I inhale one final whiff of Zach before gently stepping out of his embrace. The realization suddenly hits me that I've shared far more than I actually intended, and I cringe.

"I'm so sorry," I say in a near whisper. "That kind of killed the mood, didn't it?"

Zach studies my face for a moment.

"You haven't killed anything, Siren," he says with a warm smile. "You've flattered me with your trust."

I shake my head. "I don't know why I said all that."

A mischievous glint flickers in his eyes. "That's what you're supposed to do on a non-date, Siren: get to know each other better."

A smile spreads from one corner of my mouth to the other and I laugh softly.

"So," Zach says with a quick clap of his hands, "I'm working on a project that I could use a little help on. If you think you'd like to?"

I nod enthusiastically, grateful for the change of subject. Zach pulls the remote control from his pocket. I wait patiently for an explanation.

"A few weeks ago, I had an idea to do a cover of 'The Sound of Silence,'" he begins. "I thought it might be kind of cool to do a dark version of it. Something more gritty. More rock, less folk."

"That sounds so interesting. I'd love to hear it."

Zach grins. "That's only half of what I need, though, Siren. Or at least I think it is. I'll sing my version first, but I still find it wanting. It's missing something."

I nod. "And you want me to help you figure out what it is?"

He shakes his head. "No. I'm pretty sure I already know what it's missing. *You.*"

My eyebrows shoot up in surprise. "What?"

He laughs softly, adjusting the mic a little. "Your voice has a quality that's very unique. It's almost haunting. I think you're what this piece is missing. So let me sing my version of it first, and you'll have a better idea of where it's going. Deal?"

I grab another stool that's sitting near the drum set, pull it over, and sit down. "Deal."

With a click of the remote, Zach triggers a pre-recorded track of a piano playing the song's intro. He closes his eyes as the music plays, and he looks absolutely peaceful. He begins singing the song's opening lyrics, his voice smooth and passionate. There is a definite quality of darkness in his inflection, and it's absolutely beautiful.

As the song moves on, I watch in fascination as Zach increases his intensity with every verse. The piano track stays the same. No new instruments are added, yet Zach's voice gets stronger and more powerful as he moves from verse to verse until, eventually, he is growling out the lyrics with a savage quality that has me riveted to my seat. Finally, he sings the last of the lyrics, and I'm left breathless.

"Wow."

Zach opens his eyes and smiles at me. "Yeah?"

"That was incredible, Zach," I whisper.

He gives me a quick bow. "Thank you, my lady."

I laugh and give him a quick shove.

"I don't see how I can help. That was pretty perfect."

Zach looks thoughtful for a moment, then takes my hands and pulls me to a standing position in front of the mic.

"I'm not sure I agree," he says softly. "Your voice will add another layer of intensity. When we sing together, it's almost like magic."

I can't help but smile. "It is."

"So you'll try it with me?" His expression is adorably hopeful, and there isn't one cell in my body that wants to say no to him right now.

I nod, and you'd think I just gave him a million dollars from the delighted expression on his face. A soft laugh escapes my lips as I pull out my phone and start scrolling.

"I'm afraid I don't know all the lyrics, though."

I find the lyrics online easily enough. I look up when another delicious wave of beach bonfire scent hits my nostrils. Zach is standing closer than ever, just on the other side of the mic stand, looking down at me with darkened eyes.

"Ready?" he asks with a huskiness in his voice that makes my heart skip a beat. He takes my phone and puts it on a stand nearby, adjusting the level so I can see it.

I nod, clearing my throat.

"As we sing, we'll raise our intensity at each verse. Make sense?" His brown eyes scan my face.

I nod again. "Got it."

He hits the remote. The music begins to play. Zach turns and puts the remote down, then holds both his hands out to me. I hold his gaze as I put my hands in his, the contact warm and comforting and very, very welcome.

The music builds to the first verse, and we begin to sing. I match Zach's gentle, almost breathless quality, and a chill sweeps down my spine at the sound of our voices mixing together in this way. He was dead on when he called it magic. I couldn't describe it any other way. I feel his fingers squeeze my hands, and I squeeze back.

The second verse comes, and our voices grow louder. I close my eyes, letting myself go in the moment, opening them only when I know I need to check the lyrics I don't know. Our voices weave their own melody on a higher level than the simple piano background accompanying us. I focus on keeping my voice clear and strong for this verse, matching Zach's level of intensity.

I open my eyes and find his face full of emotion, his beautiful eyes watching me. We both grip our hands a little tighter as we add more power to our voices. The building intensity is exhilarating, sending chills across my skin and pushing me to be bolder. Stronger.

When we hit the fourth verse, Zach adds a gravelly, hard rock growl to his voice. Instinctively, I raise my voice an octave, and the combination is both beautiful and brazen. He raises his eyebrows at the change, his expression one of pure joy as he squeezes my hands harder and keeps singing. I feel a thousand different emotions as we sing. Our voices are alive with power and song, blending perfectly in a melody that's both haunting and exhilarating. The final verses of the song are pure madness of the best kind. The song ends, leaving me breathless and full of emotion.

Zach and I just stand there for a moment, breathing heavily, the air between us charged with the leftover energy of our duet. There are no words for what I'm feeling right now. The way he's looking at me tells me he feels exactly the same. Our eyes are locked on each other, anchoring us as we come back down from the complete out-of-body experience we just had during that song. I can barely think. I'm just standing here, panting along with Zach, a single tear falling down my cheek.

He lets go of one of my hands, raising it to cup my cheek. As he brushes the tear away with his thumb, I'm suddenly very aware of the fact that the mic is a very inconvenient barrier between us. I grab the mic stand with shaky fingers and move it to the side, which gives Zach room to fully close the distance between us.

Still breathing heavily, he wraps his arms around me, and I melt against him. I wrap my hands around his biceps, feeling them ripple in response. A smile teases the corner of Zach's mouth.

"Marina…"

My gaze lowers to his mouth, and I find myself nodding, wanting his kiss. Zach lowers his lips to mine, grazing a feathery light kiss there that completely ruins me. Because it's not enough. It's not nearly enough. He pulls back again, his eyes full of need, and I'm completely taken away by a wave of wanting. I need his kiss like I've never needed anything else in my life. I reach up and thread my fingers into his hair, pulling his mouth down to mine in a soft, warm, deliciously all-consuming kiss that tears down my boundaries like they're made of tissue paper.

Chapter 9

Zach

Marina is kissing me…

This isn't a dream. Is it?

Please don't let it be a dream.

Her lips are so soft as they move under mine, her nails lightly scratching over my scalp as she holds me just where she wants me. I am completely okay giving her all the control. I'm lost in this kiss, and I never want to be found.

I gently put my hands on either side of her face, and a husky little moan escapes her lips. Her hands move from my hair, and she wraps her arms around my waist, pulling me closer. My pulse is racing like I'm running a marathon. I inhale her intoxicating coconut scent and move my fingers just slightly into her hair, so soft and silky. I can kiss her all night if she wants. She's the boss. I never want this to end.

Marina's kisses slow down, and when she pulls her mouth away slightly, I dip down and nip playfully at her bottom lip. She laughs softly and comes back for more, placing a soft, slow kiss on my mouth. I dig my hands into her beautiful hair as I deepen the kiss, and I'm rewarded with another little moan as she leans into me. I feel a little tipsy, but the only thing I've had to drink is Marina. Eventually, she pulls away again and looks up at me with eyes darkened by passion.

"Wow," she says huskily, a very sexy smile spreading on her beautiful face.

I nod. "Wow."

She's still leaning on me, her hands splayed across my chest, but I see the exact moment reality starts to creep back into her thoughts. Her eyes dart around nervously, and I instinctively know she's filing through her list of excuses to run away from me again. I know I need to do everything I can to stop her from back peddling right out of my life. As much as I don't want to do it, I gently pull away from her and take both of her hands in mine.

"Talk to me, Siren," I whisper. "I see you."

Her eyes search my face. "You see me?"

"You're looking for reasons to run again." I give her hands a gentle squeeze.

To my surprise, she nods and squeezes back.

"I'm not very good at…casual…kissing," she says as a blush creeps up her cheeks.

I squeeze again.

"There was nothing casual about that, Marina," I reply with a husky laugh.

She can't be more adorable right now, and she has no idea what she does to me. She heaves a sigh and pulls her hands away, and just like that, my heart drops to my stomach.

Don't run, don't run, don't run.

She folds her arms across her middle and shakes her head.

"No, I mean," she begins, then pauses as she searches for the right words. "I don't just go around kissing men. I haven't even been on a date in years. By choice. And you don't even live here. Obviously, this isn't going to go anywhere. So…I'm sorry. I shouldn't have—"

I cautiously step into her space again, wrapping my hands around her elbows and running my hands up and down her arms. She relaxes a little.

"Marina," I interrupt gently. "Can I get a word in before you put me through a break-up when we've only been on two non-dates?"

She laughs softly, rolling her eyes at me. She nods. Good. Progress.

"Okay, yes, you're right," I admit, leaning forward and planting a light kiss on her cheek. "I don't live here. And you are on a dating hiatus for reasons you've yet to share. What if my geographical status wasn't an issue?"

She blinks. Aha! Wasn't expecting that.

"What?"

I kiss her other cheek. I'm going for broke here.

"Okay, let me put this another way," I say with a hopeful air. "What if I was independently wealthy? What if I decided you're worth all the extra travel it would take to keep coming back to San Francisco between gigs? What if things go really well between us? What if I decide to move here in the future because I simply can't stand to be parted from you?"

She shakes her head disbelievingly. I step closer and reach up to cup her radiant face with my hands. I don't miss how her eyes shutter closed just for an instant as she presses her cheek into my palm.

"Marina," I say tenderly, "what you shared with me tonight…about your family was so brave. It's helped me to understand you better."

"It has? How?"

"Life has shown you that you can't depend on anyone. You learned very early in life that the one thing you *can* count on is that most people are going to let you down," I explain.

Even as I say the words, my heart breaks for her and what she's been through.

Her lip quivers, and I'm barely holding back from crushing her in my arms and never letting go.

"What's the actual truth?" I ask softly, grazing a thumb along her smooth cheekbone.

Those beautiful green eyes that'll be the death of me glance up at me, seeking.

"You are an amazing woman, Marina. You have worked hard to build a good life for yourself. You got yourself through college, you're going to be a lawyer. You're driven, and brilliant, and funny, and disgustingly talented."

A smile lights up her face, finally. I feel like I've won the lottery again.

"Your inner circle is fiercely protective of you," I continue, raising one of her hands and placing a light kiss on the back of it. "Not to mention Merry's grandfather. Any one of them would fillet me if I hurt you."

She laughs softly and nods. "They would."

I kiss her other hand. "All right then. If I say that whatever this is between us is special, are you going to argue with me?"

Her smile widens. "No?"

"How refreshing," I tease, earning a poke in the ribs.

I laugh out loud and pull her against me once more. She wraps her arms around my waist and looks up at me with a gleam in her eyes.

"Will you let us have this chance?" I ask softly. "Can you push aside the worries over the mermaid story, my fame, and anything else that may get in the way? Because I don't know if you feel the same, but that kiss changed my life, woman."

She laughs in earnest, and it's music to my ears. "That wasn't one kiss. It was more like thirty-seven."

I smile slowly, rubbing my nose against hers. "I detest odd numbers. Can we make it an even forty?"

"Yes, and yes," she mutters, her darkening gaze lowering to my mouth.

I raise my eyebrows in question.

"Yes, let's see where this thing goes," she says in a near whisper. "And yes to forty."

That's all the permission I need to bury my hands in her hair and claim her mouth with my own.

***

Marina

I've read the same email three times and still can't get my fingers to type out a simple response. I sit back in my chair and heave an exasperated sigh. I've come down with a bad case of Zach brain. I cannot get the man out of my head. How am I supposed to function like this?

Admittedly, I'm a bit of an amateur in the dating department. I was so bent on causing chaos during my teen years, including going out with all the wrong kinds of boys, that when I finally decided to stop the chaos, I also stopped the boys. That translated to men as well. When I was trying to get my life back on track, dating added another level of complications that I just didn't need. So, I ruled it out, and I've been happy with my choice until now. Until I met a rock star, who makes me want to break my rules. No, not break them. Crush them into powder.

Rules? What rules?

I sit forward and put my hands on my keyboard, willing myself to concentrate. I type out a reply to our custodial team, explaining that the executive conference room will need detailed cleaning on the day before the Montclair meeting and that I've re-booked all the meetings scheduled in that room that week so they have plenty of time. Then I click over to the catering order form for the breakfast we're hosting that morning. During my research on Ethan Montclair, I learned he's a health nut who loves an organic, vegan cafe in the Fisherman's Wharf area, so that's where I'm ordering from.

My stomach growls, and I'm grateful I'm not in Ms. Taft's office, or I'd have to hear a fifteen-minute lecture on gut cleansing and the dangers of gluten. She'd die if she knew about my fondness for pasta. It's probably grounds for termination. I'll have to check the employee handbook.

My phone vibrates on my desk, and I look down to see a message from Zach. I don't even try to hide the ridiculous smile on my face when I see his name on my screen. If I'm a siren, I'm a siren caught in his net. Last night changed the whole dynamic of our relationship, and there's no pretending that it didn't. While most guys only ever managed to chip a little mortar from the brick wall of my defenses, Zach has the ability to reach out and remove entire bricks. That first kiss managed to knock the wall down, and it's my fault entirely. Who kissed who?

Zach: What's for lunch today, love?

I smile. Do I tell him the truth? Why lie about my not-so-awesome lunch situation.

Marina: I have an energy bar in my desk drawer that looks extremely tasty.

Okay, the tasty part was a lie.

Zach: I thought as much. Can I steal you away for a moment?

I laugh quietly, shaking my head.

Marina: Zach, no. I told you I only have about 15 minutes and even the cafeteria on the second floor takes longer than that.

Zach: Do you think I'm an amateur? I've come prepared.

What? Is he *here?*

Zach is typing...

Zach: Can you meet me in the garage?

My eyes dart to the calendar on my computer monitor. It's 12:11, so Ms. Taft has started her daily web conference with her colleagues. She won't need me for at least fifteen minutes, but probably more like forty-five. I lock my computer screen and grab my phone, setting an alarm in case I get distracted by the very handsome man downstairs. I text him as I walk to the elevators.

Marina: On my way. This better be good.

I school my expression into one of neutrality. Boredom, even. It's a challenge, given how hard my pulse is racing because Zach is waiting for me. I take the elevator down to the garage level and step out, walking over to the area where I met Dave before. My pulse goes crazy when I see Dave standing outside the SUV and the rear passenger door open. He greets me with a nod. Behind him, Zach smiles at me from inside the car.

"Hello again, Dave," I say as I get in.

Zach sits in the back with a huge grin on his handsome face. Does he know how gorgeous he is? His rich, dark brown hair is just tousled enough to be sexy, and the stubble on his jaw...how does it always look perfect? I want to lean in for a kiss, but I can't. He's set up a small collapsible table and it's covered with various takeout bags from local eateries. The inside of the car smells like a food court. I laugh out loud as Dave shuts the door behind me.

"What is all this?"

Zach points to the first bag. "I wasn't sure what you'd be hungry for, so I picked up a few things. This is a chicken Caesar salad."

He points to each bag. "Orange chicken from some Chinese place I can't remember the name of, boneless buffalo wings, a double cheeseburger and fries, or a burrito bowl with carne asada."

I just stare at him, wide-eyed. He drove all over the city. For me. I am in crazy danger of seriously falling for this man.

"I don't know your favorites yet, so I wanted you to have choices," he says, looking sheepish.

I shake my head in disbelief. "This is the nicest thing any man has ever done for me."

His eyes rake over my face. "Yeah?"

I lean over as far as I can and crook my finger at him. His eyes darken as he gets my meaning and leans over to kiss me. His lips are soft and warm and make me want to forget all about work today. As if he knows my thoughts, he pulls away and gestures at all the food.

"All right, Siren, I know you don't have long. What's your choice?"

I don't even have to think about it as I grab the burrito bowl. I sweep my hand at the rest of it.

"And what's your choice?"

He grins and grabs the burger, then yells, "Dave!"

Dave opens the door, and Zach offers him his choice of what's left. Dave accepts the orange chicken with a gleam in his eye and shuts the door, eating as he waits outside the car.

I carefully peel the foil cover off the burrito bowl and dig in.

"How's the project going?" he asks as he bites into the burger.

I nod and swallow. "I feel good about it, as long as there are no surprises. I've done a lot of the busy work that needed to get out of the way. Ordered breakfast from his favorite place, and today I ordered the supplies the supporting staff will need to put together the proposal materials."

"It's going to be brilliant," he says with such confidence. "And the Evil Queen shall grovel at your feet."

I let out a laugh. "That will literally never happen," I say as I scoop up another forkful. "But I appreciate your faith in me."

He bobs his head and takes another bite, covering his mouth as he mutters, "You'll see I'm right."

"So, what are you doing today besides buying all the food in the city?"

"Rick and I are getting together at the hotel to work on a couple new songs," he says. "And then I have to get some things ready for our date tomorrow night before I head to the television studio."

I smile. "Still not telling me what we're doing on our date?"

He shakes his head. "It's a surprise. But I am feeding you, so don't eat dinner, and the dress code is casual."

I like the sound of this already. "How casual?"

"Jeans and trainers are perfectly acceptable," he replies.

"Trainers?" I ask with a frown.

"Sneakers," he clarifies. "You might want a jumper. Uh…a sweater, as Americans say. Could get chilly."

He points to my burrito bowl.

"Eat," he commands playfully. "You need calories so you can go back in there and slay the day away."

I laugh and shake my head. "What?"

He grins like a Cheshire cat and takes a bite out of his burger, making me laugh even more. I load up another forkful and sit back, just enjoying this little bit of time with him and trying my best to ignore the occasional panic attack that tries to rise up over the personal rules I'm breaking. But they're my rules, so I get to decide when they no longer serve me. It's just going to take some time to adjust, that's all.

"Is it hard to write songs?" I ask as he takes the last bite of his burger.

He immediately shakes his head. "They just come out. I can't explain it."

"That's amazing. I'm not very creative, so I can't imagine what that's like."

He crumples up his burger wrapper, pulls a container of fries out of another bag, and throws the burger wrapper inside.

"Well, I don't mean they come out fully finished," he clarifies. "I have to work at it. So does Rick. But it usually starts with a feeling or an idea of a feeling."

I finish off my bowl and throw the trash in the bag with Zach's, then give him a perplexed look. "A feeling?"

Zach rolls his head and shoulders and pops a fry in his mouth. "How do I explain this…"

I say nothing, content to watch his face as he thinks through how to explain creativity to a law student who wouldn't know what to do with a box of crayons. His eyes are bright as he thinks, showing how passionate he is about music. And the way he's lounging with his back against the car door gives me a great view of his broad chest, muscled arms, and…I wonder what his abs look like. I fight the urge to reach out and feel for the answer.

"Tell me about a happy memory," he says quietly. "Something that still pops in your head once in a while."

I think for a minute. "One summer, my mom was waiting tables, and this couple sat in her section," I begin. "They just hit it off with her, and it turned out they owned this big theme park that was really popular. They asked if she'd ever taken us, and she said no, so they gave her passes to the park for two days, vouchers for food, and an overnight stay at the park's hotel."

Zach raises his eyebrows. "Wow! That was really nice of them."

I nod. "It was. She was so excited when she got home. I still remember the look on her face when she told us. We had the best time, just the three of us. We rode every ride at least twice. We didn't have to worry about money at all. We just had fun together. They sold this red licorice that came in huge, long ropes. My brother and I thought that was the best thing ever. Even now, I think of that day every time I see red licorice. It makes my heart happy."

I don't realize until it's too late that I have a tear in my eye. I swipe it away as soon as I feel it fall down my cheek, smiling as the happy memory hits me in full force. I wonder about my brother. About where he is. If he's okay. If he forgives me. Or does he hate me? Does he still love red licorice as much as me?

A low growl escapes Zach's throat as he sits up, making quick work of moving the remaining to-go bags out of the way. He folds the small table up and tosses it over the divider into the front passenger seat, scooting next to me. He pulls me close and cradles my head against his chest. My body fully relaxes against his, and I sigh heavily, content to just let him hold me.

"Thank you for sharing that with me," he says gently, his lips moving against my hair.

"Are you going to write a song about red licorice now?" I ask quietly, smiling against his chest. He laughs, and I love the sound of it reverberating against my ear.

"No, but it's a great example of what I meant," he says, wrapping his arms tighter around me. "I take a memory like that, and the music comes from that feeling. If it makes me feel happy, the music comes out that way. If I'm angry or hurt, that's what it sounds like. For lyrics, it just depends. Both Rick and I have written several songs just on our own if it's something we have to get out, or sometimes we get an idea and work on it together."

"Mmm," I mutter into Zach's t-shirt.

I feel completely and utterly at peace. Protected. Treasured.

"Are you all right?" he whispers, moving his hand up and down my back in comforting circles.

I nod, slowly sitting up and nestling against his side.

"Despite everything, I like thinking about my mom," I explain.

"Especially since I've lost track of Max. It feels like I'm the only one who remembers her. And I don't want her to be forgotten."

"About that," he begins, planting a light kiss on my temple. "I've had an idea."

I turn to look at him. His expression is pensive as he reaches down to take my hand.

"I want to ask you something, but I don't want you to give me an answer right away," he says cautiously. "I want you to have time to think about it."

I nod slowly. "Okay."

He considers for a moment, licking his lips. "I would like to help you find your brother."

My eyebrows knit together in confusion. "What?"

"If you are agreeable to the idea, I was thinking a private investigator would be a good place to start," he explains. "It would likely be a quick and easy case, especially if the adoption records weren't sealed."

I blink back my surprise. I always hoped I would find Max after I lost track of him, but I knew I had to get my life together first. At first, my time was completely taken up with therapy and college. I had to get off of financial aid and slowly worked my way to being independent. My search for Max has always been limited to what I can do myself on social media, and it always comes up empty.

I look down at my hands. "I can't accept that, Zach. It's too much."

Zach pulls me closer against his side. "Please don't make a decision yet. The offer stands if you would like me to help, but I don't want you to feel rushed in giving me an answer."

The alarm on my phone goes off, signaling me that Ms. Taft will be done with her meeting soon. I silence it with a frustrated sigh and look at Zach.

"I know, I know," he grumbles as he releases me. "Time's up."

I give him a sad look. "I don't like it either. I'm sorry."

I pull on the handle to open the door, and Dave is there in an instant, pulling the door the rest of the way so I can scoot out. Zach follows. Dave gets in the driver's seat and closes the door to give us some privacy. Zach takes my hand and walks with me to the elevator doors. He steps in front of me and pulls me close as I wrap my arms around his neck.

"Have a wonderful rest of your day, love," he purrs, eyes dropping to my mouth. My toes curl, and I smile up at him.

"Thank you so much for lunch," I say softly, smiling up at him. "This was the best surprise ever."

There's a twinkle in his eye as he moves closer and brushes a soft kiss on the corner of my mouth.

"You deserve all the surprises," he says with a grin.

He brings his mouth down to mine in a soft, slow kiss. Something low in my belly stirs, and I gently pull away before I'm tempted to stay longer. He reluctantly lets me go and presses the elevator call button.

"Knock 'em dead, Siren," he growls as the elevator doors open.

I step inside, hit the button, and blow him a kiss. The grin that lights up his whole face is the last thing I see before the doors close between us.

*****

The afternoon breezes by in a flurry of ad-hoc tasks thrown at me by Ms. Taft's staff, all in a frantic rush to get their parts of the presentation ready for the Montclair meeting. I handled it all with the efficiency and thoroughness they've come to expect from me, and in the few quiet moments I had to myself, my brain always looped back to Zach's offer.

I would like to help you find your brother.

I gather my belongings and head down to the lobby, stopping in the ladies room to change into my disguise for the day. I slip off my skirt and jacket and pull a pair of yoga pants, a sweatshirt, and sneakers out of my tote bag. Once dressed, I carefully fold my work clothes and tuck them into my tote bag with my heels. I leave my hair up, shove a baseball cap on my head, and head for the door.

As I step back into the lobby, I notice a group of people at the reception desk, which is odd because this building is full of corporations, and it's after five o'clock. The afternoon guard seems to have it all under control as he speaks firmly to the group. They're too far away for me to hear, and I have a ton of laundry to do before Ashley and I make dinner and get ready to watch trash TV all night so I don't slow down to investigate. The bus is pulling up at the corner as I step outside. I easily jog the distance and bound onto the bus. Thank goodness I decided to wear sneakers, or that would have been harder to do.

For once, I leave my phone in my bag and lean my head against the glass as the bus pulls away from the curb. Zach's offer rolls over and over in my mind, and my pulse quickens with excitement at the mere idea of actually *finding* Max. I could have my brother back in my life. Soon.

Would he still be angry at me? Or has he missed me? Would he want to see me? What if he doesn't want to be found? What if he doesn't want anything to do with me? Every imaginable scenario plays out in my head until I'm mentally exhausted and no closer to a decision than I was before, so it's no surprise when the bus rolls up to my stop, and I almost miss it. I bolt up from my seat.

"Wait!" I yell out as I grab my bags and head up the aisle. I mutter an apology to the bus driver as I step onto the pavement outside my building just in time to see Scarlet and Merry hurrying up the street towards me.

"Ladies!" I cry out, happy to see them, as I adjust my tote bag on my shoulder. "What's up?"

My smile falters when I see that they're each carrying huge takeout bags from our favorite Chinese food dive. Oh, no. Something's happened. Whenever any of us is going through a tough time, our standard operating procedure is to grab Chinese takeout and call an emergency conclave of the girls. Since neither Merry nor Scarlet appears to be in tears, that leaves Ash. Oh, no.

"What's happened?" I ask as they meet up with me. "Is it Ash? Did she fight with Greg again?"

That can't be. They're not just regular happy, they're Hallmark movie happy. Well, at least *she* is. There's something about him that I don't quite like. Scarlet loops her arm through mine and starts pulling me while Merry runs ahead of us to get the door.

"Let's get upstairs and we can all talk about it," Scarlet mutters, pulling so hard my bag slides off my shoulder.

"Hey!" I cry out as she drags me into the building and pushes me towards the stairs.

"Sorry," Merry says tensely as we climb to the second floor. "I'm just really hungry."

"You work in a restaurant," I remind her, giving her the side-eye.

As soon as we hit the second-floor landing, Ashley opens our apartment door. She looks completely fine. No tears, no drama. She's fine, Merry's fine, Scarlet's...fine.

This is about me.

I stop in my tracks. My heart is instantly pounding.

"What's happened?" I ask again, my voice shaking.

Scarlet hands her bag to Merry, who takes it inside the apartment and then wraps an arm around me.

"Let's get inside, and we can all talk, okay?" she says in a voice that's meant to be soothing but makes me panic more. She gently coaxes me towards the door.

Ashley watches me with a worried expression. "It's gonna be okay, Marina," she assures me.

What is? What's happened? Scarlet pulls me through the door as I look over at Ash with pleading eyes.

Just tell me.

And that's when I hear it, coming from the television in the living room.

"Well, you heard it here first, folks," the news anchor says. "The mystery of the mermaid is solved! Apparently, this sexy siren's name is Marina MacArthur, and she's one of San Francisco's own!"

Chapter 10

Marina

I'm dreaming, right? This has to be some kind of bad dream. I can't get my mind around it, but my palms don't usually sweat when I have a bad dream. And I feel a little sick to my stomach.

This is real.

As much as I don't want it to be, it is most definitely real. My ears ring as one of the girls helps me into the living room, and they start spreading takeout containers around the coffee table. Ashley is looking at me as if she's waiting for an answer, but I didn't hear the question.

"Did you say something?"

She takes my hand and squeezes. "Why don't you go put your things down, and we'll figure this out, okay?"

I nod slowly.

Yes, I should go put my tote bag and purse away.

I take a step toward my bedroom on legs that don't feel like my own, stopping to glance at the television. There's a photo of me with Zach on the screen, taken by someone hiding in the shadows as we

"

exited the recording studio last night.

It's a good picture, I numbly acknowledge in my addled brain. I'm smiling up at him, lips swollen and looking thoroughly kissed, as he waits for me to get in the car. The entertainment news reporter on TV is almost squealing at how romantic it is that the Duke of Rock found his mermaid. They're speculating now. How long has this been going on? Is it serious? They have so many questions. This is my worst nightmare.

Merry appears at my side, gently walking me the rest of the way to my room. I shut the door behind me. Only when I'm alone, do I feel the sting of tears threatening my eyes. A lump forms in my throat as I drop my bags on my bed. One bag rolls to the side, and my suit falls out and lands on the floor in a crumpled heap. I pull my phone from my purse and slip it into the pocket of my pants.

Already, there's a war going on in my head over Zach, my fight-or-flight mode trying to win in a battle with my heart. My usual response is to cut the drama off at the source. Not that Zach is the actual source here, but if he wasn't in my life, I wouldn't be in this mess. Normally, I hate messes, but he's kind of making me see that it's okay to color outside the lines. I know I'm not in any place to make decisions about it right now. I somehow manage to keep my mind from running through every horrible scenario as I shrug out of my jacket and throw it on the bed. The first tear falls as I walk to the door to join the girls. I leave my suit on the bedroom floor in a heap. I won't be needing it, or any of the others, for a while.

The girls have arranged the food on the coffee table when I get back to the living room, along with a giant box of tissues in the middle of it all. I snag a few from the box before I drop onto the couch. Ash leans over and wraps me in a hug, which I accept gratefully. If there's one thing years of therapy have taught me, it's to accept comfort when it's given and try to deal with my feelings instead of fighting them.

I'm still working on the latter.

Scarlet, ever the practical one, passes me a container and a set of chopsticks as soon as I stop hugging Ash. I don't even have to look in the container to know it's my favorite fried rice. These women know me better than anyone, and when we call an emergency conclave, we do it right. When Ash and Greg broke up because he wasn't sure what he wanted, it was her favorite ice cream and Hallmark movies. Scarlet's childhood pet dying? Merry baked her favorite cookies, and we all slept over at her mom's house. When Merry found out her last boyfriend de jour was cheating, we converged on Nonno's restaurant so she had three shoulders to cry on while she ate her weight in cannoli. Whatever any of us needs, we're here for it. Today just happens to be about me, and it's a doozy because I literally have no idea how we're going to figure this out.

"I'm so fired," I manage to choke out before digging into my fried rice.

Ashley rubs a hand up and down my back.

"We don't know that for sure," she says in a motherly tone. "We should prepare for that, but we don't know that yet."

Merry snorts. "The Evil Queen will go for the throat."

I nod in agreement as I load my chopsticks. "I've definitely lost my job. Which means I've lost law school, or delayed it significantly. And I won't make rent next month."

"They're not the only firm in the city," Scarlet reminds me. "Just the most bougie. I'll ask my mom if she has any leads. You know she'll do anything to help you, girl."

I nod and give Scarlet a weak smile. Her mom is a lawyer. She may not work for the most prestigious firm in the city, but she is a partner at a decent-sized firm, and I know she would at least write me a letter of recommendation to help with my job search. I feel myself relax a little and take another bite, not really tasting anything.

"Don't think about rent right now," Ashley tells me with a nudge. "I can float you next month, and you're not allowed to say no."

"At least it's a good picture," Merry chimes in, ogling the television. I scoff.

"It really is," Ash adds with a grin. "I mean, look at you two."

I glance at the television before throwing my chopsticks back in the container and setting it on the table. It *is* a good picture, but that's not going to help me get a job or get into law school. All it shows is two people who are clearly focused solely on each other, so much so that we both fail to see the photographer hiding somewhere nearby. I stare at Zach's image for a moment, still unsure of how to handle him.

"Hey," Ash says, pulling my attention from the television. "Don't even think about *that* either."

I don't bother trying to act like I wasn't thinking about ending things with him. Ashley knows me too well. I shrug.

"It could minimize the damage," I say all too matter-of-factly. I should really be worried about how easily the words roll off my tongue. I would be if my heart didn't plummet to the floor at the mere thought of never seeing Zach again. He's already under my skin and well on his way into my heart. I like him. I'm happy when I'm with him…and that's not a bad thing, nor is it an easy thing to give up.

Scarlet gasps. "This is not the time to make that decision!"

"And what good would it do?" Merry adds with a wave of her hand. "If you're right and you do get fired, breaking up with Zach won't get your job back."

Without even thinking about it, I know she's right. Breaking up with Zach solves nothing at this point. It's just running like a coward, and I'm done with that. That's what I did when Mom died…I ran. I haven't come this far in life just to go back to old habits. I'm going to stand, and I'm going to deal with it.

"Does he even know?" Ash asks from her perch on the couch. "We barely just found out about it as we were getting off work."

I pull my phone from my pocket and check for messages. None. I shake my head.

"He's on his way to the Channel 3 studio to be on *San Francisco Tonight*," I explain. "He must not know, or my phone would have exploded."

My heart jumps to my throat. He doesn't know…and he's on his way to a talk show appearance. I pull up his number and hit dial, my heart pounding in my ears. The girls watch anxiously as I hold the phone to my ear, waiting. Waiting. It goes to voice mail, so I hang up. I quickly text him.

Marina: They know. It's all over the news.

I put my phone on the end table and shrug.

"It went to voice mail, so I texted him."

The entertainment reports have mercifully gone on to the next story, so I don't have to see myself on the screen anymore. I reach over and grab my food off the table.

"What time is Zach's interview?" Scarlet asks. "We have to be sure to watch it."

"It's not live," I say between bites. "They're taping it tonight, but it won't air until later in the week."

Scarlet nods. "And the Evil Queen? What do we do about her?"

I laugh bitterly. "There's nothing we can do about her. I have brought what she calls unfavorable attention to the firm. I will be fired. There's no getting around it."

"Why give her the satisfaction then?" Merry muses. "Just don't show up tomorrow."

I consider it, then shake my head. "No, if I'm going to lose my job over something like this, I'm going to make her work for it."

Scarlet and Merry blink back their surprise and Ashley smiles from ear to ear.

"There she is!" Ashley cries out, holding her hand up for a high-five. I give her one.

Merry grins at me. "You got this."

I nod. "I got this. I mean…it was a shock, for sure. I would have preferred to remain a mystery, but this is what's happened. I can't run from it."

"Besides, everyone loves the mermaid story!" Scarlet says excitedly. "It's not like it's a bad thing for your boss."

"Yes, it is," I argue gently. "She thinks the whole thing is stupid. She's much too important to waste time with music or art or…"

"Fun," Ashley chimes in.

"She'll take this as a personal blow," I explain. "I'm making Taft & Kennedy a laughingstock."

"That's ridiculous," Scarlet says, chomping on an egg roll.

I take a deep breath and roll my head around to release the tension in my neck.

"Well, ridiculous or not, there's only one thing to do," I say. "I will go to the office on Monday, clean out my desk, and close that chapter of my life. I should probably start looking for jobs tonight, but I can't face it. I have the whole weekend to figure out what to do."

"No," Ashley says soothingly. "Don't think about that tonight. You can work on that tomorrow when you're fresh."

"Yeah," Merry agrees. "Tonight's about you and margaritas."

I raise my eyebrows in alarm. "Margaritas and Chinese food?"

Scarlet rolls her eyes at me. "Seriously?"

I open my mouth to reply, but a knock on the door interrupts me. We all look at the door, but nobody moves. The knock happens again.

I get up and head for the door, but Ashley jumps in front of me.

"What if it's the paparazzi?" she says with wide eyes.

I laugh and step around her, putting my hand on the door knob.

"It could be Mrs. Baldwin next door," I muse. "Or the landlord. Or a delivery. Everything doesn't have to be about me."

I open the door and the foyer erupts in white light as dozens of flashes go off in my face. I put my hand over my eyes and quickly slam the door, but it's too late. They've seen me. I couldn't see how many reporters there were, but now they're shouting through the door.

"Marina, tell us about your relationship with the Duke of Rock!"

"How long have you been the mermaid?"

"Is Zach a good kisser?"

I lock the deadbolt and step back from the door like it's on fire. I turn to Ashley, shaking my head.

"How are we ever going to be able to leave?" I ask, my voice nearly a whisper.

Ashley grabs my hand and yanks me away from the door as the reporters continue shouting in the foyer. It's only a matter of time before my neighbors open their doors and they're accosted with questions about what it's like to live next door to the mermaid. I'm suddenly thankful we have a trash chute in the building or they'd already be going through our garbage.

"This is impossible," I whisper as my hands float up to my cheeks.

"Well, we have food and margaritas. We can out last them," Ashley declares, stepping into the kitchen and flicking the switch on the blender with dramatic flair.

Merry snickers. Scarlet runs into Ashley's bedroom to look out the window because it faces the street. My room overlooks the tiny little alley behind our building. She comes back with eyes as round as saucers.

"We may be spending the night," she mutters as she heads to our tiny kitchen and starts pulling margarita glasses from the cabinet.

Merry and I look at each other and shuffle into Ashley's bedroom. I move the curtains just enough to look down, and my pulse hammers wildly. There's a crowd on the sidewalk below. It looks like a party down there, people chatting excitedly with each other. There are several reporters swarming anyone walking on the sidewalk.

"Whoa," Merry mutters as we watch the chaos.

I pull away from the window before anyone looks up and sees us. Merry and I walk back to the kitchen.

"I'm sorry, girls," I mutter, feeling terrible that we're now trapped in this building.

"For what?" Merry asks. "You didn't do this. They're the crazy ones. And none of us care if we're on TV. You're the one who works for the weirdos."

Ashley hands me a margarita. "We're not going to worry about it right now," she says. "We're just going to hang out and focus on what we can control. And if they're still in the foyer when we're ready to call it a night, I'll call the police."

I smile and take a sip, choking almost immediately. I give Ash a wide-eyed glance, and she winks at me.

"They may be a little strong," she says with a laugh.

***

Two hours later, we've watched more news footage, and the girls have had to talk me off my mental ledge twice. There were speculations on whether this is my natural hair color, whether I planted myself in that traffic jam on purpose to get Zach's attention, and an impromptu poll among the commentators about whether we've slept together yet. We finally turned off the news. Our current topic of discussion is spa pedicures, which is funny because I can't really feel my feet anymore. Or my hands. I've had four of Ashley's special margaritas, and my limit is usually two.

Another knock on the door jolts us all from our debate on gel polish. The reporters haven't budged. We've been ignoring the random knocks, but this one is a more frantic pounding than a knock. And they're not letting up.

Geez.

Ashley bolts from the couch and stomps to the door as Merry and Scarlet leap to their feet and urge her not to open it. I would as well, but I don't think I could manage it. I've always been a lightweight when it comes to drinking.

"Marina!" Zach's frantic voice sounds on the other side of the door.

I gasp, and Ashley lurches forward with a squeal. She rips the door open to let him in. Zach stands in the foyer alone. All the reporters are gone. His eyes dart nervously around the apartment until they meet mine. He looks relieved but worried at the same time. His jaw muscle is working overtime as he assesses the situation. He steps inside, and Ashley closes the door behind him.

Nobody moves. Merry and Scarlet are frozen where they are standing by the coffee table. I'm sitting up on the couch, trying to focus my increasingly fuzzy gaze on Zach. Ashley stands behind him, looking bewildered. Zach looks around at my friends.

"Hello, ladies," he says with a pensive smile. "Everyone all right?"

No one says anything. We're all like deer in the headlights. Eventually, Merry nods. Zach's gaze fixes on me.

"Are you okay?" he asks quietly, his voice laced with hurt and worry.

"Hi…here," I say, then shake my head. "Hi. Reporters are here."

He nods. "I'm so sorry. Are you okay?"

"Yep," I reply, showing him my glass. "We have margaritas."

The corner of his mouth twitches as if he's not sure he should smile. He takes a few steps towards me.

"You aren't angry with me?" he asks softly.

My mind is starting to get really fuzzy. "Where did all the people go?"

"I sent them away."

I raise my eyebrows in wonder. Wow.

"And they listened?" Merry asks incredulously.

He shrugs. "They listened to the private security I just posted outside your door."

Ashley opens the door and sticks her head out. "Oh! Hello…sorry…"

She shuts the door again and gives me a thumbs up, as if having security guards outside our door is totally normal. Zach looks at me again.

"I left my phone in the car when I went to the show taping, so I didn't see your text message," he says. "I only found out the media knows who you are when they asked me about it during the interview."

It's starting to get really hard to hold my head up. I rest my chin on the cushions.

"Come sit down, Zach," Ashley says, ushering him into the living room.

I try to move over and suddenly feel very dizzy. I sway to the left, and Zach is there to catch me. He takes the margarita from my hand before I spill it everywhere. He sits next to me, brushing my thigh with his, and I don't think about anything but sinking into his side. A look of relief washes over his face as he wraps an arm around me and kisses the top of my head.

"I'm glad everyone is all right," he says. "Certain members of the press can be aggressive."

Ashley nods. "We noticed."

I feel Zach's body tense up. "Did they try to push in here?"

"No," Ashley replies. "But they just kept knocking and yelling through the door. Like that's going to get anyone to go out there. So thanks for the rescue."

"Well, that brings up something I wanted to talk to you ladies about," he says pensively. "You don't have a doorman or any security in this building."

I scoff. "We're not all rock stars, baby!"

Merry snorts and Zach frowns at me, then looks at my margarita that he's still holding. He sniffs it, takes a sip, and nearly chokes.

"How many of these has she had?" he asks my friends.

Merry holds up some fingers, but I can't see how many.

"Maybe some water?" Zach asks, handing my glass to Ashley. She takes it with a smile and disappears.

Ashley brings me a glass of water, and I start sipping.

"I worry about your safety," Zach continues, looking from me to Ashley. "I can keep security here to keep them out of the building, but that won't stop them once you're on the pavement."

Ashley heaves a sigh. "I have to be able to get to work."

"I don't!" I shout, then frown at myself. Why am I yelling?

Zach looks at me with a worried expression.

"I'm going to be fired," I whisper.

Zach's eyes sadden. "I'm so sorry, Marina. I never meant for this to happen."

I shake my head. "Not your fault."

"She's right," Ashley says.

"If I hadn't stepped off my bus and caused that scene, none of this would be happening," he argues. "And there's no way I'll be able to relax if you two aren't safe because of me."

"What do you suggest then?" Ashley asks.

"I'd like to put you both up in a hotel," he answers. "One with security, and I'll get the car service to take you both to work."

Ashley's eyes are huge, and I wish I had my phone so I could take her picture.

"No, Zach," I say quietly, sipping more water. "It's too much. That's so much money."

He shakes his head. "They won't stop, Marina. And they'll badger your neighbors as well."

Ashley bites her lower lip, and I know she wants to say yes when she looks at me. I cave instantly.

"Okay," I say quietly. "I guess I understand."

"You'll let me help?" he asks, his hopeful expression pulling at every single one of my heartstrings simultaneously.

I nod. "We'll go to a hotel. I don't care which one. I'll leave that to you."

"Oh, not for me," Ashley jumps in. "I can stay with Greg."

Even as fuzzy as I am, I wonder how that's going to go over with Greg.

Zach nods. "Okay, then I'll let you ladies pack."

I raise my brows. "We're going tonight?"

Ashley comes over and pulls me up off of the couch and out of Zach's arms, making me frown. "Let's go pack what we need, okay?"

I shuffle off to my room with Ash, leaving Merry and Scarlet behind with Zach.

***

Zach

I sit in the back of the car with a sleeping Marina tucked into my side, watching Merry say goodbye to Ashley as we drop her off at her fiance's apartment building. I made sure to have two drivers waiting downstairs, and although it was technically illegal, I asked one of the drivers to block the road so Dave could get us safely away from the reporters outside Marina's apartment building. I wave at Ashley through the open car door as her fiancé comes to help her with her bag, and Merry gets back in the car with us.

Marina is in no condition to be left alone, so I asked Merry to stay the night with her. She insisted she could borrow something of Marina's so we didn't have to stop at her family's home for her, and I told her to charge whatever she needs to the room. Toothbrush, shampoo, bottle of champagne, I don't care. I just want someone to watch over Marina tonight, and I don't think she'd want that person to be me.

"Thank you again for doing this," I say quietly, smiling at Merry over the top of Marina's head.

She grins at me. "Well, I happen to agree with you about her current condition. Sometimes Ash gets heavy-handed with the tequila."

I nod. "That little sip I had nearly killed me."

Merry laughs. We sit in silence for a while.

"I want to ask you something," she begins, looking straight ahead, "but it's none of my business."

I nod again. "Okay. Go ahead."

"Why Marina?" she asks plainly, her dark eyes flickering over my face.

I swallow hard, my mouth suddenly dry. Marina's inner circle is fiercely protective, and I don't want to get this wrong.

"Her voice got me off the bus that day," I begin. "But then I saw her, and I was instantly attracted to her…I won't lie about that. But there's a light inside her that's intoxicating. And when we sang together? She hooked me. I couldn't have gotten away if I tried. Our voices blend perfectly, and the pure joy that shines in her eyes when she sings? What a beauty. Inside and out."

Merry smiles over at me.

"When I went to the library the next night and watched her working with the children, I knew I had to see what this is between us."

She nods slowly, and somehow, I feel like I've passed another test.

A few minutes later, Dave pulls the car up to the hotel's entrance. There's never any press allowed here, which is why I stay here every time I come to this city. I gently rouse Marina from her slumber.

"Time to get you settled, love," I say, planting a gentle kiss on the top of her head.

She grumbles and tries to snuggle in tighter, which kills me but also makes me laugh a little. She never stops being adorable. Dave opens the car door, and I slide out, gently bringing a yawning Marina with me. She sees Merry, and a big, loopy smile spreads across her face.

The concierge walks hurriedly toward me with two card keys and a big, placating smile.

"Mr. Adams, I've taken care of all the arrangements," he says quietly. "Your guests have a suite on the floor directly below yours, and I've had some complimentary noshes taken up there in case they're hungry."

I take the card keys and hand them to Merry.

"Thank you very much," I say with a nod, then turn with Marina toward the elevators. Merry keeps pace with us, and Dave brings up the rear with their bags.

Merry's eyes travel in awe as her gaze sweeps across the poshly decorated lobby.

"Of course you're staying at the Fairmont," she laughs, shaking her head.

We get in the elevator and I hit the button for their floor.

"I love staying here when I'm in town," I explain. "Specifically because they don't put up with any aggressive reporters hanging around. No one will bother her here."

She nods.

"And you're welcome to stay the whole time if you'd like," I offer gently. "It's a two-bedroom suite."

Marina looks up at me and squints. "Why are we at the Fairmont?"

Merry laughs out loud. "Dude, you can't handle your liquor."

Now it's my turn to laugh. "In her defense, there was very little margarita mix in the one I tasted."

Merry shrugs, and the elevator door opens for their floor. We all walk together, slower than normal, because Marina is concentrating on her steps like a toddler learning to walk. Merry opens the door and holds it for me to help Marina inside. Dave follows, putting the bags down in the small foyer and stepping back out of the room. I gesture at Merry.

"Lead the way and pick a room," I say lightly.

She steps into the main living area, which is lavishly decorated. Two bedrooms are visible, one on either side of the living room. Merry looks to Marina.

"Are you sober enough to pick one?" she asks.

Marina looks around and points to the one on the right. "That one's closer."

Merry grabs her bag and takes it into Marina's room. I gently turn Marina to face me, cupping my hands on either side of her lovely face. Her eyes are tired as she looks at me.

"This is where we say goodnight, Siren," I tell her, already missing her.

She wraps her arms around my waist and presses her cheek to my chest. How am I supposed to say goodnight to this woman when all I want to do is spend every minute of every day basking in her sunshine? I hold her close for just a moment before gently pulling her away just as Merry appears in the doorway.

Unable to help myself, I brush my lips against hers in a light kiss.

"I'll check on you tomorrow, okay?" I say as she nods sleepily, then turns and walks toward Merry.

"I'm so fired," she mutters, and my heart sinks.

I hope that's not true. I hope with every fiber of my being that her horrible boss doesn't hold her responsible for this mess, but all I can do is wait and see. Merry puts an arm around Marina and nods at me as she helps Marina get ready for bed.

"Thanks for everything, Zach," Merry calls to me just as I get to the door.

Yeah, I think. Thanks for everything. Thanks for bringing absolute chaos into the life of the sweetest creature I've ever met on this Earth. Thanks for probably getting her fired. Thanks for literally bringing drama to her front door, when she specifically told me she doesn't like drama. I step out into the hall and take the stairs up to my floor, hoping with everything in my heart that Marina doesn't wake up and decide none of this is worth it.

Chapter 11

Marina

I wake up at two am with a pounding headache in a bed that's not mine. I squint, even though it's completely black in this room. Slowly, painfully, it all comes back. The incessant media reports. The paparazzi outside our apartment. The margaritas. Zach coming to rescue us all. My mouth feels like someone scrubbed it out with sandpaper, and I slowly sit up, swinging my legs over the edge of the bed. When the room stops rocking, I feel around on the nightstand for a lamp and cover my eyes with one hand before turning it on. With the speed of a sloth on sedatives, I uncover them and ease the light back into my aching eyes.

I get up and slowly walk to the bathroom, cursing Ashley's margaritas the entire way. Merry, bless her heart, put all my bathroom stuff in here already. I brush my teeth and wash my face, using the softest towel in the world to dry my skin. I don't even want to know how much this is costing Zach. I can't think about it right now. I'm just going to let this be another lesson in focusing on gratitude.

I'm thankful for my friends. I'm thankful for this room. I'm thankful for Zach. I'm thankful for Zach's strong arms and the fact that every time I'm wrapped in them, all my problems seem to disappear. I'm grateful for his lips and…*whoa*. Slow down on the Zach parade, Marina. I pad back into the bedroom then venture out into the living space. I was too out of it to really look at it last night, but this room is huge. Elaborately decorated in shades of cream and light rose, it's elegant without being ostentatious. When Zach offered to put me up at a hotel, I wasn't expecting a suite in the most expensive hotel in the city, but this just shows how different our lives are.

There's a small dining room off to the side, and the beautiful mahogany table is set with an array of snacks and drinks. I look around and almost squeal when I see crackers. They always settle my stomach when I'm queasy. I grab a small plate and put a handful of crackers on it, then grab a bottle of water and pad back to the bedroom. I set the plate and water down, then root around in my bag for the bottle of over-the-counter painkillers I always carry. I pop three into my palm, chase them down with the water, and then climb back into bed.

I need to try to get more sleep, but I can't keep my mind from worrying about work. There is just absolutely no way I'm not getting fired for this. The story is everywhere, and there's no way the Evil Queen missed it. She isn't a forgiving person, and even if she was…I'm nothing to her. It's not like I'm a partner at the firm or anyone she considers truly valuable. She will kick me to the curb with the fury of David Beckham in 1997.

Briefly, I think about going in this afternoon and getting my stuff. It's Saturday. No one will be around, but I don't have the energy to face it. I swipe open my phone and check her calendar for Monday. She has a meeting at 9 am, so I'll just show up at 8 am like normal and pack up my desk. Worst case scenario, I'll get yelled at for less than an hour. She is never late for anything, so she'll have to throw me out beforehand. I'll just spend the rest of the weekend hiding away here. Maybe one of the girls will pick up some new books for me from the library.

I grab a cracker and turn off the light. I let the darkness wash over me as I try to calm my racing thoughts. I've fought hard to ensure there is no more drama in my life, and yet this week has been full of it. I used to be the one causing the drama, but I learned long ago that I want a peaceful life. Not a *boring* one, just relatively free of daily angst and worry. Perhaps I've been so focused on that I've forgotten to actually live a life. I can feel something changing in me. There is a noticeable shift in what's important. It's totally like me to grab the proverbial scissors and cut the subject of the drama right out of my life - yet when I intrinsically thought about cutting Zach out, every fiber of my being screamed in resistance. For the first time in a long time, my instincts are at war with each other.

There is something in his spirit that calls to mine. I can't explain it, and I can't define it - but whenever we're together, I just want more. My self-preservation instincts are still screaming at me to run, but I'm rooted to this spot by something stronger. Something in my core that tells me I don't need to run. Not from him. And that scares me most of all.

I chew on my cracker and take a deep, cleansing breath. I've been feeling a lot of fear lately. Fear of the mermaid story going viral, of being fired, of catching feelings for Zach, of not being able to afford to live on my own. When I was a lost, scared kid, I ran from my fear, and that took me to a thousand places I didn't want to be. I learned the hard way that I needed to face it and fight, and my whole life turned around when I learned to be brave.

I pop another cracker in my mouth and brush off my fingers. Whatever happens, I know I have what it takes to handle it. And I have a support system that will back me up. That's what I need to focus on, not the fear. So, I will walk into Taft & Kennedy on Monday morning with my head held high. I will pack my belongings and leave, knowing it's their loss. And I will have faith in myself to figure out the rest of this. I have the remainder of the weekend to get my head together, so that's just what I'll do. I burrow down under the covers and remind myself as my head hits the pillow…fear is a lie.

*****

The sound of my cell phone vibrating on the nightstand rouses me from my fretful sleep, and I roll over with a grumble, fumbling for the switch on the lamp. Light splinters through my cracked eyelids, making me hiss. Slowly, I open my eyes and swipe open my phone. 10:30 am. I groan as I stand, my head throbbing. I pad across the room to the bathroom and flick on the light. The bathroom is nearly the size of my whole apartment.

Good Lord.

I turn the shower on and search the room for my bag, then grab a pair of yoga pants and a clean t-shirt and throw them on the bed. I brush my teeth before stripping and step under the hot spray, letting the absolutely perfect water pressure rinse away my stress.

This shower is life-changing. Rich people get all the good stuff. The shower in our tiny apartment definitely can't hold a candle to this.

When I'm done, I dry off, get dressed, and head out to the living room to see if Merry's still here. Just as I'm thinking she's probably already left for Nonno's, I hear her voice…and she's not alone. Zach is here. I spend about three seconds considering whether I should check my face and immediately shut it down. I'm in crisis mode, and if he can't handle me in crisis mode, then he doesn't deserve space in my life. I made that decision long ago. I'm not changing for anyone.

I swing open my bedroom door and walk barefoot across the plush carpet, following the sound of their voices.

"No, I can't do that, Zach," Merry says emphatically, a touch of humor in her voice. "Not gonna happen."

"C'mon."

"Nope. It's top secret."

"It would be so great to have when I'm on the road," he insists. "Please?"

I walk into the dining room just as Merry folds her arms across her chest. Zach has his back to the door and can't see me.

"I am not giving you Nonno's sauce recipe. No way."

Merry looks up at me over Zach's shoulder and rolls her eyes.

"Your boyfriend doesn't know who he's dealing with, does he?"

Zach whirls around, a look of deep concern on his face, and bolts from his chair. I'm in his arms a split second later, and I don't even try to resist. I wrap my arms around his waist and rest my cheek on his broad chest. His strong, steady heartbeat reverberates in my ear. Safety. He reaches up a hand and strokes my hair.

"How are you feeling? Are you okay?"

I don't answer right away. I just stand here…wrapped in Zach's arms…inhaling that gorgeous scent of his. It's better than anything you could ever buy. Forget healing creams or vapor rubs. The relief for all that ails is Zach. Finally, I pull away enough to look up at Zach and over at Merry.

"As okay as I can be, I think."

Zach gently ushers me over to a chair, and only then do I see a huge brunch spread on a large catering cart that's been wheeled in. My eyes go wide, prompting Zach to step over and grab a plate.

"What's your pleasure, Siren?" he asks, ready to dish up whatever I want. "We have just about every breakfast or brunch item known to man."

I don't even have to think about it.

"All the bacon."

He raises his eyebrows, and the corner of his mouth twitches up. "All of it?"

I nod. "Bring it."

Merry snickers as Zach serves up a plate full of bacon and sets it down in front of me. I stare at it blankly and nod.

"Thank you."

"Well, you're semi-coherent, and you have an appetite," Merry declares. "I'm gonna head off to Nonno's before he panics. I'm usually there by now."

She gets up without ceremony and gives me a squeeze before high-fiving Zach on her way out.

"Thanks, Merry," I call after her.

"Love you!"

I pick up a piece of bacon and look up at Zach with a resigned expression, biting into the perfectly crispy strip and sighing heavily. He looks…sorry.

"So what are you doing today?" I ask between bites.

He picks up his fork and continues eating the French toast on his plate.

"Whatever you want to do."

I lower my bacon and regard him curiously.

"Do you think I'm going to leave you on your own all weekend when I know you're just going to hide away here and overthink it all?"

I try to smile back at him, but I'm not sure how successful I am.

"I forgot you were a chivalrous Brit."

He grins. "Your wish is my command, Siren. What quests would you have me do?"

I laugh softly. "I can't think of anything. Unless you want to go to the library for me and see if they have anything new. I'm almost done with what I have. Danielle would let you check stuff out on my card."

He takes another bite and pulls out his phone. "What titles would you like? Or do you want me to choose?"

I study him carefully for a moment. I have trouble thinking of what kind of fiction he'd like.

"I just started a fantasy series called 'A Throne of Crystal and Stone'," I explain. "I'll probably finish the first book tonight, but I'd love to have the next one in my hand already. I can't put it down."

"I love books like that. What's it about?"

"A young woman, thrown into a world of faeries and magic, surviving and falling in love," I explain. "Probably not your thing."

"I love fantasy books!"

I nearly drop my second piece of bacon. Or is this my third? I've lost track.

"You do?"

He nods. "Have you read 'Heart of Ash'?"

I bounce in my chair. "Yes! I love that series so much!!"

He points his fork at me. "Let me guess. Randyn, King of the High Fae, is your favorite book boyfriend ever."

I throw the bite-sized piece of bacon in my hand at him, and he bats it away with a loud laugh, then bends over to pick it up off the carpet. I don't even try to hide the laugh that bubbles out of me.

"I knew it," he declares with a cocky glint in his eye.

"I can't help it if you're jealous," I tease lightly. "He's so perfect."

Zach clutches a hand over his heart. "You wound me, Siren."

I grin and offer him the plate of bacon. He holds his hands up.

"That's the best non-verbal apology I've ever received," he says. "But I don't want to get between an American and her bacon."

I grab another piece and put the plate down as he shakes his head.

"Two things I don't understand about Americans: your weird idea of bacon and your obsession with ice cubes."

I give him a mock warning look.

"Now you've done it. You don't like ice? We can't be friends."

He looks at me with a glint in his eye, then feigns shock.

"I *love* ice. I put it in *everything*. Even my cup of tea. I *adore* ice."

I hold up a hand. "Calm down. I'd never ask you to change for me. You can keep on being an ice hater."

He laughs softly and pushes his plate aside.

"Okay, so the next book in the 'Throne of Crystal and Stone' series… what else can I bring you?"

I tilt my head and think for a moment. "I really can't think of anything else. I only need to get through today and tomorrow. That should do it."

He stands up and puts his napkin on the table, then steps to my side and plants a kiss atop my head. I fight the urge to reach out and grab him around the waist.

"Very well," he says quietly. "I'll be back in an hour or two, love. You just sit there, eat bacon, and look beautiful."

He gives me a kiss that's too quick and too fleeting, then turns and heads for the door. I laugh softly and watch him go, wondering the entire time whether he's truly real or some figment of my imagination.

***

Zach

"It looks like you picked up more than just a library book," Marina says incredulously as she steps back and lets me whisk past carrying two armloads of shopping bags.

I may have gotten a little carried away. Not that I really care. She deserves things to make her smile, and I feel like I have at least half a dozen smiles in these bags.

"One book didn't seem like enough for a whole weekend," I say lightly as she follows me to the living room. "I didn't want you to get bored."

I sit, and she sits. She looks at me as if she's not sure whether she'll want to hug me or throttle me when we're done going through all the bags.

"Did you even go to the library?"

"No, but I did go to Barnes & Noble," I reply, pulling out the large bag.

Her eyes light up, and I feel a disgusting amount of triumph at the level of joy she's trying to hide.

"Zach…"

"Marina…" I parrot. "I started thinking about how I feel when I read a great series. I want to keep certain books so I can re-read them, so I just bought you the next book instead of borrowing it from the library."

She smiles, and my heart skips a beat. Her eyes dart to the bag.

"There's more than one book in that bag."

I nod. "Yeah, well, why would I buy you the second book when you probably don't own the first either? If you also got it from the library, that is. So I went back to get the first book and ended up buying the whole series instead."

I place the bag in her lap as her surprised gaze flicks from me to the bag and back again. She reaches in and takes out the five-book series, reverently looking over each volume, and then she does something that cements her in my heart forever.

She smells them.

Something in my expression makes her give me a quick, shy grin and put them back in the bag. Then she spots the bookmark and pulls it out, running her fingers over it. No explanation necessary for the iridescent mermaid bookmark I couldn't resist. She holds it up so I can see it.

"Thank you."

I nod. "I love that you smell books."

"I always do that," she explains. "I love books."

"Me too."

"And I love bookmarks…this is gorgeous."

I lean over and plant a soft, lingering kiss on the corner of her mouth.

"A gorgeous mermaid for a gorgeous mermaid."

She shakes her head, and I decide I'm not going to argue with her about her beauty today. Instead, I reach into the next bag from a little gift shop just down the street from the bookstore and hand her the luxuriously soft blanket I picked up. She takes it from me and runs her fingers over it.

"I couldn't resist when I saw it in the window," I explain, pointing to the design that looks like mermaid scales. "It's perfect for curling up with a book."

She nods. "It really is. Thank you so much."

I point to three bags from the grocery store. "Hangover cures in those bags."

Her eyes go wide. "Wow."

I pull up the final bag from the local drug store and hand it to her.

"And finally, happy memories and snacks."

She looks in the bag, and her face slackens as she pulls out the giant bag of red licorice I bought her. Her eyes glisten a little when she looks up at me.

"You remembered."

I nod.

She puts it down, stands up, and wordlessly steps over and sits in my lap. I pull her against me immediately, looking up into those emerald green pools as I brush a stray strand of her hair back. She puts her hands on either side of my face.

"You are the most thoughtful man I've ever known," she says quietly.

I rub our noses together and press my forehead to hers.

"You deserve every good thing."

I kiss one corner of her mouth, then the other, and then our mouths just come together like two magnets. Her kiss is so full of emotion it fills me with hope. And longing. She slides her hands into my hair, and I hear a growl escape my throat. I wrap my arms tighter around her waist and squeeze her possessively.

Mine.

She's soft and pliant in my arms as we explore each other slowly, passionately. When she pulls back slightly, I'm not even sure what my name is. She's kissed me senseless. What a way to go.

She reaches up a hand and combs her fingers through my hair. The warmth and affection in her eyes catch my breath in my throat. My chest tightens.

"You were not in my plan," she whispers cryptically.

"You weren't in my plan either, gorgeous, but here we are."

She laughs softly and cradles her head on my shoulder, snuggling closer, and I think it's quite possible we just found the perfect way to spend our afternoon.

***

Marina

Sunday afternoon, Zach holds his hand out wordlessly, and I pull another piece of licorice from the bag on the couch and hand it to him. He smiles with the joy of a ten-year-old and takes a huge bite, prompting a laugh from me.

"I've created a monster," I say, giving him a mock shove.

We're cozied up on the couch in my suite, sharing the mermaid blanket, as I read my book, and he monitors social media chatter on the mermaid story. I have my feet propped in his lap, and he rests his forearms on my shins as he scrolls. We've easily slipped into a peaceful existence with each other while I hide away from the world this weekend. It doesn't feel weird or too much, it's just…nice to be together. But it also doesn't feel real.

The girls have been checking in on me via our group chat here and there, but they've been suspiciously too busy to visit. They're more than content to let Zach look after me while I bide my time until Monday morning. When it's time to face the music. My stomach lurches at the mere thought of facing Ms. Taft and all her ire. She'll make a show of it.

I haven't turned on the television or looked at social media, but I can tell the story is still trending. Possibly even more viral than before, given the scowl on Zach's face earlier. I haven't asked because it won't matter. It was already bad enough for me to be fired. Who cares how much it blows up now? The result will be the same: my name out in public and me looking for a job. For now, I'm content to cocoon myself away with Zach—although I probably should have faked an illness and kept him away. It has been far too easy to sink into a routine that feels very domestic. Intimate, even. We fit so easily together until you consider the fact that he's the world's biggest rock star and travels the world, performing to thousands, and I'm an unknown executive assistant trying to fight my way into law school without a penny to my name. We may fit as individual people, but the worlds we exist in do not mesh at all.

Zach has pampered me to no end this weekend, and I can feel myself getting more and more attached to him by the minute. Like the Grinch, my heart is growing multiple sizes because of all the feelings he's creating. But what happens to all those feelings when he rolls out of San Francisco on his giant tour bus? My head is still firmly *not* on board with any of this. My heart and my gut are focused solely on Zach, staring at him with big cartoony hearts floating up into the air.

"What are you thinking about so seriously?"

Only when he speaks do I realize I was frowning at a nondescript spot on the carpet, deep in my thoughts. His voice is a sexy, raspy growl, stirring something low in my belly. I force the corners of my mouth to turn up.

"Nothing important."

He raises an eyebrow. "Doesn't look that way from here."

Our eyes are locked on each other and I feel the pull of those depthless brown eyes, so focused on me. Zach studies me silently, looking like he wants to ask me so many questions. He reaches out and takes my hand.

"Are you worried about tomorrow?" he rasps.

My heart skips a beat just thinking about it. I really hate any kind of negative attention. It's a hangover from my days as a foster kid. From the time I left the Lewises, I was constantly acting out in a desperate attempt to feel like I had control over anything. Negative attention was all I knew. Now, as an adult who mostly has her act together, any negative attention…like losing my job because I was the star of a viral video…gives me flashbacks to a tumultuous time I would rather not think about.

"I can't help it," I admit. "I hate letting people down. Or breaking the rules."

He frowns. "Surely you deserve a little grace here. These people you work for sound horrible."

"In terms of company culture, they are pretty awful," I admit. "But their reputation is stellar, and if I can get a letter of recommendation for law school, it would give me a lot of leverage. It opens a lot of doors. So it feels worth it to me."

He nods slowly. "So that's why you fight so hard to fit in with people who are so…different."

I consider his words for a moment. Not because they're hurtful but because they're true in a way I'd never thought of before. I nod slowly.

"Well, it's over now," I say with a heavy sigh. "There's no way Ms. Taft hasn't seen the story, and that's a truth I must face tomorrow."

He squeezes my hand, and I squeeze back.

"Is there anything I can do to help?"

I shake my head. "Nothing I can think of. It's me against the Evil Queen, and she will win this one."

His throat bobs.

"I know you don't need me," he says with a wry smile. "I know you're perfectly able to fight this battle on your own, but just know that I will slay dragons for you, my lady. Evil Queens too."

I offer him a brave smile. He opens his arms to me, and I swing my legs off his lap so I can scoot closer. Instantly, he pulls me against his chest and wraps me in an embrace that feels so much like home I have to fight back tears. A picture, clear as day, forms in my mind of a life with this kind, generous, and insanely romantic man. One where I'm free of all the worry I heap upon myself. A life with a man who would slay all the monsters for me. It feels reckless to hope for such a thing, but right now, in this moment, I close my eyes and snuggle closer, locking that picture away in my heart.

Chapter 12

Marina

I step off the elevator into the Taft & Kennedy lobby in sneakers, yoga pants, and Zach's t-shirt from the day we met. My hair is pulled back in a high ponytail. The whole ensemble screams my defiance, and it actually feels good. I woke up in an eerily calm frame of mind. I thought about wearing the suit I mindlessly packed on Friday night, but I've spent all my time trying to fit in here, and I never have. If I'm getting fired today, it's go big or go home.

Out of the corner of my eye, I see a few heads turn to follow me. I hear whispers. I ignore them. I'll never see these people again. None of what's about to happen matters. I duck into the copy room, grab an empty paper box, and head to my desk. I can hear Ms. Taft on the phone as I near her office. Great. Showtime.

I cross in front of her open door and step over to my desk, setting the box down and opening the top drawer. As soon as I do, I hear her cut her phone call short.

"Something wrong with your dry cleaner?" Ms. Taft says as she stands in her doorway, looking me up and down.

I finish pulling my personal items from the drawer and drop them into the box, then I look up and shake my head.

"Not at all," I say with forced lightness.

Internally, I'm a bit of a riot, but she doesn't need to know that.

"Please step inside my office, Marina," she says coldly.

I step out from behind my desk and follow her into her office. She doesn't bother to shut the door, which shows what a wonderful person she is. She wants this to be overheard.

I sit down without being asked, prompting her to raise her eyebrows. I focus on my breath, in and out, while my heart pounds against my ribs. Conflict is hard for me to deal with, but here we are. I'm facing it. She looks me up and down again.

"What's with the outfit?"

"I'm just here to pack up my desk," I explain. "I didn't see the point in wearing Chanel for it."

She scoffs coldly. "You mean that bargain basement blue thing that hasn't been in style since I was in college? I'll be glad not to see that rag anymore, at least."

Ouch. I can see by her smug expression I didn't hide my feelings well when she landed that punch. That blow landed right where she wanted it to, and she looks really happy at my reaction.

"Is there anything else you wanted to say before I leave?" I say coolly.

"Well, at least you're efficient at being fired," she says with a roll of her eyes. "You lied to me."

I shake my head. "I've never lied to you."

"I asked you if that was you on the news that morning!"

I shake my head again. "You didn't. You said I must have a twin, and I told you I don't have any family here."

"Semantics."

"It's actually *not* semantics," I say. "And there is nothing I've seen or experienced in my time at this firm that would lead me to believe transparency would be something that's a safe choice. Besides, it has nothing to do with the firm."

She scoffs, and then her eyes dart to the doorway behind me. Someone is obviously there because the transformation on her face is immediate. I'd be shocked if I hadn't seen it a million times before, any time she was being cruel to an employee and someone important walked in the room. Her expression morphs into one of pleasant, delighted surprise as she bolts out of her chair, ready to greet whoever has just walked in. I turn in my seat, and my jaw drops in shock. I look up to see the one and only Ethan Montclair leaning down to kiss both of her cheeks. The gesture is as dramatic as it is insincere, and I'm left feeling decidedly creeped out.

"Ethan! Isn't this a wonderful surprise," Ms. Taft gushes, gesturing to the guest chair beside mine as he sits. Then she shoots me a look, "I think we're done here."

"Yes, we are," I say with feigned levity.

I start to stand, but Montclair reaches out and wraps a hand around my wrist.

Eww.

"Just because *I'm* here? No!" He looks at Ms. Taft. "Lexi, c'mon…if I'd known you had the famous mermaid on your staff, I would have cleared my calendar a lot sooner. When I saw the story on the news last night, I couldn't believe you kept this secret from me! I cleared my calendar this morning just so I could come over to say hello."

Her cold eyes drift to me and I fight against the smile I feel tugging at the corners of my mouth, despite Mr. Smarmy having his hands on me. Plus…*Lexi?* Who knew?

Montclair turns to face me.

"You must know one of my corporations owns a television studio," he croons. "Promise me you'll give us an exclusive interview."

I force a smile and gently pull away from his grip. His fingers slide along my skin, making it crawl.

"You and Ms. Taft must have a lot of catching up to do," I say, standing. "I'll let you get to it."

He holds a hand up, halting me. "No, I refuse to let you leave this room until you promise me that interview."

My gaze flicks to Ms. Taft, and I can see her fuming under that cool facade. She flicks a hand in my direction.

"Of course she'll give you the interview," she spits out. "But as you can see by her attire, Marina has a scheduled day off today. She's only come in to help me with something because she's such a dedicated worker."

She puts emphasis on *dedicated worker* as her eyebrows slightly rise in a silent challenge. Interesting. I smile at Montclair.

"She's right. I did come in to put some things together for her to sign," I say in my most professional voice. "I'll just be a minute, then she can sign them, and she's all yours."

He eyes me carefully for a few seconds. "And you'll be at the proposal meeting so we can chat?"

I nod. "As long as Ms. Taft allows it."

He grins as if it's a done deal, then pulls his phone out of his pocket and waves a dismissive hand at us.

"All right, ladies, go sign your papers," he says. "Don't take too long."

I walk out the door, followed quickly by Ms. Taft.

"All right, you can stay," she whispers when we come to a stop at my desk. "At least until the contract is signed. If the media circus dies down by then, I'll consider letting you stay permanently."

Emboldened by Montclair's enthusiasm and my own bravery this morning, I decide to really push.

"No," I say flatly, looking her right in the eye. As long as I live, I'll regret not being able to take a picture of her face. And mine. It's quite possible this is the first time anyone has told her no, and oh my lord, it was me! Little Miss No Drama.

"*No?*"

I nod. "No," I say emphatically. "It's clear Mr. Montclair wants me here, which means you *need* me here. I don't just want my job back. I want a bonus when the contract is signed."

She blanches. "That's ridiculous."

I literally have no idea how I'm doing this, but it's thrilling. My stomach is in knots, my palms are sweaty, and my pulse is pounding, but I am cool as a cucumber on the outside as I stare her down.

"It's not ridiculous," I argue, channeling my inner trial lawyer. "Remember, I've seen the bonuses you give to your staff. You've never rewarded me for being such a *dedicated worker.*"

She rolls her eyes at me. "Anything else?"

I nod. "I want a letter of recommendation from you. For law school."

She scoffs but doesn't argue when I raise my brows. She nods curtly.

"Deal," I say, then gesture at her office. "Better get back to Mr. Montclair."

She regards me quietly for a moment. "We'll talk later."

I nod, and she stalks back to her office and closes the door behind her. As soon as she's gone, I fall into my chair and let out a huge gasp.

What. Just. Happened?

I reach into the box on my desk and take my things out, putting them back in my desk drawer. All things considered, this is really a hollow victory. She will *definitely* fire me as soon as the Montclair deal is done. But at least this gives me time. Time to save up what little I can and to look for another job. The real victory was in the way I just stood up to her. Fear didn't control my behavior at all, and look where it got me.

Bravery rocks.

I pick up the empty box and put it back in the copy room. Halfway back to my desk, the heavy weight of realization hits me. If she does fire me right after the contract is signed, there's nothing to keep her from reneging on that bonus. Whether I lose my job or not, I need that money. I chew on my lip for a moment, then head back to my desk.

I unlock my computer, look for the file I need, and make the necessary edits to add my name to the form before sending it to my printer. I jump up, grab the printed document, and nearly bounce into Ms. Taft's office after giving the door a quick knock. She and Montclair both look up as I enter.

"Ms. Taft," I say in an apologetic tone. "I'm so sorry, but there was one more document I needed you to sign."

I move to the side of her desk and place the paper down in front of her. She reads it, then looks up at me with a hint of rage behind her eyes.

"I don't think this is necessary," she says coldly.

I nod. "Yes, I remember distinctly. You insisted this is done by the book."

I smile at Montclair. "She's very thorough. I've learned so much from her."

He aims what I'm sure he thinks is a wickedly charming smile at me, but I just feel like I need a shower. His gaze rakes over my yoga pants, which leave little to the imagination, and I force my attention on Ms. Taft.

She looks back to the agreement to pay me a bonus if I remain employed through the Montclair deal. It's the standard agreement she makes all her people sign when she's dangling a monetary carrot over their heads. She grabs a pen and signs it, handing the agreement back to me.

I look it over and put it back on her desk, pointing at the space she intentionally left blank.

"Don't forget this," I say sweetly.

If looks could kill. She left the dollar amount of the bonus blank on purpose. She scrawls something and hands it back to me without looking at me.

Five thousand dollars.

For her, that's chump change. For me, it's a little bit of safety. It's all I can do not to squeal in triumph, but instead, I turn to Mr. Montclair and extend my hand for a handshake.

"It was wonderful to meet you, sir," I coo at him. "I'm looking forward to seeing you in a couple weeks."

He takes my hand in both of his and gives my hand a squeeze.

"Me too, gorgeous," he croons from behind his perfect veneers. "But I'm sure I'll be around. You've given me a reason to visit more often."

I pull my hand from his and walk out the door, not giving Ms. Taft another look. I fold the agreement and shove it into my purse. As I head for the elevators, I feel the eyes of my curious colleagues on me. I don't take a real breath until I get down to the parking garage and climb into the back of the waiting SUV, where Merry is sitting in the back seat with a curious expression.

She runs her gaze over me, looking for the box of my belongings she expects me to be carrying. I fasten my seatbelt and grin at her. Her eyes grow round.

"Not fired?"

I shake my head. "Not fired. Dave, would you mind swinging by my apartment?"

He nods and begins maneuvering the car out of the parking garage while I tell Merry what happened upstairs. She listens with rapt attention as the car winds around the dark depths of the garage.

"Why do you insist on working for this woman? She is horrible. I can't believe she said that about your clothes. How cruel."

"Yeah, that stung a little."

We're driving up the last level of the garage, so it's dark in the car, but I can still tell she's frowning.

"I wish I understood why your plan has to involve spending so much time around hateful people," she mutters. "You deserve better."

Dave drives the car up the exit ramp of the parking garage, and my pulse quickens as I notice a group of photographers standing outside the exit. I know they can't see through these windows, but I still feel so exposed when they try to peer inside. Now that the story is out, I feel like I should relax a little about all of this, but I can't seem to make myself. I shake it off.

"Well, I have to go to my apartment and grab some work clothes if I'm going to keep working there," I say in a breezy tone. "At least this gives me some time to plan and look for another job."

"True."

A few minutes later, Dave pulls the car up to the curb in front of the entrance to my apartment building. There's a woman waiting outside on the sidewalk who is paying way too much attention to Dave as he gets out and opens the door for me. He steps in the way so she can't see inside the car.

"Pretty sure that woman is a reporter," he grumbles, looking at me with concern. "Let me open the door to the building for you."

"Thanks, Dave," I whisper as I ease out of the car, and Merry follows behind me.

In just a few steps, Dave covers the distance to the door and manages to shove himself between me and the woman. She has her phone out now and is obviously recording me. I put my hand up over my face and run inside the building with Merry.

"Marina, how serious are things with the Duke of Rock?" she yells as the door shuts.

Merry and I climb the stairs to my floor and find a security guard waiting outside my door. He recognizes me and nods. I smile briefly, turn my key in the lock, and Merry and I are safely in my apartment.

"Wow," Merry gasps. "That was a little crazy."

I nod slowly, trying to ignore the uneasy feeling in my gut. I look at Merry and shake my head.

"I don't know how he does it. How do you live your life being chased by complete strangers? And for what?"

Merry shrugs. "People relate to him. And let's be honest…a mermaid and a rock star having a spontaneous concert in the middle of a bridge is a pretty good story."

"And completely your fault."

She dares to feign innocence. "Me?"

"You're the one who started the whole thing."

She wiggles her eyebrows and laughs, making me giggle as I shake my head and walk into my bedroom. Merry follows, and I duck into the closet to start pulling out what I'll need.

"So what's he like?" she asks, flopping onto my bed.

I toss a couple suits on the bed next to her.

"Hmm," I muse. "Unnerving."

She laughs. "Wow, that's super romantic."

I shake my head. "No, I'm serious. When it comes to giving guys the cold shoulder, I'm pretty good, right?"

"If scaring men away was a competitive sport, you'd definitely bring home the gold."

I make a face at her. "Gee, thanks!"

Merry laughs as I head back to the closet and grab more clothes.

"Zach is different. He just looks at me like he knows exactly what I'm thinking and keeps coming at me."

Merry's brows furrow.

"Not in a bad way," I clarify. "It's just unnerving like I said. I know exactly what to do when the average guy tries to come on to me. With

Zach…"

Merry rolls over on my bed. "Awww! This is so great!"

I shake my head. "It's no big deal."

"You can say that all you want, Marina, but I know you. I know what this is."

"What is it?" I ask as I throw an overnight bag on the bed and toss clothes into it.

"He *sees* you, my friend. That's why you find him unnerving. All those other guys were just guys trying to get attention. This is a man who sees you. He doesn't just want your attention. He wants your heart. And it scares you a little."

I feel the truth of her words hit home and I swallow hard, my mouth suddenly dry. Merry pulls herself up on her knees and grabs my hands.

"Hey," she says gently. "It's totally okay to feel a little scared when you meet someone who gets a little under your skin."

I squeeze her hands in thanks and let go so I can busy myself with tucking the rest of my clothes in the bag. She's exactly right: Zach sees me. But if it *does* scare me, why can't I run? The man is like some kind of musclebound tractor beam with a British accent. I'm caught up, and I can't get away. And, let's be honest, I don't want to get away.

I zip the bag closed.

"I still have the instinct to run away from him," I say slowly, sitting on the bed. "But I think I'm just realizing I've spent too long pushing most people away. I haven't really allowed myself to get involved with anyone, and Zach…"

"Is the only one to come along who's actually worth it?"

She's grinning ear to ear and I laugh despite the tumult of feelings at war in my head and my heart. My stomach could compete for a gold medal in gymnastics right now.

I nod. "Yeah. Exactly. I don't *want* to run from him."

Merry jumps up off the bed and wraps her arms around me.

"I'm happy for you, Marina. You deserve to find someone worthy of you."

I hug her back, then pull away with a gasp.

"I forgot to tell you what he wants to do," I say quietly. "He offered to help me find Max."

She flops back down on the bed, her mouth wide open.

"Oh, Marina!"

I feel a little tear pooling in my eye when I smile and nod at her. I've thought about it a lot since he made the offer. It's so generous. And kind. And completely too much. Exactly like him.

"What did you say?"

I clear my throat. "He didn't want me to give him an answer right away, so I promised I would think about it."

"Have you?"

"Some," I say. "My first inclination is to refuse. He's offering to hire a private investigator, and that is a huge expense. We just started… whatever this is. I feel like it's too much. I feel like I'd be taking advantage."

She nods. "Okay."

"But I also know the offer comes from a sincere desire to help, and not as some way to gain my favor. And it'll be years before I can afford such a thing on my own. I could have my brother back in my life."

"So what are you going to tell him?"

I shake my head and pick up my bag. "I'm still thinking about it."

"Keep me posted?" she asks as we walk to the door together. "When do you see him again?"

I hesitate with my hand on the doorknob. "We're going out for dinner tonight, but he won't tell me where."

Merry raises her eyebrows. "Oooh! Probably someplace fancy."

I shake my head. "Casual dress. Jeans and sneaks. And he says I might get chilly."

She thinks for a moment. "I have no idea, but it sounds interesting."

We step out onto the landing together and I lock my front door, offering the guard a smile before heading down the stairs with Merry.

"With Zach, it's *always* interesting."

Merry laughs. "Nonno was right, he's a keeper."

My heart does a little flip at the idea, and I let myself imagine for just a moment that Zach and I have some kind of future together. What does that even look like? I can't imagine going to law school while living in the back of a tour bus. Nor can I imagine a scenario where he settles down and lives a quiet life in San Francisco with me. I don't know where this is going, and that's definitely feeding my fears on some level. But Zach *does* see me, and when we're together, I feel so many things I've never felt before. Cherished. Treasured. Precious. No one else has made me feel those things. Ever. So even though this is scary and things are uncertain, when I think about the way I feel as soon as I'm in Zach's arms, I know I don't need to have all the answers right now. The only thing I need to do is get back to the hotel and get ready for our date. Everything else can come later.

***

Zach

I force an interested look on my face as I listen to the lawyer drone on and on about the paperwork he's drawn up. Indeed, I couldn't care less. I've done this kind of thing a few times before when I've been inspired. There's not much to it. Yet, when I telephoned my lawyer in London yesterday, he gave me ample warning that his American counterpart assisting in my latest endeavor is very…enthusiastic. I have little patience for anyone trying to impress me at present, when all I can think of is Marina and how she's doing at work.

I pull my mobile phone from my pocket and check my messages for the hundredth time. Still nothing. I can't stand it any longer. I nod at the lawyer as he continues talking and type out a message.

Zach: Hey, beautiful. I was trying to give you time to get through it, but I find I'm too worried to keep quiet. Are you all right?

Marina is typing...

Marina: Hey, you. :-) There's way too much to type, but I'm not fired. I'll fill you in when you get back.

I can't help but heave a huge sigh of relief, which prompts a curious look from the man behind the desk. Sadly, it doesn't deter him from his breathlessly boring interpretation of the forms I'm about to sign.

Zach: And you're okay?

Marina: I'm okay. What are you doing this morning? I don't think I asked.

Zach: Just a few things I needed to take care of. I'll be on my way back shortly.

Marina: Oh? Nothing else on the *shed*ule today?

I laugh out loud at her mockery of my accent, and the lawyer stops talking completely. For once. But I can't help it, so I just let it roll out of me. This woman drives me crazy in all the good ways.

I clear my throat. "Sorry. Please continue."

Zach: Oh, my beautiful Siren...you wreck me. :-)

Marina: LOL. How long before you're back?

Zach: About thirty minutes and I'm all yours.

The chat goes silent, and I force my attention back to the attorney, holding up my hand.

"Mr. Zedner, I'm not sure if my attorney explained, but I am quite familiar with this process."

He nods, opening his mouth to continue, and I hold up my hand again.

"I'm afraid I have a full day ahead of me, so if you could just let me sign so I can be on my way. I'm quite positive everything is in order."

He nods quickly and pulls a pen from his desk drawer, handing it to me.

"If you'll just sign here, here, and here," he says, pointing to each line requiring my signature.

I scrawl my name and place the pen on his desk, standing.

He regards me pensively for a moment. "I'm just curious, sir. About the mermaid reference."

I offer him a smile and nothing more. He takes the hint and clears his throat, holding up the papers with a flourish.

"I'll make sure these are filed and sent to your attorney's office in London right away," he says with a smile.

I shake his hand.

"Thanks very much," I reply quickly, striding for the door. "Have a good day."

I text my attorney the approval to create a new account and move funds to it as I walk through the lobby on my way to the awaiting car. Everything's in place, and now I can spend the rest of the day with my favorite mermaid.

As I exit the building, a few reporters rush after me, yelling questions as usual. As if yelling at me will get a reply. It never works. The smart ones know this.

"Zach, how does the mermaid kiss?" one of them asks.

"Is it serious?"

"C'mon, Zach, tell us about the mermaid!"

I dive into the awaiting car before they can see the secret smile spread across my face. The driver shuts the door behind me and we're away in a few seconds.

How does the mermaid kiss?

I'm in so much trouble. I'm already addicted to those mermaid kisses. Something's gnawing at me, though, and I can't shake it. I'm used to the media covering everything from the band's latest album to whether I prefer American pancakes or English scones for breakfast. Marina isn't. I make a mental note to see how she's feeling now that the story is out.

It feels like an eternity before I'm actually knocking on the door to Marina's suite. I'm not ready for the growl that escapes my throat when she answers the door in yoga pants and my t-shirt. Her hair is up in a high ponytail that makes me think of all kinds of things I know she's not ready for. She smiles at me, and her whole face lights up.

"Hi."

I give her a wicked grin. "Hi."

She steps back and lets me in. I take two steps inside and pull her into my arms before the door is even shut. She laughs softly.

I lower my mouth and brush her lips with mine as she wraps her arms around my neck. Her body is soft and pliant as she relaxes against me. I squeeze tighter, and she lets out a little moan, her breath tickling my ear. I pull back enough to look into those gorgeous green eyes.

"Are you going to tell me what happened with your job, or do I have to kiss it out of you?"

She reaches up and runs her fingers through my hair. Her nails scratch lightly across my scalp, and I lose all capacity for rational thought for a few seconds. I could live my whole life right here. Never sing another song, never do another thing but kiss this woman. Her smile fills me with longing.

"That's only going to give me incentive to keep quiet."

That's all the invitation I need. My mouth crashes into hers as I lift her up until her feet are dangling, then take a few steps forward. A little squeal escapes her lips. I don't put her down until she's trapped between me and the door. She breaks our kiss and eyes me with mock suspicion.

"I'm trapped."

I grunt, she grins. She playfully tries to step around me and I block her. She steps to the other side, blocked again. I step forward, pressing the length of my body into hers as she wraps her arms around my waist. I cradle her head in my hands, turning her slightly so her mouth is at just the right angle, and I begin the most delicious exploration. She gives as good as she gets, tasting and taunting me as she fists her hands in the back of my shirt. Finally, I pull away as my resolve begins to disintegrate. Her eyes drift up to mine. They're darkened with desire, which only makes me want to push her against the door again. Before I can, I take her by the hand and lead her to the couch in the living area.

"Right," I say as I gently pull her to sit with me. "Out with it, Siren. Tell me how things went."

She takes a deep breath and nods. I don't miss how her throat bobs when she gets ready to speak. I drape my arm around the back of the couch and place a comforting hand on her shoulder. She turns her full attention to me.

"I went in to get my things and leave quietly. Ms. Taft was there, and she was pretty angry. She accused me of lying to her about the whole thing."

I shake my head incredulously. "What did you say?"

A proud smile blooms on her face. "I corrected her."

I stay silent so she can continue, but I know my eyes are glowing with joy for her victory.

"She was halfway through her speech when Ethan Montclair stopped by to surprise her."

My eyebrows shoot up. "Montclair? The man she wants to impress so badly?"

She nods. "And, apparently, he's a huge fan of mermaids."

I feel my eyes grow round as saucers. "No!"

Marina laughs and shakes her head like it's the most incredible thing to be saved by the one person her horrible boss would be afraid to upset. It's bloody brilliant, and I'm thrilled for her.

"He made it clear that he's on Team Mermaid, so I wasn't fired simply because she couldn't do it without angering him," she explains. "But I also took the opportunity to work a bonus into the situation if the meeting goes off without a hitch."

I reach up to brush her cheek with my fingers. "I'm firmly on Team Mermaid. You are so brilliant. That's wonderful news."

She shrugs. "She'll keep looking for reasons to fire me. I'm not safe…I'm just safe for now. But I'm used to that."

Her words are a shot to my heart. I can't imagine what it was like to grow up the way she did, with no one in her corner. Always fighting. I reach my free hand out and capture one of hers, causing her eyes to dart up to meet mine.

"How can I help?"

She looks surprised by my question, and I wonder how many men in her life have ever asked her if she needed help. Has anyone? Has there ever been a time when she felt safe? Remembering how she tried to push me out of her life like a tiny, glittering battering ram with fins…I think not.

"Oh, I'm fine."

I study her face. That meme of a cartoon dog in a bowler hat drinking tea in a room that's on fire comes to mind. Something about her expression tells me not to press the matter, so I don't. I clear my throat.

"I was thinking we should talk about something."

As soon as her face falls, I regret my choice of words. She always seems to be waiting for the next run of bad luck to happen. I squeeze her hand.

"About the media," I add quickly.

Her expression changes to curiosity. Better.

"It occurs to me that I'm very used to them following me around and hounding me, but you are not. It can be a lot to take in."

She considers for a moment, then nods. I lace our fingers together. A tingling sensation crackles along my skin everywhere our hands meet. Something in my gut tells me to treasure this contact like I might lose her at any moment. I can't shake the feeling that she's one small catastrophe away from trying to run again.

"I'm okay."

The smile on her face doesn't quite light up her eyes as her real smiles do. You know, the ones that turn my heart to liquid goo as soon as I see them. The ones that make me want to slay dragons for her. I remain unconvinced as far as her being *okay*. Worry pulls at me like a riptide.

"It's perfectly fine if you're not," I say gently. "You can tell me."

She shakes her head and offers a shaky smile. "I'm fine."

I decide not to push things again. The newness of whatever this is between us still feels so delicate, and I don't want to do anything to stress it too much. I force myself to let it go.

"Well, in that case…" I growl.

On impulse, I slowly lay down on the couch and pull her with me. She giggles as she slides down and leans precariously over the edge of the cushions.

She clings to me, giggling. "Help!"

I pull her on top of me for a moment, then move enough to let her slip down between the back cushions and my body. She nestles in perfectly, resting her chin on my chest and looking up at me.

"Now what?"

"We have a few hours before our date. Let's take a nap, Siren."

The sexiest smile I've ever seen spreads across her face, and I may come completely undone by it. She drapes her arm across my middle and rests her head fully on my chest. A little murmur escapes her lips as she completely relaxes against me, and I wonder in earnest whether my heart ever stood a chance against her. Marina is one thousand percent in control of it, and I'm completely at her mercy.

I reach up and smooth a hand against her hair, planting a light kiss on top of her head as sleep starts to pull me under with her. Her breathing has already evened out and I let out a light chuckle as I realize she's asleep. I give her a gentle squeeze, and she snuggles closer. As I close my eyes, I think ahead to our date tonight. Everything is in place. I've made sure of it. I've done everything I can to make it special and uniquely Marina. One thing's for sure: this isn't a date the average guy can pull off, and I'm hoping it'll be one she'll never forget.

Chapter 13

Marina

I watch the city of San Francisco pass by in a blur from my perch in the back seat of the car as Dave drives us to a destination kept more secret than whatever actually happens at Area 51. Zach's warm, strong hand is wrapped around mine, and his other arm circles gently around my shoulders. The heat of his body is a tonic against my frayed nerves leftover from my morning altercation with Ms. Taft. Everywhere that my softness meets his muscled hardness, I feel the undeniable urge to melt into him. He feels safe. Like home. A calm harbor in the storm that's become my life right now, and the feeling is equal parts thrilling and frightening.

For the past five years, I've relied solely on myself. After listening to all the wrong people giving cheap and easy (and wrong) advice, and being in relationships with people who continued to let me down, I realized that the only person who could pull me out of the hole of poverty and obscurity I'd dug for myself...was me. And that's how it's been all this time.

Have I let Ashley, Merry, and Scarlet in? Absolutely. It was hard at first, but my therapist was my lifeline through all the big changes that were necessary in the early days. She helped me find safe ways to learn to trust. Now, they're more like sisters than friends. It's different with men.

I barely remember my father. He was never around as an example, so I never learned to form healthy relationships with boys. I was either chasing the wrong ones for approval or running from the boys (and sometimes men), who were even worse. My lost years, as I call them, were a nonstop lesson in staying as far from the opposite sex as possible.

And this leads me to the gorgeous, kind, wonderful, and amazing man I'm sitting next to right now. The one who has me tucked securely against him as if I'm the most precious thing in the world. When I'm with Zach, I'm constantly torn between giving into my fear and running out the door or surrendering to the intense pull I feel whenever he's near. I could just let it take me out to sea, never to be seen again. I'll spend my life swimming in the infinite pool of Zach's affection. But I'm also petrified of what will happen to my heart if I get too close and he leaves.

My own history has taught me that this can't be real. And if it *is* real, it's not for me. I don't deserve it. It'll disappear, either because he tires of me or simply because none of this is true and he's just that good at manipulating me. I'm a novelty. The mermaid who trapped the rock star. His affection will wear off when the story's played out, leaving me alone and heartbroken. But it doesn't feel like that. *He* doesn't feel like that. And there's the source of my confusion and fear. What if I'm wrong?

Zach adjusts in his seat, brushing his thigh against mine. Warm, delicious tingles pass between us and I wonder if he feels them too. I look up at him and I'm immediately rewarded with one of his beautiful smiles. His dark brown, slightly wavy collar-length hair is the perfect frame to highlight the warm, intense brown eyes that study me closely. The ever-present stubble on his strong jaw makes him look like he just stepped out of a magazine. My eyes take a roving tour of his full lips, and my pulse immediately quickens when the memory of his feverish, all-consuming kisses flutters through my mind.

"What's going on in that beautiful head of yours?" he asks with a sexy rasp in his voice.

I feel a blush creep across my cheeks. "I'm still trying to figure out where we're going."

His smile deepens, and he pulls me closer. That delicious combination of sandalwood and salty sea air fills my senses. I will never get enough of it. I rest my cheek on his shoulder and breathe in.

"It's called a surprise for a reason, Siren. But we're nearly there. And I promise you won't be disappointed."

I tell my inner control freak to take a seat, then turn my attention back to the city outside the windows before I'm tempted to kiss that perfect mouth of his. We sit in silence, content in each other's company, until I see a very familiar sight looming outside one of the windows. I sit straight up.

"Are we going to the stadium?"

He lets out a musical laugh. "Maybe."

I look at the large marquee outside the venue, but it only shows the date of the big charity concert he plays in later this week. There's nothing scheduled for tonight.

"What's going on?"

He brings my hand up to his mouth and plants a light kiss on my knuckles, stirring something low in my gut.

"You'll find out soon enough, Siren."

I force myself to sit back in the seat as the car gets closer and closer to the stadium, then pulls into the parking lot. Within minutes, we're driving into the tunnel where I got off Zach's tour bus just over a week ago. I steal a sideways glance at him as the inside of the car darkens.

"Scene of the crime," he purrs.

"Crime?" I shoot him a mocking glare.

The car comes to a stop, and Dave opens the door for us. I stay where I am, waiting for an explanation.

"Right," Zach says with a wry grin. "Are you conveniently forgetting the speed with which you attempted to run from me as soon as we parked the bus in this tunnel on the day we met?"

Guilty, but I don't plan to confess any time soon.

"I have no idea what you're talking about," I reply lightly as I scoot out of the car. I feel his body heat right behind me.

"Wild horses can't run that fast, Marina."

I turn away and laugh nervously. He's not wrong, but I don't want to talk about my fears right now. I want to go on this date and find out what on earth he has planned. Thankfully, he seems to sense I don't want to talk about it and he doesn't push. He unfolds his tall frame as he exits the car and offers me his arm. For a moment, I swear I catch a glimpse of doubt in his eyes, but it disappears under the light of another devilishly handsome grin. I take his arm, and he leads me away from the car and further into the tunnel.

"Can you tell me what we're doing now that we're here?"

He continues leading me down the tunnel, and it begins to curve to the left.

"It's all in the presentation," he replies.

"What does that mean?"

He laces our fingers together as we approach a man who appears to be waiting for us. He's dressed casually, but I can see he's wearing a polo shirt with the stadium's logo on it. Zach kisses the back of my hand as we continue walking toward the man.

"It means you're just going to have to wait, my sweet little control freak."

I let out a sigh in mock frustration.

"I feel attacked," I tease as we come to a stop and Zach shakes hands with the man.

"Mr. Adams and Miss MacArthur, welcome," the man greets us. He nods at Zach. "Everything is ready as you requested."

I listen curiously, but I'm not rewarded with any more details. The man gestures down a smaller tunnel that points to the center of the stadium. Zach slaps a hand on the man's shoulder.

"Thanks very much," Zach says quickly, leading me down the next tunnel.

I see little glimpses of the main stadium, but we're underneath it. I think. Actually, I have no idea where we are. A slow smile spreads across my face as anticipation builds. My pulse picks up as I try to imagine what Zach has planned. I cling to his hand, letting him lead me forward into the unknown. The unknown isn't so scary with him.

We walk through the tunnel opening and I recognize where I am immediately. I've seen enough football games to know we just walked out of the tunnel the players come running out of, but there's no football field in sight. Everything is all set up for the benefit concert. A huge stage looms ahead of us, facing out into the rest of the stadium. I stop dead in my tracks so I can have a moment to take it all in. It's gigantic, and I can't even see the whole thing. We've come in on the side of the stage. Zach turns to make sure I'm alright, and I nod at him.

"I know this is no big deal to you," I begin breathlessly. "But this is so cool. I've never been down on this level before."

He leans forward and gently places a light kiss on my lips, then offers me the most mischievous grin.

"Are you hungry, love?"

I blink back my surprise. "We're eating *here?*"

Suddenly I envision a dinner of stadium hot dogs and fries. Perhaps dessert will be ice cream served in a helmet-shaped dish. Or churros? Actually, that doesn't sound too bad. I give him a curious look. Are there churros?

"Come on," he says, leading me toward the stairs to the stage.

We climb the stairs, which are painted black with yellow tape striped along the edges so everyone can see the steps in the dark. Everything on the side of the stage is black: the floors, the walls, and the curtains that divide the backstage area into wings. I squeeze Zach's hand a little tighter.

"Here we are," he says as he leads me out onto the stage, and I freeze in my tracks.

There's a dining table for two set up at center stage, complete with a white tablecloth and elegant place settings. A beautiful floral centerpiece, made of violet and pink hydrangeas and cream-colored roses, adorns the table. Candles of every shape and size decorate the space around the table in a variety of holders, on every surface. It's absolutely beautiful.

"Zach..."

He turns to me and pulls me into his arms. I go willingly, placing my hands flat against his chest as I gaze up into his eyes. I look around at this beautiful setting, and my throat constricts. He did this for me. I smooth his shirt under my fingers, and his pectoral muscles flex slightly, sending a little thrill up my spine. I shake my head as I glance over at the table again, my eyes filling with tears as my emotions hit me full force. No one has ever done anything like this for me. It's overwhelming in a way I didn't expect.

"Hey, there," he says in a voice laced with concern. "It's just dinner."

I sputter out a laugh, wiping away a stray tear.

"Only a rock star would say *this* is just dinner."

He watches me cautiously for a moment.

"Have I gone too far?" he asks quietly. "If this is too much, I apologize. Truly."

His expression is a mix of concern and regret, and a pang of guilt nudges at me. I glance around at the beautiful setting, something I know he did just for me, and the fear hits me full force. All the what-ifs, too. It comes at me like a tidal wave. I close my eyes.

"Things like this don't happen to me," I say with a shaky voice.

I take in a shuddering breath as his large hands gently rub up and down my back. He presses his forehead to mine, and we're silent for a moment. It's surreal to be in this gigantic stadium, the ghosts of 80,000 seats surrounding us on all sides, and yet we're entirely alone here.

"I'm so sorry, Marina."

I shake my head and fist my hands in his shirt, shaking him a tiny bit.

"Do not apologize for doing something so incredibly romantic."

He brushes a tear from my cheek as I stare up at him. He looks as confused as I feel. I can practically hear my therapist screaming in my head, begging me to tell Zach about my fears. About the fact that almost everything good has been taken from me in my life. About how hard it is for me to trust that good things can happen. I can't make myself do it. Instead of baring my soul, I clam up. And I hate myself for it.

"This is the sweetest, most wonderful thing anyone has ever done for me," I say with a sniff.

I quickly pull myself together and place a soft kiss on the corner of his mouth. He accepts it with a look like he's not sure whether I'll implode or I'm truly all right. I smile up at him.

"I was just a little overwhelmed. I'm okay."

He watches me carefully as if I'll break at the slightest touch.

"You keep saying that," he hedges. "I'm not sure I believe it."

We're interrupted by a tuxedoed waiter wheeling a linen-covered cart towards us from the other side of the stage. Slowly, I pull away from Zach and smile at the waiter.

"Right," Zach says in resignation. "For now, let's have our dinner. But we're going to have a proper conversation later."

He takes my hand and leads me to the table, pulling my chair out for me, then he sits. We both put our napkins in our laps as the waiter makes a show of uncorking the wine before pouring it. Before long, a sumptuous dinner is plated and served. There is a beautiful Caesar salad, followed by an appetizer of Dungeness crab cakes, and finally a platter of grilled seasonal fish to choose from. Mushroom Spatzle and seasonal vegetables round out the feast.

"This is incredible, Zach," I say as I dig in.

He eyes me warily. "I'm sorry if the big reveal was overwhelming."

I shake my head and hold up my hand to stop him.

"No, I'm okay. And, as you said, it's just dinner."

He nods and takes a bite. I don't want him to feel like he has to walk on eggshells around me, so I point over my shoulder at the empty stadium.

"I can't imagine what it's like to perform when this place is full."

He raises his brows and grins at me. "There's nothing like it."

I love how he lights up when he talks about his passions, and performing is definitely on that list. I may not have been a super fan when we met, but I have my share of favorite songs from The Royal Rebels. He is electric on stage, and it's mostly because you can just tell he's having a great time. In my whole life, I've never been able to let go like that. Well, at least not without negative results. My teen years were nothing but acting out and letting go, but I was never having a great time...I was just lost.

"So many famous bands and singers will be on this stage soon," I continue, "and here I am having dinner on it."

We both laugh softly.

"Not only them. You're eating dinner where Lady Gaga has performed."

My eyes grow wide. "And Taylor Swift."

He nods, then I let out a gasp.

"Justin Bieber!"

He lets out a rich, hearty laugh and I take another bite of my grilled salmon.

"I'm feeling a little jealous, Siren. You said his name with such reverence."

I wink at Zach. "He's married. I missed my chance."

Zach takes a sip of his wine and his eyes darken as he slowly smiles.

"No, beautiful. *He* missed his chance."

Suddenly the air in the whole stadium changes, all the way up to the nosebleed seats. My throat goes dry. I'm not sure if my knees would work if I stood up right now. Just call me noodle knees. To have a man like Zach look at me this way…well, it's another thing I'm just not used to. It's not just that he's handsome on a criminal level, but he's thoughtful. And kind. And he smells incredibly good. There must be something wrong with him, but I can't possibly try to figure it out right now while he's looking at me like this. I swallow the heavenly bite of salmon in my mouth.

"I'm sure he's devastated," I chide.

Another devilish grin. "He would be if he were smart."

I officially have no saliva left. I'm out. I feel my throat bob.

"Actually, he's quite a nice bloke," Zach offers lightly. "I met him at an awards show a few years back."

I blink a few times.

"Marina?"

I shake my head. "Sorry. I just realized for the first time…you actually know them all, don't you? Famous musicians and singers."

"Some, yeah. It's not like we all live on the same block."

Another question pops into my head, but I decide not to ask it. It must be written all over my face, though.

"What was *that* look for?"

I smirk. "I sort of thought you lived on the bus."

He makes an adorable, shocked face. "What? With the guys? And the bunks? Siren!"

I laugh hard. "I'm sorry! From what I gather, you spend most of your time on the road going from concert to concert."

He nods. "Well, I do happen to own a home, thank you very much."

I bow my head slightly, smiling softly. "Please accept my apologies and tell me about your home."

He shakes his head. "Only if you can tell me where it's located, Little Miss Know-It-All. Where do you think I live?"

I laugh again, and it feels wonderful to have this kind of silly, laid-back conversation with him. Maybe this is why I'm having an increasingly difficult time seeing him as the royal millionaire rock star he is. He's so normal despite it all. I decide to go for the obvious answer.

"L.A."

He scoffs. "Try again."

"Hawaii."

Another shake of his head. "Three strikes and you're out, gorgeous."

"London?"

He makes a game show buzzer noise and gives me a thumbs-down sign. I throw my hands in the air.

"I give up!"

I put my knife and fork down and toss my napkin onto the table, unable to fit in another bite. I turn to face the empty stadium, trying to imagine it filled with screaming fans. It must be an incredible rush. I hear movement behind me and Zach is out of his chair, holding a hand out to me. I put my hand in his and stand, walking with him until we're standing at the edge of the stage.

"I can't imagine what it must be like," I say quietly. "To stand here and sing in front of so many cheering fans."

He steps behind me and pulls me back against his chest. The warmth from his body wraps me in its own embrace as his arms create that familiar, safe cocoon I'm quickly learning to gravitate towards whenever we're in the same space together. He rests his chin on top of my head.

"When a stadium is filled with fans, the energy of it is a living thing. Different shows have different energies, depending on the music and the performer's dynamics. I can't speak for others, but the guys and I have worked hard to create a really good vibe at our concerts. It's positive and outrageous and just…fun."

I nod, trying to picture it. He reaches in front of me and points out into the floor seats directly ahead.

"For a Rebels concert, there would be a large catwalk out there," he explains. "It's an extension of the stage, protruding into the audience to give us more space to play."

"Play?"

He moves his lips close to my ear. "You've never been to a Rebels concert?"

The most delicious chills cover every surface of my skin, and I shudder, then inch closer to the shelter of his body. He wraps his arms tighter and places a whisper-light kiss on the shell of my ear. This is it. Right here. This is my favorite place in the world. I'm not gonna lie…it scares me. A lot. I don't want to like it here. I don't want to feel these feelings for him. I mean, I don't want to catch feelings for *any* man, especially not one of the world's biggest rock stars. But those feelings are here. What do I do when he leaves? What happens to me? Who picks up the pieces of Marina after he's gone?

I've spent years picking up the pieces of me that my childhood trauma sprayed everywhere. I close my eyes and shove it all down like I know I shouldn't.

I turn my head to steal a glance at him. "I would have gone to a Rebels concert, but I've been foolishly wasting my paychecks on rent and food."

He pulls me even closer, gently rocking us back and forth.

"I don't know," he says in a raspy voice. "Maybe you dated some chap who had excellent taste in music, and he got you tickets for the best date ever. But since I don't like thinking about you on a date with anyone but me, I'll drop that. Luckily, I know a guy who can get you really good tickets."

I laugh, and he swings me out of his arms and leads me in a slow dance to no music. Not that we really need it. When we're together, we're a force all our own. A force that makes me throw all my rules right out the window. One that has us dancing on stage in the middle of a huge stadium like it's just an average Tuesday. Not for other couples, perhaps. But normal for us. If there is an us. Is there? I want there to be. There, I said it.

"The catwalk enables more of the audience to get a better view of us when we're performing. Especially if I'm just doing vocals and I'm not on an instrument. I love running out there to engage with the fans."

He spins me around again, then pulls me close.

"What's it like to sing in a stadium like this?"

He places a soft kiss on my temple. "Sssh. Let's finish this dance first."

I smile and follow his lead. "There's no music."

Zach begins humming a soft melody against my ear. I recognize it, but can't place it. Whatever it is, it's perfect, and my heart is in mortal danger here. He's tearing down my resolve in every way possible. He hums the song beautifully, and I want to ask what it is, but I don't want to break the spell, so I just let go for once and let him lead me around. As he turns us around and around, I look at the candles on stage, the beautiful table, and the empty stadium…committing them all to memory. Whatever happens, I never want to forget that someone went to all this trouble for me. This is the most special night I've ever had.

I still can't name the song when it's over. Zach places his hands on either side of my face and brings his nose to mine. His gorgeous scent envelops me.

"I really want to kiss you," he rumbles. "But we'll make dessert late, and then the second part of my surprise will start late."

I pull away slightly, eyes wide. "There's dessert?"

I'm rewarded with a husky laugh and a quick, soft kiss before he leads me back to the table. At some point, the waiter cleared all our dishes without so much as clanging a plate. Our napkins are refolded at our seats, and there is a particularly delicious-looking personal-sized dessert at each of our place settings.

"Oooh! That looks amazing!"

Zach waits for me to sit, then pushes my chair in for me. He walks around to his side of the table and sits.

"I thought a proper English trifle might be fun."

I pick up my fork. "I agree already, and I've never had one before!"

Zach sits back in his chair, and a brilliant, beautiful smile spreads across his face. He looks like he's having the best time, and I laugh softly under my breath.

"What?" I ask, my fork still paused in mid-air.

He shakes his head. There's a secret shining in his eyes, and I want to ask him a million questions to sniff it out, but I also don't want to know. With Zach, that seems to be the theme of my feelings: equal parts wanting to know and wanting to run.

Well, if he's not going to tell me what he's thinking, I'm going to dig into this rich, creamy looking thing. There are layers of what looks like pudding, jam, and whipped cream over a base layer of ladyfingers. I load my fork with a little of everything and take my first bite.

"Wow," I moan, still savoring the scrumptious simplicity of the dessert.

"Well, I can relax now," he teases, taking a bite of his own trifle. "The King could have my head if I failed to represent my country so miserably that I couldn't get an American to appreciate trifle."

I only nod as I go in for another bite. This is too good for words, but movement out of the corner of my eye distracts me, and I look up in time to see Rick, Jimmy, and Sam walk on stage from the wings. Ricky's got his electric guitar, and Jimmy's holding his bass guitar. I blink back my surprise and lower my fork.

"Well done, Duke!" Sam says, slapping Zach on the shoulder. He eyes the table appreciatively. "You pulled out all the stops to impress her."

I stifle a giggle as Zach gives him the side-eye. I sit back in my seat and wave to all the guys, then look to Zach.

"The second part of your surprise is inviting your friends to join us?"

Rick winks at me, throws his guitar strap over his head, and starts flipping switches and connecting things in the background. Sam snickers under his breath as he pulls a pair of drumsticks from his back pocket, walks to the drum set, and sits down.

"They're fifteen minutes early," Zach explains, raising his voice and offering them a mock scowl. "But I spoke to them about it earlier, and we all agreed it would be fun to get you to sing with a proper band."

I set my fork down with a thud. "What?"

Zach nods. "Hey, you've already sung in a recording studio. I wanted to elevate your experience this time."

My gaze flicks to Jimmy, who is picking out a few notes on his bass guitar. He bobs his chin in my direction.

"C'mon, Marina, let's have some fun!"

Sam beats on his drums. "Yeah!!!"

I laugh out loud, my heart suddenly pounding wildly at the idea of singing with a band to back me up. The thirteen-year-old Marina in my heart is squealing with excitement. And not just any band…The Royal Rebels. When will I ever have this chance again? And doing the brave things has been working out for me lately, so I'm totally going to go for it. As soon as I stand up, Zach jumps out of his chair.

"That's my girl!"

I clap my hands with excitement as Zach steps into the wings and comes back with a mic and a stand. I step back and watch Zach and the guys set everything up. Finally, Zach motions for me to stand at the mic. He taps it with his finger, and I hear the sound amplify out of the speakers.

"Now, this is just for fun, so we don't have the proper setup," he explains. "The rest of the sound system will be set up at the benefit concert, but we don't need that for tonight. If there were fans with paid tickets up on the highest level, they'd be rioting over sound quality."

I nod, unable to get the idiotic grin off my face.

"All that to say, what shall we play for you, my lady?"

My mind goes blank again. I shake my head.

"I'm so excited I can't think of a thing."

"Let's warm up our voices first. Something simple?"

I nod, and Zach grabs a rhythm guitar from somewhere, then comes back to me at the mic stand.

"Ready?"

I smile up at him. "Go for it."

Jimmy shouts from behind us. "That's the spirit, Marina!"

Zach begins playing "You Are My Sunshine" on the guitar and I laugh out loud, then immediately join him in singing it. The band joins in, exchanging curious looks with each other, but they just go with it. In the background, the waiter is cleaning up the dishes and linens. Two assistants come out to move the dining table and chairs off stage, and I silently lament the loss of that trifle. I keep singing with Zach because even that trifle is no temptation compared to any time Zach and I sing together. We end the song with a light, playful kiss on one side of the mic stand. I distinctly hear Jimmy snickering again, and I roll my eyes at him. He is definitely a nine-year-old in an adult's body.

For the next several minutes, we get pretty silly. The guys just start playing random songs, and Zach and I jump in to sing them. Country, rock, pop, you name it. We sing it all, sometimes laughing through half of it, but it's such great fun to be on a real stage with a real band behind me. It's an experience I'll never forget.

Zach takes one of my hands in his. "Siren...I have an idea."

I turn to face him fully. "Tell me."

"We're going to sing it at the benefit concert this week as our closing number," he explains, looking like he's not sure I'll like his idea. "The Sound of Silence...just as you and I sang in the studio."

"Oh yes!"

I don't have to consider whether I want to sing it with him or not. Our voices are perfect for it, and we sounded so beautiful that time. The night I threw all caution to the wind and kissed him. My heart flips just thinking about it.

Before I know it, we're all set up to sing. Zach stays at the mic with me, so Rick switches to piano. The music begins, and I close my eyes. I feel Zach take both my hands in his as he begins singing the first notes.

Zach's voice is so unique when he sings this song. It's honeyed, smoky, and rich. It's an instrument in itself. I open my eyes to watch him sing, and our eyes meet. His expression is still as he expertly brings a solemn, haunting quality to his performance. My part comes up, and I close my eyes again. I've been singing it around the apartment ever since that night at the studio, so I don't worry about looking up the words anymore.

I lift my voice to meet Zach's, keeping my energy in check for this first part, and then we gradually increase the power of our voices as we move through to the end of the song. I don't think about our surroundings, the band, or anything else as we sing together. The perfect blend of our voices is what carries me through. When I open my eyes at the end, Zach is smiling with pride, and Rick, Jimmy, and Sam are still as death.

I shrug at them. "What?"

Rick gets up from the piano stool.

"That's a real powerhouse of a voice you've got there, Marina."

Sam and Jimmy shake their heads in agreement. Sam gets up and walks over to us, motioning for Rick and Jimmy to follow.

"Time for a company meeting."

I raise my eyebrows in question, my gaze flicking between all of them. Zach pulls me into his side and wraps an arm around me, and I slip my arm around his waist, which feels like the most natural thing in the world.

"Fancy talk for saying that the band needs to make a decision," Jimmy explains with a smirk. He looks at Sam. "So what are we deciding?"

Sam looks at the guys one at a time, then lands his gaze squarely on me. He looks at me with a glint in his eye that makes me nervous. Apparently, Rick is a mind reader because he suddenly smacks his hands on top of his head.

"Yes! I vote yes!!"

Jimmy grins wickedly. "If we're talking about what I think we're talking about? Absolutely."

I shake my head at all of them. "What *are* you talking about?"

Zach pulls me in tighter as if he's afraid I'll run when I know. I look up at him as I feel my pulse picking up, somehow knowing their plans include something about me.

"Marina, darling," Zach begins, that same proud smile on his face. "Would you like to be the first-ever guest vocalist when the Rebels perform at the benefit this weekend?"

***

Zach

I could fall into the endless, emerald green pools that are staring at me in utter disbelief, but I'm torn between deciding whether I need to give Marina more details or talk her off the ledge. Her eyes can't get any bigger, and her mouth pops open slightly as her gaze flicks between the four of us. Once again, I feel a strong urge to cover the exits in case she decides to bolt. Sam speaks first.

"Marina, don't look so freaked. It's all just for fun."

She just blinks at him and turns to me, shaking her head.

"I can't do that," she says in almost a whisper. "It's thousands of people. I can't."

I nod slowly, giving Marina a little squeeze. "That's completely fine, Marina."

Rick nods. "Yeah, it was just an idea. We didn't mean to...do whatever we did."

I give Rick a look. Not helping. Gently, I turn Marina to face me.

"Hey," I say gently. "There is no expectation, Siren. None at all."

She nods quickly, her throat bobbing hard as she gulps. I know she's thinking about her job again, about the loss of her income, her apartment, and everything she's fought so hard to achieve. And I know her well enough to know that offering to make it all irrelevant, financially speaking, is not going to do me any favors. Money isn't an issue for me, and it hasn't been for years. I would help in a heartbeat, but that's not the road to take here. Marina is fiercely independent and very proud of what she's accomplished, as she should be. But she still believes it's all on very shaky ground. I'm not sure how to make her see that I won't let her fall.

Her eyes scan my face, searching for truth. I reach up and brush my fingers over her cheek, then pull her in close. I hold her for what feels like an eternity before I feel the tension starting to leave her body. I make eye contact with the guys over her shoulder, my sigh of relief lessening their alarm at her reaction to what they thought was no big deal. We're laid-back people, but our childhoods were all vastly different from Marina's. I get it. She's fought hard to get here. I don't know how to make her see that she isn't fighting alone anymore. She hasn't been for a while. Ashley, Merry, and Scarlet are proof of that. Any one of them would come out guns blazing if anyone tried to hurt her. And now she has me as well. I just don't know how to make her see that.

"Thank you," she whispers against my chest.

My heart twists into knots at the guilt in her voice, and I know it's there because she still doesn't think she can ask for what she needs. I give Rick a look over Marina's shoulder, and he motions for the guys to get back to their instruments. I stay where I am, holding her, and soon the simple strains of "Joy to the World" by Three Dog Night come from the band.

I feel Marina pull away from me slightly, and I'm relieved to see her fighting back laughter. I grin and swing her away from me as I sing the opening lyrics, then motion to her to follow me to the mic.

"Let's go, Siren," I growl. "We're not done playing yet."

I see relief flood her face when she realizes no one is angry, no one is offended. No one will try to talk her into doing something she doesn't want to do. There is something shining in her eyes that looks an awful lot like gratitude, and I feel hopeful that she'll come to realize I'm one hundred percent Team Marina. I push everything else out of my mind as she steps up to the mic. That familiar light of pure joy shines from her face as she sings, and I lose myself inside it. I go willingly, like a moth to a flame.

Chapter 14

Zach

Hours later, Marina and I walk into her suite at the Fairmont, still laughing from our night on stage, which sold absolutely no tickets, and no one will ever know about it. The memory will remain ours, and ours alone, and I'm chuffed I could give her such a unique experience. It got a little rocky for a moment, but we recovered nicely. Now, I just want to spend a little more time with her before I fall into my bed exhausted.

She leads me to the couch, and I go willingly, sinking to the cushions with her and pulling her against me. I nuzzle her hair as she rests her head on my shoulder. The scent of coconut and some kind of exotic flower is intoxicating.

"I had so much fun tonight. Thank you, Zach."

I relax a bit more. I know we turned the tide back to a fun vibe after she panicked at the idea of singing at the benefit concert, but it's a relief to hear it spoken aloud. I reply with a kiss atop her head and she snuggles closer. Heaven.

"I'm sorry I can't sing on stage."

I lean back a bit and turn her head gently so she can see my face.

"There is nothing to be sorry for," I say soothingly. "I meant what I said, and so did the guys. I worry that you feel you're not worthy if you don't blend in and do what everyone expects."

She studies me for a moment.

"I just really hate disappointing people."

"I would only be disappointed if you told me you were never going to sing with *me* again. Whether that's in an empty studio, in a closet… on a bridge. Doesn't matter. I love singing with you. I don't care if we never sing in public. Your answer is your answer, and that's all I need to hear. If you should ever wish to change it, all you need to do is say so."

I rub our noses together and hover inches from her lips, looking at her with pleading eyes. My heart sinks at the sadness reflecting back at me. I brush her lips with mine once, twice. She closes her eyes and brings us together. Her lips are warm and deliciously soft against mine, and I swear I feel a little tremor just before she pulls away. Her coconutty scent envelops me as she studies me carefully for a moment.

"Thank you," she says with a pensive look on her face.

"You are an incredible, strong woman. I think sometimes you forget it's all right to ask for what you need."

"Speaking of that, can we talk about my brother for a minute?"

I nod. "We can talk about anything you wish."

She considers her words for a moment, then turns to face me fully.

"I've been thinking about it, and I'd like to take you up on your offer to help me find him."

I beam at her. "Yeah?"

Her gaze flicks over my face. "If it's okay, yes."

"I'll make the call to the private investigator tonight."

She begins to reply, then thinks better of it, then changes her mind again. I give her the space to work things out in her head, then she watches me hesitantly.

"Sometimes it's hard for me to accept help from people."

I nod. "I can understand that. Thank you for letting me help you find him."

She looks at me as if I'm from another planet, and I want to tell her everything I'm feeling. That the time I spend with her is so special to me, but that's not all I want. I want to be in her *life*. And I already know I'm at the point where I'll move my life around to fit whatever that looks like to her. I'll take whatever I can get. But she's already been through enough emotions tonight and I'm not going to push my luck.

"May I ask you something?" I reach out and play with a loose strand of her hair.

She nods with an open and curious expression.

"Ever since we had that moment on the bridge, I've felt drawn to you. Yet I feel like you always have one foot out the door. Is that in my head?"

She regards me with a look I'm now familiar with. I see her, and she gets it. She licks her lips nervously, then looks down at her hands.

"Not entirely."

I raise my eyebrows in question but stay silent so she has time to elaborate.

"I'm not sure how to put it into words right now," she hedges. "I spent my growing-up years completely out of control, and when I realized I wanted a better life, I had to fight really hard to get free of a lot of toxic relationships. I completely swore off men in order to focus on myself. I found Ashley, Merry, and Scarlet on the way, so I have three amazing friends. But I haven't ever had a functional relationship with any man. Ever."

I nod slowly.

"I guess what I'm trying to say is…I feel the same pull, but I am in very uncharted territory. It's scary, especially when I'm one paycheck away from losing all the ground I've fought to gain. If I lose my job, it won't take long before I'm in financial ruin. My head is screaming at me not to lose focus, or I'll lose everything I've built. But my heart and my gut are telling me I'm crazy if I don't explore…whatever this is between us."

I smile and wrap her in my arms. She feels the same attraction. Mentally, I heave a huge sigh of relief at that. This isn't some fluke, and it isn't one-sided. My gut tells me I just need to be patient, and she'll work this out. She'll realize there's no need to run anywhere…unless it's straight into my arms.

***

Marina

After lunch, I step out of the elevator and head to my desk, feeling a dozen sets of eyes following me.

Again.

It's fine.

It's expected, since I didn't actually get fired, that I'd now be the source of all office gossip. I'm the famous mermaid, and the aftermath is slightly worse since I've worked hard not to form any personal relationships here. No one knows me. Not really, thanks to the protective shell I keep around myself. So, no one knows how ridiculous most of the stories on the news are. Now that I've been identified, the media chatter has changed to whether Zach and I have a romantic relationship. I can't even watch the news right now because there are whole segments of talk and gossip shows breaking down our body language in the photo outside the recording studio, trying to show whether we're in love.

Love?

We've known each other for a week and a half. Is that long enough to fall in love? Of course, the fact that I've never *been* in love complicates the issue even more. Not to mention, we met in the weirdest of circumstances, and we're not just from two different worlds. Two different universes, really.

Regardless, I feel more hunted now than before. The media's getting sneaky. One of them actually got hired as a temp in our accounting department just so she could sneak up here and snap photos of me. She was caught, of course. So was the reporter posing as a Fed Ex delivery driver, as was the maniacal fan who got past lobby security and up fifteen flights of stairs before she was caught.

Ms. Taft is already fuming about all of it, and we still have a little over a week before the Montclair proposal meeting. I've given up the hope of ever hearing a civil word from her again. The only thing that keeps her in check is Ethan Montclair, who insists on stopping by every other day for lunch or a quick coffee chat with Ms. Taft. He takes every opportunity to find me wherever I am in the office, trying to get little tidbits about Zach. I've made a point to stay out of our cramped supply closet ever since he found me in there on Tuesday and made sure to physically bump into me, suddenly clumsy. My skin crawls just thinking about it.

Still, I've managed to build better boundaries with Ms. Taft, and it feels really good. I'm taking regular lunch breaks now, at least. It's actually nice to get out of the office to run an errand or, like today, have lunch with Zach in the back of the car. Restaurants are too public to deal with right now, so we have takeout picnics in the garage where we chat over takeout and make sure to squeeze in plenty of kisses.

Tonight we're staying in. It's two days until the benefit concert on Sunday, and Zach has to preserve his voice. It's not as big of a deal as it will be when The Royal Rebels concert opens the following weekend, but he still has to be careful. The benefit concert is a collective performance of a dozen artists, with The Royal Rebels closing the show. The other concert at the end of this month is part of the band's U.S. tour, so it's all The Royal Rebels. They're playing something like forty-four songs each night. Performing is more physically demanding than most people think, and he's going to need his voice to be in the best shape.

I look up in time to see one of the other executive assistants coming towards me. She stops at my desk with a smile.

"Hi, Hillary," I say lightly. "How's your day going?"

"Hey, Marina. Let's just say I'm glad it's Friday."

I nod. I get it.

"Look," she hedges, "I know we're not close or anything. I've always felt that you're not really interested in office friendships. That's totally fine, I just…I wanted to tell you that I'm really impressed."

I raise my eyebrows. "About what?"

She looks behind her to make sure we're alone.

"You didn't get fired for the whole viral video thing," she explains. "We all know how Ms. Taft feels about those things. First, I was shocked that you're the mermaid, and then I was really bummed because I knew you'd be fired for it—and you've always been helpful and kind here, unlike some of the other assistants. So I stopped by to say I'm glad you're staying and completely impressed by whatever you did to keep Ms. Taft in check."

I smile at her warmly. I've always known Hillary to be a genuine, kind person with a strong work ethic, and I'm grateful for the compliment.

"Thank you so much. That's really sweet of you to say."

She nods and gives me a little wave.

"Well, have a nice weekend, Marina."

"You too."

She starts to walk away, and I'm overcome by another flash of bravery.

"Hillary?"

She turns to face me.

"Would you like to grab lunch next week?"

Her face lights up, and she nods. "I'd love it. Maybe Monday or Wednesday?"

I smile back at her. "Either works."

She nods. "I'll come by, and we can decide what we're in the mood for."

"Great. See you then."

She waves again and walks away, and I click open the next document I need to work on. I just broke another one of my die-hard rules, and now I'm making friends at work. It feels good…and I can't stop smiling.

***

"I can't believe it. *You?*" I ask incredulously.

Zach nods, then adds sarcastically, "It's my deepest shame."

"You never shy away from anything, but you're afraid to fly?"

He nods again. "It's true. I'll still do it, but I'm a wreck the whole time."

I consider this an absolutely groundbreaking bit of information. Fearless Zach is not fearless after all. In fact, he's afraid to do something I love to do. I shake my head.

"What part of it is scary to you?"

His eyes widen. "It makes no sense. You're basically in a chair…on a giant bus…hurtling through the air."

I purse my lips together, trying not to laugh. He grins at me.

"You can laugh, Siren. I know how ridiculous it is."

I shake my head and take his large hand in mine. He laces our fingers together and pulls me against his side. I go willingly, and he wraps his arms around me as we lounge on the couch in his suite.

"It's not ridiculous at all," I say as I rest my cheek against his chest. "Lots of people are afraid to fly. I just wasn't expecting that."

"I met a pilot when I was flying Patriot Airlines once," he explains in a gravelly voice. "He explained everything so logically to me. I felt all right about it for a while, but then all of that just goes away when I'm actually on an aeroplane. I can't help it."

I plant a loud, squeaky kiss on his cheek, and he laughs.

"What's that for?"

I grin up at him. "For finally having a flaw and showing me you're human."

He laughs again. "I am a man of many flaws, Marina, I can assure you."

"Okay, tell me about one of your flaws," I challenge him, sitting up and facing him on the couch.

Zach tosses his head back for a moment, thinking.

"Well, I'm quite a challenge for my parents."

I raise my eyebrows. "Yeah?"

He nods. "Surely their lives would be easier if they had a son who wanted to go to Cambridge, work as a solicitor or banker, and was well on his way to being married and settled, though they would never admit it."

"Are you close to your parents?"

"I am," he says fondly. "I won the parental lottery. My parents are loving and supportive, which is why they let me go to Julliard. They support my love of music, although I doubt they had The Royal Rebels in mind when they let me go."

"Have they ever been to one of your concerts?"

"Lord, no!" he laughs. "It would create too much of a stir for the

Duke and Duchess of Wendly to be seen at a Rebels concert. But Mum insists on having me autograph every new album we release, and they're all proudly displayed in the music room at Allenton Hall."

He strokes his fingers across the back of my hand as we chat, lazy circles creating warm, delicious tingles on my skin.

"Is that where you grew up? Allenton Hall?"

He nods. "It's quite beautiful there."

"What was it like…growing up in a place like that?"

He makes a face, and I tilt my head.

"I'm not sure I can tell you without sounding like a privileged brat."

I squeeze his hand. "You might have grown up privileged, but I won't think that. I just want to hear about your childhood, that's all."

"Very well," he says. "Allenton is a very beautiful place. I'll tell you more about it later, but for now I think you'll love that my favorite room on the estate was always the library. I loved to read and could spend hours in there. Whenever my parents, or the nanny, or anyone was looking for me, it was the first place they looked. They usually found me."

"You had a nanny. Wow."

Could our lives be any different?

He shrugs. "It's not that different from home schooling in the States, really."

I roll my eyes at him.

"Okay, so you loved it there. And yet here you are…halfway across the world."

He flashes me a devilish grin. "The world is a big place, my darling. I want to see some of it before I return home."

I can't help the blush that crawls up my cheeks. Sometimes, that sexy British accent really hits me in all the feels. Every single one. But something he said prompts a question that must be asked.

"So your plan is to go back some day?"

He gives me a lazy nod. "Eventually, yeah, but not for a long time. My dad's healthy and quite happy managing his title and everything that goes with it, and I'm quite happy being the family rebel."

"But someday you'll go back," I say softly. "Probably marry a princess."

He growls and sits up, his lips instantly on mine in a soft, slow, painfully perfect kiss. I sink into him as I surrender myself completely to it. His hands cup my face so gently. He pulls back to gaze into my eyes, and I see that look again, like he knows exactly what I'm thinking.

"Why would I want a princess when I have a mermaid?"

Swoon.

This man is a force to be reckoned with. Gorgeous, sexy, and incredibly sweet. Romantic. And I don't want him to go home. I don't even want him to leave San Francisco, I realize. It's so irrational I want to scream. Suddenly, a thousand thoughts are rushing in. They're all different versions of what-if, worst-case scenarios.

Zach's expression sobers.

"You have that look again," he says quietly. "What's troubling you?"

Just for a moment, I start intrinsically shutting down all the questions in my head. Don't rock the boat. Don't make waves. And then I remember. *Hey, Marina...we're not doing that anymore.* We're singing on bridges. We're standing up to tyrant bosses. We're letting a good man into our life.

I hesitate a moment longer.

"I have questions."

He nods. "Ask me anything."

"What happens after you leave town? What happens to...us?"

The smile that blooms on his face could light a thousand Christmas trees.

"Wow," I say with a little laugh. "Not the reaction I was expecting."

He shakes his head. "I'm sorry, love. I'm just so chuffed you used the 'us' word."

I smile. "Yeah?"

"Yeah," he says. "I like it."

"There's an us?"

He cups my face in his hands and concentrates, locking my gaze with those gorgeous brown eyes.

"There is definitely an us," he growls. "I am crazy for you, Marina."

My heart feels like it's going to pound right out of my rib cage. I lean in and capture his mouth with mine. His kiss is eager and passionate, and I'm being devoured in the most delicious way. His lips are soft yet firm as they trail from my mouth and make their way across my jaw line. If he gets to my ear, I'm a goner. I break away reluctantly.

"What does this look like when you leave town?"

He brushes his fingers down the side of my face, and I have to fight the urge to kiss him again when I see the pure emotion behind his eyes.

"Well, we have shows in Los Angeles, San Diego, Phoenix, and Dallas before we're done this year," he begins, playing with the ends of my hair. "The tour won't officially end for five more weeks. Since you're not afraid of hurtling through the air at fantastic speeds, I was thinking that you could come to see me during the tour as your schedule permits. When the tour is done, I'll come straight back here."

I feel some of my anxiety slowly fading away.

"You'll come back here?"

He grins, and my whole heart flips over like a puppy showing its belly.

"Well, my brilliant and beautiful girlfriend lives here," he croons. "Why would I want to be anywhere else? Is that all right with you?"

I nod, speechless. He reaches out one hand and buries it in my hair, pulling me closer until our foreheads meet.

"Hey," he says breathlessly. "Thank you."

"For what?"

He rubs our noses together, a thing I'm really beginning to love. Nose rubs for the win.

"For asking me questions instead of running."

I brush his lips with my own. Little goosebumps bloom down my spine.

"My boyfriend loves it when I don't overreact."

He throws his head back and laughs that deep, raspy laugh I love so much. I laugh right along with him. He pulls me into his arms and kisses the top of my head.

"Oh, Siren," he says, his lips moving against my hair. "You wreck me."

I raise my eyebrow mischievously.

"Isn't that exactly what sirens are supposed to do?"

*****

Zach

Halfway through my morning shower, I realize I haven't stopped smiling since I rolled out of bed. I hurry through my routine, eager to get downstairs and have breakfast with Marina. We had a bit of a breakthrough last night, and I'm chuffed beyond reason. She trusted me enough to talk through her feelings instead of shutting me down and running. Score one for Team Zach.

I grab my phone off the charger and send her a quick text that I'm on my way, then I exit my suite and take the stairs one flight down to her floor. Today is our last full day together for more than a week, and I want to make the most of it. The benefit concert is tomorrow, then the guys and I have to hit the road for a mini press tour around southern California and Nevada before we get back to San Francisco. We'll be gone for days, and I hate it, but she'll need to focus on work. Her big meeting is less than a week away.

Just as I raise my hand to knock on her door, she opens it and pulls me inside. I turn around and back her up against the door as she throws her arms around my neck and brings me in for a soft, slow good morning kiss. I pull away slightly and smile down at her.

"Good morning, love."

She beams up at me. "Good morning. Hungry?"

I give her a flirtatious look, and she kisses me again, then leads me into the dining area.

"For foooood?" she teases.

The brunch spread is back and looking quite delicious, so I hand Marina a plate and let her dish up while I pour two cups of coffee from the carafe on the cart. Once that's done, I quickly fill my own plate, and we take our seats.

"Are you ready for our day?"

Marina nods, an adorable smile on her face as she chews. "I'm up for anything."

"Skydiving?"

She gives me a look and I chuckle to myself.

"Actually, I was thinking a picnic in Golden Gate Park might be just the thing. How does that sound?"

I'm rewarded with a luminescent smile.

"I love the park," she replies between bites of bacon. "That sounds fun."

"Excellent. You can choose the spot, then."

I pull my phone out of my pocket to text the plan to the concierge. The hotel puts together wonderful gourmet picnic hampers and I've asked them to try to throw a few British picnic items in this one. Perhaps some scones instead of those giant cake-like muffins. We'll see how they do. I put my phone on the table and dig into my French toast.

"So the benefit concert is Sunday night, then you're leaving for Los Angeles on Monday morning?"

I nod. "We have three talk shows between Monday afternoon and Tuesday morning. Then we're doing some radio station appearances on Tuesday. Wednesday morning, we have a few fan events, and then we'll head back to San Francisco. I'll be available on Thursday, but you'll be preparing for the proposal meeting. Maybe we can have breakfast that day?"

She nods, her expression a little sad. "I'll miss you."

"Did you ever think you'd say that to me when you were running down the tunnel at the stadium, trying to escape me?"

Marina giggles. "I can see I'll be paying for that the rest of my life."

As I stab another piece of my breakfast, my mobile phone vibrates. I take a bite, put down the fork, and look at the screen. I recognize the number immediately, my heart is instantly pounding as I answer.

"This is Zach."

I listen carefully, occasionally looking up at Marina. She's watching me curiously. When all my questions are answered, I ask the caller to email all the information to me so I can access it on my mobile. I thank him and hang up, then I turn my full attention to Marina.

"I don't think you're going to want to go to the park today, Siren."

"Who was that? Is something wrong?" She watches me with a concerned expression.

I reach across the table and take her hand in mind.

"Would you like to go to San Diego instead? That's where your brother is."

Chapter 15

Marina

I stare blankly at Zach. It feels like there are a million words on the tip of my tongue, and I can't voice a single one. Max has been found. In San Diego of all places. For the first time in what feels like forever, I have the ability to see my brother. Zach gets up from his seat across the table, comes to my side, kneels next to my chair, and takes my hands in his. His thumbs make lazy circles on the backs of my hands as every imaginable scenario runs through my head. But none of them matter. Not really. All I can think about is seeing my brother again, making sure he's all right, and making amends. I close my eyes for a moment to gather my strength, then open them and nod at Zach.

"Tell me."

His throat bobs. "He's a student at San Diego State University on a baseball scholarship. He lives on campus and works part time at a local coffee house. He appears to be living a happy life and is a good student."

Baseball. Instant tears fill my eyes. He always loved baseball so much. When I left, he was on a team, and Mr. Lewis was an assistant coach. I can still remember the glow on his face when he suited up in his uniform. Right now, at this moment, I feel like my heart might explode from happiness. He is chasing his dream.

"Is that it?" I ask, unable to control the ridiculous smile on my face. "Anything else?"

Zach hesitates just for a moment, then reaches over, grabs a napkin, and gently puts it in my hand as if he knows more tears are coming.

"He also volunteers on Sundays," he says, his expression full of emotion. "As an assistant coach on a baseball team for foster kids. He's giving back to them…just like you."

I feel my face crumple and let the tears fall as Zach's arms wrap around me, pulling me off my chair and into his lap. I drop my head to his shoulder and don't even try to stop the happy sobs that shake my entire body. I don't care what I sound like or look like, I'm not interested in holding anything in. I slide my arms around Zach's neck and let out what feels like a thousand years of pent-up worry and hurt over how I left things with Max. I squeeze Zach as hard as I can.

"Thank you, thank you, thank you," I whisper in a voice that's so wobbly I don't even recognize it.

His arms are like steel bands around me as he rocks me gently back and forth. I cling to the warm, solid wall of Zach's body and breathe in his beachy scent. It's a balm to my overwhelmed emotions, anchoring me while the pure emotion of what's just happened hits me like a tidal wave. The warmth of his body gradually settles me until I can finally breathe normally.

I pull back to study his face and find the clear tracks of tears on his cheeks. My heart swells, and fresh tears threaten my eyes. I place my hands on his face and gently wipe them away. He smiles softly and places a gentle, sweet kiss on my lips. I press my cheek to his and take a deep breath. I am absolutely 100% going to fall in love with this man. There's no denying it any longer. I'm already well on the way. My inner control freak is being loved right out of me.

"I am so happy for you, Marina," he rasps as he rubs his strong hands up and down my back.

I laugh softly, joy overflowing. "All because of you. Thank you, Zach. I can't believe it."

He beams up at me. "I'm glad I could help."

I nod. "Me too."

His arms slacken a little, but he still holds me securely on his lap.

"What will you do now that you know where he is?"

I don't even have to think about it.

"I want to see him," I answer succinctly. "As soon as possible."

With that, Zach gently nudges me off his lap, stands, and pulls me with him. He pulls my chair out for me, and I sit, then he takes a seat next to me.

"Right then, let's make a plan."

I shake my head at him, still unable to fathom how this incredible man came to be in my life. I grab a piece of bacon and take a bite, focusing on the logistics of getting myself down to San Diego.

"Well, this could be tricky," I hedge. "San Diego is five hundred miles away. I know Ashley would let me borrow her car, but it takes too long to drive down there. The benefit concert is tomorrow. There's no way we'd be back in time."

His gaze rakes over my face as he considers what I've just said. The corners of his mouth tip up. I take another bite of bacon.

"So I'm coming along, then?"

I lean forward and press a kiss to his cheek, then pull back and regard him with pleading eyes.

"You don't think I can do this without you, do you?" I ask quietly. "I don't *want* to do this without you."

He bows his head just slightly. "My honor, my lady."

I point my remaining piece of bacon at him. "We still have to figure out if we have enough to time to get down there and back. We have the benefit concert tomorrow, then you hit the road for your media stuff in L.A. and I'll be busy prepping for the Montclair meeting. Then we have the big Rebels concert that next weekend."

He waves a hand at me like it's no big deal. "Easy, Siren. I've got this all figured out."

I sit back in my chair and give him a curious look, tossing the last bit of bacon in my mouth. He shakes his head and slides a hand over his face, then runs it back through his hair.

"When I said I'd slay dragons for you, I didn't think they'd be my own," he mutters. "We're gonna fly down there. Today."

***

For more times than I can count over the past two weeks, I'm having one of those moments where I'm wondering how this is my life. This time, it's because I'm looking out the window of a private jet, letting my hot rock star boyfriend squeeze my hand to death as the pilot lands us in San Diego just two hours after we got the phone call about Max. I'm not sure which part of it is the strangest, but I'm going to go with the whole having a boyfriend thing since I had previously sworn off all men for the foreseeable future until I met a rock star in the middle of the Golden Gate Bridge.

Yep. That definitely trumps the whole private jet thing.

Zach's jaw muscle constricts a few times, and he swallows hard when the wheels touch down. I reach over and cup his cheek with my free hand, softly kissing him over and over again as the plane slows and comes to a halt. He looks at me with darkened eyes.

"I may get used to flying if we get to do that every time."

I laugh softly and kiss him again, my heart full of every good feeling in the whole wide world. The pilot steps out of the cockpit as the steward lowers the plane's stairs for us. We take our seatbelts off and stand. I wrap my arms around him and give him a huge hug.

"That wasn't so bad, was it?"

He lets out a low growl and pulls me closer.

"At the risk of looking a coward in front of my brave, beautiful girlfriend, I'm going to decline to answer that."

The steward clears his throat from the doorway and we reluctantly let each other go. I grab my bag, and we make our way to the exit. The pilot smiles kindly at us both and shakes Zach's hand.

"Just send me a text when you know what time you'd like to head back, Mr. Adams," he says coolly. "We'll have everything ready."

Zach nods as he shakes his hand, smacking him on the shoulder. "Thanks so much, Jeff."

"Thank you," I say as we begin our descent down the plane's stairs.

It's a beautiful day in San Diego, but southern California weather is usually mild. They don't have to deal with as much fog and murkiness as we do up north, and I feel a little jealous as I look up at the blue sky. White puffy clouds are dotted around, looking so perfect it's almost as if they were placed there by an artist.

Zach is right on my heels as I step onto the tarmac, and we walk over to the terminal building at the small private airport. He holds the door for me, and I don't miss how his eyes drag down my body and back up again. When I realized I'd be seeing Max today, I ran back into my room and changed into a favorite sundress that I rarely get to wear. The fabric is a very light pink with beautiful red and pink flowers sprayed across the hem line just above my knee. I opted for a pair of pink espadrilles to go with it.

"I love that dress on you," Zach says as he laces our fingers together. "You look even more beautiful than usual."

I smile my thanks as we walk over to greet the car service driver holding a sign that reads *Walker*. For obvious reasons, Zach uses a fake name for things like this. I find it completely adorable that he uses the name Brett Walker when he travels because it "sounds like a really cool American guy".

After exchanging a few pleasantries, we follow our driver out to an SUV waiting at the curb. Zach lets me in first, then he scoots in behind me before the driver closes the door and gets in the front seat.

"Our destination is about twenty minutes away, folks," our driver, Michelle, informs us. "Would you like the privacy screen up or down, Mr. Walker?"

"Up, please," Zach replies. "Thank you, Michelle."

The privacy screen slides into place, and I can see by the way she nods at Zach in the rear-view mirror she knows exactly who he is. Zach reaches over, covering my hand with his.

"How are you feeling?" he asks, his eyes roving over my face.

I take a big breath and let it out.

"Okay, I think. Excited. Nervous." I squeeze his hand. "Unbelievably grateful."

He pulls my hand up to his lips and kisses the back of my hand, his eyes lit up with excitement.

"I'm excited for you," he says. "Are you sure you don't want me to wait in the car, Marina? If I'm spotted, it could bring a level of attention to the situation that you really don't want."

I shake my head firmly. "I want you with me, Zach. Especially if it doesn't go well. It'll kill me if he's angry, even though I deserve that from him. I need you to help keep me together."

He squeezes my hand. "You deserve no one's anger. I have all the faith in the world that he'll be happy to see you. I just don't want my presence to ruin things."

I grin and reach into my bag, pulling out my Alcatraz Swim Club ball cap and handing it to him.

"I brought you a disguise."

He laughs out loud when he sees it, and he slips it on as my phone starts vibrating like crazy in my purse. I pull it out and swipe it open.

Ashley: Sending you all the love and happy vibes, Marina! So happy for you!

Merry: Send us an update as soon as you can...I'm so excited!

Scarlet: Extra points for selfies. You got this!!!

My heart is so full right now. I sent a message to the girls via our group chat when Zach and I were on the way to the airport. The amount of joy, love, and support I get from these women is something I will never take for granted. While I'm still worried about Max's reaction when he sees me, I feel more than equipped to bear the weight of whatever happens because I have them in my inner circle—and now Zach as well. I feel like the luckiest woman in the world.

Marina: Thanks, guys. I'm nervous, excited, scared, and about a hundred other emotions right now. I promise not to leave you hanging.

I slip my phone back into my bag and lean into Zach's solid warmth. Hard muscle and that lovely beachy scent is the perfect place to cuddle against right now. He wraps an arm around me and kisses the top of my head as the car winds its way through the city streets, bringing us closer and closer to my brother. I've dreamed of this moment for so many years. I can barely believe it's happening now. There are so many things to say. I have so many questions. I've tried to picture the adult version of the boy in my memory, but I can't quite get there. The image of him cemented in my heart all these years is of him in his baseball jammies, tucked into bed with his big blue eyes watching me as I sang him to sleep each night. That memory has both tortured me and kept me going all these years.

"You have no idea what it means to me that you're coming with me," I murmur against Zach's shoulder.

He pulls me closer. "As if I could ever refuse you anything, Siren."

I smile. "I'm glad you're here."

I feel his lips press a sweet kiss on my temple.

"Zach?" I say softly.

"Yes, my darling Marina?" I can hear the smile in his voice.

"You make me feel safe."

He reaches up a hand and gently cups my face, turning my head so I can look into his eyes. I see such warmth every time he looks at me. And longing. Joy. Love? There are times when I could almost swear I see that too.

"That is probably the greatest compliment you could ever give me," he says quietly. "I want you to *know* you're safe. I want you to know deep down that you can reach any goal, any dream you want. And you will never fall simply because I will not allow it to happen."

Tears threaten my eyes again as I get lost in the pure emotion lighting his face. Gratitude fills my heart.

"How did I ever want to run from you?"

He lets out a growl and rubs our noses together.

"I'm about three seconds from ruining your lipstick, gorgeous."

I let out a little laugh and kiss the tip of his nose just as the car slows, then turns into a small parking lot along Ocean Front Blvd. I look out the window, my heart instantly pounding. We're in a quaint little shopping center. The buildings are all covered in gray, blue, or light yellow siding with cheerful white trim and shutters. There's a definite beach vibe going on. I can see a surf shop, a small convenience store, an art gallery, and…there it is. The Bean & Biscuit, the coffee house where Max works. According to the report from the private investigator, he works every Saturday before heading over to coach his baseball kids in the afternoon. Michelle pulls the car into a parking space, stops the car, then gets out and opens the door for us.

Zach gets out, then waits for me to follow. I scoot across the back seat and step out of the car. The warmth of the late morning sun hits my shoulders, and I tilt my face up to the sky. Such a gorgeous day. Surely nothing bad could happen on a day like this.

Right?

I feel my confidence waver just a little as Michelle shuts the car door behind us.

"I'll be right here when you're ready to go," she says with a smile.

We both nod at her, and I think Zach says thank you, but I'm suddenly not able to focus on anything happening around me right now. Zach reaches out and places his hands on my shoulders. My gaze flicks up to meet his. The warmth of his hands on my bare skin is hypnotic, and he gives me a little squeeze.

"All right?"

I take a deep breath and nod. "It's finally hitting me. He's right there in that coffee house, working. He has no idea I'm here, getting ready to walk in and…"

I feel a tightness in my throat as the raw emotion of this moment overcomes me. My eyes fill up, and I look away for a moment, shaking my head.

"What if he doesn't want to see me? What if he won't even let me apologize?"

Zach gently nudges me under the chin with a single finger until I'm looking up at him. His eyes are full of concern for me as he brushes a stray bit of hair away from my face.

"I don't believe for one minute that you have anything to apologize for, Marina," he says gently. "You were a kid. I think he'll be overjoyed to see you, but it's completely your call. Say the word, and we'll go back to the airport right now. You don't have to do anything today."

He pulls me into his arms, and I'm enveloped in his warm, comforting, beachy scent. I wrap my arms around him and breathe him in, working through the possibilities in my mind. He's right. I don't have to do anything today. I could get back in the car right now, and

Zach would follow. We would fly back home, and I could save this, and all the emotion that comes with it, for another day. But I don't want to. I know in my heart I want to do the brave thing.

I am tired of the guilt. Tired of punishing myself. I'm tired of wondering whether Max is angry at me or even cares what happened to me. My need for closure is pressing me forward. I need to know he's okay and to see it with my own eyes, even if he wants nothing to do with me. I need to see my brother.

I feel the decision settle in my gut and I know it's what I need to do. I pull back slightly and look up into Zach's eyes.

"I want to see my brother," I say almost hoarsely.

Zach brings our foreheads together. "Then let's go see your brother, Siren."

I nod, and we pull apart. Zach laces our fingers together as we turn toward the coffee house and start walking. My legs feel almost wooden as we get closer and closer to Max.

The Bean & Biscuit looks charming from the outside. There's a large wood sign with their logo hanging above the door and a spacious and inviting patio area on the side of the building. Customers are seated on white wood chairs at tables covered in blue and white checked tablecloths, enjoying coffee and pastries on this gorgeous morning. So many people just going about their day while I walk toward my reunion with Max.

A waiter steps out onto the patio with a loaded tray, and I freeze dead in my tracks. He's tall, with short blond hair. The same shade as Max. I squint, trying to get a better look as my heart threatens to pound its way right out of my rib cage. Out of the corner of my eye, I see Zach looking from me to the waiter on the patio and back again.

"I don't know," I whisper, shaking my head. "I don't know if that's him."

Zach squeezes my hand. "Shall we move a bit closer?"

The waiter goes back inside, and I come back to my senses. Yes. Closer. I step forward again, and we get to the sidewalk that leads up to the coffee house. I pause again. The large windows are tinted with something, making it hard to see through. What if he looks through the window and sees me? Would he recognize me? I'm kind of hard to miss with my long red hair. If he doesn't want to see me, he could be out the back door before I'm even inside. Zach pauses with me, giving me the space to do this how I need to. Or change my mind.

I look up at him. "Time to do the brave thing," I say breathlessly.

He nods, and the pride shining in his eyes fortifies my courage. He's proud of me, I can see it clear as day.

"The very brave thing," he says, planting a soft kiss on my mouth. "Ready?"

I squeeze his hand and nod, stepping forward again and closing the distance between us and the front door. Zach pulls the visor of the ball cap down over his eyes a bit more and reaches for the front door, opening it for me. I summon all the bravery I can and step inside.

The door closes behind us, and I take a look around. The inside of the Bean & Biscuit is just as charming as the outside. Walls covered in white shiplap contrast with charcoal gray concrete floors and natural dark wood tables and chairs. Quirky, brightly colored pots are filled with various plants and flowers around the space. Straight ahead, a large bakery case displays a tempting array of pastries and cakes. Coffee house staff rush around behind the case, filling orders for coffee, tea, and food. The smell of coffee and pastries is intoxicating.

Zach nudges me, and I look over to find him pointing at a chalkboard sign halfway down the counter.

Barista of the week: Max

It is written in brightly colored chalk. I give Zach a wobbly smile as I search the coffee house for any sign of my brother. I don't see anyone who looks like him, and the blond waiter I saw outside is nowhere to be seen. The edges of doubt begin to creep in, and I wonder if he did see me and left abruptly. I have to face the reality that this visit might not have a happy outcome.

I nearly jump out of my skin when the bell on the door dings, signaling the arrival of more customers coming in behind us. Zach keeps his head slightly lowered to avoid recognition, and he leans close.

"Perhaps we should get a table so we're not standing out in the open?"

I nod. Good idea. But my feet are firmly planted in the entryway, and I can't seem to move. I feel Zach's large hand wrap gently around my elbow. I look at him, and he smiles encouragingly. My heart is racing as I let him lead me to a table in the corner by the windows that overlook the beach. He pulls my chair out for me just as movement out of the corner of my eye pulls my attention away. The blond waiter pushes his way through the door that leads inside from the patio area.

Except that's not a blond waiter. It's my brother.

It's Max.

Chapter 16

Marina

My breath catches just as our eyes meet, both of us frozen in time. He blinks rapidly as if I'm a hallucination. I feel like my heart might just burst right out of my chest. It's pounding so hard. I look at Max from head to toe, so tall now. And so grown up. I feel my lips tremble as I take him in, unable to speak because of the lump that's formed in my throat. He takes a step toward me, his crystal blue eyes locked on me.

"Marina?" he says, almost a whisper.

A sob escapes my lips as I nod at him, and he launches himself at me. Suddenly, I'm being lifted up in the biggest, most amazing hug I've ever had in my life. I wrap my arms around my brother as he swings me around and around so fast that I actually squeal.

"I can't believe it!" he says in a voice trembling with emotion as he sets me down.

I step back and look up at Max, both of us laughing and crying as we take each other in. I realize too quickly as I look at this adult version of my little brother that I've missed so much of his life. I've missed baseball games and first dances and so many things I should have been there for.

"Max, I'm so sorry," I blurt as I place a gentle hand on his tear-stained cheek. "I'm so, so sorry. I don't even have words—"

He looks down at me in confusion, putting his hands on my shoulders and shaking me gently.

"Sorry for what, Marina?" he asks with a slight frown.

I gulp down the lump in my throat. "For leaving. For losing track of you. For—"

"No," he says softly, shaking his head and pulling me back into his arms. "No, Marina."

I sob against my brother until he pulls away again.

"Hey, Marina," Max says gently, making sure I'm looking up at him. "There is nothing you need to apologize for, okay? I—"

I know the moment Max has recognized Zach, who's standing behind me with his eyes looking more than a little watery. Zach extends a hand to Max.

"Hi, Max," he says quietly. "It's nice to finally meet you."

Max shakes his hand and then looks back at the bakery counter for a moment. He turns back to me and motions to the table.

"Okay, sit right here and don't move," he says excitedly. "I'm going to go tell them I need a minute."

I nod and watch him walk away, then turn back to Zach with a smile so big it hurts. He beams back at me and winks.

"Told you, Siren."

I laugh softly. "You sure did."

Max comes bounding back to the table, and Zach steps away. I look at him curiously.

"I'm going to be right over here," he says, pointing to a table on the other side of the bay of windows.

I start to shake my head in protest, but he stops me with a quick kiss.

"No, you two need a proper catch-up. I'm right over there if you need me."

Zach smiles at us both and retreats to the other table as Max and I sit down. Max watches Zach leave, then leans over the table close to me.

"After we catch up, I have to hear the story about how *the* Zach Adams is following my sister around," Max says incredulously.

I laugh softly, wiping another stray tear from my cheek.

"How is it possible you haven't seen us both on the news? It's been ridiculous."

Max shrugs. "That's easy. I don't get out much between school, baseball, work, and other stuff. I don't even have a TV in my dorm room."

I reach out and take his hand, squeezing it. "I'm so happy to hear that you're still playing baseball. You always loved it so much."

He beams at me, and I'm overcome at how big he is. I just can't get over it. He's been frozen in time in my mind for ten years. I've missed so much.

"Turns out I'm pretty good at it," he says. "Dad was a great coach. He had a real talent for seeing what I needed help with and getting me the training I needed to work on it."

"Yeah, you two were pretty inseparable almost as soon as we were placed with the Lewises," I say softly, remembering how Max loved having a father.

He watches me pensively for a few moments before replying.

"What happened, Marina?"

I feel my throat bob as I try to swallow the lump in my throat. I chew on my lip and look away, shaking my head.

"I was just so angry, Max," I whisper. "And so young. I was angry at the whole world. For everything. I don't know if it was teenage hormones or the culture shock from growing up struggling and then living with a wealthy family or…I don't know. But it felt *good* to break all the rules. I thought I was controlling things when I was losing control the whole time. I didn't really think of the consequences until one night when I heard the Lewises talking about how much they loved you…but how bad my behavior was. I was worried you'd lose the dad you always wanted, and I decided the best thing to do would be to run away so they could keep you. I told our case worker I didn't want us to be together. I told her I'd just keep running away, and I did. And eventually, they let the Lewises adopt you. I felt like you had a better life."

He's silent for long moments, mulling over my words. Finally, he leans forward and braces his forearms on the table.

"How much of a better life could I have without my big sister," he says, his voice thick with emotion. "I missed you so much, Marina."

My eyes fill again, and I blink back tears, wiping a few that fall down my cheeks.

"I'm sorry, Max. I thought I was doing the right thing for you. Can you ever forgive me?"

He stands up and pulls me into a hug. "You were forgiven the minute I saw you."

Is it possible to get dehydrated from crying? I think I'm in danger. We stand there, hugging, for what seems like a blissful eternity. I don't think about anything other than the fact that I have my brother back…and he's *happy* to see me. Suddenly I wish we could put the world on pause for Max and me to do ten years' worth of catching up. Someone clears their throat behind us, and Max and I break apart. We find a petite brunette in a Bean & Biscuit apron watching us curiously.

"Hi there," she says, smiling up at Max with puppy dog eyes.

Oh boy.

"Can I get you guys anything while you're catching up?"

Max looks at me with a grin, then gestures to the young woman.

"Marina, this is my friend Daisy," he says. "Daisy, this is my sister. Marina."

Daisy smiles at me and nods. "It's so nice to meet you, Marina. Can I get you anything?"

I look at Max, eyebrows raised. "What does my brother recommend?"

He turns to Daisy. "Two 'Max Specials' please, Daisy," Max says with a mischievous glint in his eye. He points over at Zach. "Can you see what this gentleman would like as well please?"

Daisy nods and steps over to Zach's table to take his order. I grin at my brother.

"I think Daisy has a little crush on you."

He bites his lower lip and nods at me. "Yep. The feeling is mutual. I'm just not sure what I can do about it right now."

I tilt my head. "What do you mean?"

He shrugs. "School, baseball, work, and I do volunteer coaching. Trying to date with all that going on feels like a lot. I don't think it'd be fair to her."

I laugh softly, watching Daisy putter around behind the counter as she puts our order together.

"I'm not sure she cares about all that."

He looks over his shoulder at her and smiles, then turns back to me and holds out his hand.

"Okay, hand over your phone."

I grab my phone and hand it over with glee. Max taps in his info and sends himself a text message, so he has my number. He swipes open his phone and saves my number.

"I am never going to stop texting you, little brother."

"Good." He chuckles. "You're never getting rid of me again."

My stomach dips at the guilt I feel, and his expression changes when he realizes what he said.

"I didn't mean it like that," he says softly. "But will you do me a favor, sis?"

I nod emphatically. "Name it."

He takes my hand and squeezes it again.

"Next time you get any bright ideas about what's best for me…ask me what I want?"

I squeeze his giant hand with both of mine and smile up at him. "Deal."

Daisy comes over with a tray that looks way too heavy for her, but she handles it like a champ. She sets down two delicious-looking lattes, a plate loaded with assorted pastries, and two plates with silverware.

Max smiles his thanks, and she moves over to Zach's table with a cappuccino and a croissant. I look over at Zach. His eyes are already on me, and I can tell by his expression that he's happy for me. He winks, and I blow him a kiss before turning back to my brother.

"I don't know how I'm going to be able to walk out of here and go back to San Francisco," I say quietly. "There's so much I want to know. There's so much to say!"

He nods. "I know. We can do video chats, though. And I can find time to come up and see you after finals."

"And I will definitely come down here to see you."

He takes a drink of his latte and lets out a satisfied sigh, then raises his chin. "Try it!"

I pick up my cup and blow on it to cool it off a little, then gingerly take a sip. Oh, that is delicious. I taste chocolate and cinnamon mixed in with the rich coffee flavor. It's divine.

"I am definitely a fan of the Max Special." I sigh, taking another sip.

He laughs softly. "Zach might not thank me later. It has two extra espresso shots in it."

My eyebrows hit my hairline, and I burst out laughing.

"Oh well…it's too good to ignore. He can suffer the consequences if I can."

Max looks over my shoulder at Zach. "Something tells me he'll be okay with it."

"I can't wait for you to know him."

Max dips his head. "He seems nice."

I nod. "He is everything that is good and decent in this world."

"And he's clearly crazy about you."

I bow my head slightly. "Yes, there is that."

Max laughs and looks back at Zach again.

"Should we invite him to join us?"

"I would love that if you're okay with it," I answer.

Max nods, then stands. "I'll be right back."

He goes off in the direction of the counter, and I step over to Zach's table. He looks up expectantly.

"Would you like to join us?" I say, stepping close and stroking my fingers down his cheek. "Because we would love that."

Zach's expression is soft and seeking as his eyes scan my face.

"Are you sure?"

I nod and grab the plate with his croissant on it. "Yep. Let's go, dragon slayer."

I hear him laugh behind me as he picks up his coffee and follows. Max is already back at the table. He stands when we approach and shakes Zach's hand again, then tells us he's found someone to cover the rest of his shift so we can spend more time together.

He coaches his baseball kids at three o'clock, which is about the time we need to head back anyway. It definitely gives us more time to visit. While we drink our coffee, Zach entertains Max with the story of how we met, and we're all laughing by the time he's done with his very sensationalized version. I roll my eyes at him.

"Well, I'm glad you kept singing, sis," Max says. "I always loved your voice."

I nudge his arm. "And I always loved singing you to sleep."

Zach bobs his chin at Max. "What was your favorite thing for her to sing?"

"Brave." Max and I answer at the same time, grinning like idiots.

Zach is obviously surprised. "The Sara Bareilles song? Here I was thinking of songs like 'Twinkle Twinkle Little Star' and you're turning top 40 songs into lullabies."

Max laughs out loud. "She softened it up, gave it more of a gentle vibe, but she can really sing that song."

Zach laces our fingers together and rests them on my lap.

"He was getting bullied in school," I explain. "I was trying to help him be brave."

Max gives me a light shove.

"And it worked. Thanks, sis."

I sit back and take in the amazing young man my brother has become. I'm overwhelmed with gratitude, and still not quite sure I've connected with the fact that this has really happened. Max and I are reunited, and I will never lose him again. I actually have my brother back.

"So, have you two decided what's next?" Zach asks. "I'm sorry you don't have more time to catch up."

Max shakes his head and gently tugs on a bit of my hair.

"We have all the time in the world. The most important thing is we're back together and I don't have to wonder anymore."

I feel my face fall as soon as the words hit me. I did that to him. Max is instantly shaking my arm.

"Hey," he says gently. "Enough with the guilt. I was never mad, Marina. I just missed you. But even through all of that, I knew we'd find each other. If you didn't find me, I would definitely have found you. I've looked on social media a few times, but could never find you."

I nod and pull out my phone, tapping and swiping to bring up one of my social media accounts. I hold it up and show him the problem. He leans forward to see, then bursts into laughter.

"Yeah, it never occurred to me to look for Marinara Princess," he says, pulling out his own phone. "We are definitely siblings."

He holds his phone up and I can see his social media name. *Thanksamillion Maxamillion.* No wonder I couldn't find him.

Zach grins at us both. "Two peas in a pod, you two."

I tell Max the story of how we found him, that it never would have happened without Zach's help. Max thanks him, and Zach gives him his cell phone number just in case he ever needs anything. My heart squeezes at how much Zach wants to help the people I love.

We spend the rest of our time hearing about Max's baseball dreams, and it lightens my spirits like nothing else ever has. He plays first base and had a stellar record in high school, which led to him getting a full scholarship to college. He's a business major, even though his dad was hoping he might want to follow in his footsteps and be a doctor. He hopes to play in the major leagues and could have worked his way up from the minors, but he doesn't want to skip college. The kid has a good head on his shoulders for someone so young, and I mentally thank the Lewises for raising him to be a strong person. Our mom would be so proud of him.

My phone vibrates in my purse, and I suddenly remember the girls. I jump in my seat.

"Oh no! I forgot to send the girls an update!" I cry, pulling my phone out and looking at Max. "We need a selfie!"

He laughs, and we stand up together. He gets behind me and I snap a quick picture, then text it to our group chat.

"You better text that to me too," Max says as he pushes in his chair and looks at us with regret in his eyes. "I hate this, but we have to say goodbye for now. I have to be at the park in half an hour. I'm sorry."

Zach stands as well, and I wrap my arms around my brother. He lifts me up and spins me again, giving me the giggles. He sets me down again and ruffles my hair.

"I am so proud of you, Max," I say in a wobbly voice. "Mom would be proud too."

He gives me another hug. "She'd be proud of you, too, sis. And I'm so happy you found me. Thank you. From the bottom of my heart."

Max shakes Zach's hand and pulls him in for a hug, slapping him on the back.

"Thanks for giving my sister back to me, man."

Zach bows his head. "I was honored to help, Max. I'm so happy for you both."

Max walks us out to the parking lot, and we wave at Daisy as we walk out the front door. Plans are made. Regular video chats on Tuesday and Thursday nights, and one on Saturday mornings—plus all the texting. Now it's time to say goodbye, but I'm not sure I can. Max can see it on my face, and he puts his hands on my shoulders.

"It's just goodbye for now, sis," he says gently.

I nod, but I can't make myself move.

"I know, I just…I can't be the one to walk away from you. I don't want to walk away from you."

Max chokes up a little but nods in understanding. Zach pulls me into his side and kisses the top of my head. He and Max exchange a look.

"I'll see you Tuesday night on our first video chat, okay?" he says as he pulls his car keys out of his pocket.

I smile and nod. "It's a date, little brother."

He ruffles my hair again and gives me a quick hug before turning and walking to a blue pickup truck a few spaces away. He waves at us before he gets in, and we watch him drive away. Zach's arm around my shoulders tightens a little.

"You okay, Siren?"

I look up him with tear-filled eyes. His arms are instantly around me, and I'm pulled against the shelter of his body. I inhale his scent and wrap my arms around him, this man who has tunneled his way right into my heart. I feel his lips place a kiss on my temple.

"Shall we get you to the car?"

I nod, and we move down the sidewalk together towards the section of the parking lot where the car is parked. I can feel my emotions rising like the tide, filling me with gratitude for everything that's happened. The sidewalk ends in front of a crowded cafe, the patio brimming with diners enjoying the beautiful weather. Zach moves to step off the curb and I pull him back. He turns to face me with a quizzical look.

"You…" my lip trembles. "You are the sweetest, most amazing man I have ever known in my entire life."

His gaze flicks over to the crowded patio. "Let's get in the car, love."

I look at the patio and see several people staring, their eyes moving between Zach and me as they realize who we are. I shake my head at Zach.

"I don't care."

His eyebrows shoot up in surprise, and I laugh and throw my hands up.

"I literally don't care," I say joyfully. "I can't let one more minute go by without telling you how grateful I am for you. I feel so…so…*lucky*."

Emotion clogs my throat at the look on his face as he steps closer to me. He runs his fingers down my arm and takes my hand in his. He shakes his head.

"I'm the lucky one, love."

I step forward and wrap my arms around his neck, overjoyed at the delicious feeling of his arms wrapping around my waist. I lean into him and pull the baseball cap off his head, laughing at the shocked expression on his face. I can see cell phones out of my peripheral vision and I still don't care.

"No," I whisper for his ears only, running a hand through his hair. "It's me. And I'm sorry I fought it and made you really work for it because you're one of the best things that ever happened to me. And I'm grateful for you."

His eyes dart to my mouth just as I brush my lips against his. I nip at his bottom lip, then pull his mouth down to mine in a soft, slow, sweet kiss. He groans against my mouth as the kiss deepens, taking on a life of its own. I feel his hands dive into my hair as our mouths explore each other. I drink him in completely, from his beachy scent to the soft, firm lips I can never get enough of, to the strong arms holding me tightly. I'm here for it. All of it.

The sudden sound of people cheering finally pulls us apart and we both turn to see half the people on the patio giving us a standing ovation. Cell phones are out everywhere, and Zach looks at me with a worried expression. I beam up at him and kiss him playfully.

"I don't care, Zach," I declare loudly. "I'm done hiding. I've done so many brave things lately, I'm addicted."

He looks taken aback. "To bravery?"

"Yep! I'm doing all the brave things now. There's no stopping me."

I bow to the cheering diners and pull Zach towards the car as he busts out a laugh. We run to the car together, thanking Michelle as she holds the door open for us. The car pulls out of the parking lot as my phone vibrates again. I nestle into Zach's side and pull my phone out of my bag.

Max: Hey, sis...just making sure you got out of the parking lot okay. :-)

Marina: We're on our way to the airport now, bro. No words

for how happy I am!

Max: Me too. Best day EVER. Time to coach some littles. Talk soon!

I hold my phone up and show Zach our text exchange. He plants a sweet kiss on the top of my head.

"I'm so happy for you two I think I could probably fly the plane home myself," he jokes lightly.

I look up at him and run a finger across his gorgeous mouth.

"Look at us," I whisper sweetly. "Doing all the brave things."

He leans down for a kiss, then rubs our noses together.

"Yep. Look at us."

***

Zach

I'm in love with Marina. There's no denying it anymore, not that I would have really tried. I've always been able to be fairly honest about my emotions. Right now, the big two I'm feeling are love (the head over heels kind) and fear (the what will I do if she runs kind). Because I don't think she's quite there yet, and I don't want to frighten her or make her turn around and head the other way. It seems like she's done running, but something gives me pause. I'm not sure what.

I will myself not to focus on the clouds outside the window or the fact that we're thousands of feet in the air right now. I think back to Marina's revelation outside the cafe and hope with all my heart that it sticks. I've never cared what the media thinks or says, but I understand why she does. I hope she doesn't end up regretting that kiss on the sidewalk because I'm sure it's all over social media already. I haven't wanted to face the reality of checking to see how widespread it is.

I look down at the beautiful creature tucked into my side as she texts her friends, catching them up on the events of the day, and I wish I could crawl inside her head and have a look around. This is one of those times when being able to read minds would really pay off. Alas, my only super powers seem to be musically based. Well, I know one thing: I'm not going to tell her tonight. We've had enough raw emotion today.

Tomorrow is the benefit concert, which I'm really looking forward to. I love performing, but this is the first time Marina will see us on stage. I feel a ridiculous amount of pressure to impress her, when my head knows there's no such need. I really want her to enjoy it. And I know she doesn't want to perform with us on stage, but with her new self-professed addiction to bravery I'm thinking that might actually change.

I don't even want to think about Monday, when the guys and I have to leave town for various press engagements. I already miss her. Imagine that. I miss her, and yet she's right here with me. Will she feel the same? I mean, I'm pretty sure she'll miss me, but she'll be occupied with the final preparations for the big meeting she's managing. Will that be enough to distract her from missing me at all? And don't get me started when it comes to the kind of people she works for. It's a viper den, and I have very distinct feelings about leaving town while my girlfriend is navigating all of that by herself. I know she can do it, but I would much rather be here at home base to give her support at the end of the day.

I feel her stir and look down to find her looking up at me, those brilliant green eyes burrowing a path right to my soul. I lower my lips to touch hers, and she relaxes into the kiss with a soft sigh. I deepen it and she opens for me, letting me explore her with slow, sweet abandon. I get completely lost in her, reaching down to touch her face and bring her in even closer, hating every bit of space where we aren't touching. I need this woman like I need air.

I feel our speed slow way down and break off our kiss to find we're on the ground already. I completely missed our descent and the anxiety I always feel as the ground looms closer and closer out the window. Marina looks up at me with a smile that's as sweet as it is conniving. She knew exactly what she was doing. My Siren lured me again and I regret nothing. I gaze into those gorgeous green eyes and laugh.

"I really love flying."

Chapter 17

Zach

I miss my girl. And I'm nervous. A little. A lot, actually. All right, I'm a bit of a mess right now.

Marina's having brunch with the girls this morning, which is great because the inner circle needs a proper catch-up after the big reunion yesterday. They were all waiting in the lobby of the Fairmont when we got back from the airport, ready to wrap her in congratulatory hugs and carrying takeaway bags of Chinese food. What is it with these women and Chinese food, anyway?

As emotional as Marina's reunion with her brother was, I have to admit to getting a little teary-eyed when I saw Merry, Scarlet and Ashley waiting in the lobby, brimming with excitement for her. It means a lot to me that she has such a fierce circle of friends who support her, especially since I have to leave town and finish this tour before we can really decide how to manage our new relationship. Between my busy schedule and her entrance into law school, it'll be a challenge…but one I am fully ready to conquer.

I'm not sure how late they stayed up last night in Marina's suite. I kissed her goodnight in the lobby and left them to it. She texted me this morning to let me know of their brunch plans and then stopped by my suite on her way out because she didn't want to leave without kissing me good morning. Lord, help me. Actually, strike that. There is no helping me. I am 100% Team Mermaid. The fact that she made a special trip upstairs just to kiss me? I could die happy right now. While I still have too many reservations to relax entirely, I am starting to believe I've actually caught this mermaid. She's a little bit hooked.

I pad across the suite, swiping open my mobile and tapping out a quick text to the guys in our group chat. I feel a bit guilty that I haven't spent much time with them while we've been in San Francisco, but we're a tight bunch and I know they understand. In spite of the stories the media like to spin, I don't chase after everything in a skirt, and the guys know none of my past relationships hold a candle to what I've found with Marina. I've never experienced the instant click that happened between us on that bridge with anyone else.

Zach: Morning, gents! We're ready for tonight, yeah?

Rick: Duh.

Sam: What? What are we doing tonight? :-)

Jimmy: Absofreakinlootly, mermaid boy.

I laugh under my breath.

Zach: Got a text from the event manager last night confirming our call time is 7, but I'd like to be there by 5. I want to check out 'Kraze'. They have a great vibe and might be a good warm up band for the next tour.

Sam: Already thinking about the next tour? I thought maybe you'd be ready to buy a house, settle down, and make little mermaids with Marina by then.

Rick: Wow, Sammy. Wow.

Zach: I already own a house, Sam...and don't get creepy with the mermaid thing.

Sam: Whatev! I'm going for a run. See you at the stadium, Rebels!

Jimmy: Does Marina's blond friend like bass players?

Zach: Which blond friend? There are two. And no.

Jimmy: The gorgeous one

Rick: She's engaged

Zach: Alright then. I'll see you gents at the stadium at 5

Rick: It's really too bad Marina doesn't want to sing with us tonight. That would've been so cool

Zach: Don't count her out yet, bud. She's been on a mission to "do all the brave things" lately. She might still change her mind. I told her she could let me know

Rick: If she does, I'm making her an honorary Rebel

Zach: Stay away from my girl, Rick. I'll fight you

Rick: Bros before mermaids, buddy. You don't have to worry about me

Jimmy: ...

Zach: Alright then. See you gents tonight!

✳✳✳

Marina

"I am *not* getting this. It's too expensive!"

Ashley raises one perfectly manicured eyebrow at me and turns me around to face the mirror. I stare at my reflection. Merry and Scarlet pop up behind me, their faces absolutely shining with delight over the way this top looks on me. Okay, I'll admit I look great in this thing…but it's a hundred dollars. There is no way I'm spending that kind of money.

"It's perfect on you," Merry says emphatically. "You're getting it."

Scarlet nods. "Even I think it's perfect, and I'm the realist. It's the perfect top for a mermaid."

I look over my reflection. It's a simple halter top, accentuating my toned shoulders and exposing more of my back than I'm used to, but it's covered in iridescent disc sequins that give off the slightest shade of lavender and sparkle like crazy. It's beautiful, and if I wasn't facing impending financial doom, I would find a way to afford it. It's not happening today, though.

"It *is* perfect," I admit, much to their collective satisfaction. "But I can't afford it, and I'm not getting it. Final answer."

Merry blows out a frustrated sigh. Ashley nods in resignation, which is a relief because the girl loves to argue. Scarlet steps up next to me, turning around to look at the pants she's considering.

"Nope," Merry deadpans. "Your whole butt disappears in those."

Scarlet frowns. "Yeah, it's a little scary, isn't it? Let's go take this stuff off so we can find Merry's boots."

I nod and follow Scarlet to the dressing room we're sharing in the packed boutique. I carefully remove the gorgeous top and put it back on the hanger, then turn away to get dressed while Scarlet shimmies out of the butt flatteners. I turn around just in time to see her throw the sparkly halter over the door and into Ashley's waiting hand. I'd recognize that manicure anywhere.

"Hey!"

Scarlet puts a finger up and gives a look that instantly silences me. It's her *I'm not fooling around and do not even mess with me* look. We all know and fear it. I close my open mouth and await her next command. She dips her chin at me as she buttons her jeans.

"Okay, let's go," she says, holding the door open for me.

Scarlet and I walk out to find Ashley just leaving the register with a small bag in her hand. She gives me a self-satisfied smile as she hands the bag to me.

"We all pitched in," Scarlet explains. "It's a sweet little pressie because you've been doing a lot of the brave things lately…and we're proud of you."

I bite my lower lip and look at my three ride-or-dies with gratitude, throwing my arms open for a group hug. They all step in and we squeeze each other silly. Merry lets go first.

"Okay, time for boots!"

I thank them as we follow her out of the boutique to the shoe shop next door. She knows exactly what she wants because she's been passing these boots in the window for weeks and hasn't stopped drooling over them, so we sit on a bench outside while she gets them. I glance at my watch. Our impromptu shopping trip after brunch has ensured that I won't get to see Zach before he leaves for the stadium, so I'm extra glad I stopped by for a kiss this morning.

My stomach does a few little flips just thinking about that kiss. I loved his look of pure surprise when I knocked on his door this morning. He didn't need an invitation to pull me into his arms, and I sank against him as I pulled his mouth down to mine. His hair was still damp from the shower, and his skin smelled like the sandalwood soap he uses. By the time we came up for air, I was seriously questioning whether I wanted to go to brunch with the girls.

"Thinking about Zach again?" Ashley coos next to me.

I look over at her with a smirk. "That obvious?"

She nods. "You definitely get a look on your face."

I lean back on the bench and sigh happily. "My boyfriend is pretty dreamy."

Ash nods at the bag in my hand. "Tell me you're wearing that to the concert tonight."

I look in the bag, then back at Ashley. "You don't think it's too much?"

Her eyebrows shoot up. "For a concert? No. For *the* mermaid?

Also, no."

A group of women walk by on the sidewalk, and one of them suddenly stops and rushes over to us.

"Wow, she's right…you're the mermaid! Oh my gosh, I can't believe it!"

I look up at her like a deer caught in the headlights. Ashley whispers an apology next to me, but the woman isn't scaring me or anything. She's just excited. I give her a little wave.

"Hi there," I say, feeling a little lame.

"Can I get a selfie with you?" she gushes as her friends wait to see what happens.

I look over at Ash. Not for permission, but more to see what she thinks of the idea. She shrugs and nods like it's not a big deal.

"Sure," I say lightly, standing up.

Her friends come rushing over to us and the woman thrusts her cell phone at Ashley.

"Actually would you mind taking one of all of us?" she says as the group of women arrange themselves around me.

Ash takes the phone with a smile and frames the shot. "Say cheese!"

We all say cheese, the picture is snapped, and the woman and her friends seem way too excited about getting a picture with me. I nod and shake hands as they're offered, telling each of them it's nice to meet them.

"So, how's it going with Zach? Is it serious? I mean…that kiss looked pretty hot!"

I flick a nervous gaze to Ash, and she steps to my side in a heartbeat.

"I'm sorry, I can't comment on that."

She looks a little disappointed but doesn't push. "Well, I hope it works out. You could be a duchess, girl!"

She waves and walks away with her friends, and I move back to sit with Ashley. We both look dumbfounded at each other.

"I guess I never thought about that before," she says quietly. "You could end up being a duchess!"

I look at her as if she has a turnip growing out of her forehead.

"I can't be a duchess. You're crazy."

She tilts her head. "Hey, I'm just saying…if you and Zach work out, eventually, he's going to inherit his father's title. Didn't you say he would go back, eventually?"

I slowly turn to face Ashley. "Yeah, I did."

She nods. "So it's a possibility."

I don't respond. I don't say anything, but I feel a prickling feeling at the back of my neck.

You could be a duchess.

It's like those words just reached into my life and pulled Zach farther away. They wash over me again and again. I feel a nudge on my arm.

"Hey," Ashley says next to me. "Get that look off your face."

I blink. "What look?"

"That look you get when you think something is beyond your reach," she explains. "Like you're not good enough to get what you want."

I study her for a moment. "I have a look that says that?"

She smirks at me. "It's just a dumb comment. Don't let the whole duchess thing push you away from one of the best things that's ever happened to you."

She's right. I know she's right. I think about that kiss this morning. And the fact that Zach helped me find Max. And when he took care of me after my identity was revealed. How he makes me feel safe, like nothing bad could ever happen when he's near. I think about the look in his eyes when he's about to kiss me, or his beautiful laugh when I say something ridiculous. If he was looking for a duchess, he wouldn't be hanging out with a fake mermaid who shops at thrift stores and loves red licorice. That's all I need to think about right now. I am his mermaid, and he is my dragon slayer.

"So, what should I wear this top with tonight?" I ask, nudging her shoulder. "I'm thinking my white jeans and some strappy sandals?

Ash gives me a single nod. "Perfect."

***

"I'm not sure how I feel about this, Dave," I joke lightly. "I'm used to *you* driving."

Dave looks back at me from the front passenger seat with a wry grin.

"Sorry, Miss MacArthur. I just do what Mr. Adams tells me to do."

I smile back at him and turn my attention to Merry, who's fidgeting in the seat next to me as she adjusts her new boots.

"Blisters imminent," Scarlet declares from her seat across from us in the limousine.

Yeah, *limousine*. Apparently, it's just one of the surprises Zach is planning for tonight. I knew Dave would be driving us, but I didn't expect him to roll up in a limousine with a second bodyguard driving it. Zach ordered Dave to accompany us into the stadium and watch over us tonight, which is something I didn't think of at all. With my identity revealed, it might get a little crazy if I'm spotted in the crowd. I think it's a safe bet to assume that's going to happen at some point tonight.

Ash nudges me with her foot. "You look gorgeous. How do you feel?"

I wiggle in my seat. "Excited! I can't wait to see Zach in his element."

Merry breaks away from watching the many fans weaving their way through the packed parking lot to the stadium.

"This is one of the things I love about The Royal Rebels," Merry shares. "They're never too big to give back to the communities they play in. This foundation is going to raise so much more money for mental health outreach tonight because the Rebels are here. They didn't have to roll into town early to do this benefit. They could have said they're on tour and too busy. But they never do. They always give back."

I feel more than a little pride swell in my heart for Zach and the guys. Granted, I don't have any other celebrities to compare them to, but they're all genuinely nice people. And good humans. And one of them is an insanely good kisser.

The limo slowly makes its way up the VIP lane, passing excited concert goers as they try to peek in the windows and see who's inside.

"They'd be so bitterly disappointed to know it's just four regular girls here to have fun," I joke as we watch them from behind the safety of the darkened glass.

"And see your insanely hot boyfriend perform in front of fifty thousand people," Scarlet murmurs with a wicked grin.

I sit back against the seat and let out a contented sigh. Yep. That's my boyfriend. As if he's reading my mind, my phone vibrates against my hip, and I pull it out of my jeans pocket to find a text from Zach.

Zach: Hey, beautiful. I can't wait to see you tonight. I'll bet you look gorgeous.

I hold my phone up to show Ashley, and she winks at me. I told Zach the girls pitched in and bought me something to wear tonight, but since we missed seeing each other this afternoon, he has no idea what. Even in the dark confines of the limo, this top sparkles like crazy. Paired with my favorite white jeans that hug me in all the right places and a pair of Ashley's strappy heels, this outfit makes me feel pretty sexy. I have no idea where the seats he has waiting for us are or if he'll be able to find me in this huge crowd, but when he does see me, he's going to love it. I am so getting kissed into oblivion later and I am here for it.

Marina: Hey, handsome. I can't either. I'm so excited to see

you perform on stage!

Zach is typing...

"So…what's up with Greg, Ash?" Scarlet asks boldly.

Merry and I exchange looks.

Ash shakes her head in disappointment. "He said he didn't have time to come with us. Too much going on at work."

"I'm sorry," I tell her with a nudge on her shoulder. "I know you're disappointed."

She shrugs it off, but I know he's hurt her feelings.

"His loss," is all she says.

I agree and look back at my phone.

Zach is typing...

Zach: You know…if you're feeling like doing all the brave things tonight, you can still get up on stage with us.

Marina: I'm not sure I'm *that* brave, but I'll think about it.

Zach: Just give me a sign if you change your mind, love. But if you don't, I'm still #TeamMermaid all the way.

Marina: A sign? Will you be able to see me?

Zach: Oh, don't worry. I'll be able to see you. Enjoy the concert, Siren. Xoxo

I slip my phone back into my jeans pocket just as the limo pulls up to the VIP entrance. Because this is a charity event, there's a small red carpet area with a step and repeat backdrop for celebrities to walk and pose for pictures. Paparazzi line the ropes, and it looks like a hundred cameras are aimed at the celebrities walking through it. Flashes erupt periodically, lighting up the night all around us.

Dave gets out, opens the door, and steps back. We exit the limo, and I step nearer to the shelter of Dave's massive form, pointing to the red carpet.

"We don't have to walk through that, do we?" I rasp, my mouth and throat suddenly dry.

"No, ma'am," he says firmly, gesturing for me to follow him.

I keep my face turned away from the press area as Dave ushers us around the back and through the VIP entrance, showing the stadium employee a QR code on his phone. They scan it, and we're admitted. An employee with the letters VIP on the back of his jacket motions for us to follow him. Subtle. He takes us to a kiosk where we're given VIP event bracelets that light up with the music. There's a QR code for the foundation on each one, so we can scan it and donate money during the concert.

Clever!

Dave motions for us to follow him. I look behind me to make sure the girls are there. We're guided down an escalator from the entrance level to the stadium floor, which is teeming with people. I reach back for Merry's hand, and she grabs Scarlet, who grabs Ash.

Ahead of us, the stage looms just as large as I remember from my dinner date with Zach. I feel the corners of my mouth tip up just a little as the memory of that special night hits me. He went through such trouble to create a unique and romantic setting. His caring nature is one of the most irresistible things about him. I can safely say that, in a stadium that will seat fifty thousand people tonight, I am the one and only person here who's had a romantic dinner with Zach Adams on that stage. It feels special in a way I never imagined.

Zach explained earlier that there were three bands designated as opening acts for tonight's concert, and I can see the last band is clearing the stage now. The stadium lights lighten just a little to allow people to move around, and a countdown clock is projected on a screen on stage to show everyone how much time is left until the main event begins. Thirty minutes to go. As we weave our way through the stadium, I try to stay hidden behind Dave, but I occasionally hear the word "mermaid" from people we pass.

"Did you see that woman? I think that was the mermaid!"

"Hey, that's her! The mermaid!"

"Whoa! She's so pretty! She looks like a real-life mermaid…"

I don't look up when I hear the chatter, but I mentally send all the good vibes in the universe to the lady who thought I looked pretty. You too, girl. You too.

There are two bands and two solo artists that will all perform short sets before The Royal Rebels take the stage for the finale. Zach and the guys are performing five songs tonight, the last being his beautiful, scorching version of "Sound of Silence".

I see a few cell phones aimed at me out of my peripheral vision, but I don't look up. I wonder if there will ever come a time when I don't notice them. I sure hope so. Dave walks us through a barricade that a stadium employee opens for us, and I look back at the girls in shock. We're not just close. We're standing at the edge of the stage close. There are several square sections of the floor divided up for VIP ticket holders, and we're in an area just to the left of center stage. When Zach is on stage, I will literally be able to reach out and grab his foot. Well, I'm sure the black-clad security guards standing between us and the stage would probably stop me, but that's how close we are. Ashley squeals with excitement.

"This is amazing!" Merry cries out.

I don't disagree. This is going to be such a fun night, made even more fun by the tuxedo-clad waiter who appears in front of us. I look around and see waiters attending to all the VIP sections on the floor. I wonder how much these people paid for these tickets. Actually, I'm not sure I want to know.

"Good evening, ladies," he says with a polite nod. "Can I get you anything to eat or drink before the show begins?"

The girls rattle off their orders like we do this every night and this is no big deal. I just ask for a bottle of water. I didn't have much to eat for dinner, and I'm too much of a lightweight to drink on a fairly empty stomach. I want to enjoy the concert, not sleep through it.

The waiter heads off to retrieve our drinks while the girls and I busy ourselves with checking out who's sitting in the other sections. It's a who's who of celebrities out there, which doesn't surprise me because this is for a great cause. There are sports stars, award-winning actors, and politicians in the crowd tonight.

And they're all here to see my boyfriend.

Before long, the stadium lights dim, and the crowd goes wild. A screen behind the stage is illuminated with a ticker showing how much money has been raised for tonight's mental health foundation fundraiser. It's over fifty million dollars so far, which is a compilation of ticket and merchandise sales and extra donations from the crowd, including the super wealthy VIP section.

The first band, an indie folk group, takes the stage, and cell phones light up everywhere, looking like fairy lights in the dark. The main attractions are well-known artists, and the girls and I know all their hits. We dance and sing to the music, along with the rest of the crowd, as each artist takes the stage and gives a message of support about the importance of mental health for everyone. The ticker dials up as more money is donated.

The bands and artists performing are making it really special by performing songs that are either not released yet or special to them in some way. Through it all, we have a blast. We even take a few group selfies when the artists are on stage so we can look back and remember this amazingly fun night.

My pulse picks up in a big way as the last act before The Royal Rebels closes out their final song. It's one of my favorites, and I sing along enthusiastically, occasionally exchanging looks with my friends. We haven't had fun like this in a long time, and it just feels so good to cut loose and enjoy the music. The band takes their bows and exits, with their lead singer flamboyantly announcing The Royal Rebels as

Zach and the guys take the stage. He hands Zach the mic and gives him a big bro hug before walking off. The girls and I go absolutely wild, cheering for The Royal Rebels.

Deafening cheers shoot up from the crowd as Zach walks up to the front of center stage, holding his hands up and waving at the fans. He keeps his hands waving but looks down until he finds me…and he gives me the sexiest grin I've ever seen in my life. His eyes drift over my body and he takes in my outfit and closes his eyes for a moment, then he clutches his heart and winks at me. If it wasn't for the security guards lining the stage, I would climb him like a tree right now. Instead, I just cheer at the top of my lungs as I beam proudly, hoping my pounding heart survives watching him perform up there. He is absolutely beautiful, dressed in black jeans and boots and a t-shirt that looks like it was custom made for him. It hugs his shoulders and pectorals in a way that should be illegal. The Royal Rebels logo is emblazoned on the front. He turns and gestures towards Rick, Sam, and Jimmy, and they all wave. Then he pulls the mic up to his mouth.

"Hello, San Francisco, we've missed you!"

The crowd goes absolutely bonkers again, and the guys start playing one of their biggest hits. Everyone is instantly on their feet, dancing and singing along. No one is prouder at this moment than I am, watching Zach thrill and entertain this massive audience. The joy on his face is a thing to behold.

Song after song, the crowd never sits down. The entire stadium buzzes with a heady vibe as Zach and the guys play their hearts out. Their third song is a popular ballad of theirs, and Zach sits at the piano to perform it. Once again, he gives off majorly sexy vibes as I watch his fingers move elegantly across the keys, his forearms flexing with the movement. Those are the arms that make me feel safe, special, and cherished. My heart is so full right now. Occasionally, Zach looks down at me from the stage and winks or blows little kisses at me. I hope he knows I plan to collect all those kisses at the end of the night.

I see a few cell phones aimed in my direction as the night goes on, and I just ignore them. There is nothing that can take away my fun tonight. I am one hundred percent all about the brave things, especially as I see my amazing man up there, bringing joy to so many with his beautiful voice. The fourth song ends, and I can't believe their part of the show is almost over.

"The Sound of Silence" is next, and then they're done, except for an encore that includes any of the acts that want to come back on stage for it.

The crowd cheers, and Zach thanks them again for their support of the foundation. The fundraising ticker on stage occasionally clicks up as people watching on a special streaming channel continue to donate as well. It pauses at fifty-three million dollars.

"You guys have been so great tonight," Zach says into the mic as he looks out into the crowd. "Our last song is a special one. You've heard it before, but this is our take on it...and we hope you love it."

More cheers erupt. Zach looks down at me for a moment, and I have no idea what comes over me, but I nod at him. He's so surprised he does a double take, raising his eyebrows at me. Out of my peripheral vision, I see the girls all turn to stare at me. I nod at Zach again, a secret glint in my eyes meant only for him.

"Yes, girl!" Merry yells at the top of her lungs as Ash and Scarlet squeal uncontrollably.

Zach turns back to look at the ticker, and then he turns to me and winks, making me wonder what on earth he's about to do. He looks out at the crowd.

"But before that, I have to say...I really hate odd numbers," he says with a wicked grin. "I think we can do better than fifty-three point five million, don't you?"

The crowd cheers, and the ticker moves up another fifty thousand dollars. I shouldn't be shocked at how much money is pouring in, but I am. There are millions of people watching online, and we all have QR codes on our bracelets in the audience so we can donate extra funds. Zach turns a determined gaze on the crowd and pulls the mic back up again.

"I don't know if you've seen the news lately," he begins. "But I recently caught a mermaid."

The roar that comes up from the stadium literally vibrates my bones. Goosebumps erupt all over me as I hear the crowd screaming, and the concertgoers nearest us have all trained their cell phones on me now. My eyes are as big as saucers as I laugh with the girls over the crowd's reaction.

"If you can get that number to fifty-*four* million, I'll get her up here to sing with me."

I clap my hand over my open mouth as the crowd cheers and the ticker starts to move. It goes up fifty thousand more, then one hundred fifty thousand. It's moving, but Zach's not satisfied. He moves up to the edge of the stage and starts pointing at celebrities.

"Jack Boyer, owner of the Dallas Longhorns football team," he says with a gravelly laugh that curls my toes.

We all look over to see Jack Boyer grinning and laughing as he waves at Zach. Zach wiggles his eyebrows at him.

"Have you ever seen a mermaid, Jack?"

Ashley turns to me with wide eyes and shakes her head. "This is incredible!"

I stand with my friends as we watch Zach work the crowd. Jack Boyer makes a show of pulling out his cell phone and scanning the QR code on his bracelet. The ticker goes up one hundred thousand dollars, and the crowd is screaming again. Zach bows his head in thanks and moves down closer to us, pointing at an A-list actress and her director husband.

"Have you two ever made a movie about a mermaid? I've got one right here."

They laugh, and she pulls her phone out, making a show of it to the audience. They eat it up, cheering her on, and the ticker goes up another hundred thousand dollars. We're getting close to the fifty-four million mark. I feel a hand on my elbow, and it's Dave, ready to escort me over to a small set of stairs that lead up to the stage. The security guards at the foot of the stage motion for me to come through the barrier they're opening. I look back at the girls, and Ashley runs over to hug me.

"I am so proud of you!" she yells over the noise of the crowd. Merry and Scarlet excitedly throw me a thumbs up and I blow them a kiss. I turn back to the secure area and wait for Zach at the base of the stairs, hoping I don't trip in these high heels and fall over.

Don't even think like that, Marina.

Zach turns and looks at the ticker.

"Fifty-three-point-nine million," he growls into the mic. "C'mon, San Francisco, make me proud."

The ticker starts moving again as people all over the stadium pull out their phones and scan the QR code. The crowd begins chanting, but I can't quite tell what they're saying at first. Then it hits me. They're chanting "mermaid" over and over.

If I die right now, it's going to be very anti-climactic for everyone, but it's possible with how fast my heart is pounding. The ticker rolls to fifty-four million dollars and keeps going. Zach throws his hands up in the air and waves at the crowd, jumping around the stage with joy, and I know in my heart he's completely undone me. I will never be the same after this. Ever. I am one hundred percent falling in love with a dragon-slaying rock star.

"All right, San Francisco," Zach says into the mic as he walks to the side of the stage where I'm waiting for him. "I was going to sing this last one myself, but you've won yourselves a mermaid."

The crowd cheers again, and he stops by the side of the stage, holding a hand out for me. Our eyes meet, and he raises his eyebrows just slightly to ask if I'm okay. I laugh nervously and give him a quick nod as I take his hand and let him help me up the steps and onto the stage. I look back at the Rebels, who are all beaming ear to ear and pumping their fists in the air. I wave at them as Zach laces our fingers together and walks me to center stage while fifty thousand people go absolutely wild.

Chapter 18

Marina

Don't look at the crowd.

Don't look, don't look, don't look.

I looked.

There are stage lights in my face, making it hard to see the darkened stadium, but I can see enough. The effect of those little lights on everyone's event bracelets is beautiful. It looks like fireflies have taken over the whole stadium. I can clearly see the VIP seating area and the seats just beyond them, thanks to the stage lights. So many cell phones are aimed at us, and it makes me giggle with nervous energy at how ridiculous this mania is over the story of the mermaid and the rock star. We're just two people, yet so many people are invested in our story.

Zach looks out at the crowd and grins devilishly.

"I need a minute," he growls, then turns the mic off.

He steps into my space and looks down into my eyes, then moves his lips to my ear.

"Look at you, Siren," he says. "Doing all the brave things."

259

I squeeze his hand and nod, incapable of words at the moment. The energy of the crowd is intoxicating and intimidating all at the same time, and I feel a little tremble move through my body.

"Just close your eyes and sing," he coaches me. "Or look at me. But forget about them. We're all that matters."

I smirk up at him. "Forget about fifty thousand of our closest friends?"

"Just focus on this, not them. I know you can do it."

He squeezes my hand, and I squeeze back. I'm as ready as I'll ever be. It's time to do the brave things. Zach turns the mic back on.

"All right, my friends, Marina's a little nervous," he says to the crowd. "I'm sure you can understand, and I know you'll be kind as we sing this last song for you."

Applause erupts, but the screaming and cheering is subsiding. The audience calms, and I look out to see people smiling and nodding at me as if to encourage me. And it works because I definitely feel a little less nervous than when I first walked on the stage.

Zach puts the mic on the stand and adjusts the height so it's right between us, but we can see each other's eyes. He looks back at Rick, who's moved to the piano.

"We must take mental health seriously," he says to the crowd. "Depression lies to you. If you or someone you love start having feelings of helplessness…it's important to speak up. If they start to isolate…check on them, okay? If you start to isolate, find a friend. Or a stranger. But talk. We've made a huge step towards providing mental health treatments for so many tonight. Communication is important, and silence can be deadly. With that, here's our take on 'The Sound of Silence.'"

Rick begins to play the simple background on piano, and Zach and I lace our fingers together on either side of the mic stand. I look up into his eyes, and my heart begins pounding again for an entirely different reason. Because I'm sure I see love in there, and the way he's looking at me makes me want to kiss him until two weeks from Sunday. I squeeze his hands and close my eyes, willing my crazy pulse to calm just a little.

Zach begins singing the first verse. His voice is low, soft, and husky. It moves around us like a living thing, cocooning us together and helping me to focus on us instead of the throng watching just outside the stage lights. Soon, I merge my voice with Zach's, and we're making magic, just like that night in the recording studio. I don't think about anything but *us* as we sing, drawing strength from our joined hands and intertwined voices.

Like every time before, I match the power of his voice with my own. There's a palpable energy in the stadium and an eerie silence in the audience as if they're all entranced by our haunting version of the song. As we bring it to a close, I open my eyes to find Zach looking down at me. His eyes are filled with raw emotion, and I can't help but reach up and trace the side of his face with my fingers. The audience erupts in applause as Zach and I step away from the mic to take a bow.

We keep taking bows for what feels like an eternity because the audience will not quiet. They're cheering and stomping their feet, and they're chanting "mermaid" again, so Zach and I just keep taking bows. We move around the stage, so we bow for each section, and I'm just taking my lead from him. Finally, they quiet when he holds a hand up in the air.

"I'd love to ask all the artists who performed tonight to please join us on stage for one final song. Thank you so much, San Francisco. We'll never forget you!"

Various artists from tonight's concert enter the stage from the wings on either side as Zach pulls me close to him and moves his mouth next to my ear.

"You'll stay? Sing this one with us?"

I nod as the band starts up the introduction to "Joy to the World" and Zach belts out the opening lyric. The stage instantly turns into one gigantic party, and there are artists from many different genres of music, all singing and dancing together. At some point, Zach and I let go of each other, and he ends up singing with a popular boy band while I dance with the tenor from The Five Wingmen. I look down to the VIP section and see my friends dancing and singing along, blowing me kisses, and being completely ridiculous.

When the song is over, all the artists wave and walk off the stage. I turn to go back down the stairs to the girls, but Zach grabs my hand to stop me.

"Stay?" he asks. "Stay with me, Siren. I'll get you back to the girls."

I nod, and he leans over to give Dave instructions. He'll bring the girls backstage. I let Zach lead me off stage and into the wings, where we descend the stairs and walk back through the tunnel under the stadium.

Linen-covered tables line the large tunnel, covered in an array of food for the artists. Several bar stations are dotted around the area, serving drinks. Only artists and special VIP pass holders are allowed in this area, so it's a who's who of celebrities.

Many of tonight's artists wind their way toward us to tell us how much they loved our performance. I'm so flattered by all of their praise that I'm not sure my head will fit through the door when I get back home. One thing's for sure, I will never, ever forget this night as long as I live.

A pair of hands close around my shoulders from behind, and I'm turned around to find Ashley pulling me into a hug while Merry and Scarlet pile on the sides. They're all literally squealing. We come up for air just in time for me to see Zach getting pulled away by an A-list actor, so I turn back to my friends.

"I am so freaking proud of you!" Merry sighs, giving me another hug. "That was the best thing I've ever seen in my life. I feel like I could climb a mountain or something after that!"

I can't keep the stupid grin off my face.

"It was scary at first, but it felt good to conquer that fear," I admit. "Really good."

Scarlet flicks one of the disc sequins on my top.

"And you looked perfect up there. Wait till you see the replay. You're gonna love it!"

My face falls when I think of seeing myself on camera. I don't think I want to see it. What if I don't like it? What if I hate the way I looked up here…or I sound off-key? Yep, not sure I'll be watching any coverage of this.

We end up staying at the after-party for another hour, and I'm not sure I'll ever get the girls to calm down. We meet movie stars and award-winning recording artists. We take a selfie with our favorite boy band. I'm a little miffed Justin Bieber was nowhere to be found, but apparently, he's on tour. So many people want selfies with me and Zach. We say goodnight to the girls at the stadium since Zach and I are going to the same place and Dave has to get everyone else home. It was an incredible night, but now I'm happy to be in the car with Zach on the way back to the hotel.

I snuggle closer to Zach, delighting in the feel of his arm around my shoulders as he murmurs something unintelligible against my hair. We're both exhausted after all the excitement of the evening. He is more than I am since performances take a lot out of him.

"What did you say?" I whisper into the silence of the car.

"I don't want to go to L.A. tomorrow," he grumbles adorably.

I slide my arm over his middle, stealing a feel of his abs on the way. The ripple I feel under my fingertips sends tingles snapping up my arm like little electric sparks. I'm almost asleep when the car pulls to a stop in front of the hotel. Zach groans as he steps out, pulling me with him. Arm in arm, we walk into the hotel together and take the elevator to my floor. I feel my spirit getting heavier and heavier the closer we get to my door. The closer we get to saying goodbye for several days.

Zach pulls me in for a final hug, and I feel like I might cry. I bury my face in his neck. He lets out a low growl.

"Siren…" he purrs into my ear.

"Mmm?"

"Can we just stay together tonight? Just to sleep."

I pull away from him enough to look up at his face. His eyes are tired and pleading. He reaches up to smooth a strand of hair from my face.

"I promise to be on my best behavior," he says softly. "I just…I have to leave in the morning, and I'm not ready to let you go. I don't want to let you go."

I'm already not sure I can fall any faster for this man, but I can't think about that right now. Realizing that I'm rapidly falling in love with him has me feeling a little scared, and I don't want to ruin it by thinking too much about it. I stand on my toes and place a soft kiss on the corner of his lips.

"I'm not ready for more than that," I whisper. "Is that okay?"

I lean into his hand as he cups my face.

"It's more than okay, beautiful," he says gently. "I just want you in my arms as long as possible."

I rub our noses together. "Then let's have a sleepover."

He lets out a husky laugh as I open the door with my key. We agree to sleep in my suite, but he goes upstairs to grab some clothes for tomorrow and take a shower. I put my phone on the charger and head into the bathroom to wash my face and change for bed. Usually, I sleep in a tank and panties, but I'm not about to do that tonight.

Promises aside, I don't think I could be on *my* best behavior if I did that. I opt for a tank and a pair of pajama pants with mermaids all over them that Merry bought me as a joke.

I hear Zach softly knocking as I'm running a brush through my hair. I pad across the suite and open the door to find him standing there with rolled-up clothes in his hand and an exhausted expression. Without a word, I take him by the hand and lead him into the bedroom.

"Do you care which side you're on?" I ask as we pass through the doorway, but he's already on his way to the bathroom to change.

"No, baby," he says hoarsely, yawning as he reaches behind his head to pull his t-shirt off.

My gut goes on an epic rollercoaster ride as I get a glimpse of his muscled back just before the door snicks shut. Be still my heart and…other things. Is the air in this room actually electric? Feels like it is.

Oof.

I climb under the covers just as he comes out of the bathroom in a thin pair of sweats and no shirt.

Hello, Mr. Six Pack.

At least, I think there are six. I'm trying and failing not to stare. Maybe I should count them. How on earth am I going to sleep next to this beautiful man?

"Nice pants, by the way," he growls with an adorable grin as he slips under the covers, grabs me around the waist, and pulls me over to him.

I settle in against his chest and take a deep breath, his wonderful beachy scent filling my senses as he wraps his arms around me.

"I thought you were too tired to notice."

He growls again, which is the sexiest thing I've ever heard, and plants a kiss on the side of my head.

"I'm never too tired to notice you, Siren."

Be. Still. My. Freaking. Heart.

"I knew we'd fit perfectly together," he murmurs, stroking my back gently.

Exhaustion claims him quickly, and I lay awake in his arms for a while, thinking about the tumultuous journey it's taken to get here. I still can't see a solid future for us. It's still so foggy. But I know what I feel in my heart, and that has to be good enough for now. Everything else can wait, so I nestle against the hard wall of Zach's warm body, safe in his arms, and sigh heavily. That's the last thing I remember before sleep claims me too.

***

Zach

I rest my forehead against the window and watch California go by as the bus makes its way south, farther from Marina. Jimmy and Sam are playing cards, and Rick is messing with a song that's been in his head, leaving me on my own devices, which is probably not the best idea right now. Marina got a little teary this morning when we finally said goodbye, and although it's a great improvement compared to her original desire to run from me, I hated leaving her like that. Especially when she's heading back into the viper den where she works during a week that's going to be stressful.

Thursday can't get here fast enough. That's when we'll be rolling the bus back into San Francisco after all the events in southern California. I did think about flying us all down there, but I truly believe the only way I could actually handle it would be if Marina was with me, and that's just not possible. I take another sip of my tea, not really tasting it. I hate the sense of foreboding I'm feeling right now.

Rick plops down in the seat across from me and throws a wadded-up napkin at me. I easily bat it back to him and give him a curious look.

"I can hear you thinking all the way across the bus, man," he explains. "What's up?

I consider my answer for a moment. Anything that comes to mind sounds crazy.

"For what it's worth, she's pretty nuts about you."

I cock my head to the side. "Why do you say that?"

Rick bobs his head, pulling his phone out of his pocket and showing me his screen.

"She texted me this morning to make sure I know to watch over you. She's yours, buddy. You got her."

I blink back my surprise, not even looking at the screen. "What? She didn't. And why are you texting her?"

He rolls his eyes at me. "Calm down, Duke. She asked me for my number at the after-party. She thought I might be able to help her friend Ashley with some kind of music thing for her third graders."

A slow grin creeps up my face. I wonder if my girl has noticed that Rick can't keep his eyes off Ashley whenever she's near. I certainly have. Although she's engaged, apparently, so maybe there really is a school thing she needs help with. Regardless, the fact that she wants Rick to watch over me is ten thousand kinds of adorable. I meet Rick's assessing gaze.

"She's the one."

He smirks. "Duh. Anyone can see that."

I take another sip of my tea, cursing this giant mug and making a mental note to buy a proper cup and saucer for the bus. I don't care how much the guys tease me about it.

"So she's not freaking out about the media stuff anymore?"

I turn back to Rick. "She says she's not, but I'm not sure how solid she is."

Rick nods. There's something suspicious about his silence.

"Why?"

A muscle in his jaw ticks, and he looks away for a minute. Bad news, then. He's a pretty straightforward guy, so there's something he doesn't want to say.

"They're calling her 'The Million Dollar Mermaid' now."

I sit up straight. "What?"

He nods again. "Last night was awesome. What you did was genius, and we raised so much more money. Most of the stories are the typical fluff, but some of the snarkier suspects have come out to play now."

I pull my phone out of my pocket and start scrolling. It's everywhere. He's right, though, the stories I find are positive. They're focusing on the romantic aspect of how we met and speculating on the stage of our relationship. I can't fault them for that. Neither of us tried to hide our feelings on that stage, and after all the footage of our kiss outside the Bean & Biscuit aired it's pretty obvious that there's something going on.

"Which usual suspects?" I ask, not taking my eyes off my screen.

"Gossip Tonight on G-Net."

My eyes go wide at the mention of the most notorious celebrity gossip show on the worst network on TV. "Bloody…"

"They discussed the story on the show," Rick explains. "Most of them loved the romantic aspects of the story. Much of it was focused on the angle of you shaking down celebrities to impress your new girlfriend."

I laugh out loud, relief flooding over me.

"I guess I did that, didn't I?" I sigh happily. "Let them come for me. I don't care about that."

Rick spends too much time trying not to pay attention to my reaction. I know there's more.

"What else?"

There goes that muscle in his jaw again.

"They had a healthy debate on the whole duchess angle."

I close my eyes against the wave of dread that hits me like a brick wall. That's not good. Not good at all. I'm not ready to have that conversation with Marina yet. She really *will* freak out if she thinks she'll ever be expected to fill the duties of a royal. It doesn't work that way. Not for our family. We're not closely related to the royal family, and my parents are not what anyone would call "working royals". We're invited to weddings and funerals, but that's really it. There's nothing for Marina to worry about. Eventually, we will have a conversation about it - but I don't want to have it now at the beginning of our relationship. She'll slap those track shoes on so fast I won't see her run…she'll just be gone.

I turn and look out the window, wishing we were going in the opposite direction and Marina and I could go back to hiding out in her suite, away from the rest of the world.

***

Marina

I've never been so grateful to see Dave in my whole life. I give him a feeble wave as I crawl into the waiting SUV, and he closes the door behind me.

What. A. Day.

The Montclair meeting is in four days, and everyone in the office is acting like we just found out about it today. No one is ready but me, I've completed all but one task: assemble the portfolios for the meeting. Those include the agenda, the proposal, and anything else Ms. Taft decides to throw in there. The problem? I can't put the portfolios together until everyone else has their piece of it done.

It was nothing but fire drills today, with nearly every department head under Ms. Taft running to me for help with this or that. I didn't even get a chance to get to anything on my plate except the bare essentials. And I was ten minutes late because I couldn't pull myself away from Zach this morning. An understandable problem to have, not one that's defensible to the Evil Queen. I feel dangerously close to dropping the ball, and I never *ever* drop the ball.

At least I get to video chat with Zach later. We have a date at six tonight, so I plan to get home and take a nice hot bath in that gorgeous tub, then tuck myself in early and see my man. Wait, did I just call the Fairmont *home?* Calm down, Marina. Don't get too big for your britches, girl.

I enter my suite and put my bags down, then pick up the phone and order a burger from room service for dinner. I don't feel like going anywhere to get food. I miss having a kitchen. Actually, the level of service here is so outlandish I'll bet they'd build me a kitchen if I called downstairs.

Jeeves! Build me a kitchen! I want to make my own dinner!

I plug my phone into the charger, happy to leave all screens behind for the night. Well, until my video chat with the hottest Brit ever. Tomorrow will likely be another crazy, stressful day at work. Made even more so by the fact that Ethan Montclair is now stopping by every day and always tries to put his hands on me. Just a little while longer, and I can collect my bonus and either get fired or leave on my own. Either way, I only have to put up with it for another month or so. Just let me get through this meeting and then give me time to find another job.

Since it'll take an hour to get my overpriced burger, I fill the tub and take an absolutely fabulous hot bath. I sink into the steaming water and burrow down to completely submerge my shoulders, then stick my chin in for good measure. While it does feel good on my tired bones, it does nothing to lighten my mood. After about thirty minutes, I get out, towel off, and just put my hair up in a loose bun when room service arrives. At least someone has perfect timing today, thank you.

The porter sets it all up in the dining room and leaves me to it, so I eat my dinner in peace and quiet. I don't feel like watching TV, plus I'm trying to avoid seeing myself on the news. I know I'm a media sensation again because I received several compliments on my concert performance at work today. It happened the first time in front of Ms. Taft, and I thought she was going to explode. She kept it together because Ethan Montclair complimented me. I'll bet that really killed her.

I finish my dinner just a little before six, so I stack my dishes together and head to the bedroom to grab my phone. I flop onto the bed, swipe the screen, and see a missed video call from Zach. Early! Squeal!! I dial him back and he answers on the first ring.

"Hi!" I cry out with a huge grin.

His smile is electric and gorgeous as he waves at me.

"Siren, I miss you so much."

I smirk. "Same to you."

"How was your day?"

I roll my eyes. "Ugh. Don't ask. It was awful. No one is ready!"

His eyes widen. "How is that possible?"

I shake my head in frustration. "No idea, but they're not. So I've been herding cats all day and trying to do my own work in the process. The whole week is going to be like this because I'm going to have to chase everyone down to make sure they're making their deadlines. I've had to reject so much work already because the teams left out crucial information."

A muscle ticks in his jaw, and I can tell he's frustrated for me. "I'm sorry, love."

I shake my head. "I don't want to talk about work. How was *your* day?"

"Not awesome because I'm without a certain mermaid," he grumbles. So sexy. "We taped an interview for 'Thursday Night with Jimmie Kaylon'. It's always fun to see him. We start early tomorrow, and I'll likely be running pretty ragged. The guys want to do what we call a Random Rebel Run, so we have to find a way to squeeze that in as well."

I laugh softly. "What on earth is that?"

"Basically, we look for events or places to crash…and we either play a couple acoustic songs or sign autographs for fans. We usually just prowl social media to find something we want to do, and then we make it happen."

"I had no idea this was a thing. What have you done in the past?"

"I think my favorite one was when a couple was getting married at a venue we played in our early days," he explains. "They met at that concert, so they got married at the venue and hired a Royal Rebels cover band to play at their reception. We happened to see their post, and we were in town, so…we crashed their wedding."

I burst into laughter. "You are incredible. That is so cool! They will never forget that."

He sits back against his pillows and rubs a hand over his face. "That's why it's my favorite!"

I heave a sigh. "I wish you were here, dragon slayer."

His lower lip juts out adorably. "I wish it more, Siren. How many more days?"

I hold up four fingers, and it's his turn to let out a frustrated sigh.

"Oh! I have to tell you. I was getting barked at by Ms. Taft today when Ethan Montclair walked in. He started gushing at me about how amazing our performance was at the concert right in front of her. I could tell it was killing her, but she couldn't say anything in front of him."

"Was he at the concert?"

I shake my head. "No, he's not the type to spend money on charities. He saw it on the news."

Zach licks his lips, looking a little nervous. "Have you watched the news at all?"

"No, I don't need the frustration. I have too much to focus on this week. Why, is there anything bad?"

"Not at all, I just worry about you lending too much importance to what they say. You're still new at this. I don't want you to get upset by anything."

I smirk. "I won't even watch. And Dave is doing a great job looking out for me."

His expression grows serious. "Will you promise me something? If anything—"

A loud knock on the door to my suite interrupts him. I frown and listen. Another knock, this one even louder.

"What on earth? Hang on, Zach."

I take my phone with me and trot to the door, looking out the peephole. Ashley? I swing open the door, and there she is, a crying mess holding a bag of Chinese food.

"Ashley!" I exclaim as I pull her into a hug. "What's happened?"

She inhales a few sobs, trying to get enough air to speak. I take the food bag from her hands and set it on the entry table, then guide her to the couch. Quickly I run into the bathroom and grab the box of tissues, then run back out and sit next to her.

"Greg says I'm smothering him," she sputters.

I gasp out loud. That jerk. She's only staying with him because of the media circus. That's my fault. She's innocent. She blows her nose and throws herself against the couch cushions.

"The engagement's off. Can I stay here with you?"

Chapter 19

Marina

I set Ashley up with her Chinese takeout, make the excuse of running to the bathroom, and duck in there with my cell phone. I hold it up and see a very concerned Zach looking at me.

"I know," he says quietly. "You need to go be with Ashley."

I nod. "I really do. I'm so sorry."

He sighs heavily. "I miss you so much."

My heart clenches at the resigned tone in his voice. "I do too. What time can we chat tomorrow?"

He thinks for a moment, shaking his head in frustration. "I'm not sure. Can we leave it open? I'll just try when I can, and don't answer me if it's not a good time. Vice versa."

I nod. "Okay, that sounds good. Let's really try to meet up. I miss you."

His eyes soften as he nods and waves.

End video call.

I text Merry and Scarlet to let them know what's happened, then put my phone back on the charger and head back to the living room.

I want to punch Greg for what I find when I get there. There is such heartbreak and defeat in her eyes as she sits with her carton of orange chicken, staring blankly at the carpet. Honestly, when I see her in this state, I can completely see the sense of my plan before I met Zach. No boys allowed. If they're going to cause this kind of pain, they can all stay away from me. Thank goodness Zach is one of the good ones.

"All right, Ash," I say softly as I take the spot next to her. "Merry and Scarlet are on the way. Tell me all about it."

***

I wake up in a foul mood, which is really something because I am *never* in a bad mood. I'm just pissy at so many things right now. At Greg, for breaking Ashley's heart. At Ms. Taft for being extra horrible this week. At her team for not having their work done. And at the universe for taking Zach away when I need him most. Ten minutes in his arms, and I'm sure everything would be rosy. But his arms are over three hundred miles away right now, and that makes me mad too.

I'm sure Ashley's still in bed, but I'm quiet as I get ready. Just in case. We were up until after midnight talking. They've had their troubles in the past, but after the last time, he assured her that she was the one. He wanted her forever, and she was safe with him. But he's such a control freak, things started unraveling. Nothing is ever good enough for him. So when Zach and I brought a media circus down on all our heads, Ashley thought her fiancé's apartment would be a safe place to run. They're getting married, anyway. Why wouldn't she think that? Now he says she's smothering him.

Jerk.

I slip into my high heels and check my reflection in the bathroom mirror before grabbing my purse and my work bag and heading out to the living room. Leaving my bags on the couch, I tip-toe over to Ashley's open bedroom door to check on her. Yep, knocked out. Television is on, there's an empty takeout container on the bed, and her phone is on the floor. What a mess, girl.

I step over to the bedside table and plug in her cell phone for her, then carefully reach over to pick up the empty takeout container.

"...c'mon now, let me play devil's advocate for a minute," the female newscaster says. "Does anyone really think Marina MacArthur is *duchess* material?"

I look up at the television in time to see her laugh cruelly and shake her head at the camera before it cuts to a commercial. I stand there in the darkened room for a moment, dumbfounded. Is that what's being said out there? Is there a whole debate going on about me being a duchess?

"Marina?" Ashley mumbles from her stupor.

I turn to her and plaster a smile on my face.

"Good morning," I whisper. "I was just checking on you before I go to work. Go back to sleep, okay?"

She turns over and pulls a pillow over her head, mumbling something. I walk out of the room in a sort of half-daze, grabbing my bags and heading downstairs to meet Dave. I'm just buckling my seatbelt when my phone vibrates.

Max: Morning, sis! Can't wait for our first video chat tonight!! See you soon.

My spirit lightens a bit, even if the text doesn't quite bring a smile to my face. At least I get to see Max today. It'll make up for possibly missing a call with Zach if we're both too busy. This week really sucks.

Marina: Hey, bro! Can't wait to see you and start ten years of catching up. :-)

I settle back in my seat and heave a frustrated sigh. Intuition tells me I'm not going to spend much time with Zach tonight, and I already hate it. My phone vibrates in my hand, but it's not Max. I toggle out of his messages and find one waiting from the Evil Queen.

Ms. Taft: Pick up Starbucks on your way in. Don't be late again.

I roll my eyes. Now she's actively throwing roadblocks in my way. This is one of her favorite things to do. As far as she knows, I'm still taking the bus to work. Making me go to Starbucks has always been a kind of punishment she likes to inflict when she's mad at me, because she knows it's impossible to carry it all with my work bag and purse. Lucky for me, I've used a workaround for months. I pull out my phone, open the Doorway Delivery app, and solve at least one of my problems this morning. It should arrive about the same time I do.

I look out the window at the waking city and feel…unsteady. I'm used to walking into work wearing my work persona like a suit of armor. It shielded me from anyone knowing much about me, but she's gone now. Ripped away by a viral news story. Now I'm a singer. A mermaid. A rock star's latest fling. I'm exposed, and now I'm afraid I may even be a joke. The American nobody who wants to be a duchess. I'm a topic of conversation, and I really don't like not knowing what's being said. Dread coils in my gut like a viper waiting to strike. I know I have to look at the news at some point. It's been gnawing at me since I heard that reporter this morning. I just need to get through today.

Dave pulls into the parking garage at Trans United Tower and stops in the usual place, getting out of the car and opening my door. I get out with much less energy than usual, taking a minute to collect myself and get my bags together.

"Everything all right, Ms. MacArthur?" Dave asks.

I offer him a feeble smile. "Sure, Dave. Just looking forward to Friday."

He gives me a look like he's not quite buying it, but I start walking for the elevator. The memory of Zach walking me to this elevator the day he brought me all the takeout food in San Francisco floats to the front of my mind, and my heart skips a beat. I get in the elevator, press the button for the lobby, and close my eyes. I miss him so much it hurts. It's been barely three weeks, and I hurt just being away from him for a few days. Is that love? I have no idea. I just know I've been unsettled since we met, and I can't seem to get back in my own groove. I feel like I don't know who I am anymore. Unless I'm with Zach, then I just feel safe and…priceless. But I can't live my life only to be around Zach. I have to have my own space in this world.

The duchess thing is grating on me. I'm thinking all kinds of thoughts I don't want to think. I want to go to law school so I can be a lawyer and fight for kids in the foster care system. Kids like me. I have a plan, and that plan does not include garden parties and hosting dinners for thirty. Ash is addicted to anything about the British royal family. I've seen plenty of documentaries about all the stately homes, gala balls and charity benefits. It's laughable to put someone like me in that world. That's not me. I have to talk to Zach about this.

You weren't in my plan either, gorgeous, but here we are.

Zach's words haunt me. He's so good at just taking things as they come. He's never unsettled. Maybe that's what growing up in a functional, well-to-do family gets you. I, of course, would not know.

The elevator doors open, and I walk through our sterile, cold lobby to find the delivery guy with my Starbucks order, who is walking up to the security desk right on time. I collect the order, say thanks, and take the lobby elevators to my floor.

"You're almost late!" Ms. Taft barks as I walk past her door to put my things down.

That's called being on time.

I pull her coffee from the drink holder and walk into her office with a forced smile.

"Here you are, Ms. Taft," I say as lightly as possible, setting the cup on her desk.

She looks up at me from behind her laptop, her eyes roving over my appearance. I'm wearing the Chanel suit she made fun of, and I don't miss the smirk she gives me. If I waited for her to say thanks, I'd be standing here until I die, so I turn and head for the door.

"I need the draft of the proposal on my desk before you leave today so I can review it first thing tomorrow."

I turn and give her another forced smile. "Of course."

Great. So many departments are still dragging their feet. I don't even have half the content I need to get it ready. Today's going to be a long day. I'll be here till at least 8 pm, probably longer.

I turn and walk back to my desk, fighting tears. There's no way I'm getting to video chat with Max or Zach tonight. Not now.

***

Zach

If spidey-sense was a real thing, I think I'd have it when it comes to Marina. Or maybe I'm just paranoid. Something's off. I feel it stretching from San Francisco all the way to Los Angeles and into the recording booth at the radio station where we're finishing an interview. I fidget through the last fifteen minutes of our chat with one of the country's most popular DJs, getting the side-eye from Rick a few times. Finally, we finish and stand there for a few minutes making small talk with him and his staff before we step out into the hallway.

As usual, radio station employees are milling about just outside the recording booth, waiting to say hello…which also further delays our departure. I feel a hand come down on my shoulder and look over to find Rick giving me a look like he knows exactly what's going on.

"Why don't Sam, Jimmy and I go chat with these guys while you step into that hallway and see if you can get Marina on the phone for a few?"

I don't even try to act like she's not on my mind, so I give him a guy hug, pull out my phone and stride far enough down the hall that no one can see me. Rick heads the other way with Sam and Jimmy. It's just after lunch hour, but I'm hoping to catch her at a good time. I dial her number and my heart gets jumpy just hearing it ring.

"Zach?" her honey-sweet voice sounds in my ear. I breathe a sigh of relief.

"Hey, gorgeous," I say with a stupid smile on my face that she can't even see. "How's your day going?"

I hear a heavy sigh and what sounds like a stack of papers being slammed down.

"Not awesome," she says in almost a whisper. "It's like the whole office got a memo to put me through the wringer this week."

"I'm sorry. I wish I could make it better."

Another sigh. "Well, you're making it a little better. Just hearing your voice is a nice surprise."

"What's going on?" I ask pensively. "Talking about it might make you feel better."

"I wish I could," she says. "I'm at my desk and the Evil Queen is in her office, so no details. She's being a real terror today and I probably won't get out of here until late. I'm going to have to reschedule my first video call with Max."

My eyes nearly bulge out of their sockets.

"You're going to be *that* late?" I gasp. Her video call was supposed to be well after dinner.

"She wants to review the proposal draft first thing in the morning, which means I have to have it on her desk tonight. And that means I have to harass five different teams into giving me their content before I can put it together. A few of them have already told me they won't have their parts done until at least 7 pm. I'll be lucky to crawl into bed by 10 pm."

I'm not a violent man, but I'm thinking all kinds of bad thoughts about the Evil Queen right now.

"Marina," I tread cautiously. "Are you sure this job is worth it?"

I wish I could take it back as soon as I say it. Even over the phone, I feel her hackles rising.

"What?" she says quietly. "Do you know how hard I had to try just to get this job? Do you know how many people would kill to work here?"

I cringe. "I didn't mean it exactly like that."

"It's easy for someone with a huge amount of wealth to have the luxury of asking those questions," she begins tersely, making me mentally curse myself with every syllable. "Not so easy for people like me. Or did you forget about where I came from?"

"Of course I haven't forgotten," I say gently. "I'm so proud of you for all you've accomplished, love. I just…I could help you, if you'd let me. So you don't have to struggle so much. So you don't have to *worry* so much, or put up with people like this."

I feel like I dug the hole deeper when I hear her exasperated sigh on the other end.

"This is my fight," she says determinedly. "I've gotten this far without help."

My gut clenches. "I wish we could have this conversation in person," I mutter. "What you've done is amazing, my darling. But you're in a relationship now. You don't have to fight alone. You have a dragon slayer on Team Mermaid, and he's crazy about you."

She hesitates, and I swear I hear her relax a little on the other end of the line.

"Zach," she whispers, a little need laced through her voice.

"Yes, Marina?" I coo back to her.

Come back to me...don't shut me out.

"I'm sorry," she sighs. "I'm just tired and frustrated. And I wish you were here."

My heart wrenches at her desperate tone. "Me too, baby. Just a couple more days."

"It's been terrible here," she says in a low voice. "The Evil Queen is determined to throw roadblocks in my way, giving me stupid errands and extra things to do. And the media's getting really out of hand."

My pulse hammers rapidly. "What do you mean?"

"There was a reporter talking about me on the news this morning. She wasn't very nice about it. And three people in the office have jokingly called me 'Duchess' as they've dropped work off on my desk today."

I close my eyes and pinch the bridge of my nose for a minute. I swear, I want to cancel everything and race back up there to be at her side. But I know I can't do that, and she wouldn't want me to.

"Ignore them, Marina," I say gently. "Your colleagues are just jealous, and reporters can be real jerks. They don't know who *we* really are, and they never will."

She's quiet for a moment as she considers my words.

"Just do me a favor, please?" I beg softly. "Stay away from the news until I come home. Let's deal with it together."

"I would love to promise you that, but with the proposal happening this week, I need to have my A-game ready, Zach," she says as dread pools in my gut. "I need to know what's being said about me."

I bow my head. "Siren, please don't."

"I'll watch it with Ash, how's that? I won't watch it alone."

I shake my head. "That still doesn't make me feel any better."

"That's the best I can do for now," she says with finality.

"Tell me you miss me, Siren."

She laughs softly on the other end. "Of course I miss you."

"The next time someone makes a joke or you feel stressed about anything, just think about all the kisses that are going to happen the second you're back in my arms."

"Oh?"

I growl a little. "Up your jawline. Down your neck. On your nose. And your mouth…"

She sighs. "What about my mouth?"

"I'm going to worship that mouth, Marina."

It's barely audible, but I hear a little whimper.

"Just get back here soon, okay?"

"I will, love," I say heavily. "I promise. And we'll talk about everything."

"After the kissing, please."

I laugh out loud, feeling a little relieved at that. "After the kissing. I'll check on you later, all right?"

"Okay," she says with a much-needed lightness returning to her voice. "Bye for now."

"Bye for now, baby."

I disconnect the call and lean against the wall for a moment, unsure of where things are between us right now, and absolutely dreading the idea of her watching the news without me there. But at least I left her thinking about the kissing…so there's that.

***

Marina

Dave pulls the car up to the front of the Fairmont just before 10 pm.

I feel ready to drop. If Zach was here, I'd let him carry me upstairs. I'm *that* tired. But the proposal draft is on Ms. Taft's desk, as ordered, so all is well. My stomach growls as I walk across the lobby, but I'm so stressed out right now I don't even want to think about food. I actually would have skipped lunch, but Merry miraculously appeared at my desk with an order from Nonno's again. My girls, they take good care of me.

Luckily, Max was very understanding when I told him I had to postpone our video chat. We'll try again tomorrow night, but I am utterly disappointed that we had to put it off. I swipe my key and enter the suite, hearing Ashley gasp from the living room.

"Finally!" she trots over to me in her pajamas and gives me a worried look. "They're working you to the bone, Marina. What happened?"

I drop my bags in the entry and purse my lips.

"I believe the word you're looking for is retaliation, my friend."

Ash frowns. "Well, that's ridiculous. Retaliation for what?"

She follows me as I walk into my bedroom, taking my suit off as I go, needing to be in comfy clothes and out of this ridiculous corporate costume as soon as possible. I put the suit in the pile for dry cleaning and grab my yoga pants and Zach's t-shirt.

I never get tired of this t-shirt. It makes me happy just by looking at it, and I need a little happiness right now.

"For being a viral media sensation that she can't get rid of?" I answer in a tone much lighter than I feel.

She follows me back to the living room, and we sit on the couch.

"For making it worse by being photographed in the dark with a rock star? And then getting on stage with said rock star and performing at a charity concert? Name it."

"You can't let them get away with this," she says firmly, and I'm glad to see some of the fire back in her eyes. She was so torn up last night.

"They just did," I say with resignation heavy in my voice. "Tomorrow will be more of the same."

She shakes her head at me, her expression incredulous. "I don't understand."

I open my mouth to explain, but she holds a hand up. "Do not even bother if you're going to tell me about the five thousand dollar bonus you *might* get unless she finds a way to make you fail, which is exactly what she's trying to do."

I shrug tiredly. "What am I supposed to do?"

Her eyes go wide. "QUIT! Lean on the people who love you, girl. I can float you on rent. I've got a feeling your boyfriend would help if you let him. Has he offered to help you?"

I don't have to answer. She can see it on my face.

"Marina," she pleads. "You don't need these people. Why can't you let us help you?"

I shake my head. "I'm okay, Ash. I don't really want to talk about work anymore. How are you feeling?"

She swallows hard, narrowing her eyes at the attempt to shut down the conversation. I know she's not done, but I just need a little break from it.

"I'm okay," she says. "I pretty much cried through breakfast, then I got in the shower crying and came out mad."

I raise my eyebrows. "Mad?"

She nods emphatically. "Mad at *myself*, for falling for him again. I mean, c'mon, the writing was on the wall the first time he felt smothered. I just didn't see it. Mad at *him* for being a poster child for commitment issues. Just *mad*."

I reach over and grab her hand.

"I'm sorry he hurt you," I say softly. "You deserve better."

Her lower lip trembles for a minute, then she reels in her emotions.

"I do deserve better," she says. "I think I'm going to spend some time figuring myself out before I jump back in the dating pool, though."

"That sounds like a smart plan."

"I've become a meme," she rants. "You know that one where the person says, 'Didn't you see all the red flags?' and the woman says, 'I thought it was a parade'? Yep. That's me. I was at the Greg Parade watching all the red flags go by."

I reach over and give her a long hug. We stay like this for a while, then she lets me go and pats my knee.

"I'm going to bed," she says as she stands. "There's a sandwich platter in the dining room if you're hungry. I asked Dave to text me when you were leaving the office. It's fresh."

I blink back my surprise. "That's so sweet, Ash. Thank you."

She pauses at her bedroom door and gives me a long, pointed look.

"You deserve better, too, Marina," she says softly. "You have a whole bunch of people in your corner, ready to back you up when you need us. That includes Zach, and now your brother, too. It's okay to need help once in a while."

I give her a feeble smile and wave goodnight. I turn toward the dining room to grab some food, hoping I can get something down before I pass out. My heart swells at the thoughtfulness of my friend as I see the sandwich platter and a small basket of various bagged chips. There are bottled waters and soft drinks as well. I choose a turkey sandwich, skip the chips, grab a bottle of water and make a beeline for bed. I put everything down on the bedside table, then pad into the bathroom to take off my makeup and scrub my face.

On the way back into the bedroom, I duck into the closet and pull out the pillow I hid from housekeeping. It's the one Zach slept on the last night we were together. I didn't want the maids to take it away and leave me with nothing that smelled like him. Kind of pathetic. I feel like it makes me needy, and I hate that feeling. I don't hate it enough to leave the pillow for the maids to take away, though. I toss it on the bed and land on it like an amoebe, wrapping myself around it and inhaling his familiar scent with wild abandon. My heart squeezes painfully because he isn't here. I miss him so much. I hate that I miss him so much. And I'm not sure where that leaves us.

After a while, I get up and take a bite of my sandwich. I plug my phone in and close my eyes, trying to mentally run through the events of tomorrow. More edits of documents I've already printed and added to the proposal folios, but will need insignificant changes for no reason. More deadlines her teams will miss, causing me to chase after them. More unreasonable demands from the Evil Queen. I'm hoping to get back at a decent hour so I can video chat with Max and then Zach.

Zach.

Only now do I realize I never answered his last text message, which came through as I was just putting the proposal on Ms. Taft's desk so she could read it first thing in the morning. I pick up my phone and unlock it.

Marina: Sorry, I got sidetracked. I'm back at the hotel. Exhausted and going to bed. I miss you so much. Chat tomorrow. xo

I stretch out beneath the cool, crisp sheets and wrap my arms around my Zach pillow, inhaling one more time. I let that beautiful, beachy scent wash over my frayed nerves as I wonder what on earth I'm even doing with my life...and drift off to a fitful sleep.

Chapter 20

Zach

My phone pings on the nightstand as I'm getting ready for bed. I swipe the screen and see a goodnight text from Marina. My heart sinks. I was really hoping to get another phone call before her head hit the pillow, but she's probably already sleeping. She's exhausted, thanks to a bunch of people who don't have a brain between them and certainly don't deserve her.

She didn't mention watching any news or anything. And she didn't seem distant or upset. I wish I knew for sure what was going on in that beautiful head of hers. We're away from each other at the worst time. I should be there to help her deal with how insanely stupid the press can be. I wouldn't worry so much if it wasn't for her being under such pressure at work and her boss having issues with the whole viral video thing.

I step into the bathroom and turn the shower on, then just stand there a minute and try to focus. I can feel all of this slipping through my fingers, and I can't get a grip on it. I keep trying and trying, but it feels like we're on a runaway train, and the tracks are out ahead.

One of Marina's greatest strengths is also one of her weaknesses: that lovely stubborn streak. She's a fighter. Fierce and passionate. I'm not entirely confident that the media and the circus that comes with it won't push her from fighting them to fighting *me*.

***

Marina

This week feels like it's a month long, and it's only Wednesday. The meeting is on Friday, and I'm still putting out fires all over the office.

I slow my steps as I near Ms. Taft's door. She's on the phone and has strict rules about being interrupted during calls. I have a document she needs for her next meeting, and there's not much time. I could leave it on my desk for her to find, but she'll just make a snide remark about me not doing everything as it should be done.

"I had no idea…you're kidding me," Ms. Taft says in what she thinks is a whisper. She never whispers, which is why I always close her door when I leave her office. "A group home for *bad kids?* I can't believe it. Are you sure? She's so…boring. I can't imagine her being anything but disgustingly wholesome."

Instantly, my heart leaps to my throat. Granted, I've been avoiding the news lately, but I'm pretty sure the girls would have told me that the gossip mongers on TV are reporting that I was a foster kid. This feels like it's coming from somewhere else. This feels less like it came from a news station and more like it was born from a gossip rag.

"Well, now it makes more sense. She practically grew up on the streets. I'm sure she buys those ghastly suits at some thrift shop somewhere, trying to fit in. And now she's found herself a duke! What a little manipulator."

I'm rooted to the spot where I'm standing, tears of frustration welling up in my eyes.

"It's laughable," she continues. "Ethan, can you see the royal family inviting her to garden parties and high tea? She clearly has no idea the pedigree she needs to have in order to be accepted in that world. They're all about bloodlines and titles over there. She's literally nobody! This will be fun to watch."

I finally push myself away from the doorway, so furious I can't listen to another word. What a horrible, cruel person. I am definitely quitting after the meeting on Friday. Well, after I'm sure my bonus has been paid out. Then I'm quitting. I know Ashley means what she says about the rent, and she's right. I need to accept help once in a while. I would be crazy to stay here after this, but I've worked so hard for this bonus I want to be sure I have it when I walk out of here forever.

I walk back to my desk and check my email. I have all the documents I need now except for two from the worst offenders on Ms. Taft's team. Not a shocker, but I can see that it's almost time for me to head to lunch with Hillary. With everything going on in the office, we agreed that she'd order takeout, and we'd meet in the employee cafeteria downstairs. I open a new email, send a reminder to everyone to have their documents to me by 2 pm, and lock my computer. Then I lock my desk and leave Ms. Taft's document where she can find it before heading downstairs to meet Hillary.

The employee cafeteria is teeming with people at this hour. It's a shared space between three firms at the top of Trans United Tower, so it's a mish-mash of lawyers, accountants, and uniformed mailroom employees. Hillary waves at me from a table against the windows on the far side of the cafeteria, and I head straight to her. I face the window with my back to the rest of the cafeteria, thinking it'll be more peaceful than looking at a bunch of people I don't know each their lunches. I smile at Hillary as I sit.

"Hey there," she greets me. "I'm glad for a little break right now. Are you going as crazy as I am with this whole proposal?"

I nod. "You have no idea. It's pretty bad in our department."

She reaches into the bag and starts distributing takeout containers. What is it about burrito bowls that are so delicious? Maybe I'm just *boring*, as Ms. Taft put it.

"Are you okay?" Hillary asks softly.

I look up quickly, and a tear escapes my eye. I wipe it away and manage to force out what I hope is a light laugh. It might sound a little maniacal, actually. Hopefully not. I rip open a utensil packet that came with our food.

"Yeah, I'm fine. Allergies probably."

The look on her face tells me she's not buying it, but she's too nice to push. She opens her utensils as I take the lid off my bowl and dig in before I open my mouth and say something else stupid.

"How late did you work last night?" she asks softly. "You were still here when I left, and I was here till eight o'clock."

I look up. "You were? I had no idea anyone else was here that late."

She smirks and leans forward. "I think sometimes they have a contest to see who can make their assistants work the latest."

I laugh and nod. "Maybe."

"You looked…sad. So I didn't want to bother you, or I would have stopped by."

I swallow hard. "It hasn't been an easy week."

She nods slowly. "Well, no one should have to stay that late. Next time, let me know, and I'll come and help."

I give her a genuine smile and dig into my bowl, realizing sadly that she's the first person who's ever offered to help me here. We eat in relative silence for a while, then her phone chimes. She has to do something for her boss and apologizes, but I wave my hand at her to go ahead. She hunches over her phone, scrolling and typing a message to him. Suddenly, I hear Zach's voice behind me on someone's cell phone.

"...I recently caught a mermaid."

My ears perk up. I can't turn around to see who it is, but they're watching Zach work the crowd at the benefit concert and snickering about it.

"Like…seriously…I'm so embarrassed for him," a man's voice says. "I used to have such respect for him, but this is pitiful. He made an ass out of himself for some chick who's just manipulating the situation to get at him."

"Do you really believe that?" a woman asks.

"Hands down, yeah," he says. "What is anyone doing dressed up like a stupid mermaid in the middle of the bridge? She put herself there on purpose."

"I feel sorry for his family," another woman adds. "I saw a post in a Rebels fan group that his parents are furious."

"Oh yeah, don't forget he'll be a duke someday. Can you see her at Buckingham Palace in her mermaid suit?"

The whole group laughs.

"Pathetic."

I take a deep breath, and another tear falls. I wipe it away and look up to see if Hillary saw it, and she's looking at me with absolute compassion in her eyes. I will myself not to cry right now, in a crowded cafeteria, where I would certainly make the people behind me very happy. Hillary leans forward.

"Let's move somewhere else," she whispers, looking over my shoulder at the mermaid haters like she wants to push them all out the window.

I shake my head. "It's okay. I'm fine."

She tilts her head. "No one would be fine after that."

I shake my head again and take a bite, focusing on chewing and breathing. She watches them over my shoulder. It sounds like they're packing up.

"They're wrong," she offers, taking a bite of her lunch. "What he did was…"

I raise my eyebrows as she holds up her fingers and starts ticking off a list.

"It was fun to watch because the crowd was eating it up. It was all in the spirit of the evening," she says defensively. "It was heroic to raise over half a million dollars more for mental health. Epic, even. And it was freaking romantic, my friend. I mean…wow. I loved it."

The corners of my mouth tip up a little bit as I take another bite, not really trusting myself to speak.

"They're just jealous," she continues. "But let's talk about something else. I wanted to ask you something, but you have to promise not to tell anyone that I asked."

My eyes widen. "Of course."

She licks her lips and looks around to make sure no one is close enough to hear.

"Has Ethan Montclair ever…well, does he ever accidentally bump into you? Or touch you? On purpose?"

I feel my blood boil instantly. That creep. That smarmy, disgusting creep.

"Yes," I say quietly. "I thought I was the only one."

She shakes her head. "And I think there are more women in the office this is happening to. He's so gross."

"I'm sorry it's happened to you. It *is* gross."

She nods, and a shudder ripples through her body.

"We have to tell someone," I say, still keeping my voice down. "Otherwise he'll just keep doing it."

"I did," she whispers. "I reported it to human resources two weeks ago, but he's still lurking around."

If I wasn't fuming before, I am now. I can't stand this kind of thing.

"Let me think about it," I say carefully. "But I promise not to tell anyone what you said."

"Why is he even here? He doesn't work here, and the meeting isn't till Friday," she muses.

"That's my fault too, I guess," I mutter. "He keeps gushing at me, trying to get Zach and me to give him an exclusive interview for his gossipy network."

Hillary makes a face. "As if!"

I nod. "Yeah, there's no way I'm doing that."

"Good," she says. "And thanks for listening. I really appreciate it, Marina."

***

I manage to get out of the office at a decent hour tonight, so I practically run to Dave and the open door to the car. He gives me a nod and closes the door behind me. Max and I can't video chat tonight after all. His partner on a project bailed on him, so he'll be busy working on it all night. We're both hopefully free tomorrow after work. I pull out my phone and text Zach.

Marina: Hey...are you there?

Zach: Always for you, love. Just about to go in for our last television interview. I'm so happy I'm on my way home to you tonight! We won't be back to the city until late, but I'll be able to see you in the morning before your big day.

Home. I pause for a minute. San Francisco isn't home for him, though. And he's only coming back for a few days before leaving again. And we'll be back on this treadmill. Again. And I'll still be the laughingstock of the office. I stare at my phone, not sure of what to say.

Zach: Marina?

I decide to just rip off the band-aid.

Marina: Are your parents angry because you're seeing me?

My phone rings immediately.

"Hi," I answer.

"What's happened, Marina?" he asks in a strained voice. "No, my parents aren't mad. Who said that to you?"

I feel my lip tremble and bite it to keep it still, swallowing hard.

"Some people were gossiping in the employee cafeteria today," I explain, my voice wobbly. "One of them said they saw something about it in a fan group on social media."

He sighs into the phone. "Well, I can confirm that there is absolutely no truth in it. Please don't pay—"

"Have you seen any stories that talk about my past? About me being a foster kid?"

"What?" he asks in an incredulous tone. "No. I would have told you immediately, and I would have handled it."

I blink back a tear. "What does that mean?"

"I always hit back if the media starts getting ugly," he explains. "I've set firm boundaries and they usually respect them because I let them get away with a lot before I start pushing back. I give them a lot of access to me, so they don't have to fight to get an interview. There's a give and take to these things, but none of that matters right now. I'm really bothered by this."

The car winds its way through the darkening streets of San Francisco, and I can tell from the view out the window that we're close to the hotel. Hearing the Evil Queen talk about my childhood like that was such a violation. To have the worst person imaginable get access to my personal history is something I'll never forget. I've tried to shake it off all day, but it clings to me like an oily residue I can't scrape off.

"Apparently the big topic in the world isn't politics or hunger or anything important. It's whether I can be a duchess," I continue, still finding the entire notion ridiculous. "About how I've trapped you because I have an agenda and how embarrassing it would be for your family."

"I've seen some talk about me inheriting my father's title, but it'll die down soon. Let's talk about this when I'm home tomorrow, and we're together," he says soothingly.

"It's a valid argument, though."

"It's ridiculous," he insists. "On many levels. Marina, please let me explain all this when I get there? I know Friday is booked, with your big meeting and opening night for the Rebels concert, but we'll have Saturday morning and afternoon together. We can stay in and talk it all through."

I nod. "Okay."

The car pulls to a stop outside the hotel. Dave gets out and opens the door for me. I remain inside for a minute.

"Just got to the hotel," I murmur into the phone.

He sighs. "Yeah, two minutes, Rick..."

"And you have to go," I say.

"I do, Siren, but I'm worried about you."

"I'm fine."

He laughs softly. "Do you remember that scene from 'The Princess Bride' when Inigo Montoya says, 'You keep using that word. I don't think it means what you think it means'?"

I roll my eyes. "Yes."

"Well?"

"Zach," I sigh in frustration. "I'm doing the best I can, but I'll be honest...I'm stressed out right now and exhausted."

"I know, love," he says in a husky voice. "Just sit tight a little longer, and we'll tackle this together. Stay away from the news until then, yeah?"

"You know I can't do that," I say emphatically. "Especially after overhearing Ms. Taft. She's been horrible all week, but I think it was Ethan Montclair who went digging into my past. When we first met, he was trying to get me to give an interview to one of his networks. I need to know if he's blasting my personal history all over. I *have* to know. I told you I wouldn't do it alone, and I won't. I'll watch the news with Ashley."

I hear his resigned sigh on the other end and Rick calling to him in the distance.

"Go do your interview," I say gently. "I'll be fine. I'll see you soon."

He hesitates for a moment.

"All right, my darling Siren. I'll be counting the minutes."

I disconnect and scoot out of the car, then walk into the lobby and head upstairs. I roll my shoulders as I press the button for my floor. I'm wearing the stress and apprehension of this week on my shoulders and there's just no shrugging it off. Life at work has gotten ugly in a way I never could have predicted. I always knew Ms. Taft wasn't a nice person, but she is also heartless. For the first time, I'm starting to understand why everyone thinks I'm crazy for continuing to work there. I unlock the door to my suite and drop my bags where I stand.

"Hey, girl!" Ashley calls from the living room. "Glad to see you back at a decent hour. How did work go?"

I drag myself to the couch and plop down next to Ashley, telling her about the conversations I overheard today. As expected, she's in full battle armor and ready to wage war for me.

"And what did Zach say about all of this?" she asks calmly, watching me with concern.

I shrug. "Zach wants to wait to talk about it when he's back so we can be together."

She nods. "That sounds like a good plan. What did you say?"

"I agree, for the most part," I say. "But the fact that the Evil Queen was talking about my childhood like that really bothers me."

"All the more reason for you to quit immediately, Marina. She's a horrible person."

I turn to face her, propping my feet up on the couch.

"I plan to give my notice next week," I share. "After the proposal is done and my bonus is paid."

She smirks, obviously not believing that I really do mean it. I can't fault her for that.

"Can you do me a favor?" I ask pensively.

She nods. "Anything."

"I want to watch the news, on the network Ethan Montclair owns," I explain. "He's the one who told the Evil Queen about my past, and I can't relax about it. I need to know if that's out in the open."

Ashley regards me for a moment, twirling a piece of her hair around her finger.

"Will it make a difference if it is?"

I consider for a moment. "Not in some ways," I say. "I'm not ashamed of it. But he's horrible. And if he's spewing hate about me, I want to know—especially before I go into that big meeting with him tomorrow."

"Okay then," she says cautiously, reaching for the remote on the side table. "Let's watch some news."

***

Four hours later, I've learned a lot about the media. Every network, sometimes every show, puts their own spin on things. They all have an agenda.

I'm a gold-digger. I'm adorable. I'm a cold, calculating opportunist. Zach and I are so romantic. He's a victim, and will end up in ruin because he's fallen for me. I think I'm Meghan Markle. We even have the same initials. I'm a law student because that'll help me *change the royal family*. What? That last one really made me laugh.

Montclair's network is the least complimentary by far. They created a list of duchess duties and then showed an animated cartoon of a resume so they could slap big red X marks on each requirement, followed by a loud game show buzzer. The obnoxious buzzing sounded every time they found me lacking. Spoiler alert: it's every duty on the list. Every time they cover a story about me, they show a picture of me laughing on stage at the benefit with the banner, "The Duchess of San Francisco". There are no words for how much I hate it, or how violated I feel by all of this.

But the worst of it has come from the most heartbreaking source: Zach himself. We're watching an interview he did for a Rolling Stone documentary last year and they asked him what happens with his life in America when it's time for him to assume his father's title.

"From the moment I landed my feet on American soil," he says with a glint in his eye, "I've felt like I was in my home away from home. I've learned so much and have gained so much from living here. I love this country. But, yeah, when that time comes I will return home and fulfill all those responsibilities."

"Do you think people back home will accept a rock 'n' roll duke?" the interviewer asks, prompting a laugh from Zach.

"I will always love music, and there's a special place in my heart for rock, but I was raised a proper little gentleman," he says. "My mum is quite happy that I still remember all the right manners when I go home for a visit. So I'll settle down and find myself a proper duchess. I won't do anything to embarrass the people at home."

Ashley shuts off the TV, but it's too late. My entire world has already crashed and burned all around me.

"Hey," Ashley says from her spot on the couch. "Talk to me."

I keep my gaze focused on the TV, even though the screen is blank. The image of Zach smiling and talking about his proper duchess is burned in my brain. I close my eyes and still see it.

"This is awful," I say hoarsely, fighting back tears. "What was I thinking?"

Ashley tilts her head at me. "About what?"

"I let him in," I croak. "I let him into my heart. Not that anyone could ever resist him."

I laugh bitterly. This sucks so much.

Ashley shakes her head at me, eyes wide. "What are you thinking?"

"I have to let him go, Ash," I cry. "I can't let this happen. This is so bad."

I let my tears fall freely, and Ash reaches over and pulls me into a hug.

"No, you don't," Ashley says, squeezing me tight. "Don't you dare."

I pull away and sit up, wiping my tears. They're immediately replaced with fresh ones.

"I cannot do this," I say emphatically. "I have no control over anything right now. People are openly mocking me at work. Everything I've worked for is slipping away from me. *Everything* I fought for."

She takes my hand and squeezes it. "The only thing you're going to lose is a horrible job working for horrible people, and that's only because you're quitting. As you should!"

I point to the tv. "Who's going to hire the Duchess of San Francisco to work at their law firm? What law school is going to open their doors for a gold-digger who's addicted to social media? I have been absolutely trashed."

Ashley regards me quietly, biting her lip and shaking her head. "You're reaching. That's not all they'll focus on."

I pull one of the sofa cushions into my lap and hug it for support, then gesture at the room around us.

"And look at this ridiculous suite. I'm living here like this is my life now. This isn't real life. This is a fantasy that I got sucked into. A hotel isn't a home. I'm so sick of takeout and room service. I miss having a kitchen."

Ash crooks the corner of her mouth up. "You literally never cook. Marina, you need to take a step back and calm down. You're ranting. It's gonna be okay."

I shake my head. "It's not okay," I say hoarsely. "I avoided Zach in the beginning for this very reason. I had a very neat, ordered life and now there's just chaos everywhere. I feel like someone put my whole life in a blender and hit puree."

"And what about Zach?" she asks pointedly.

My heart cracks just thinking about him now. My lip trembles.

"I grew up in one of the poorest neighborhoods in the city, he grew up on an estate. I had a one-bedroom apartment and was a latch key kid, he had a nanny. I am as far away from a 'proper duchess' as you can get."

She frowns at me. "Do you think that matters to Zach?"

I roll my eyes at her. "Not now. But it will later when he has to go back home. Because *that* is his home, Ash, you heard him say it. So if we stay together, what happens to me then? What happens to my career as a lawyer? I just stop advocating for kids and start hosting tea parties? No."

Ashley smirks at me and holds a finger up.

"I love you, girl, but I need you to not talk for a minute."

I nod, then reach over and grab a tissue from the box on the side table.

She takes a huge breath.

"No one is trying to begrudge you the praise you should always get for what you've done with your life," she says. "But it's pretty obvious to me that you've become so focused on the original goals you set for yourself that you've forgotten how to be flexible. You are not thinking outside the box. You're so locked onto the goal of working for the most prestigious law firm and getting into law school that you're failing to see the other, possibly bigger, opportunities that are laying themselves at your feet. All you see is the goal that Marina from five years ago set."

I blow my nose and wait for her to continue, not sure if I should speak.

"I'll give you one example and then I'm done, because I know you well enough to know there is no changing your mind once you've made it. Picture yourself in three years. You're a lawyer, and you're advocating for the foster kids who are near and dear to your heart. Are you with me?"

I nod. "Yes."

"You have a case load of maybe thirty kids," she says. "And how lucky are those thirty kids to have an amazing lawyer like you to fight for them! But here comes Taylor Swift."

I blink. "What?"

"Taylor dedicates one song on her concert tour to foster kids and gives her fans an opportunity to donate to a special fund every night. She raises millions of dollars for foster kids on her tour. She makes a huge difference to a lot more than thirty kids, and she's not a lawyer."

I blow my nose again.

"Does she do that?" I ask breathlessly.

Ash rolls her neck and squares her jaw. "I don't know, it's an example of what fame can do for someone who wants to help others."

"Ash, I am not Taylor Swift."

She gives me a look. "My point is…there are all kinds of ways to do what really matters to you: advocate for children less fortunate than others."

Zach's words ripple through my body like a physical ache.

I'll settle down and find myself a proper duchess. I won't do anything to embarrass the people at home.

Ashley stands up and offers me her hand. I look at her dumbly.

"If you miss the apartment and having a kitchen so much, then let's go home," she says. "Maybe you'll feel better to have a little bit of normal back. We'll deal with media stalkers and all that stuff later. But please save the Zach stuff for when he gets back so you can talk about it together."

I let her pull me up off the couch, then turn toward my room to go pack. But the happy glow on Zach's face as he spoke about his future life back home and finding a proper duchess punches a hole in my heart. I can't bear the thought of disappointing him. Or worse, him sacrificing his image and reputation when it's time for him to take his father's title because he's with me. There's no doubt in my mind that he would stick by me to the bitter end, and that's why I have to be the one to let go. He would ruin himself for me, and I would never forgive myself.

I step into my bedroom and pack up my things, not even trying to stop the tears. Ash is right about part of it: going back to the apartment will feel better. I need some normal back in my life. I need my control back, and I need space to think my way through the catastrophe that my life has become. And I need to end this and get out of here before Zach comes back because if I have to see him face to face, I'll be even more destroyed than I am already.

I check the clock on the bed table. We've been watching horrible videos and talking for hours and hours. Zach is well on his way back now. I need to get this over with. I nearly jump out of my skin when Ashley sticks her head in my door.

"Hey," she says. "I'm going downstairs for one of those cart things for our bags and I'll be right back."

I offer her a feeble smile. "Perfect."

She disappears from the doorway and I listen carefully for the sound of the front door. Once it clicks, I prop my phone up on the dresser instead of holding it in my hand like usual. There's no way I can do what I have to do and keep my hand steady. I'm already a wreck. But this has to be done now before I talk myself out of it.

I press the video call button and wait. One ring. Two. On the third, his handsome face, with that beautiful smile, comes into view. My eyes instantly fill with tears.

"Siren, you should be in bed," he croons. "We're just about…an hour outside the city. It'll be after midnight bef—"

"Listen to me."

He stops talking, and only then does he see my tears.

"What's wr—"

"I need you to listen to me," I say with a calm I most definitely do not feel.

He swallows hard. His eyes seek answers in mine, and I see the moment he realizes what's happening. I see a little piece of him break. He shakes his head.

"Marina…"

"I am so grateful to you for so many things," I begin, my voice wavering.

"*Don't.*"

I know I have to push forward. The only way for us to heal is for this to move ahead. I lick my lips and take a deep breath.

"You have to let me go."

He flinches at my words. "No!"

I tilt my head as the tears begin to fall anew. "It's for the best, Zach. Our schedules are making this an incredible challenge already. It'll be so much worse when I'm in law school. And I can't be a duchess."

"We can make our schedules work. And the duchess thing…that is not a conversation to have now," he pleads. "It's something we can deal with much later. In a year or two."

"I disagree."

He nods, and a single tear falls. I hate myself to the core for that tear. I will never be okay again.

"You disagree because you're being a coward right now, Siren."

I shake my head. "The *brave* thing is to let you go before you get too hurt."

He rubs a hand over his face. "You're much too late for that."

I lower my head so he can't see my face crumple.

"Can't you at least wait until I get there?"

I shake my head. "There is nothing you can say that will make me believe I can live up to everything you need."

"*I get to decide what I need,*" he growls. "Not you or anyone else."

"I saw an interview you gave," I confess. "You talked about your duties back home, and that you'd marry a proper duchess. Those are your words."

He groans like a wounded animal. "Those were my words to a reporter who doesn't matter in an interview I gave a year before I ever met you, Marina."

"That doesn't change anything," I say, pushing back. "I am *not capable* of being a duchess. I can't be what you need me to be. It's easier if we walk away now."

"You're already everything I need. And I will *never* walk away from you."

Silence. He hangs his head, shaking it disbelievingly.

"I won't be here when you get back. Please don't come find me. I need to focus on the proposal meeting tomorrow."

"Oh, Marina," he laughs bitterly, his voice a mere rasp. "I wish you'd fight for us as hard as you fight to fit in with people who don't deserve you."

"Someday you'll understand," I whisper. "I'm sorry, Zach."

As I press disconnect, my heart shatters in a million pieces.

Chapter 21

Zach

I wake up to the sound of a forklift horn honking. I slept on the bus last night, and it sounds like the stadium staff are moving things around to get ready for The Royal Rebels concert tonight. It's a new day, and everyone is moving, while I am unable to make myself set one foot in the real world. Maybe if I stay in here, I won't have to face the fact that my heart was ripped clean from my chest last night. One thing's for sure: I can't go to the hotel.

I don't doubt for a minute that Marina isn't there anymore. And, while I would love to go crashing through her apartment door to profess my undying love for her, she specifically told me to stay away. She doesn't want to see me and I'm not going to force myself into her life, as much as it breaks my heart. Is it too much to hope that the reality of being without me will be enough to send her running back into my arms? I think, for once, I may be reaching too high. But if there's a way to get her back in my life, I know it's not by force.

I'll have Rick go get my things from my suite. I can't set foot in that building. I don't want to see the lobby where I helped her walk a straight line after too many margaritas the night her identity was revealed. I can't go to my suite, through the doorway where she just had to kiss me good morning. And I can't be anywhere near the elevators….where she walked with me the morning I left, kissing me goodbye like her life depended on it.

Our last kiss.

I can't be bombarded with all the memories of her sweetness and light if I don't get to have her in my life anymore. So I will stay in this bus…tunneled under a stadium…until Rick, Sam, and Jimmy drag me out by my hair. End of story.

I've thought of texting her a million times and I still don't know what to say. She didn't specifically tell me not to text her, but how much of a jerk am I for getting *that* detailed. The message was clear: walk away.

I cannot do it.

She is my whole heart. How do I walk away from her?

I roll over and pull a pillow over my head to block out the day. I know eventually I'll have to face it. I honestly don't know how I'm going to get on stage tonight and sing, but I have to find a way. Personal heartache aside, there's no way I'm letting down my band mates or our fans. So I close my eyes and try to drown out the hurt that's hurtling through my veins. For the first time, I wish I'd never stepped off the bus on that bridge.

***

Marina

I walk into the Trans United building with five reporters on my heels. I speed up my stride, making a beeline for the security desk, because they won't be permitted to chase me further.

"Marina! When's your next concert?"

"Are you going on tour with The Royal Rebels?"

"What's next for you?

They're still yelling at me as I step into the elevator and hammer at the button to close the door. I hate that they're able to get closer to me now, but I felt it only right to get on with my life as it was before I met Zach. That means taking the bus to work.

I wonder if my life will now be divided in my memory as Before Zach and After Zach. Before Zach there was order and peace, After Zach there is disorder and heartbreak. Will I ever get over it? Will I ever get myself back together after this?

I don't know why I was surprised, but Dave was parked outside my apartment building this morning, waiting to give me a ride to work. Fresh tears fell just seeing him. Because it meant Zach sent him. Even after I hurt him last night, his first concern is still my safety.

I shook my head at Dave and said no thank you as I stepped past him and got onto the bus, feeling incredibly guilty for the look of utter confusion on his face. The poor guy is just trying to do his job. It would have been hypocritical to accept that ride, as much as I would have loved the safety it provided. I felt so exposed just leaving my building and stepping onto the sidewalk this morning. It was a harsh return to reality, but it's one I have to make.

The security guard was still stationed outside our apartment door when Ashley and I got home last night, and another was on shift when I left this morning. I'm not sure what to do about it. Maybe they'll stop showing up when Zach and the band leave town on Sunday, headed back to southern California to continue the end of their concert tour. I don't have to worry about it right now. I need to focus on getting through today and tomorrow. And I need to figure out a way to smooth things over with Ashley.

She was furious this morning when I stepped out of my room. I never told her last night that I broke things off with Zach. I figured I'd tell her after work on Friday because the proposal meeting would be over, and I'd have to explain why I wasn't going to The Royal Rebels opening night concert. I can't go now, for obvious reasons.

Unfortunately, I'd forgotten that I put her in touch with Rick, and he texted her this morning to see if she knew why a heartbroken Zach was sleeping on the bus at the stadium. He won't get off the bus. That nearly killed me. I wanted to run to him as soon as I heard that. I wanted to throw my arms around him and make it all better, and never leave his side again. But that would only make us feel better in the moment. We would still have the impossible situation of the duchess disaster looming over us. I can't do that to him.

I make my way to my desk, noting with a lump of dread in my stomach that Ethan Montclair is in Ms. Taft's office. Great. It's going to be a long day. They're laughing, thick as thieves, as I walk by, so I hope that's enough to distract her from seeing my arrival.

I log into my computer and see half a dozen revisions to the proposal deck. Great. More fun for today. And I'm sure these aren't the only ones. Does she surround herself with bumbling idiots so she can feel smarter? Some of these edits should have been caught days ago.

Montclair comes slinking out of the Evil Queen's office and heads straight for my desk. A chill runs down my spine as he half sits on the edge of my desk and smiles down at me. I sit back in my chair and look up at him with as much of a pleasant smile as I can muster.

"Good morning, Mr. Montclair," I say with forced lightness. "Can I help you with something?"

His eyes narrow at me for a moment. "If only you would," he coos at me.

"I don't know what you mean."

"I would really love to book you and Zach Adams for an exclusive interview," he says, practically drooling. "What do I have to do to lock that in?"

I hate hearing Zach's name on his lips. Ethan Montclair could live a thousand lifetimes and never be worthy of even sitting in the same room with Zach. I lock down the shudder that threatens to run through my body.

"I'm sorry, Mr. Montclair," I say quietly. "We don't discuss our personal lives with the media."

His brows fly up at my reply while I fight an internal struggle over the fact that there is no *we*. He doesn't need to know that, but I feel the crack in my heart widen, regardless.

"That's so boring, Marina, really," he croons. "Surely there must be something I can do to sweeten the deal."

He reaches out a finger and starts tracing a line down the back of my hand. I pull away immediately and he smirks at me. His smugness, his absolute sliminess, grates on me. I turn to face him, narrowing my eyes.

"I can understand how you'd expect more from the Duchess of San Francisco," I say pointedly. "But I'm not interested."

He scoffs and pushes himself off my desk.

"I'm not done with you, *Duchess*," he says in a slithery, low tone as he turns to leave.

"Mr. Montclair?"

He turns back to me with raised eyebrows. I set my jaw and look him square in the eye.

"Please don't touch me again. It makes me extremely uncomfortable."

He smirks and walks away without answering, and I take in a long breath. He walks back into Ms. Taft's office.

"Marina!" Ms. Taft calls from inside her office.

I grab a pad and pen, curse under my breath, and enter her office. Montclair winks at me as I walk in and I fight the urge to hurl my note pad at his head.

"Mr. Montclair will need a workspace for today and tomorrow," she explains. "He's working on some things for a client of his and there's too much going on at his offices right now. Find an open office here and set it up for him before you get started with the rest of your work."

"No problem," I lie. Big problem. We don't have any open offices.

Montclair reaches up and runs two fingers down my arm.

"Do you need any help?" he says, looking me up and down with a predatory gleam in his eye.

I pull away from him. "No, sir. But thank you."

He laughs, then stands and strolls toward the door.

"I'll be back around lunch time," he says lightly. "Can't wait to see the space you set up for me, Duchess."

He walks out with an air of superiority, leaving me alone with Ms. Taft. I decide to go for broke.

"Ms. Taft, I feel like you should know some things going around in the office," I say carefully.

She puts down her pen and raises her brows, motioning for me to go on.

"Mr. Montclair is making excuses to touch women in the office," I say. "Myself included. It's…creepy."

She scoffs. "That's ridiculous. Why would he bother with someone like you?"

I pause and consider my answer before speaking. "That's your response?"

She rolls her eyes. "Marina, I know you're used to getting the attention of a social media darling, but not every man in the world is interested in you. Get over yourself. And get back to work. Now."

I go back to my desk, wondering why I even bothered.

***

It's after 6 pm when I finally walk out the doors of the Trans United Tower, dogged by more reporters as I run for the bus. One of them actually gets on the bus with me and tries to get me to talk the entire way home. By the time I get to the apartment, I'm in a horrible mood. I step off the bus and duck into my building as quickly as possible. I don't miss the fact that there's now a second security guard on the ground floor to make sure no one follows me inside the lobby.

Zach.

The reminder that he's still trying to take care of me reaches into my ribs and wraps around my heart like a warm blanket. I hesitate just inside my apartment door, closing my eyes against the wave of emotions that hits me. A throat clears and I jump, opening my eyes to see Ashley, Merry, and Scarlet watching me from the living room.

"Hi," I say simply. "Is something going on?"

Merry walks toward me.

"Yep," she says, grabbing my hand and pulling me to the living room. "This is an inter-friend-tion."

She pushes me to sit on the couch, so I obey.

"A what?"

"We're here to talk to you about your life choices," Scarlet deadpans. Always the realist.

I look from one to other, waiting for one of them to start so we can get this over with. No one speaks.

"Guys," I plead. "I really don't need this right now."

"Why not?" Merry asks. "What's more important than your friends making sure you don't totally screw up your life?"

"You're looking at this wrong," I try to explain. "I'm thinking of the future."

Ashley steps forward. "You're running."

My lip trembles. "I am literally just trying to hold everything together until this proposal is done."

Merry nods. "And we're literally just trying to get you to see some sense. What's all this duchess stuff about? Ashley says you think you can't be a duchess. Why not? You would be an amazing duchess."

I openly scoff. That is the most ridiculous idea ever.

"I'm serious. You're smart, beautiful, determined. Why not you?"

Something inside me breaks a little more, and my throat closes up. I don't have the energy to list out all the ways I don't measure up here, especially after a long day of working with people who enjoy reminding me that I'm lacking in some way. I stand up and turn to my friends.

"I appreciate what you're trying to do," I say in a voice that's way too wobbly. "But I finally have a video call with Max in twenty minutes, and I want to take a shower first. I love you guys."

With that, I walk into the bathroom and shut the door, leaving them to figure out how to deal with me. I turn on the shower and strip out of my suit, then start pulling my hair out of the tight up-do. I step under the spray, letting the hot water pour over my skin. No matter what I do, I can't scrub the unsettled feeling out of my head or my heart. I let the shower spray wash away fresh tears. I'm not sure I'll ever feel normal again.

I put my wet hair in a towel and wrap another one around my body, then pad out of the bathroom and head for my bedroom. The girls are huddled on the couch, their hushed voices silencing when I emerge. I say nothing as I open my bedroom door.

"Hey," Ashley calls.

I turn and look at her. Her eyes are full of concern, as are Merry and Scarlet's.

"We love you too."

I manage a wobbly smile as I step inside my bedroom and close the door. Once inside, I check the time. Five minutes to go. I rush through toweling myself off, get into my pajamas, and throw my hair up in a messy bun, then sit on my bed just in time for Max's call to come through. I hit the connect button and his face lightens my heart like it's loaded with helium.

"Hi!" I say excitedly, feeling happier than I've felt all day.

"Hey, sis, what's…what's happened? Bad day at work?" Max asks, no doubt when he gets a look at my red, blotchy face.

I manage a weak smile.

"It's been a rough one," I say. "How about you?"

He looks concerned but decides to answer me.

"Pretty average, except for my project partner bailing like that," he says. "Rocking all the math stuff, have to work hard at all the floofy stuff."

I laugh, and it feels good.

"Floofy stuff?"

He shrugs. "English, history. You know."

"I remember," I say fondly, thinking back to what it was like trying to get him through his homework after school. "You always needed a lot more help with those subjects."

He nods. "And you were always great about helping me."

"Yeah, well," I grin. "You weren't much trouble."

He laughs at that, then raises his chin at me.

"So what's up? Really. You seem a little down."

I shake my head. "I'll be a lot better after tomorrow is done."

"The big proposal at work?"

I nod. "Yep. My boss is really awful, and she's been really rude and demanding. The guy who runs the firm we're trying to sign a contract with is even worse."

I tell him about the creepy touching and he looks like he's going to crawl through the phone so he can go strangle Montclair.

"That's terrible, Marina," he says, frowning. "What does Zach say?"

My lip quivers, and he catches it.

"Hey, sis," he says, his tone cautious. "What's really going on? Now you have me worried."

So I tell him. The whole story. The horrible gossip shows. The media scrutiny. Zach's interview. My decision to set him free. I lay it all out. Max is quiet for a moment, then he shakes his head.

"You've done it again, haven't you, Marina?"

I look at him quizzically. "Done what?"

He smirks at me, and it's a little like looking in the mirror. It's hard not to feel a sense of pride that he takes after me in a small way.

"You've made a decision that wasn't yours to make," he says, his voice laced with sadness.

"No, that's not—"

"Ten years ago, you decided I was better off without you in my life," he says.

His words cut deep. He's right. I did do that.

"Did you ask me what I wanted?"

I shake my head.

"No, you sure didn't. You thought you knew better. And I spent ten years without my only sister."

I inhale sharply at the pain that punches through his words, and he looks chagrined.

"Hey," he says gently. "I'm not trying to make you feel bad. I'm trying to stop you from making a really bad decision. I saw you two together for just a few hours and I could see you have something special."

I shake my head. "The decision has been made, Max. It's done."

"Oh, and you can't take it back?" he pushes.

I don't want to think about any of this right now. I'm at my emotional threshold. And I am so, so tired of crying.

"Marina, if I could make one wish in this world, it would be for you to truly believe that *you* are worth fighting for. You fight for everyone else. Fiercely. But you don't think you're worthy of the same. You are."

Tears again. I put my head back against my headboard and let them fall, then grab a handful of tissues from the box on my nightstand.

"I've missed you so much, Max," I say in a wobbly voice. "Thank you for all that."

He nods firmly. "No problem, sis."

"Can we talk about something else? Otherwise, I'm going to get severely dehydrated. I've done nothing but cry for days."

His eyes fill with concern again. "As long as you promise to think about what I said."

I nod.

"So what do you want to talk about now?" he asks.

I think for a moment, then grin at him and say, "Red licorice."

***

Marina

This day will never end.

It's finally Friday. Proposal day.

Initially, the plan was to have breakfast here at the office during a meet & greet for the staff, then go over the proposal, and then out to a fancy lunch to celebrate. The end.

That all changed yesterday when Ms. Taft decided that she wanted a whole dog and pony show after breakfast in order to tout the many services available at the firm. Lunch was changed to a different location, which was difficult to manage last minute, and we added a fancy dinner tonight. Since I'm not going to a certain concert tonight, I guess it's no big deal.

I ended up falling asleep right after my video chat with Max, so I missed seeing the girls again. I meant to go back out there and smooth things over, but I didn't get that far. Instead, I sent them a text from my seat on the bus this morning.

Marina: Fell asleep after my video call last night, guys, I'm so sorry. Didn't mean to leave you hanging.

Scarlet: We know. We checked on you.

Marina: You did?

Merry: Who do you think put you under the covers and turned off the light?

Marina: I really love you guys.

Ashley: Enough to go to the Rebels concert with us tonight?

Marina: You know I can't do that, Ash.

Merry: You can do anything you want to.

Marina: You girls go and have fun. I'll be exhausted anyway. Love you.

Ashley: :-/

Now I'm sitting in the executive conference room, fighting to keep my focus. Ms. Taft is seated at the head of the table, and Montclair is to her right. Department heads from both firms are seated around the table, and several executive assistants are in chairs against the wall. As per usual, I'm in the hot seat to Ms. Taft's left in case she needs anything.

Someone touches my arm and I jump out of my reverie. I glance to my left to see a concerned look from Kat, one of Montclair's team. She's around my age and seems nice enough. I have no idea why she works for a jerk like him. Then again, I work for the Evil Queen.

I give her a curious look.

"I just wanted to say how excited I am," Kat whispers. "I've loved following your story in the media. It's so romantic."

"Thanks," I say quietly, looking over at Montclair.

He's certainly drawn this out as long as he can. The man loves to be the center of attention. I look up at the clock on the conference room wall. It's after 6 pm, and we're officially going to be late for our dinner reservation at a very exclusive restaurant in Nob Hill.

"Maybe we'll get to work together a little now that our companies are besties." She grins.

I offer Kat a bland smile, stealing a glimpse at Ms. Taft out of the corner of my eye. She's practically drooling as she fixes her eyes on Montclair. His hand hovers above the contract he's about to sign, and he looks at Kat and me.

"What are you two talking about in such hushed tones over there?" His tone is teasing, but I don't like being the focus of any kind of attention from him.

Kat waves a hand. "Oh, I'm just sharing with Marina how excited I was to meet the famous mermaid. I just love her story."

Ms. Taft narrows her gaze at me. She looks furious that I've stolen the attention away from the big moment.

"I couldn't agree more, Kat. But I never much cared for The Royal Rebels," Montclair drawls, picking a bit of lint from his jacket and giving me a pointed look. "Their music is just okay."

I hate how defensive his words make me feel. How insulted I am on Zach's behalf, even though I don't have the right to be anything on his behalf anymore. Not after what I did. Even if it was for his own good.

Wait, *what?*

"Are you kidding?" Kat argues. "They've had some great hits. 'All You', 'Take My Hand', and my favorite is 'You Are My Heart'. That song is so beautiful!"

Suddenly, it feels like an electric current is passing over my skin. My pulse picks up, and I feel flushed.

You Are My Heart.

Something clicks inside my addled brain. *That's* the song Zach was humming in my ear that night as we danced on stage in the empty stadium. I recognized it, but couldn't place it. As if it's happening right now, I hear his voice humming the melody to the song. I feel his arms around me as we slow danced in the middle of the stage. The lyrics spin through my head as Ms. Taft tries to bring the focus back to Montclair and the big signing.

And for you, I'd walk through fire. My heart lurches. He would have, wouldn't he? *I'd sell my soul, burn with desire.* One look from Zach was enough for me to catch fire. *I'll swim oceans, fly across the sky.* Our impromptu flight to San Diego comes to mind. *Just don't leave me, don't say goodbye.* I literally did that. I did that. And I stomped on his heart on the way out.

I'm vaguely aware of someone calling my name, but my mind just keeps burning through the lyrics, finding meaning in each and every word. *I fell for you from the very start.* And he did. I know he did. My mind wanders back to his expression when he stepped through the crowd of onlookers in the middle of the bridge. I try to remember what he said to me on the bus.

Unbothered...but completely bewitched. That's what he said.

An overwhelming wave of regret and longing sweeps over me. *What have I done?*

Max was right. I did the same thing to Zach that I did to Max: I made his decision for him and completely discounted myself in the process. I made myself the problem and shoved him away because I thought he'd be better off without me. He's the one who gets to decide what he can handle and what he can't. And he's the one who gets to decide whether I'm worth sticking around for. And I'm worth it to him, I know it in my very core. I'm worth it to him.

"Marina? Helloooo?" Ms. Taft says loudly, making me jump.

I look over at her. She's absolutely incensed. "I'm sorry...what?"

"I asked you to call the restaurant and tell them we're running late," she says in a patronizing tone. "Honestly."

My mind drifts back to Zach, who wanted me to fight for him. Instead, I fought to be in this room with these people who don't deserve a place in my story. Well, maybe Hillary, who's seated at the back near her boss. But the rest of these people haven't done one thing to earn an ounce of the energy I've spent working for them. What am I even doing here?

Something touches my leg under the table, and I jump in my seat, earning me a scathing look from Ms. Taft. I mouth an apology automatically and settle back down. That is until I look across the table and find Ethan Montclair raising an eyebrow at me. Something brushes my leg again, and I realize it's him. He's reaching his foot across and is touching my bare leg. Every inch of my skin feels like it's crawling. Unable to stand it another second, I stand up and shove my chair back.

Ms. Taft glares up at me. "What has come over you, Marina? Sit down."

I make eye contact with Hillary at the back of the room. She gives me a determined nod as if to say *I'm with you.* I turn my attention to Ethan Montclair.

"You need to keep your hands and feet to yourself, Mr. Montclair," I declare boldly. "Don't ever touch me, or any other woman in this office, again. Ms. Taft seems to be the only one here who wants your slimy attention."

He laughs loudly, looking me up and down as if he's enjoying this immensely.

Ms. Taft scoffs loudly. "That is enough! What is going on?"

"I told you what is going on, and you wouldn't believe me," I explain, pointing at Montclair. "This man has been disrespecting my personal boundaries since the day he stepped into this office.

He's been banking on me needing my job so badly that I wouldn't say anything about all the creepy touches and bumps. But I did. I told you, and you refused to do anything. You belittled me instead. Honestly, I think you two deserve each other."

Pure anger flashes in Ms. Taft's eyes. "How dare you, I—"

"Has anyone else here had to endure Mr. Montclair's creepy behavior?" I ask loudly, raising my own hand. "I'm betting there's more than just me."

Hillary slowly raises her hand, and I want to run over and hug her. So do three other women, including Kat. I put my hand on her shoulder and give her a little squeeze. Montclair looks at her and scoffs.

"Wishful thinking, ladies," he drawls. "I'm just a little clumsy."

I roll my eyes. I've had enough. These aren't my people. They don't deserve one more second of my time or energy. I'm done wasting my life with people who don't see my value. Because there are people who do see it. That's who I should be with.

"I'm sorry, but there's somewhere else I need to be," I interrupt breathlessly. I gather my things but leave the copy of the proposal on the table. I turn to Ms. Taft. "For the record, I quit."

"Without notice? How typical," Ms. Taft bites back. "And you call yourself a professional? You have a lot to learn, Marina."

I turn and give her a cold look.

"No, I am most definitely a professional, which is why I will not tolerate this kind of behavior for one more second," I say coolly, and then I look at the other women in the room. "I will, of course, be filing the appropriate paperwork with the California Civil Rights Department. If any of you would like to join me, I'll be in touch."

The last thing I see is Ms. Taft's mouth fall open as I turn on my heel and walk out of the conference room.

Chapter 22

❦

Run, don't walk.

Run, run, run.

And so I do.

I go straight to my desk to grab my bags while dropping my ID badge and assorted keys in the top drawer. Then I pull out my phone as I run to the elevator.

Good riddance, horrible people. I'm done.

It's late, so I'm betting Dave is at the stadium already, since he was picking up the girls tonight. I can't count on him for a ride this time. I start weighing my options.

The concert starts in less than thirty minutes. I order a rideshare to take me home since there's no bus due for another fifteen minutes, and I take the elevator down to the garage level.

Yes, home first. I did think of just rushing straight to the stadium, but I won't be able to see him until the concert is over, anyway. I've hurt Zach deeply. Amends must be made, and I have an idea. I just need a little help to execute the plan. If there's one thing I've learned this week, it's okay to ask for help. My inner circle and I will knock it out of the park.

It feels like forever, but the rideshare driver pulls into the garage six minutes later. I verify his ID and get in the back of the car. As soon as we clear the garage, which makes cell coverage spotty, I open the group chat with the girls.

Marina: Are you guys at the concert?

Merry: We just got to our seats.

Marina: Is there room for me?

Ashley: SHE'S BACK, LADIES & GENTLEMEN!

Scarlet: You rock, girl!

Merry: Yassss! I knew it! I had faith!!

I laugh out loud and swipe a stray tear away. A happy tear, for once.

Marina: I need your help, guys.

Ashley: Oh, just get here and we'll talk about whatever it is.

Marina: No, I have wardrobe questions.

Scarlet: What? Why? Who cares what you're wearing?

Ashley: We're listening.

And that's when I tell them my plan.

The rideshare pulls up to my apartment, and the driver agrees to wait for me to come back down. Then, he'll take me to the stadium. Anything to save time at this point, because I need hugs from my girls before I pull the trigger on this plan. I get out of the car, and the security guard at the door keeps two reporters from getting in my way. I run into the building and race up to my apartment, not caring if anyone is taking my picture. I don't hear the questions they are yelling. I'm on a mission.

Once inside, I run straight for my closet and pull out the dress we decided on in the group chat. It's a white, form-fitting cocktail dress with tons of sequins and crystals on it. We each have one in our size, as we bought them for our little side hustle when we perform together. As soon as Merry suggested this dress, I knew it was the perfect choice. I run to Ash's room and grab the shoes she said I could have since they were intended for her wedding with Greg.

The jerk.

They're simple white high-heeled pumps, but they're fancy enough to look fabulous with this dress. I grab a clutch out of my closet, throw in my phone, wallet, keys, and lipstick, and I'm back out the door. Hopefully, I can check my hair at the stadium.

Reporters snap more pictures of me as I get in the back seat of the rideshare and hand the driver my phone so he can show me how to update my trip in the app. He punches away on the screen, then verifies the stadium address with me before handing my phone back to me. With that done, I settle in and open a new text message.

Marina: Are you there, Dave? I need a big favor.

***

The concert is well underway by the time the rideshare pulls into the parking lot, so the outside of the stadium is pretty calm. The driver pulls up to the VIP entrance, and I see Dave's hulking form waiting for me. My heart pounds with excitement as I jump out of the car, thanking the driver and running to Dave.

"Dave!" I squeal happily, throwing my arms around his neck and giving him an impromptu hug.

I feel his hands pat me on the back hesitantly as my very open display of affection takes him by surprise. I step back quickly and smooth my dress with shaky hands.

"Sorry," I say with a quick laugh. "I'm just so happy to see you. Thank you for helping me."

He bows his head, looking slightly embarrassed, and hands me my VIP credentials for the show. "Of course, Miss MacArthur. Are you ready?"

I nod and walk with him as he starts toward the entrance. My pass is scanned quickly, and I follow Dave to the upper level. Zach's powerful voice fills the stadium as the band performs one of their many hits to the screaming crowd below. I desperately want to run over to the railing so I can see him, but I stay with Dave. Little tingles break out all across my skin. That's my man down there, thrilling eighty thousand people.

Most of the fans are in their seats, but a few are milling around, and I see some of them take notice out of the corner of my eye. Cell phones come out. I may never get used to this, but it's enough that I no longer care.

"Hey, it's Marina!"

Since I'm doing all the brave things again, I turn and wave at them as Dave and I walk around the corner. He leads me to an elevator that takes us down one level to the suites. We're still well above the floor seats, so it's quite different from the benefit concert. It's perfect, though, since I don't want Zach to see me until I'm ready to be seen. I can stay hidden away in the suite with the girls.

We're stopped by fans a few times as people recognize me and rush over to ask for selfies and handshakes. I say yes to all the things, no longer worried about what anyone is thinking. Because that's my boyfriend out there…playing his heart out for them, and his fans deserve my best. Finally, Dave leads me to a door and opens it for me to reveal a posh-looking suite.

I'm quickly pulled into the arms of my three ride-or-dies. Gratitude fills my heart as we hug each other. There aren't words for how much these women mean to me. I'm so lucky to have friends who will lift me up and be real with me when I need it. And I do the same for them.

"You look amazing!" Merry says breathlessly. "Oh, I love it when I'm right! That dress will look beautiful under the lights."

Scarlet nods. "We need to amp up the make-up just a smidge if you're going to be under a spotlight."

Ashley tilts her head at me. "Yeah, maybe a little. And touch up the hair."

"Sorry, girls," I say as I hold up my tiny clutch. "I only have a lipstick."

Merry shrugs it off. "We got this. Check your purses, ladies. What do we have?"

Within minutes, my eyes are lightly lined, my cheeks tinted, my lipstick reapplied, and my hair is loose and flowing. I am officially deemed ready for the grand gesture of all grand gestures. We sit down inside the suite, where there's a plush leather sofa and several chairs.

The suite is decorated in a beautiful navy and cream color scheme, with high-end logos of all the local teams that play here. On the far side of the suite, a sumptuous buffet is set up and waiting for us. There's also a bar with a bartender, just waiting to pour whatever we want.

"I sent a text to Rick as soon as you told us your plan," Ashley shares. "He's taken care of everything with the crew. Dave will come and get you when it's time, and he'll be with you the whole way."

I nod slowly, a secret smile spreading across my face. "So you guys think this'll work?"

Scarlet cocks her head. "Girl, do you think he's going to do anything but run right into your arms when you do this?"

Merry wiggles in her seat and squeals.

"I am so proud of you, Marina," she says, her eyes a little damp. "I had faith you'd come around. What you have with Zach is too good to walk away from."

My own eyes cloud up. "It really is," I say softly. "I don't know what I was thinking, trying to let him go."

Ashley scoffs. "That man was not gonna let you let him go. I'm not sure what he would have done if you hadn't come around, but he's got it bad."

The crowd in the stadium cheers loudly, and we all look up at the huge video screen inside the suite. Zach smiles at the fans in the stadium as he and the guys take their bows after performing one of their many hits. My heart lurches at the look behind his eyes. I can see the hurt he's trying to hide, and I feel terrible that I'm the one who put it there.

Just hang on a little longer, baby.

I can't wait for him to see me.

I take a minute to watch him on the screen. He gives so much of himself to every performance, running around on stage so every part of the stadium can see him. Depending on the song they're performing, sometimes he's at a mic stand with his guitar. Sometimes, he's at the piano. Right now, he's walking down the catwalk that juts into the audience, and he pauses occasionally during the song to engage with the audience closest to the stage. It's no wonder his voice is hoarse, and he's physically exhausted when he's done with a show.

One of the things I admire most about him is the fact that he lives his life out loud. He doesn't really worry about what others think of him. But he's a kind person and a good man, which makes it a challenge for the media to report anything negative. So I smile up at the screen, watching him have fun on stage with the guys and feeling absolutely proud that he's mine.

"So you're really okay with…everything?" Ash asks me with a hopeful expression.

I tilt my head and think about my reply.

"I'm not okay with the media being jerks," I say. "And I still have a lot of doubt about the future, but I'm prepared to acknowledge that my sweet and gorgeous boyfriend knows a lot more about it than I do. I will be listening to his expert opinion in the future."

We sit there for the bulk of the concert, watching the band on the monitors and using the breaks between songs to chat.

"How did the big meeting go?" Scarlet asks.

"Everything went to plan for the most part," I explain. "Until I finally realized that those are not my people."

"Yes!" Ashley cheers.

"Once it dawned on me, I didn't want to waste any more time where I wasn't valued. So I quit."

"Did they pay you the bonus?" Ash asks.

I shake my head. "I have no idea. I guess we'll find out, right? If they don't, I'm gonna need some help."

Ash's expression softens, and she nods at me. "I've got you."

Zach leads the band through a mash-up of some fan favorites and we stay silent for a while, enjoying the concert and each other's company.

The door to the suite opens and Dave fills the door frame. A uniformed security guard is right behind him. He dips his head.

"Miss MacArthur," he says stoically. "It's time."

Merry squeals again and pulls me in for a hug, then Ash and Scarlet take their turns.

"Good luck," Ashley says with a huge grin, rubbing her hands up and down my arms. "You're going to be amazing."

I nod my thanks, knowing I'll need all the good luck I can get.

Don't let me forget what to do. Don't let me trip in these heels.

I head for the door, ready to follow Dave so he can take me downstairs, and then I pause. I turn around to face the girls.

"Hey," I say with a conspiratorial grin, "you guys want to come with me?"

***

Zach

The crowd cheers wildly as the guys and I bring "Highway to Love" to a close. As one of our biggest hits, it gets the audience going every time, and we always play it toward the end of our shows. Every once in a while, I turn my back to the audience to relax my face and pull myself together. I usually have as much fun as the fans up here, but I'm not feeling it tonight. Honestly, I don't know how I've gotten through this entire concert without making a stupid mistake or just crumbling from the huge hole that was blown straight through my heart when Marina ended us. I do know one thing. Our final song of the night before the encore is "You Are My Heart," and there is no way I'm making my way through the entire song without a couple of tears falling.

It's a ballad, and it's perfect for winding the crowd down before we get them riled up again with an encore.

I do not want to sing it.

I wrote it on my own last year when the inspiration came to me, and singing my heart out about a love like no other will break me. There is one hundred percent certainty that I'm going to lose it. If it wasn't for the eighty thousand fans in this stadium, I'd scrub the song completely. But I can't let them down, and I'm a stand-up guy. Especially when it comes to our fans. We owe them everything. My heart may lie in a thousand pieces right now, but as the saying goes…the show must go on.

The fans are still cheering when I step back up to the mic, ready to set up "You Are My Heart", but I pause when I feel a hand clamp down on my shoulder. I turn to find Rick standing next to me, with a look on his face that I can't quite identify. We're used to clowning around together on stage, so I give him a big smile and lean over to the mic.

"What's up, Rick?" I say with a lightness I definitely don't feel.

I can see from his expression he knows I'm having a hard time. His hand gives my shoulder an extra squeeze.

"How much do you trust me, bud?" Rick asks, winking at the audience and prompting more cheers.

I force a laugh. "I trust you implicitly, my friend."

The crowd cheers again. I knit my eyebrows together and give him a confused look. He doesn't explain. He just reaches behind him, where Jimmy is handing him a stool that must have come from backstage. Rick makes a show of sliding it next to me and steps aside, gesturing at it.

"Have a seat," Rick says, smiling at our fans and then giving me a secret look, which I read instantly.

Just go with it.

I play along and sit down, folding my arms across my chest and winking at the front row. Laughter bubbles up from the audience, and cell phones are coming out to capture this off-script moment.

"Okay, just relax," Rick explains. "We've got a surprise for you, so just sit here and enjoy it. But don't sing. All right?"

I'm confused, but Rick would never do anything to ruin a show or anger our fans, so I know whatever this is, I can just let it happen. I shrug and nod.

"Yes, boss."

This prompts shrieks of laughter from the fans.

As Rick steps away, he gives my shoulder another squeeze, and I wonder what on earth he has planned. I turn to face the audience and smile. If I truly don't have to sing this song, maybe it's a blessing. The heaviness in my chest feels like it could drop me right through the stage floor. I kind of wish it would. Then, I could stop forcing myself to smile.

Behind me, I hear Rick take my usual spot at the piano. He begins playing the opening strains of the song, which, at the risk of sounding like an egomaniac, are beautiful. I've always been so proud of this song. It won a lot of awards, and I love playing it, but tonight it'll wreck me. The lyrics could have been written about Marina and me, and my throat gets tight just hearing the opening.

Just as the first verse approaches, I hear some loud cheers coming from somewhere out in the stadium audience. Is something going on out there? We never have that kind of response at this part of the song. I have about three seconds to wonder what's going on before a voice I know all too well begins singing the first line of the song.

"All my life I've waited, baby..."

My heart nearly explodes in my chest as Marina's voice fills the stadium while applause and screams erupt from the fans. I bolt from the stool and turn to face the stage, expecting to find her standing at a mic behind me, but she's not there. She's nowhere on stage. My eyes dart to Rick, who is grinning at me like the proverbial cat that ate the canary. He nods in the direction of the audience.

"...for someone to call my own..."

I whirl around and look out into the crowd, but with the stage lights on my face, I can't see anything. Several fans are yelling at me, and I start running toward their voices, heading down the long catwalk part of the stage that stretches fifty meters into the audience. They're pointing to the left, and I shield my eyes from the lights as I scan the crowd. It's a sea of black out there, but when my eyes focus a bit, I can see some kind of commotion in one of the main aisles of the floor seats.

"Always thought that maybe I was meant to be alone..."

As she begins the second verse of the song, a spotlight illuminates a lone figure slowly walking towards me up the main aisle. My pulse is a riot in my veins, and a guttural sound escapes my lips as I see Marina. She's wearing a simple white dress that comes to just above her knees, and it's covered in iridescent sparkles. The light from the spotlight dances off her dress and makes it look like she's covered in fairy lights. She looks like an angel. Her beautiful red hair flows in soft waves, framing her face as she slowly makes her way through the crowd, singing "You Are My Heart". She's not holding a mic, so she must be wired with one. I realize for the first time that someone in my inner circle has been plotting this behind my back. Rick is definitely one of them, but this is more than Rick. I owe them all a raise.

As she gets closer to the catwalk, I can just see a couple of shadowed figures walking behind her. Security. Good. As she walks, fans hold up their mobile phones to catch a video of her. Others are holding out their hands for high-fives or handshakes, but her eyes are fixed only on me. The dam inside me finally breaks.

Tears fall down my cheeks just as a lump the size of a Tesla parks in my throat. She's here. Singing *my lyrics* with her hauntingly beautiful voice, walking towards me with hope in her eyes and a little smile that's just for me. My face crumples, and I hit myself square in the chest with the palm of my hand a few times, trying to hold it together. I'm failing miserably, and I just don't care…because that's my girl.

She pauses at the end of the catwalk, and I realize there's no way for her to get up on the stage. Before I can make a move, Dave and a security guard step out of the shadows and lift her onto the stage as if the entire thing was choreographed. I blink back my surprise, which prompts a huge smile from Marina.

I want her to come to me. I need her in my arms more than I need the air I'm breathing, but she stays where she is as she sings the end of the verse she's on.

As she gets to the second chorus, I can no longer contain myself. I shake my head at her as I close the distance between us, the crowd going absolutely wild as I pull her into my arms. She wraps her arms around my neck as she smiles up at me, and I've never seen anything more beautiful in my entire life.

"Hi," I say simply, rubbing my nose against hers.

"Hi," she answers, her eyelashes fluttering closed for a moment. When they open again, I'm lost in an emerald sea. "I quit my job today."

Cheers erupt from the crowd, and we both laugh.

"Good."

We stand in each other's arms for a moment, just gazing at each other as if there aren't eighty thousand fans watching. After a few seconds, I realize that Rick has continued to play, looping the music over and over in case Marina wants to continue the song. I look over at him, and he raises his eyebrows in question. As if reading my thoughts, Marina gets a mischievous look in her eye.

"So, should I finish the song, or would you rather go somewhere and talk?"

I throw my head back and laugh. "Maybe we should finish the song first."

When I start to let her go, she steps closer to me and wraps her arms tighter around my neck. "No, no. This is good. Don't let me go."

I reach up to stroke a strand of hair away from her face. "Never again."

Her lip trembles, and she swallows hard, blinking back tears. "Good. Because I'm not going anywhere."

Keeping one arm wrapped firmly around her, I reach down and take her other hand in mine as I move us in a slow dance to the music. I'm vaguely aware of more cheering, applause, and mobile phones recording this ridiculously amazing moment. Marina's eyes meet mine as she picks up the chorus and begins singing again.

"And for you, I'd walk through fire," she sings, and I'm mesmerized. "I'd sell my soul, burn with desire. I'll swim oceans and fly across the sky. Just don't leave me, don't say goodbye. I fell for you from the very start. Because you, baby…you are my heart."

When the chorus repeats at the end, I distinctly hear female backup singers, and I whirl us around to face the stage. There, standing at the mic I left when I ran out here, are Merry, Scarlet, and Ashley singing a harmony to back up Marina. They finish the song with thunderous applause from the audience, and I don't wait one second longer to claim Marina's mouth in a soul-searing kiss.

I hear nothing but my own heart, ready to pound right out of my ribcage as we kiss each other like we've been apart for years. I claim her with this kiss, and she claims me right back. I feel her tremble as she tightens her grip on my neck and digs her fingers into my hair. When we finally come up for air, I press our foreheads together.

"I love you," I whisper over her ear, but I don't know why I bothered whispering. Her headset mic picks it up, and everyone hears it. "I love you so much."

The audience is screaming so loud it sounds like they're ready to riot. Marina doesn't seem to notice. She traces my lips with light, feathery kisses as she gently wipes the traces of tears from my face. "I love you, too."

I crush her in my arms and swing her around. She squeals, and I set her down after a while, taking her hand in mine and beginning the walk back up to the main stage as the crowd begins to chant "encore" over and over and over again. I pull her hand up to my lips and kiss the back of it as we come to a stop center stage.

I look into her beautiful face. "Say it again. Tell me again."

She beams up at me. "I love you, Zach Adams."

"Siren," I say breathlessly. "That is music to my ears."

Her smile could light up the whole world.

"Just to make it official," she asks as she smooths her hands over my chest. "Does this mean you forgive me for trying to end the best thing that's ever happened to me?"

I feel a growl escape my throat as I bury my hands in her hair and bring her mouth to mine. I don't care about the cheer of the crowd or the fact that I can hear our friends whistling from behind their mics. I only know that she's mine. She came back. And she's *mine*. And I am most definitely hers. Body and soul.

We break from our kiss, and I look down at Marina. "Well, Siren? Shall we sing them an encore?"

She nuzzles into my neck for a moment, then moves her mouth close to my ear. "If you think you're getting rid of me now, you're crazy."

I laugh out loud and squeeze her tighter as I look over at the guys and give them the signal for the encore. They begin to play, and the opening notes of our biggest hit, "All You, All Day, All Night" fills the stadium. I look down at Marina as I move us closer to the mic, bringing her with me. I know the A/V team will turn her headset mic off when they see what I'm doing.

"Do you know this one?" I ask softly.

She rolls her eyes like I just asked the dumbest question ever.

"Of course," she says with a gorgeous grin. "I'm your biggest fan."

And with that, we turn to our audience and give them an encore none of us will ever forget.

Chapter 23

Marina

I try to roll out of bed, and two arms tighten around my middle like steel bands, not budging an inch. I'm hauled back against a hard, warm, muscular body that smells like…home. Beachy sandalwood bonfires.

Zach.

I laugh softly, my heart feeling light and full of joy.

"It's getting late," I whine softly. "I'm hungry."

I feel Zach's body relax in resignation behind me. I said the magic word. The man will not let me go hungry. He'd go out and hunt pigs for me if the hotel ran out of bacon, which might actually happen if we stay here much longer. Zach requested plenty of it last night when he ordered breakfast to be delivered to the room by ten this morning. And it's almost time for that magical room service cart to come rolling in.

His lips tease little kisses on the side of my neck and I tilt my head farther back, granting him all the access for all the kisses. Best way to wake up ever. Warm, comfy bed. Gorgeous Brit wrapped around

337

me. Neck kisses. I'm here for all of it.

My stomach growls, and it sounds like a T-Rex is loose somewhere in the hotel. Zach laughs softly, his breath tickling my neck, and he lets me go. I instantly regret it.

"All right, beautiful," he groans. "Let's get up. We've much to do before the concert tonight."

I roll out of bed and stretch. I don't know how he does it. The Royal Rebels have two more concerts at the stadium this weekend before the whole show packs up and moves down to southern California for a series of shows down there, then on to a few more stops before it's all over. It must be exhausting.

Zach lets out a low whistle behind me and I turn to find him eyeing me appreciatively.

"You really rock those mermaid pants, Siren," he says with a wink. "I'm going upstairs to take my shower, and I'll be right back down."

I smile at him as he throws his t-shirt on and walks out of the bedroom. I turn on my heel and head to my bathroom to get ready, even though I'd love nothing more than to just lounge around in my jammies with Zach all day. He's right: we have a lot to do. I have no idea what it is, though, because he won't tell me yet. I imagine some of it is talking through how we're going to manage our relationship going forward. And maybe he'll finally tell me where he actually lives. I reach into the shower and turn it on, then grab some towels and strip while I wait for the water to warm up.

Last night, after the girls and I sang three encores with The Royal Rebels, he wouldn't let me leave his side (not that I'm complaining one bit). So he had Dave take the girls home when it was time, while I was glued to his side backstage. Ashley packed a bag for me and gave it to Dave, who came back to the stadium to take the rest of us back to the hotel. Zach never altered the hotel arrangements, even though he was sleeping on the bus, so my suite was exactly as I left it.

That's probably a good thing because I accidentally left behind three suits that were meant to go to the dry cleaners. Naturally, the housekeeping staff had them cleaned and left them hanging in the closet because the service here is insanely awesome. I move quickly in the shower, eager to get on with my day and, of course, to be back in Zach's arms. That's something to celebrate because I can't remember the last time I was actually excited about my day. Another realization brought on by doing all the brave things. I was so used to keeping my nose to the grindstone that I never allowed myself time to look up.

It's funny how completely at peace I felt the moment I decided to walk away from the things that are no longer serving me (mainly my horrible job) and chose the people who choose me every day. I thought I'd feel some level of angst or guilt about quitting my job, but I'm just happy. I feel free. And I have a whole new level of gratitude for the people who love me.

I dry off and change into the yoga pants and oversized sweater Ash threw in the bag for me. What can I say? The girl knows me. I brush out my damp hair and pull it up on my head with a clip for now. I'll fuss over it later.

A brief knock at the door has me running for it because it's either Zach or bacon, and I want to devour both. I hold the door open for the porter with the magical cart full of all things breakfast. He nods at me as he pushes the cart into the little dining area. He checks to see if I need anything else and then leaves quickly. A few moments later, another knock. That's the one I want most.

I open the door, and Zach steps through it, right into my space, wrapping me in his arms. I wrap mine around his neck and breathe him in, fresh from the shower and smelling of sea salt and sandalwood. I line his jaw with soft kisses and feel victorious when he tilts his head back to give me all the room I need. My stomach growls again, and I squeal as he picks me up in his arms and carries me into the dining room.

"Eat, woman!" he growls with a hearty laugh.

He sets me down in my usual spot, then grabs two plates and starts dishing up for both of us. Of course, mine is piled with way too much bacon, but I see he's also observed that I like grapefruit with a little sugar on it, and when he adds that, I feel another ping of gratitude. Lucky, lucky me. How did I ever want to run from a person who makes me feel like the most treasured woman in the world?

We eat in silence for a few minutes before he pauses and tilts his head at me.

"Do you eat that much bacon every day, Siren?"

I nearly choke on a bacon strip, but I recover and finish chewing the piece in my mouth before answering.

"I'm afraid I gave you the wrong impression with my bacon love fest the other day," I say lightly. "I don't eat bacon every day, and when I do, it's usually four pieces at most. Sometimes I just…want more bacon."

His expression lights up when I mention my bacon love fest, but he doesn't reply. I pull my legs in so I'm sitting criss cross in the chair and dig into my grapefruit.

"So what are we doing today?" I ask. "You still haven't told me."

There's a delightful glint in his eyes and he holds a finger up, then bolts out of the dining room. He reappears in a few seconds, holding a manila envelope in his hand. He holds it up with a little flourish and sets it down next to his plate, then digs back into his breakfast without a word.

I raise a brow. "What's that?"

He feigns ignorance and looks around. "What?"

I smirk and point at the envelope. "That."

He points to it as well. *"This?"*

I wiggle in my seat. "Zach!"

My reward is a throaty, full laugh as he throws his head back. He composes himself and then levels his gaze at me. The pure love in his eyes reaches into my heart and squeezes out a few extra beats. Suddenly, I want to crawl into his lap and set up camp.

"It's a present," he says simply, passing the envelope to me.

I hold his gaze as I take it, then finally look down to see it's in an envelope from a lawyer with an office in San Francisco. I slip my thumb under the flap and gently tear it open. There's a legal document inside, and my eyes dart over the words on the paper carefully. I shake my head slowly, still reading.

"I don't understand…"

I look up to find Zach smiling softly at me. "Which part?"

"What's the Mermaid Foundation?" I ask breathlessly. I think I know what this is, but…it can't be.

He grins and sits back in his chair. "It's a charitable foundation."

Slowly, I lower the document to my lap. "What kind of charity?"

He shrugs. "That's up to you, Siren."

I raise my eyebrows. "I'm sorry?"

He nods. "That's your call. It's your charity."

My jaw goes completely slack. "What?"

He chuckles under his breath and puts down his fork.

"Do you remember the night I showed up at the library?" he asks. I nod.

"In the car, I asked you about little Brandon's situation," he explains. "And you told me how his Aunt Grace is struggling."

I nod again, feeling a little silver lining my eyes.

"I just really felt for her," he says. "She's his only remaining family. She could have said no and let him go to foster care. She obviously didn't, which is likely because she loved her brother and loves her nephew. Should she have to struggle the rest of her life because she's doing something selfless and brave?"

"No?" I squeak around the sizeable lump that's formed in my throat. He shrugs again. "That's up to you. It's your charity. If you want it." "If I want it?"

He nods. "Sometimes I give terrible gifts," he says with a grin. "You should probably know this about me from the start, Siren. I may hit the mark with a book or a bag of red licorice, but someday I'll show up with something you may want to throw in the bin."

I look down at the papers again, flipping through all the legal verbiage. I can't believe he did this for me. I look at the date of his signature. This was done weeks ago. Right after the library. My eyes dart down when I see a dollar amount and I freeze.

"A million dollars?" I gasp. "You funded it with a million dollars?"

"Well, there's a lot required in running a charity," he explains. His eyes dart nervously around my face. "I wasn't sure if you'd be interested in running it full time yourself, and your law school aspirations would make that impossible. So there are salaries to consider before you begin fundraising efforts. You may wish to hire a consultant to help you set things up. You'll need staff to help you. Whatever you decide to do with it, you have the funds to get it off to a good start."

I close my eyes and shake my head. This is one of those life moments where the path I've been on for years dries up and narrows, while a wider, more beautiful stretch of road appears before me and I want to change directions. It's a little humbling to realize that everything I thought I wanted isn't really what I want at all. I want more.

I open my eyes to find Zach watching me with a guarded expression. I feel a little guilty when I realize he's not sure whether I like his present or I'm upset about something.

"You don't give terrible gifts," I say quietly, breaking off a piece of bacon and putting it in my mouth.

His eyes light up. "No?"

I shake my head. "No. This is the most amazing gift anyone has ever given me."

Instant relief floods Zach's face. I laugh softly and stand up, making my way over to him and sitting in his lap. I feel his strong arms wrap around my waist as I put my hands on either side of his face and tilt his face up to look into my tear-filled eyes.

"Thank you," I whisper, slowly lowering my mouth to his and brushing a light kiss on his lips. I press kisses to the corners of his mouth. His lips are soft, warm, and one thousand percent intoxicating as his familiar scent envelops me. His arms wrap tighter around me, pulling me close against his muscular, warm body, and a low growl escapes his throat.

I pull away and press our foreheads together.

"I'm never going to find a gift I can give you to equal anything you've given me, am I?"

He smiles softly and rubs our noses together.

"I already have everything I want, Siren," he rasps, his deep brown eyes burning into mine. "I have you. You're all I need."

I kiss him again, soft and slow and full of promise. We give and take equally, exploring each other's mouths without hurry.

This is fine for today. We don't really need to do anything else, do we? I'm good just staying here and kissing this amazing man for the rest of my day. Eventually, our lips break apart and Zach leans over to slide my plate next to his.

"Eat, beautiful," he says, planting a soft kiss on my cheek.

I reach for another piece of bacon from my perch on his lap, realizing this two chairs kind of thing is way overrated. Breakfast on Zach's lap is infinitely better on multiple levels. I take a bite of bacon and offer a piece to him, laughing out loud at the face he makes.

"That's not bacon," he says with a grimace.

"Um, you're on this side of the pond, my friend," I remind him playfully. "This is bacon."

He shudders and loads his fork with eggs and sausage.

"Just you wait until I take you to England, love," he says softly. "You'll have proper bacon there."

I shake my head and take another bite, emphasizing my point by making yummy sounds as he rolls his eyes.

We finish breakfast with me on his lap, then move to the couch to plan the rest of our day. Zach lounges on one end and I wedge myself into his side as he wraps an arm around me. Perfection.

"What time do you have to be at the stadium?" I ask as I rest my head against his shoulder.

"The guys and I agreed on 5 pm," he says quietly. "So we have all day. I thought we could brainstorm a little on the Mermaid Foundation if you wanted, and then I was wondering if I could talk you into Nonno's for lunch?"

A huge grin lights up my face as I turn to look at him. He laughs.

"I really want some breadsticks."

I plant a loud kiss on his cheek and snuggle back in. "That sounds perfect."

I pull away and stand up, then pad into my room to grab my phone. I come back and lean into Zach again, then open a text to Merry.

Marina: Is a table for two at noon possible?

I put my phone on the coffee table in front of us, then lean against Zach and sigh happily.

"So tonight," Zach hedges, catching my interest.

I look up at him with a curious expression.

"Would you like to sing with us?" he asks hesitantly. "You were so amazing last night, beautiful. I want you to have the opportunity if you want to, but it's completely fine if you'd rather not. Your choice, love."

I think for a moment, checking in with my gut instinct. What do

I really want to do here? No longer tethered by a mortal fear of bringing too much attention to Ms. Taft and her ridiculous world, I feel like I have endless possibilities ahead of me. And I do love to sing with this man right here next to me.

"How about one song?" I say softly, feeling pretty confident about that.

He raises his eyebrows and gives me a gorgeous smile.

"Yeah? Which one?"

I purse my lips in thought. "Well, that's a harder question. I'll let you figure it out."

"Nothing to figure it out if it's up to me." Oh, the confidence.

"Oh? What are we singing then?"

He palms the side of my face with his free hand, moving me slightly so our faces are inches apart.

"You Are My Heart," he answers, placing a light kiss on my nose between each word.

And I'm done. Or undone. I can't decide which. Both, probably. He is the most wonderful man in the entire world and I feel so lucky that I went against all my better judgment and sang on the bridge that day.

"Done deal," I say contentedly.

We sit in silence for a few minutes, happy in each other's company.

"Shall we talk about what happens on Monday?" Zach ventures quietly.

I sit up slightly so I can look at him. "When you and the guys leave town to finish the tour?"

He nods.

"Yes, let's. What's that look like?"

He works the muscle in his jaw for a bit, looking thoughtful.

"Well, I was thinking you might want to come to one of our San Diego shows," he begins. "You could bring Max."

"I'm in!" A chance to see my brother and hangout with my boyfriend? Yes, please.

"We also have Los Angeles, Las Vegas, Phoenix and Dallas," he explains. "So you can come to any shows you want and fly back here when you need to. I have a personal assistant who makes all my travel arrangements, so she'll handle yours as well. Once we leave on Monday, I won't be able to come back to San Francisco until the tour is completely over."

I nod solemnly. "And when it's over?"

He tightens his arm around my shoulders. "Right here back to you, beautiful."

I narrow my gaze at him. "Are you ever going to tell me where you actually live?"

He laughs softly. "Is it killing you?"

I smirk. "Slowly."

"Very well," he says. "When I was a boy, I loved Halloween so much. And my favorite story was written by an American named Washington Irving."

I gasp. "Sleepy Hollow? I love that story!"

He grins from ear to ear. "Ichabod Crane and the headless horseman."

"So, wait…you actually live in Sleepy Hollow, New York?"

He nods. "I bought an estate there after we ended our third tour."

I try to imagine how our relationship is going to work if we're flying across country to see each other. I know Zach never has to worry about money ever again, but it still sounds insanely expensive.

"I can see you overthinking," he says gently, nudging me.

"How will this work?" I ask bluntly. "You'll be on the other side of the country when you're at home."

He scoffs. There's a warmth in his eyes that sets my heart pounding. "When the tour is over, I fully intend on shopping for a second home here," he says casually, as if he's just said he's looking for a piece of furniture. A mischievous glint flashes in his eyes. "I'll be here most of the time, but I hope you'll also come and stay with me on my estate."

Now he's just being obnoxious. I make a face.

"An estate, huh?" I say with a smirk. "You can take the almost-duke out of the UK, but—"

He reaches down and tickles me, making it completely impossible to do anything but squeal at the top of my lungs. I'm about to retaliate when my phone begins vibrating so hard on the table it actually starts moving. Zach releases me and I grab my phone and unlock it. Merry has replied, but in our group chat.

Merry: Hi, New Marina! You can have a table if you want it...but your girls would like to have lunch with you instead. My cousin's working at Nonno's today. Unhand that man and go out with us.

Scarlet: Is that what we're calling our fearless friend now? I vote for Marina 2.0

Ashley: It's the same Marina, just...braver.

Scarlet: Lame.

Ashley: Marina, can you unattach yourself from the handsome rock star long enough to have lunch with your girls? We have so many questions.

I am stupid-grinning at my phone right now, I can feel it. More gratitude flows over me as I realize how lucky I am to have these amazing women in my inner circle. Zach eyes me expectantly and I hold my phone up so he can read.

"The girls," I explain.

He smirks. "They want the details."

I nod. "Totally."

He tilts his head. "If you'd rather go spend time with them, darling Siren, you're not going to hurt my feelings."

I feel torn now, but I expect that'll be a side effect of this new path I'm forging for myself—at least for a while. It'll take some time before this feels real. Normal.

"I think I'll kiss you until eleven and then go have lunch with the girls," I say, inching my mouth closer to his.

His eyes drop to my lips and a slow, sexy smile spreads on his gorgeous mouth.

"Is that so?"

I nod, then nip at his lower lip. He steals a quick, soft kiss. I sigh against his mouth, then pull back and smile devilishly.

"Talk British to me."

I'm rewarded with a throaty laugh.

"Gladly," he growls. "I agree to this plan of kissing all morning. As long as we can go to Nonno's tomorrow. Can we meet back here at 4 pm and go to the stadium together?"

I nod, scooting closer. He leans over and scoops me up, sliding me into his lap as I burst out laughing and throw my arms around his neck.

"Good," he says, rubbing our noses together. "Because you're mine after that. Concert, sing together, straight back here, curl up with you in my arms."

"Perfect," I purr softly as I surrender my mouth to his kiss.

***

"Well, this better work out because he has ruined you for all other men," Ashley laughs out loud.

The city is busy and full of life on this perfect afternoon, and we're enjoying it all from our table on the patio at Baja Burrito on Bay Street. I take a sip of my watermelon margarita and revel at the contented feeling in my heart.

Merry shakes her head incredulously. "The Mermaid Foundation. Think of all the good you'll do for people! I love him so much."

Scarlet raises her eyebrows.

"Platonically, of course!" Merry adds with a wave.

"Have you had any ideas about what you want to do with it?" Scarlet asks as she dips a tortilla chip in the salsa at the center of our table.

I nod. "Tons. And that's what I wanted to talk about. Can you guys help me think this through?"

Merry smacks the table. "We're here for it!"

I take a deep, steadying breath and smooth my palms down the top of my thighs.

"I just want to make sure my idea doesn't sound too crazy," I say hesitantly.

They all nod. Eager faces await my next words.

In my heart, I know this is right. I know this is what I'm meant to do. An inkling of it hit me when Ashley tried to talk some sense into me during my meltdown about the duchess thing. Then a crack formed in my previous plans when I realized the people at Taft & Kennedy were not actually my people, and that was not the best path. When Zach gave me The Mermaid Foundation, he also gave me a better purpose.

"I'm thinking that this," I hold up the Mermaid Foundation legal documents I brought with me. "Is a better job than what I had at Taft. With the money Zach gave the foundation, I can take a modest salary and hire a small team to help me with outreach and fundraising. This is a huge chance to keep families together that might otherwise be broken apart. And it can also support kids in foster care by providing funds for programs they need."

I'm met with three expressions so full of love and approval I feel like I could burst into tears. It inspires me to press on.

"Zach was inspired by Brandon's story, and how his aunt has made a home for him but is struggling financially," I continue. "Not to mention her aspirations before she adopted him. Did she have a career in mind? Is she able to pursue it now because she's suddenly working to feed and clothe two? Not to mention school costs, day care, and everything else. Social services wants them fed, housed and employed. Nothing else matters because there are so many other cases. The Mermaid Foundation could provide the extra help family members need so they can confidently step up and say yes to adopting family members who would otherwise go into foster care."

I finally stop babbling long enough to let my friends speak. Ashley shakes her head, her eyes lined with silver.

"Well, well, well," she says breathlessly. "Look at you. I'm so proud of you, Marina."

I bite my lower lip and fight back tears.

"You started it," I choke out, wiping a stray tear. "When you gave me that speech about there being more than one way to advocate for kids. And then this past week at Taft was so horrible. I kept pushing harder and harder. It took me breaking up with Zach to realize how stupid I was being. I was fighting so hard for the approval of people who were never going to get me."

"And never could have deserved you," Merry chimes in.

"So goodbye, law school," Scarlet says, raising her margarita glass. "And hello, philanthropy!"

We all clink our glasses together.

"I wasn't sure if I was being realistic," I share. "I thought maybe it was crazy to give up law school, even though my feelings about it have changed. And I knew you guys would be concerned if I was on the wrong track. I just want to be sure I'm looking at this with a level head."

Scarlet scoffs. "Girl, we'll always tell you if we think you're acting crazy. But in this case, I am totally on board. I was starting to worry that you were working yourself to death for the wrong people."

I tilt my head with a wary expression. "I may be about to work myself to death for the *right* people, though," I joke. "There's a ton of work to do."

Ashley beams at me. "And no one better to do it."

Merry holds a salsa loaded chip in the air. "Here, here!"

"And what about the rest of it?" Scarlet asks as our waiter brings our orders.

We stay silent as he sets everything in place, and we mutter our thanks when he's done. I watch him leave, making sure he's out of ear shot before speaking.

"The rest of it?" I ask her.

She picks up her fork and nods.

"The singing stuff," she says. "Are you joining The Royal Rebels or going solo or…what?"

I nearly drop the street taco I'm holding.

"No to all those things," I gasp. "Yikes."

Ash puts up a pouty lip. "But you and Zach are so freaking awesome on stage together! How can you not want to sing with him again?"

I chew on the bite that's in my mouth and consider how to phrase my reply.

"I wanted to be famous when I was a kid," I explain with a smirk. "This whole experience has made me realize what living with fame is like. And that's only in a small way. I'm not ready to jump straight into all of that, and I still need some kind of normalcy. I can't deny that I love performing, especially with Zach, but I'm content to let him be the only rock star."

We enjoy our lunches in relative silence for a few minutes. There's the normal grabbing little bites from each other's plates so we can try all the things, but that's standard protocol in the inner circle. Allowing the sneaking of samples off our plates is our love language.

"Are you singing with him tonight?" Merry asks.

I nod. "Absolutely. I let him choose one song."

Merry shoots me a knowing look. "He picked 'You Are My Heart', didn't he?"

I laugh softly, little chills running up and down my arms. "He did."

A delighted groan from Ashley. "You guys are so cute!"

I swallow the bite in my mouth and beam at my friends.

"I'll never stop singing," I say happily. "I love the idea of getting on stage with him and the guys once in a while, I just don't want it to be my job. And it doesn't matter if it's on stage, in a car, or at home…if Zach asks me to sing with him, the answer will always be yes."

Merry wiggles in her seat and squeals. Enough talking about me, though. I'm good. I'm really good.

"Scarlet," I say, giving her a playful nudge. "How's the interior decorating thing going? That's coming up, isn't it?"

She nods and waves her hand. "Girl, I've got this! Decorators Showcase is about to meet the best thing that ever happened to them."

"Yeah they are!" Merry croons from her seat as she takes another sip of her margarita.

As Scarlet fills us in on her genius plan to win San Francisco's biggest home decor challenge, I sit back in my seat and listen with gratitude. I'm so grateful for my friends and my life in this city I love. And I am especially grateful for that ridiculous mermaid tail.

***

The Royal Rebels bring another of their hits to a close as Zach jumps off the top of the piano and lands on the stage with such flourish it has 80,000 people standing and screaming their heads off. Their performance has been amazing tonight. Sam gets quite a workout on the drums, and Jimmy never holds still. Rick is almost as mobile as

Zach when it comes to running around on the stage. They all love their fans and it shows.

Zach's been giving me secret looks all night, and it sets my heart pounding every time. While he's made sure to move around the stage and engage with his audience at every angle, he's also taken quite a few opportunities to sing directly to me. There have been a few moments that have made me want to bust through the security team guarding the stage and kiss him for the rest of the concert, but I've resisted thus far.

I feel a slow smile spread across my face as he walks up the catwalk towards me. Our eyes meet and it's like we're the only two people in the whole stadium. Keeping my eyes locked on his, I step forward and the security detail in my section opens the barrier for me. Zach leans down to offer a hand and I slip my fingers into his. Immediately, my racing heart steadies as he gives my hand a reassuring squeeze. Applause and cheers erupt from the stadium as soon as they see me stepping up onto the stage with him. I wonder if I'll ever get used to it.

I finally break my gaze from Zach's and look out into the crowd with a huge smile, waving in every direction. His fans are going absolutely wild. I look behind us and wave to the guys. They all wave back, and I see Rick is seating himself at the piano as he gets ready to accompany us. In the audience to my right, Ashley, Merry and Scarlet are cheering as well.

I look out at the crowd and wave again, flashing them a huge smile when I'm rewarded with thunderous applause. Zach moves his lips close to my ear.

"You're not as nervous as the first time," he notes, leaving a trail of tingles where his lips touch my skin. "You're getting them all excited. Well done, you."

I shrug and wrap my hand around the back of his neck, pulling him towards me. I put my mouth against his ear.

"Well, I am a mermaid, after all," I say with no small amount of sass. "And mermaids make waves."

We share a secret smile as we pull apart and he brings the mic into position between us. We face each other, lacing the fingers of both our hands together, and let our voices make magic once more.

Chapter 24

One Year Later

Marina

"I can tell we're by the water," I tease from behind the blindfold that Ashley tied around my eyes as soon as Merry and Scarlet showed up at our apartment. Thank goodness I don't get motion sickness.

"Stop trying to guess," Merry scolds as she takes my hand and helps me out of the car. "You'll know where we are in just a sec."

"And what you're wearing," Scarlet says cryptically.

At least I know it's not the mermaid tail because I'm walking normally. Actually, they let me wear my yoga pants and sneaks, but I have no idea what's on the sweatshirt they pulled over my head when we got dressed right before we left.

"Well, it better be good," I warn. "I should still be sleeping in my cozy bed, not out here in the chilly morning."

"You were alone," Merry pipes in. "You couldn't have been doing anything that interesting."

I laugh under my breath. Indeed, I was alone. Zach had to go out of town overnight and won't be back until this evening.

I'm led across flat pavement, then the girls help me step up onto a sidewalk that's got a bit of an incline to it. I'm holding onto them for dear life as we walk. It's going to be a warm day later, but I'm grateful for the sweatshirt as a gentle morning breeze blows past. My hair is up in a high ponytail, so it's not getting in my face. Not that I can see yet anyway. The sidewalk levels off a bit and the girls pull me to the side so we can stop.

"Okay, it's time for the big reveal!" Merry says enthusiastically.

"Well, it's not really a big reveal," Scarlet scoffs. "More like—"

"Can we get to the part where you take this blindfold off of me, please?" I plead with a wave of my hands.

"Okay," Ashley says excitedly. "I think we're ready."

I feel Merry pull the blindfold off, and I'm surprised to see the south tower of the Golden Gate Bridge towering above us. We're standing on the pedestrian sidewalk for the bridge, but it's just after sunrise. There aren't many people out this early.

"Oh!" I say, looking around at their faces to see if I can get any clues as to why we're here. "We're going for a walk on the bridge?"

Scarlet nods. "A symbolic walk to the place where it all started…to applaud your many accomplishments with the Mermaid Foundation."

I gasp. "What a fun idea! I love it!"

Ashley grins. "We thought you might. And you haven't even noticed our shirts!"

Ash, Merry and Scarlet all line up in front of me so I can see them. Instant tears line my eyes as they show me. They're wearing dark purple long-sleeved shirts with the Mermaid Foundation logo over the breast pocket, but the back of the shirts are emblazoned with iridescent metallic words that read *Be a Mermaid…Make Waves.* I look down at my own shirt and I'm wearing the same. Tears well up in my eyes.

"You guys, this is amazing!" I cry, hugging each one of them. "Thank you so much."

"We're so proud of you," Ashley says. "We wanted to do something special this morning before your day gets crazy. Something just for us."

Right. Because tonight is the Inaugural Mermaid Ball. It's our first large scale fundraising event with a silent auction and performances from famous music artists, followed by an evening of dancing. My amazing staff of ten will be going for free since this is also a celebration of all the work they've done for the good of others, but the ticket prices are hefty for everyone else. The who's who of celebrities and politicians lined up to come when we opened the ticket sales. I couldn't have asked for better results.

I jump when someone rushes over to us and jumps to a halt in our haphazard circle. *Max?*

"Morning, sis!" Max greets me, giving me a quick hug. He looks at the girls with a satisfied grin. "Right on time!"

"Max, you're joining us?" I cry out, giving him another hug. "This is awesome!"

He shrugs. "Well, I was going to the ball tonight anyway, so… couldn't miss this."

I notice Max is also wearing a shirt to match ours and my heart swells again.

"You guys are the best," I say as we start walking up the rest of the incline. "This is so fun."

When we get to the gift shop, which is closed this early, the sidewalk levels out and we step onto the bridge. The sky glows a beautiful golden pink as the city begins waking up behind us. We set out for our special, early morning walk and I listen to my brother catching up with the girls on what's been going on with them.

Max has been up here to visit me several times in the past year, and

Zach and I have been to a few of his games in San Diego. We have plans to spend Halloween at Zach's estate in Sleepy Hollow so we can see everything the town has to offer. Apparently they take their reputation very seriously.

And I'm officially an international traveler now. Zach and I went to England last month so I could finally meet his parents. They were every bit as wonderful as he said they would be. His mother is incredibly kind and infinitely patient with Zach, who spends much of his time teasing her and trying to make her think he's going to do something embarrassing. But he never does, of course, because he loves his family. I got to see how important it all is to him, including the legacy his family upholds. I discovered a new level of admiration for Zach on that trip, as he's managed to forge a life of his own and pursue his dreams while always keeping his duty in mind. While a duke with a rock star past would be a new thing, when it comes time for him to assume his father's title, the people will embrace him. The reputation he's built as a rock star with a heart for those less fortunate will serve him well it comes time to retire from touring and cutting records.

It won't likely happen for many years, but Zach shared that plan with me. He'll step away from the Rebels. He'll move back to the family estate and assume his duties in England, but music will always be a part of his life in some way. He has plans for outreach programs for disadvantaged kids - and he may even agree to the odd performance here and there if it raises money for charity.

The thought of him moving back home to England used to fill me with worry, but it doesn't anymore. I know it'll be okay because we'll be together still. Yes, I'll go with him when the time comes. There are children and families who need help in England just like there are in America, and by that time, the Mermaid Foundation will be something I can run from across the pond.

For now, Zach spends most of his time in San Francisco. When The Royal Rebels tour was finally over last year, Zach returned to the city, and I helped him look for a house to buy. Or that's what I thought he was going to buy. Instead, he bought a whole building. It's a vintage four-story building that used to hold newspaper offices and is no longer in business. It was empty and not generating much interest, but Zach had a plan.

He turned the first floor into the office space for the Mermaid Foundation. The second floor was turned into eight small apartments that will be part of the Mermaid Foundation's emergency intake center. We'll use them for people who are being evicted or have no place to go, giving them a safe space until we can connect them with services that will help them long-term.

He turned the third floor into a beautiful two-bedroom apartment where Ash and I now live. And the top floor is his. Oh, what it is to be rich and brilliant. But that's my boyfriend.

"Marina!" Ash calls from ahead of me.

I realize I'm bringing up the rear, daydreaming about my new life. I hurry to catch up with them.

"Yes, Ash?"

She spins around and wiggles her eyebrows at me as she walks backwards.

"Are you singing at the Mermaid Ball tonight?"

I nod. "Zach and I are doing something special."

She looks happy with that answer and turns around.

This walk is always invigorating. We're just at the first tower, so we're still walking at a slight incline. A few boats are cruising around the bay already, and I can see Alcatraz Island in the distance. The bay air is crisp and clean, making this day seem full of promise and possibility.

Scarlet tells Max all about the process she used to design the

Mermaid Foundation headquarters. Yeah, I hired her to do it. Because when you have a friend who lives to make the world a beautiful place you hire her to use those talents whenever you can. We were her first major client, and she got some great press coverage from all the news articles about it. The office space is incredible. Not to mention our apartment, which she designed for free as a gift to me and Ash.

Yes, Ash is still very much turned off of men. After Greg broke her heart, she decided she was going to harden her heart for a while and just be by herself. Every time one of us tries to set up her up on a date, she says, "I'm a dragon lady. I don't date." Some day that wall has to come down, though.

Merry is still blowing through boyfriends at the speed of light. She doesn't let anyone get too close. Lately, she is working on Nonno to let her re-open her Nonna's old bakery next door to the restaurant. She died five years ago, and sweet Nonno just can't even talk about opening her bakery. Merry's not giving up any time soon, though.

When we hit the center of the bridge, we all stop and walk to the railing and look out at the bay. For a few feet, the bridge is flat here, and then it begins to decline as we go further north. I flag down a jogger and ask him to take our picture. He is very kind, snapping pictures for us and then handing my phone back to me. We keep walking as my mind wanders back to tonight's festivities. We don't just have celebrities and politicians coming. CEOs and top figures from prominent businesses in the city will be there. I gave the guest list a good look. Ms. Taft and Ethan Montclair were not listed, much to my relief. I know they were invited. I left that up to my Director of Events. Taft has money, and we don't turn down anyone's money. If they were on the guest list, I would have had Dave make sure they weren't able to get near me. He's my new full-time security guard, and he does the job brilliantly. The only good thing that came from my time at Taft & Kennedy was the friendships I forged with Hillary and Kat, who I still see every day because they work for the Mermaid Foundation now.

I'm really proud of how much I've developed it in just a year. After hiring a consultant to help set it up, I reached out to little Brandon's Aunt Grace at song night at the library. Zach kept Brandon busy, teaching him how to play guitar while I explained to his aunt what the Mermaid Foundation would be built to do. I must say I recognized the relief and the gratitude in her eyes when she realized that there are people who care about people in her situation. She accepted my invitation to be our charter case. She's now finishing college. She had to leave during her final year when Brandon landed in her life. So she's back in school and receiving financial assistance from the foundation in order to live in a decent neighborhood while she completes her education. And Brandon has been able to join a local scouting program because they're not pinching every penny.

As we near the north tower, my friends slow down and start making a fuss over me. I'm dragged to the front of the group and told to walk ahead of them because I'm the leader of the Mermaid Foundation. I do as they say because, honestly, why not? I love them all so—

I freeze in my tracks as I come around to the other side of the north tower. Someone has put up a beautiful floral archway in a beautiful blend of cream, blue and lavender flowers, and I caught a quick glimpse of a man in a suit pacing behind it. I whirl around and put my hands up.

"Some guy is going to propose!" I whisper excitedly. "We can't go over there."

I look behind our group to see if I can see any women walking on the bridge, but there's no one. I look the other way. None. Where is she?

"Some guy?" Scarlet asks in that famous deadpan voice we all love.

I shrug. "I didn't get a good look. I only saw his elbow."

They all exchange incredulous looks and move towards the man's beautiful floral arch. I try to push them back.

"No, you guys, we can't just walk through it."

Max pulls me off to the side and braces his hands on my shoulders, looking down at me with such brotherly love.

"*We* can't," he agrees. "You can."

He turns me around to face the archway, and only then do I see the man is Zach.

My Zach.

Looking indecently gorgeous in a suit that was cut just for him, standing in front of two foot high light-up letters that spell out "MARRY ME?" Beautiful baubles are arranged all around him, glowing in the soft morning light. There's a purple mermaid tail sticking up from the center of them as if a mermaid is splashing down through the bubbles.

Everything happens in slow motion as Max leads me under the arch and brings me to the man I love. Zach's warm, strong fingers close over mine as tears form in my eyes.

"Good morning, love," he says in that delicious British accent. He gets down on one knee.

"Baby, I—Zach," I say with a tremor in my voice.

I close my mouth, realizing I don't have any coherent words to say right now.

"Darling Marina," he says huskily. "You have brought me such joy from the moment I met you. Not far from this very spot."

Now my lips are trembling. I desperately need to be in this man's arms. Right now. A little sob escapes my lips.

"I have loved every minute of our life together so far. You are good, and kind, and so very brave. A fierce friend and a warrior for the less fortunate. And you love me, with all my imperfections. Please promise to be mine forever. Marina, will you marry me?"

He pulls a ring from his pocket and presents it to me. It's a beautiful emerald-cut amethyst ring with diamonds encircling the band. I look at him with a stunned expression.

He winks. "It matches the mermaid tail."

Tears fall in earnest now, and I find myself nodding as I struggle to find my voice.

Then, finally, I choke out, "Yes! Yes, I will marry you."

He stands, and I throw myself into Zach's arms. My friends and brother throw themselves around us. I don't know who is hugging who, but Zach's hands are holding my face and he's kissing me tenderly while the celebration goes on around us. The group breaks off, and I'm mildly aware of them dancing around and cheering like maniacs.

I focus my attention on Zach's warm, soft lips devouring mine. Heat spirals down my spine and into my belly as he holds me tightly against him. One of his hands holds the back of my head, giving him total control over the exquisite torture he's administering. I fist my hands in his shirt and hold on for dear life.

After a few moments, he pulls away slightly and reaches for my left hand.

"Let's get this on you before one of them knocks into us, and it flies into the bay," he says, laughing softly and sliding the beautiful ring onto my finger. A perfect fit.

He pulls me back into his arms, and I splay my hands across his chest so I can see my gorgeous ring. I look up into his eyes.

"It's perfect," I say, struggling around the lump in my throat. "I love you so much, Zach."

He places a light, reverent kiss on my temple.

"I love you too, Marina," he says, his voice husky with emotion. "You're never getting rid of me now."

"Nonno said it best," I coo into his ear. "You're a keeper."

I look over at Max and the girls, then back at Zach.

"So, what's the plan for today?"

He nods in Max's direction.

"Since your brother's here for the ball tonight, perhaps we should go back to your apartment and hang out till lunch," Zach suggests. "Then we definitely need to take him to Nonno's."

I nod enthusiastically. I love that idea. Zach pulls away from me, then spins me like we're dancing, and pulls me back into his arms. He moves us around on the part of the sidewalk closest to the base of the tower so we're not in anyone's way. The rest of our group is chatting excitedly and looking out at the bay.

Zach wraps an arm around my waist and locks our hands together, dancing me slowly around as he begins to hum the melody to "You Are My Heart". All the feels, every single one of them, washes over me in a rush. I tilt my head and look up into Zach's eyes.

"I am the luckiest woman on earth," I say quietly. "Because I get to love you."

He shakes his head, pulls me in, and holds me tight.

His lips touch the shell of my ear as he whispers, "I'm the lucky one. I finally caught myself a mermaid."

***

Zach

I pause from puttering around Marina and Ashley's kitchen for a moment, stealing a look at my girl sitting on the couch, surrounded by her friends and brother. They're listening to Max talk about stealing two bases at his last baseball game, and the glow of pride lighting Marina's beautiful face fills me with such happiness. Watching her renew her relationship with Max has been a wondrous experience that I feel honored to have taken a small part in.

I pull a wood serving platter off a shelf above the refrigerator and set about creating a charcuterie display. I called Rick, Jimmy, and Sam to invite them over as well. They'll be here shortly, and we'll all have a nice, proper catch-up. It'll be awhile before we get to thrill Max with his first Nonno's experience, and our early morning walk certainly made everyone a bit peckish. Not to mention my proposal. That's something else to celebrate. I wonder if Merry should have paramedics on standby for Nonno when he hears the news.

My blood stirs as the sound of her lyrical laughter drifts over to me. If I live a thousand years, I may never truly believe I pulled this off. When I think back to the beautiful ball of pure sass I met on the bridge, who wanted absolutely nothing to do with me, I silently thank the powers that be for my lot in life. The past year with her has been one of discovery and wonder, from watching her work on the Mermaid Foundation from the ground up to just being a new couple together and building a life with each other. Our love has grown stronger each and every day, and I haven't worried once that she might decide to run from this…not from the moment she surprised me at the concert, singing "You Are My Heart" to me as I cried like a baby on stage. I regret nothing.

Every once in a while, I see Marina look down at her hand and admire her engagement ring, and my heart soars with pride. I knew it was the right ring as soon as I saw it. The memory of that sparkly purple tail flashed in my mind immediately. I knew she'd love it.

"Zach?" Marina calls from her perch on the sofa.

I look up from the sausage I'm slicing. "Yes, love?"

Her eyes twinkle with hidden meaning. "Did you call the guys and invite them over?"

Nobody's looking at me right now, so I flash her a wink.

"They'll be here in about twenty minutes, gorgeous."

Satisfied, she turns back to the conversation, which currently consists of Merry telling Ashley it's time to let the dragon lady idea go and be open to new things. I let out a low chuckle. Good luck, Merry. Of course, that isn't stopping Marina and I in our diabolical plan to nudge Rick into Ashley's line of sight. There's no need to push him at all. He's already noticed her, and it's quite obvious how smitten he is. The problem is, she's friend-zoned every man in her life and shows no signs of letting anyone back in after her cad of a fiancé broke her heart. Still, my money's on Marina when it comes to who will win this chess match.

I want everyone I love to be as happy as I am right now at this moment. I'm so full of joy I feel as though my skin is the only thing keeping me together. When I picture her in a white dress, walking down the aisle of a church, making her way toward me and our happily ever after, I feel my eyes line with tears.

This is the key to happiness right here: find yourself a mermaid. Perhaps I'll write a book about it someday, giving hope to people who think they'll never find love. I'll call it "How to Date a Mermaid" and provide three easy steps to success.

Step One: Heed the call of her beautiful siren's song. Don't waste one minute sitting around. Run to her, wherever she is.

Step Two: Be patient. Don't frighten her, or she'll swim away and be gone forever.

Step Three: Show her love. Shower her with it. Make her see that she is the most special creature that ever existed. Show her in everything you say and every action you take. Show her she's your whole world.

Easy peasy, right? There's only one problem standing in the way of a book like that becoming an instant best seller: there's only one mermaid. And she's mine. All mine. And I am never, ever letting her go.

THE END

You saw Zach's side of the story.
Now see Marina's.

When Marina stepped onto that stage in front of 50,000 fans, she didn't just risk humiliation—she risked everything she'd spent her entire life protecting.

You watched Zach performing with a broken heart. But what was Marina thinking as she walked toward that stage, singing in the spotlight? What did it feel like to choose love over fear when the whole world was watching?

Get Chapter 22 from Marina's POV—the grand gesture you never got to see from inside her head.

It's free. It's exclusive. And you can't get it anywhere else.

Grab your bonus chapter here!

Paperback readers: scan the QR code below!

Ashley's next...

꧁꧂

Marina and Zach's wedding is coming. Ashley needs a date. Rick's been waiting a year for this moment.

Read what happens next!

Chapter 1: Fake It Till You Make It

Ashley

I watch the too-perfect, too-handsome, well-dressed stranger retreat to the bar to lick his wounds, giving his friends a disappointed head shake as he sits down. Another victim of the Dragon Lady. #SorryNotSorry

"Time?" Scarlet asks from our booth in the stylish restaurant.

Merry looks up from the stopwatch app on her phone, flipping her dark brown hair over her shoulder.

"Twenty-two seconds. A new record."

I smirk.

They can tease me all they want, but after my fiancé stomped all over my heart last year and made me question my ability to judge good humans from bad ones, the whole Dragon Lady thing has worked well for me. I don't see the sense in even letting them get a complete sentence out of their slick-talking mouths when it's not going to do any good. I think this one got four words out before I shut him down.

My friend Marina, the one we're celebrating tonight, nudges me from her seat to my right. She's fighting back a shocked grin.

"You can let some of them get a whole sentence out, can't you?"

I shrug. "Why? When they're not going to get anywhere? It's better to put them out of their misery quickly."

Merry holds her drink up in a salute. "Smashed like a bug on a windshield!"

We all burst into laughter, and I look up to see how my latest admirer is doing. He's already off to another table, where a very pretty brunette smiles up at him like she's the luckiest woman on Earth. All is well. They'll probably toast to me at their wedding.

At the risk of sounding completely full of myself, I'm very blessed when it comes to good looks. I'm really *not* full of myself - but when you're born the only child of parents who look like they won some kind of genetic lottery, well...I definitely benefited from it. I remember the first time a stranger approached my parents in a restaurant, presenting a business card from a modeling agency and asking if I had representation. It only got worse as I got older. I've always gotten attention from strangers for my looks, and I'm pretty used to it at twenty-five. Looking back, it never really bothered me before Greg broke my heart. I always took it as a compliment when I was approached by men before, but something changed in me when Greg broke up with me the *second* time. I got...mad. And I can't seem to get *unmad*. So until I figure this out, I'll keep guarding my heart like a dragon guards treasure.

"Anyway, tonight is not about me," I begin, holding my drink in the air. "Tonight, we're celebrating Marina and Zach's engagement. To true love and mermaid tails!"

Marina laughs softly as we all clink our glasses together in her honor. She's glowing with happiness, and my heart is full just looking at her. A few days ago, we helped her fiancé pull off the ultimate surprise engagement right in the middle of the Golden Gate Bridge. There were times when I thought Marina's fear of going against her rigid rules would derail the relationship before it even started, but I was wrong. Zach charmed her right off her feet—or, I should say, mermaid tail.

We were all dressed up in costume that day, having just come from a singing gig at an engagement party, when we met him. Marina was dressed as a mermaid. And now, since Zach is a world-famous rock star, she'll never have to wear that mermaid tail again. Ever since she and Zach were in a viral video, she's too famous to wear it. And we only do the singing gigs occasionally now, but if she shows up anywhere in that tail, I think the whole world will stop to record it.

"I'm so happy for you guys," Merry says wistfully.

She's our little ray of sunshine, forever positive. Always looking on the bright side. It's all rainbows and unicorns in Merry's world, and we love her for it. She was born on Christmas day, so I'm pretty sure it's in her DNA.

"I'm super happy for you and just a little jealous," Scarlet chimes in with a laugh, taking another swig of her mojito.

She's the realist. If you want honesty, you go to Scarlet.

"I think that's the first time anyone's ever been jealous of me," Marina replies with a head tilt in Scarlet's direction.

Scarlet shakes her head. "Not just you. I'm jealous of Ashley, too."

My eyebrows shoot up to my hairline in surprise. "Why me?"

"You get to be maid of honor," she replies, sagging her shoulders dramatically. "I've never been one!"

Merry nudges her shoulder. "Stop whining, Scarlet...you can be mine."

She sits straight up with a wide grin. "Oh! Well, okay then."

I look at Marina and smile. "So when do we get to go dress shopping?"

Merry lights up like a Christmas tree. "Oooh, yes! I can't wait to see you trying on all those dresses!"

"You'll be gorgeous no matter what you pick," Scarlet says as she takes another sip of her drink.

Indeed. With Marina's beautiful, long red hair and startling green eyes, she could wear a burlap sack down the aisle and look like a queen. It won't matter, but we'll have fun shopping anyway. We always do.

"More importantly," I say lightly, "what color are you making us wear?"

She laughs. "With Merry's dark hair and you two blondes, I think some kind of blue or purple is a safe bet. But I want to see what we think when we start looking at dresses."

"And for you?" I ask.

Marina shrugs. "I'm not sure if I'll even wear a proper wedding dress," she says softly. "It might be just a nice dress. I don't want a big wedding."

"You can wear a proper dress and have a small wedding," Merry says, sitting up straight. "But definitely have the wedding you want, and don't be pressured into doing anything else."

"No pressure happening," Marina says with a glint in her eyes. "Everyone's been wonderful, but I should probably give you guys one tiny detail right away."

That's enough to silence the table. No sips are taken, no rolls are buttered. We're all watching Marina expectantly.

"I didn't grow up going to church or anything," she begins. "So there's no place that's special to me in that way. I'm marrying the right man, and that's really all I care about, but Zach grew up—"

"Oh my God!" I exclaim.

I look around the table and can see by Merry and Scarlet's expressions they've made the same realization.

Marina laughs. "So, yeah, I'd like for us to get married in England," she says. "It means a lot to Zach."

Scarlet, Merry and I exchange excited looks. We're completely speechless.

"Zach is paying for everyone's travel expenses because he's...him," she says with a smile. "So get those passports, ladies."

"This is amazing!" Merry cries excitedly. "How exciting!"

Marina nods. "I'm definitely excited. And his mom has been so sweet. She's over the moon about it all, and she's going to be such a help from a planning aspect."

"Who did Zach choose for his best man?" Merry asks.

I know the answer without having to hear Marina say it. Rick—a present-day Viking god and Zach's best friend. The lead guitarist for their world-famous band, The Royal Rebels, Rick, is six feet two inches of luxurious blond mane and gorgeous muscles. He and Zach write most of the songs the Rebels perform. And despite his rock star status, he's a really nice guy. I know because I asked Zach to come speak to my third graders last year during music week at school, but there was a scheduling conflict, and Rick very graciously volunteered to take his place.

The kids loved every minute of their time with him. He made sure every child had time to hold his guitar and try it out, and he brought guitar picks for all the kids to keep. Finally, he played a couple acoustic versions of Rebels songs for the class and...wow. As much as I've shoved every man I meet into the friend zone, Rick was dangerously close to breaking out of it that day. I've managed to keep him contained, but he's...beautiful. And sexy as hell.

"Ash?" Marina asks, bringing me out of my thoughts.

Everyone is looking at me, waiting for an answer. Answer to what?

"Sorry?" I say quickly.

Merry gives me a knowing look. "Marina jokingly asked if you'd find it terribly trying, working with Rick on the wedding, but we all know the answer to that question now."

I scoff. "Oh, please," I answer lightly. "I consider Rick a friend, nothing more. And it won't be terrible at all. He's super sweet."

I avoid eye contact with Merry, who is obviously not convinced.

"A friend?" Marina asks.

I shrug. "We text each other once in a while," I explain, leaving out the fact that our banter borders on flirty more often than not and my pulse hammers like crazy any time his name appears in my incoming messages. "He was so great with my third graders last year."

Merry levels her stare at me. "So, you text each other about your third graders?"

I smirk at her. "Of course not. But once in a while, he'll see something funny and text it to me or something. I do the same. It's meaningless. Just silly things."

Like the time I got a random text from him telling me that no one can hear a pterodactyl use the bathroom because the p is silent. I got the giggles so bad I had to step outside my classroom for a few minutes.

"I think it's sweet that you keep in touch," Marina says, giving me a little squeeze on my hand. "I'm glad to see you're getting to know him better."

I level my gaze at her. "Don't get your hopes up, Marina. Rick will remain firmly in the friend zone."

Marina gives me a look I can't quite identify. I'm not sure if she's accepting my words or taking the whole thing as some kind of challenge.

"Even Rick? Seriously?" Scarlet scoffs, shaking her head at me.

Merry laughs out loud, which of course only encourages Scarlet further.

"I mean…look at him," she says boldly. "And look at you! You both look like supermodels. Think of the gorgeous kids you'd have."

"Oh, yes, please!" Merry sighs as if Rick and I are already walking down the aisle.

Just as I'm about to say enough is enough, another man steps over to our table and right into my space. Too close. I nearly choke on the cloud of Axe body spray that hits my nostrils as he settles his gaze on me. I feel my skin crawl.

"Hey, ther—"

"Don't speak," I say sharply, jabbing him hard with my index finger. "And step back."

He takes a step back in surprise, and I hear Merry suppress a nervous chuckle.

"No," I say emphatically. "Not interested."

He opens his mouth to argue, and I hold up a hand.

"Bye bye now."

He rolls his eyes at me and walks away. I turn back to my friends to see them all watching me with wary expressions. Merry speaks first, eyes wide.

"I didn't even have a chance to time that one."

Scarlet giggles and gestures at the man's retreating form. "Look at the poor guy. Walking away with the air of a man sentenced to prison."

Marina shakes her head at me. "And what was his crime?"

Scarlet answers before I can. "Not being Rick."

I swipe my hand at her playfully. "Stop making something from nothing. Rick is a friend."

Merry wiggles her eyebrows at me. "The only friend of the male persuasion you're nice to."

I point a finger at her. "Not true. I'm nice to Zach."

Marina smiles. "And thanks for that."

Scarlet is undaunted. "The only single man friend—"

"Okay, enough!" I scold them, trying to keep a straight face. As ridiculous as they're being, I definitely need to nip this in the bud.

Out of the corner of my eye, I can see Marina trying to hide a smile.

"They're not wrong," she mutters. "You *are* nice to him. It's not a bad thing. And you two look really good together."

"Back to the wedding preparations," I say slowly, giving everyone a warning look. "Have you decided where you're having the engagement party?"

Merry snorts. "Oh, she didn't get to decide that."

Marina laughs. "I sure didn't. The party will be at Nonno's. It's not in my heart to tell him no, even if I wanted to. He's so excited for us."

Merry's grandfather, Nonno, is really a grandfather to all of us. He's full of nothing but love and joy, although I have seen him yelling in Italian at some of the kitchen staff a time or two. Most of them are Merry's cousins. His restaurant serves the best Italian food in San Francisco, and it's the perfect place for our group of friends and family to celebrate Marina and Zach.

"Well, we all know how hyper-organized you are," I say to Marina. "So my job as maid of honor will probably be easier than most. But tell me when you need help with something, okay? Whatever it is."

I'm rewarded with a side hug as the waiter comes swooping in with our plates. Once everyone is served, a comfortable silence settles over us as we dig into our entrées. I try to shove all thoughts of Rick out of my head, but they keep rolling back in. Rick with the kids at my school. Rick on stage performing with Zach and the band. Rick smiling at me while we're talking. He really does have a gorgeous smile.

Get out of my head, you huge, perfect Viking god.

"How's your dad doing, Ash?" Merry asks as we eat.

I finish the absolutely perfect bite of steak in my mouth.

"He's good," I offer. "His doctor says there's no evidence he ever had a heart attack. And he's keeping me busy with that fundraiser dinner party for his 'Have a Heart Foundation'. He may have gone a little overboard."

"In what way?" Scarlet asks.

"Well, it's a foundation for heart patients…on Valentine's day, so he wants a Valentine-themed dinner," I explain. "Hearts everywhere."

Merry lights up. "That doesn't seem overboard. It sounds perfect."

I tilt my head at her. "Yes, but I'm the one coordinating this thing, and I really hate Valentine's day right now."

Merry sticks her lower lip out at me. "C'mon, Dragon Lady, that cold heart has to soften up someday. You liked Valentine's Day last year!"

"Don't remind me," I grumble. "My plan is to just focus on the task at hand and be there for my dad, but I dread being at the dinner. I don't want to be surrounded by hearts and flowers right now. We're having lunch tomorrow, and I just know we're gonna talk about it."

"Of course he'll want you there," Marina chimes in. "He's proud of you. And you've worked really hard to create this charity dinner. You know he'll want to acknowledge you."

In our friend group, my dad is everyone's dad, just like Nonno is our grandpa and Scarlet's mom is the mom. My mom passed when I was still in high school. Merry's parents live in Silicon Valley and are not very present in her life. But everyone knows my dad well, and I'm afraid Marina is right. He will definitely want me sitting there with him, surrounded by all the ridiculous reminders of Valentine's Day. Ugh.

"I know, I know," I moan over my plate. "I just don't feel very Valentiney this year."

Marina nudges me and whispers, "Sorry, girl."

I busy myself with buttering a roll while I try to get myself in the right mindset. Greg broke up with me a little over a year ago. The hurt has faded, but the anger remains. Anger at myself, not Greg. He was just being who he really is, and I was looking at the whole thing through rose-colored glasses. He works at the investment firm that's been in my family for generations, and we met at the company retreat two years ago. He was quickly becoming a sales superstar, and he ended up being paired with me at the retreat's golf tournament. He was handsome, witty, and showered me with attention. I was swept off my feet so fast I failed to see a lot of red flags. I feel like that meme that says, "Didn't you see the red flags?" and the woman is gasping, "I thought it was a parade!"

What upset me most about the Greg red flag parade is that I really thought I loved him, but when I look back, I can see he never really loved me. He just wanted the boss's daughter. I was just another goal to achieve, and when he had me, he got bored. My instincts were so off track that it was laughable, so my plan is to just be the Dragon Lady and keep them all away until I figure myself out. Like the Taylor Swift song says, I'm the problem. It's me.

Marina gasps, and I look over to see her smiling down at her phone. She looks up to find all of us watching her curiously.

"The guys got home early!" she says with a huge, disgustingly sappy grin.

Merry tilts her head. "Aww, you're so in love. It's gross!"

We all laugh…mostly because it's adorably true. They are so in love it's enough to make me want to sing show tunes and throw flowers whenever I'm near them. They're the cutest thing ever, and I'm so happy for my friend. Friends, actually. Zach has been fully integrated and I consider him a friend as well. He'll either be in our apartment when we get home, or she'll run straight up to his. We're all under the same roof, so to speak.

Last year, when Zach and Marina became a couple, he bought a building. Yep, a whole building. Because that's what multi-millionaires do, I guess. Even my dad, who is also extremely wealthy, has never bought a whole building, but he's not a rock star in love with my best friend.

It's four stories of classic Victorian architecture that was in dire need of some love. So Zach had the ground floor turned into offices for The Mermaid Foundation, Marina's charity that supports families in crisis. The second floor was made into two temporary apartments for said families. The third floor was transformed into an apartment for Marina and me, and Zach took the top floor for his own apartment. I thought it might be weird at first, but it's actually been really great. For one thing, Marina is at Zach's half the time, and it's almost like I live on my own. And I love me some quiet time!

I nudge Marina. "If he's going to be at our place when we get home, can you get him to make those cheese chip things?"

"Done!" she replies, pulling up her phone and tapping a message on the screen.

"Thanks," I say with a quick nod. "I love those things, and I can't figure out what I'm doing wrong when I try to make them."

"Hey, Scarlet's got a great plan for the San Francisco Beautiful Home competition," Merry brags.

We all turn to Scarlet.

"Tell us," Marina says with a smile.

Scarlet wiggles her eyebrows excitedly. "I got my mom to let me redecorate her office, so that'll be the project I show on my application this year. I feel like the faux corner window I designed last year wasn't enough. Hopefully, this is enough of a boost to get me on the show."

We'll all be cheering her on, too. Scarlet is an interior designer, and she's laser-focused on getting a spot as a contestant on the Decorator's Showcase television show. The winner gets $250,000, and Scarlet has her eye on the prize.

I wink at Scarlet. "You got this."

She winks back, and she thrills us with her ideas to make her mom's office the most gorgeous space in the city. The conversation shifts to Merry's mission to rediscover her beloved Nonna's cookie recipe, and before we know it, the check is paid, and we're hugging each other goodbye on the sidewalk outside.

The restaurant isn't far from our apartment, so Marina and I walked here. We fall into step beside each other, chatting easily about her wedding plans as we cover the three blocks home. There's a chill in the air and I didn't bring a coat, which I'm really regretting in the damp San Francisco night air. There's a thick fog rolling in off the bay. I thought this sweater dress would be enough, especially with boots. So wrong, but kind of a thing I do frequently. Someone's always scolding me for forgetting a coat. Just a little further and I can curl up with a hot cup of tea and get warm.

"You're freezing, aren't you?" Marina guesses correctly from under her warm coat.

"Of course. But I look cute, so there's that."

Marina nudges my shoulder with hers. "You always look cute."

I stop abruptly just before we start up the steps of our building.

"Maybe that's it!" I exclaim. "Next time we go out, I'm putting my hair in a messy wad on top of my head, not wearing make-up, and wearing baggy, mismatched clothes."

Marina rolls her eyes at me, then grabs my elbow and pulls me up the stairs to the front door. She puts her key in the lock, and I keep going.

"Too bad it's not Halloween. I could buy some fake warts at one of those costume shops that pop up all over town."

"Wow," she says coolly. "I almost wish I could see that. But you'd need about thirty-seven fake warts to scare most men away. You're just that gorgeous."

We step inside and take the stairs up to our apartment.

"I don't think that's true, but thanks for the compliment, girl."

As soon as Marina opens the door to our apartment, she runs to

Zach. He's in the kitchen, making the aforementioned cheese crisps I can't stay away from. Snacks for tomorrow. Yay! I look over at my friends with a huge grin. Zach has cow print oven mitts on his hands as he scoops Marina into his arms and kisses her passionately. Freaking adorable.

I rub my hands together as I step into the apartment, averting my eyes from the display of affection in the kitchen. A tiny ping of longing knocks against the iron door to my Dragon Lady heart. I miss that feeling, even knowing what Greg and I had wasn't real. My head was full of home decor ideas and naming our children when I should have been focused on the fact that Greg's actions and words didn't line up. He knew how to say all the right words, but he just wasn't present. And I guess that's the biggest lesson I learned from him. I want someone who cares enough to show up for me. In all the ways a person can show up for another person.

I walk across the expanse of our generous living room, decorated in cream and rose, and start down the hall to my room so I can put my bag away. While I'm there, I shimmy out of my sweater dress, ditch the boots, and throw on some cozy gray leggings, my favorite pink over-sized sweater, and a pair of fuzzy socks before darting back out to hang out with Zach and Marina. Right after I grab a big steaming mug of spiced chai tea, of course. I pad down the hallway and hear Marina laughing.

"All right," I call out before I'm even in sight of the kitchen. "Don't block my kettle with your make-out session, I'm freez—"

I skid to a halt as I get to the kitchen. My jaw drops open in surprise. Because there, standing in the kitchen next to my tea kettle, is the Viking god himself…holding my favorite mug out to me and flashing me a knowing grin that makes my pulse jump.

"You forgot your coat again, didn't you, Ash?"

What happens next?

Marina & Zach's wedding is coming. Ashley needs a date. Rick's been waiting for this moment.
Read *Fake It Till You Make It now!*

(And don't miss the exclusive bonus scene waiting for newsletter subscribers at the end.)

Acknowledgments

Like Marina, I love practicing gratitude - and I am grateful for so many people in my life. First, to you…my readers. Thank you for buying this book, for reading it, leaving reviews and supporting a dream I've had ever since I was nine years old. I appreciate you so very much.

To my husband Kevin, for being the one person who looked at me like I was crazy when I told him I couldn't be a writer (thanks to years of brainwashing). For years, he was the only voice telling me yes when everyone else said no.

To my friend and fellow author Tomi Tabb, thank you for so many midnight emails telling me to keep going. Thank you for sharing your thoughts and wisdom and suggestions with me.

To my editor, Victoria Straw, thank you so much for giving me the absolute best first experience with an editor. I appreciate your patience and guidance more than you know. Thank you for making this mermaid tale shine. See what I did there?

To the Mermaids!!! Throughout this process, these four ladies really knocked it out of the park. They read my early chapters, gave me feedback, found a ton of typos, and lifted me up. Thank you, Christine R, Linda A, Linda B, and Tammy C.

Thank you to Bookstagram rockstar Hillary aka @hil.literate for naming Zach's band! You can thank her for The Royal Rebels. She won a contest I had for my readers and her prize was to have a character named after her. As a result, Marina's first office friend is named Hillary!

Sweet clean hugs to the amazing rom com authors Aven Ellis and Emma St. Clair for being available for questions, being supportive, and freaking inspiring. Confession: every time you've graciously given your time and energy to answer any question I've asked, I was totally fan-girling nonstop in my head and I don't think there will ever come a time when I'm not starstruck in your presence. I appreciate you both so much.

And finally to the friends and family who have been supportive and patient, thank you. I know sometimes I can't stop talking about something funny Nonno said or how absolutely delicious Zach is…or the horrible funk I fell into when I had to write the part where Marina broke Zach's heart. Thanks for putting up with all that. I really hate making my characters get sad. It will happen again, so just remember to shove some red licorice under my office door and back away slowly. I'll be okay.

And to all of us who've had to make ourselves small in order to fit in where we don't belong: Be a mermaid. Make waves.

If Marina and Max's experience as children touched you, I encourage you to check for a CASA organization in your local community. During the pandemic, I volunteered as a CASA (Court Appointed Special Advocate) for kids in the foster care system, and it was extremely rewarding.

CASAs are specially trained volunteers who advocate for children in foster care beyond what Social Services and other agencies do for them. In fact, a foster child's CASA is the only unpaid person who is fighting in their corner. CASAs form relationships with the kids in their case, they check on their needs to be sure they're all being met, write reports for the judge to review, and speak up for the child in court.

There are many CASA organizations across the United States, and I encourage you to see whether there is one in your community that you can volunteer with.

This book is specially dedicated to the amazing team at **CASA of Tarrant County**, where I volunteered as a CASA advocate for two years. Thank you for your tireless dedication to children.

About the Author

Dianne Oren writes sweet rom coms and lives in Texas with her husband, crazy doggos Duke & Daisy, Finn the cat, and an 8 pound murder muffin named Rebel. She loves embroidery, travel, and is completely addicted to iced coffee.

You can connect with me on:

https://dianneoren.com

https://www.facebook.com/DianneOrenOfficial

Subscribe to my newsletter:

https://dianneoren.com/subscribe

Also by Dianne Oren

Fake It Till You Make It

Ashley

My ex-fiancé jilted me twice—proof my taste in men is deeply questionable. So I'm done with relationships. Permanently.

Just call me the Dragon Lady. I guard my heart like a dragon guards treasure. Unfortunately, when the jerk shows up again, I need proof I've moved on. Fast.

Enter Rick: six-foot-two, absurdly attractive, and the sole surviving resident of my friend zone. One fake Valentine's date. No feelings. Definitely no complications.

Except we're also best man and maid of honor at our best friends' wedding. And pretending is getting harder than I expected.

Rick

Ashley thinks I'm safely tucked in the friend zone. She's wrong.

I've never been passive about what I want—and what I want is *her*. Agreeing to be her fake date isn't a favor. It's strategy.

When she accidentally face-plants her strawberry mask onto my white shirt? I keep it. Wear it as pajamas just to mess with her. She calls it The Great Ashley Shirt War. I call it phase one.

She thinks I'm patient. She has no idea I'm playing the long game.

And I always win.

Merry & Bright
Merry

A runaway car. A twisted ankle. A very serious police officer who keeps calling me ma'am.

I'm turning thirty—not eighty—and Officer Nicholas Bright is not amused by my objections. He's buttoned-up, stoic, and completely unprepared for my nonstop commentary…until I finally make him laugh.

He insists on driving me home.
Then he keeps showing up.
"Just checking in."

I'm a baker—specifically, a Christmas-cookie maximalist. When Nick mentions that his adopted grandmother used to bake with him every Christmas, something shifts. She has Alzheimer's now. Most days, she doesn't remember him at all.

So I suggest cookie decorating.

And somehow, I end up going with him.

Nick

I don't believe in optimism. Life cured me of that.

Merry is sunshine and chaos—too cheerful, too talkative, and far too determined to see past my badge and dark sunglasses. I tell myself we're just friends. I have nothing to offer her. My grandmother is slipping away, and Christmas—her favorite season—feels like salt in an open wound.

Then Merry comes with me to the care home to decorate cookies. And for a few precious minutes, my grandmother remembers me.

I break every boundary I built. I don't care anymore.

I want Merry. And I want more than friendship. For the first time, I'm willing to risk my heart to get it.